are true masters of page-turning terror guaranteed to shock and awe you." —*Reader to Reader*

"Edgy . . . a flashy romantic thriller."
—*Publishers Weekly*

"Shocking . . . with a vibrant cast of characters."
—*Fresh Fiction*

Close Your Eyes

"Gripping . . . The authors combine idiosyncratic yet fully realized characters with dry wit and well-controlled suspense that builds to a satisfying conclusion."
—*Publishers Weekly*

"Mind-blowing . . . The scenes with Adam and Kendra ooze sexual tension, making this thriller a titillating delight." —*Booklist*

"Intrigue at its best." —*Reader to Reader*

Shadow Zone

"A sexy thriller peppered with enough science and mysticism to make any beach seem a little more exotic."
—*Kirkus Reviews*

"In this adrenaline-accelerating tale of a high-stakes, high-seas conspiracy, the Johansens adeptly juggle multiple points of intrigue, smoothly balancing the prerequisite whirlwind pacing with plausible, even restrained, personal relationships." —*Booklist*

NIGHT WATCH

IRIS JOHANSEN

&

ROY JOHANSEN

St. Martin's Paperbacks

NIGHT WATCH

Copyright © 2016 by IJ Development, Inc. and Roy Johansen. Excerpt from *Look Behind You* copyright © 2017 by IJ Development, Inc. and Roy Johansen.

For information address St. Martin's Press, 175 Fifth Avenue, New York, NY 10010.

ISBN: 978-1-250-07600-7

Our books may be purchased in bulk for promotional, educational, or business use. Please contact your local bookseller or the Macmillan Corporate and Premium Sales Department at 1-800-221-7945, ext. 5442, or by e-mail at MacmillanSpecialMarkets@macmillan.com.

Printed in the United States of America

St. Martin's Press hardcover edition / October 2016
St. Martin's Paperbacks edition / June 2017

St. Martin's Paperbacks are published by St. Martin's Press, 175 Fifth Avenue, New York, NY 10010.

10   9   8   7   6   5   4   3   2   1

PROLOGUE

Big Bear Lake, California

THOSE CHAMBER OF COMMERCE brochures were right on the money, John Jaden thought. It was freezing, and he was practically up to his ass in snow, yet surfers and sunbathers preened on a warm beach less than ninety minutes away. He'd seen them as he'd driven up the highway on his way to Big Bear.

A little longer than ninety minutes, he reminded himself. The highway patrol had made him turn around to buy tire chains before they let him up Bear Mountain. Annoying as hell. He knew how to handle himself on ice and snow, even if these other sunbaked idiots didn't.

It didn't matter. This was going to be the best day he'd had in a long time.

He pulled his jacket tighter around him as the snow fell harder. He'd left his car in a parking lot a mile back. Couldn't risk getting stuck. Not today.

The snowplows hadn't found their way to this cluster of rustic vacation houses on a street called Starvation Flats.

He shook his head. What the hell kind of name was that? Probably a story there, but not one he'd care to explore once his business was done. Most of the houses appeared deserted on this Wednesday afternoon, with no fresh footprints coming or going from any of them. He'd only seen one car since he'd set out on foot, a group of pretty-boy ski bums on their way to the slopes.

Perfect.

He looked ahead to a two-story wood cottage at a bend in the road. The Bavarian-influenced structure reminded him of one of his grandmother's old cuckoo clocks, just as it had when he'd first been shown the photo at dinner the night before.

A bit kitschy for its resident, a man he'd always respected for having taste and intelligence. He smiled as he pushed his white hair back from his forehead. Of course, if Shaw was all that smart, Jaden wouldn't be standing in front of this house right now.

He steadied himself on the path to the front door. His jeans were wet from the snow, and his athletic shoes were better suited for running than protecting him from the elements.

No biggie. In just a couple of hours, he'd be tossing back whiskey shots in front of the fire pit at Gracias Madre.

He rapped on the door and waited.

No answer.

He tried again.

Nada.

Shit. He'd been told that Shaw was always—

Wait. He listened.

Squeaky hinges and hurried crunching footsteps on fresh powder.

Around back.

He bolted around the side of the house and leaped over the short fence. A stocky man was running away from the cabin, slogging through a snowdrift and pulling a long coat over his T-shirt and sweatpants. Jaden ran faster and overtook him.

"Dr. Shaw!"

Shaw stopped and looked up at him. His round face was red and covered with sweat. He was out of breath. "Jaden . . ." He finally wheezed.

"What the hell? Do you know how far I came to see you?" He looked down at Shaw's bare feet in the snow. "No shoes? You were in that much of a hurry to get away from me?"

He glanced around nervously. "I wasn't sure if you were alone."

"Of course I'm alone. You see anyone else here?" He smiled. "How important do you think you are?"

He shook his head. "I'm not going back to London."

"No one's asking you to."

He studied him for a long moment. "How in the hell did you find me?"

"I had help. It's hard for people to hide and stay hidden these days. No matter how smart you are."

"Does he know where I am?"

"Sure. Who do you think sent me?"

"That's why I ran, Jaden. I don't trust him. I don't trust any of them. If you're smart, you shouldn't, either."

"Stop being paranoid. He just wants to talk. To consult with you occasionally. If it's a matter of money . . ."

"The money was never a problem."

"Then you can stop running. He'll find you wherever you go anyway. He just wants to know that you'll be available when you're needed."

3

His eyes narrowed on Jaden's face. "That's it? That's why he sent you all the way here?"

He nodded. "He's just looking for assurances. You know how he is."

Shaw stared at him for a moment. Then he nodded, and his fingers ran through his rumpled gray hair. "Okay. But I'll never go back to London. He has to know that."

"He understands. And now I'm glad that you do, too. Thank you." He extended his gloved right hand.

Shaw half smiled as he started to take a step forward to shake his hand. "What would you have done if I'd said no?"

He shrugged. "Same thing."

Two shots fired from his glove, muffled by a silencer.

Shaw dropped to his knees. A bloody stain spread across his chest and drizzled onto the pristine white snow.

His lips moved as if he was trying to speak, but no words came forth.

"Shhh." Jaden put away his gun. "You're a smart man, Dr. Shaw. You had to know it would end this way."

Shaw fell facedown into the bloody snow.

As his last breath left him, the wind whipped up and blew fresh powder from the snowdrifts around them.

CHAPTER
1

"ANY QUESTIONS?"

Kendra Michaels looked out at the four-hundred-odd seminar participants at Pepperdine's Elkins Auditorium. She'd just delivered her latest research paper at a conference on aging, and it had seemed to go well. She'd documented several success stories using music therapy to treat Alzheimer's patients, but there was still resistance in the medical community. Not as much as there had been only a couple of years ago, when most academics still put her in the alternative-therapies woo-woo column.

She had helped move that needle, one study, one paper, one boring academic conference at a time.

Try not to go on autopilot, she told herself. Stay in the moment.

But how could she, when she knew that the man in the front row was obviously angry with his colleague about something. His pursed lips, narrowed eyes, and clenched fingers told the story as she watched him make small talk before the presentation. And how about that female brain surgeon who clearly hadn't operated on anyone in months? And, sadly, probably wouldn't again, if the slight tremor in her left hand was any indication.

Stay in the here and now. Answer the questions with crystal clarity and politeness even as condescending as some of them were. She'd show them.

She looked up toward the back of the auditorium.

She froze.

It couldn't be.

A man stood in the doorway, partially silhouetted by the light from the corridor beyond. She couldn't make out his facial features, but she didn't need to.

His ramrod-straight posture, impeccably tailored suit, crossed arms, and slight tilt of the head told her all she needed to know.

Dr. Charles Waldridge was in the room.

How long had it been since she'd seen him? Four years, maybe five. And then it had only been an accidental meeting at a conference. She felt the usual rush of excitement and intimidation. Suddenly everyone in the room faded but the man in the doorway. No one on earth had changed her life more. Why was he even on this continent?

Concentrate.

Get through with the questions.

She finished the Q & A, and as the participants left the auditorium, Waldridge moved down the aisle toward her.

"Well done, Kendra."

He spoke in his British accent that always sounded distinctly upper-crust to Kendra, though she knew he'd grown up in a working-class neighborhood in South London. Waldridge was in his late forties, and he had a few more lines and gray hairs since she'd last seen her. But his an-

6

gular good looks hadn't faded, and the added maturity only made his face more intriguing.

And there was that ever-present fierce and intelligent spark in his dark eyes that had held her captive since the first instant she had seen him.

She smiled and came toward him. "Dr. Waldridge . . ."

"Please." He made a face. "I thought we'd moved far beyond that. Why do you keep forgetting? It's Charles."

"Charles . . . I can't help it. I still have trouble being informal with you, dammit. You catch me off guard and I'm that starstruck kid again." She gave him a quick hug. "I didn't see your name on the attendee list."

"Because I'm not an attendee. This is a bit out of my specialty, you know."

"Don't tell me you're teaching here?"

"Hardly. I haven't taught anywhere since I left St. Bartholomew's." He stared deep into her eyes. "Everything okay?"

His stare made her uncomfortable even though she knew he was looking at her clinically. She fought the urge to look away. "Yes. My eyes are fine. No cloudiness, no watering."

"Good. Have you been examined lately?"

"About a year ago. Still almost twenty-twenty."

"Excellent." He looked from right to left and back again, then spoke softly. "Everything I could have hoped for, Kendra."

"I didn't think doctors made house calls anymore."

He smiled. "Only for very special patients. And you'll always be very special to me."

Kendra finally forced herself to look away. She'd been born blind and spent her first twenty years in the darkness. She knew she'd still be there had it not been for Waldridge and his experimental stem-cell procedure. She was nineteen when her mother had seen mention of the Night Watch Project in academic journals and brought her, uninvited, to the front door of Saint Bartholomew's Hospital in London. Her mother had ruthlessly browbeaten Waldridge and his staff until they agreed to see Kendra and eventually grant her a spot in their test group.

"It's been over nine years," she said. "But this all still feels new to me. I don't take it for granted. I never will."

"Sight, you mean?"

"Yes. I'm still making discoveries. All the time."

"You have a wonderfully inquisitive mind, Kendra. You always have. I could tell the first time I met you."

"So why aren't you in England poking around in that lab? There are a lot of other people in this world who need your help."

"Oh, it's the eternal problem. Finances. Research is expensive. There are occasions I have to leave the lab, hat in hand. This time it has brought me to your shores. But when I learned you were here, I knew I had to come see you in action."

"You've seen me work before."

"I've seen you working with your patients, which was miraculous. But here, watching you hold your own against some of the top specialists in the world . . . It's a side of you I hadn't seen." He added quietly, "It made me very proud."

Her face flushed. "Thank you. That means a lot."

"I was hoping I could take you to dinner if you know a decent place nearby."

"We're in Malibu, California. There are *dozens* of decent places nearby." She gathered her presentation materials and gestured toward the door. "And, just so you know, I'm taking *you* to dinner."

WALDRIDGE FOLLOWED KENDRA half a mile up the Pacific Coast Highway to Geoffrey's, a restaurant offering a large Mediterranean-themed patio and a spectacular view of the ocean. They arrived just in time to enjoy the sunset, a pale orange orb shimmering over calm waves, and an excellent dinner.

They followed the meal with coffee, and, after a few minutes of small talk, Waldridge folded his hands on the tabletop. "Okay, Kendra . . . time for me to say something that's been on my mind for a long time. I don't believe I've ever given you a proper apology."

Her eyes narrowed on his face. "Apology for what?"

"For the way I treated you in those first few years after your procedure. I turned you into a show pony, trotting you out for the media, medical conferences, fund-raising dinners . . . I know it couldn't have been fun for you."

She looked away from him. "I tried to cooperate. But not always gracefully. I was going through a lot at the time."

"Of course you were. Your reality changed overnight. And I was too wrapped up in my project's success to even think about that. I wanted everyone to see what was possible. For someone to go from total blindness to near twenty-twenty vision, that was a dream come true for so many of us who had been working for years. You were our first great success. There have been several since then, but at the time, you were totally unique. You were the key to showing people that this was the path worthy of all their attention and funding."

Kendra nodded. She was silent, remembering that time. "I'm sorry I didn't handle it better. I guess I just kind of . . . rebelled."

"I didn't blame you. None of us did. You probably don't know about the others who came after you, but many of them had a difficult time after gaining their sight. A life-changing experience like this has completely redefined who they are, along with every single one of their relationships. There have been divorces, family estrangements, bouts of severe depression . . ."

"That actually doesn't surprise me."

"Because you lived through it yourself. One would think that a gift like this would bring nothing but joy. But as you found out, it doesn't solve all of life's problems, and that disappointment can bring some hard feelings."

"Exactly. It took me awhile to find out who I was. I call those my 'wild days.' I wanted to experience everything I could, no matter how risky or dangerous it was. I know I scared the hell out of my friends and family."

"And me," he said ruefully.

She shrugged. "I came through okay. I'm grateful for the time and effort you were able to give me while I was fighting my way out of the dark. And I don't regret those wild days one bit. It helped to make me who I am."

"Which is an extraordinary young woman. But you always were that." He leaned forward in his chair. "Since the last time I saw you, you've become distinctly more extraordinary."

She cocked her head. "As much as I enjoy hearing you call me 'extraordinary' in that British accent of yours, I don't know why you would say that."

"I'm referring to your fascinating sideline, of course."

He smiled teasingly. "You've become Kendra Michaels, crime fighter."

She cringed. "Oh, don't say it like that. Better still, don't say it at all."

"Why not? It's the truth, isn't it?"

"I've consulted with the FBI and a local police department on a few cases." She shook her head emphatically. "Believe me, it's nothing I've ever asked for."

"Success breeds demand, and from what I understand, you're very much in demand."

"Crazy, isn't it?"

"Not at all. In a way, it makes perfect sense."

"I'm glad *you* think so."

"I do. Almost all the vision-impaired people I've known have developed their other senses to compensate. They know who's in a room from the particular sound of each person's footsteps. From a mere whiff, they can identify one of dozens of colognes, soaps, and even tobacco brands. They make themselves aware of their surroundings in a way that few other people can, just as a survival mechanism. I imagine that gives you quite an edge in the investigative arena."

Kendra nodded. "I've found that most detectives only go by what they can see. They don't pay enough attention to the sounds, the smells, and the textures. A lot of answers can be found there."

"But I'm sure you also see things they don't."

"Sometimes. Because I didn't have sight for so long. I now savor the things I see. I try to absorb every detail just because I can. I suppose that helps in the investigative work, too."

He shook his head. "Like I said, extraordinary. Are you working on anything now?"

"No. I still haven't quite recovered from my last case. It was a serial killer, probably the worst I've ever come across. I spent months trying to find him, and it took a real toll on me. As I said, it's nothing I've ever asked for."

"Then why do you do it?"

She thought for a moment. "When there's a killer out there who can and will strike again, it seems wrong to refuse if I know I might be able to help catch him."

Waldridge nodded. "You have a good heart, but you're right to take care of yourself, Kendra." He was silent a moment, gazing out at the ocean. "I'm sorry I even brought it up."

"It's okay." But she wasn't sure it was okay. There had been something odd about that hesitation. She shifted uneasily in her seat before changing the subject. "So what have you been working on?"

"I'm afraid I can't talk about it."

"Aw, come on. I practically bared my soul to you."

He smiled. "And I felt honored by every word. But I really can't return the favor. I wish I could."

"I heard you abandoned your corneal-regeneration work."

"I keep abreast of the latest developments, but I leave it to others to refine the techniques I pioneered. I get more satisfaction from exploring new frontiers."

"Frontiers you can't tell me about."

"Not right now."

She wrinkled her brow. "Now you have me curious."

"There's an old adage about a cat and curiosity. Drop it, Kendra."

She stiffened. "I'm not a cat, and I'm uneasy about the idea that my being curious about what you're doing now could cause me to be killed."

"Of course it couldn't. I shouldn't have used that term." His smile was full of charm. "I was merely trying to shift you away from interrogating me. You always were persistent. It's really much better for you that we don't discuss it."

"Better for *me*?" Her gaze narrowed on his face. "What in the hell is that supposed to mean?"

"Nothing." He shook his head. "I suppose I'm just being overly dramatic. It's really not all that interesting."

"Everything you do is interesting. You're a groundbreaker. Look what you did for me. You're one of the finest minds in medicine." Kendra studied him. "I don't believe you. What's going on, Charles?"

"Nothing. Just fund-raising meetings, as I said."

"Where?"

"Downtown, Pasadena, Century City."

"Anywhere else?"

"No."

"Please don't lie to me, Charles," she said quietly.

Waldridge looked as if he was about to protest, but he caught himself. Then he looked away, then back. "Of course. What, exactly, do you know, Kendra?"

"You arrived here from London only in the last couple days. Since then you've been in the local mountains. Big Bear or Baldy, I would guess."

Waldridge cursed under his breath.

"Am I wrong?" she asked.

"What else?"

She shrugged, then continued, "You drove straight from there to see me. You've spent a good deal of the day talking on the phone. You've been under an incredible amount of stress."

"You don't think asking foundations for money is stressful?"

"That isn't what you were doing. You were telling Porter to stay out of sight until it was safe. Whoever the hell Porter is."

He stared at her in shock. "How do you know all this?"

"Same way I always do. I pay attention."

"That's too vague. I need to know *now*. It's important."

He spoke with such desperate urgency that Kendra felt compelled to explain herself quickly. "Fine. Take it easy. Your car has a nice dusting of rock salt all the way around. That may be common in other parts of the country at this time of year, but it's extremely rare in Southern California. The San Bernardino Mountains have had record snowfall this week, and it's probably the only place within hundreds of miles that has been salting the roads. You also have some on your shoes and the cuffs of your slacks. If you hadn't come straight here, I know you well enough to know that you would have changed clothes or at least tried to wipe it off."

Waldridge looked down at his shoes. "I didn't think that it was that noticeable."

"It isn't. And I know you were just in London from your haircut. You're very particular about the cut, and your stylist also has a specific way of sculpting the eyebrows. I can tell it's just been cut. Within days of each of your haircuts, a stray lash or two appears between your eyebrows. There are none there. You've been in London in the past three or four days."

"What about my phone calls?"

She could tell that was really bothering him. She hadn't realized that it would upset him. She had known him so long, she had felt as if she could trust him to understand. "The opening of your right ear is red and slightly chafed. It's a small area, just about the size of an earbud. If you had been listening to music, you probably would have been using both earphones, not just one. You pretty much confirmed it when I looked in my rearview mirror on the way here and saw you talking on it at a stoplight."

"How did you know what I was talking about?"

She said simply, "I read your lips."

He gazed at her in disbelief. "You can do that?"

"I guess I never told you. When I got my sight, I was amazed to discover the visual aspect of human speech, the whole interplay of tongue, lips, and teeth. It was fascinating to see what caused the sounds I'd been hearing my entire life. I just paid attention to what movements caused what sounds. After a couple years of studying that, I was pretty good at lipreading. It's nothing I planned to do. It just happened."

"Pretty good is right, but you're not infallible," Waldridge said sourly.

"I never said I was. Did I get a word wrong?"

Waldridge stared at her for a long moment. "Clever as always, Kendra. You're always a surprise and experience for me. But you could get yourself into trouble."

She grinned at him. "Well, I'm *always* doing that."

"I'm serious. I shouldn't have come. This was a bad idea."

Her smile faded. "*Talk* to me. What's going on?"

He shook his head. "Drop it please. It was a mistake."

"I know you have a right to say that this is none of my business." She was silent a moment, then she said with sudden passion, "But you're wrong. You became my business when you gave me my sight. Nothing can ever change that. But if you don't feel comfortable talking to me about this, so be it. I'll try to back away."

He pulled the napkin from his lap and tossed it onto the

15

table. "Things aren't as simple as they once were, Kendra. I wish they were, believe me. I think that's why I wanted to see you. Seeing you takes me back to a happier time, when things were more clear-cut, black-and-white."

"They were never that black-and-white for me."

"Of course not. But from a purely scientific point of view, we saw a problem that needed to be solved, and we fixed it. You're my greatest success, Kendra, and I will always feel good about that."

"Even if you don't feel good about what you're working on now."

"You're guessing, and I'm not confirming." He made a face. "I've said too much. Perhaps we should call it a night."

She didn't want to let him go. She felt frustrated, and the uneasiness was growing by the minute. But she could see by his guarded expression that he wasn't going to tell her anything more. "Perhaps we should."

Kendra paid the check, and they walked out to the valet stand in silence. After they handed their tickets to the attendant, Waldridge turned toward her. "Things aren't always what they seem, Kendra. The Night Watch Project was formed to do great things, but there was more going on than any of us were aware. Even I didn't know until much later that I couldn't take pride in all of it. I hope you can forgive me."

"Enough, Charles. *Forgive* you? You gave me the greatest gift anyone could ever give me." She took a step closer, her eyes holding his own. "You have to talk to me about this."

"I'm afraid I can't."

"Bullshit."

"I'm afraid it's not. This was a mistake." His rental car

rolled to a stop in front of them. Waldridge embraced Kendra and kissed her gently on the forehead. "I'm sorry. I know I must be driving you mad, but it's for your own good. Trust me. It's better for you."

"That's my decision. You don't call the shots any longer in our relationship, Charles." She gripped his arm. "Whatever is going on, I can help. *Try* me."

"All that intensity. How I've missed it." Waldridge pulled away and looked down at her for a long moment. "No, Kendra. You can't help. I can't let you."

He climbed into his car and drove away.

JADEN STOOD AT HIS HOTEL room's floor-to-ceiling windows and stared out at the twinkling lights of West Hollywood. His mobile phone was on speaker while he finished changing his clothes.

"No problems?" Hutchinson asked. His voice on the phone had a slight echo.

"No problems," he replied. "The snow will melt off before anyone finds him. There will be no footprints, no trace I was ever there."

"Good."

"I'll be out on the early flight tomorrow. I'll be back with the team by early afternoon."

"That's what I wanted to discuss with you. He needs you to stay a few more days."

"It was supposed to be in and out. He promised me."

"I know, but there's been a development. Dr. Waldridge has reached out to an old friend. We're still not sure why, but we'd be foolish to ignore it. Sit tight until we can check it out."

Jaden muttered a curse as he turned from the window. "I don't like this."

"Nothing to worry about. Just a precaution. You haven't asked me who the friend is."

"I didn't ask because I don't give a damn."

"You will."

"I doubt that."

"It's Kendra Michaels."

Jaden froze. "Are you sure?"

"They were having dinner together less than an hour ago."

"Kendra Michaels . . . That's a name I haven't heard in a long time. I really hate unfinished business." Jaden sat on the edge of the bed and smiled. "Okay. I'll stay. This just got interesting . . ."

CHAPTER
2

"IT'S NICE TO MEET YOU, Kendra. I'm—"

"Dr. Charles Waldridge." Kendra crossed her arms before her and placed them on the small conference table. "I know. How do you do, Dr. Waldridge."

Waldridge closed the door behind him. "How do you know who I am? We've never met before, have we?"

"No. I listened to one of your lectures on YouTube. Even before you just spoke, I recognized you from your footsteps. And from the jingle of keys in your pocket. You have some kind of charm on your key ring that makes a tinkling sound when you walk."

"Very good. It's a little souvenir dolphin my niece brought me from Grand Cayman."

"You also like to rock back on your heels every time you make a major point."

"You could hear that on the video?" he asked, amused.

Kendra adjusted her Ray-Ban sunglasses. "Yes. You did it eight times in a fifty-minute lecture."

He sat in a chair on the other side of the desk from her. "Hmm. I didn't realize I did that. Is it effective?"

"I'm not sure what it looks like, but those pauses work for you. It gives your students time to think about what you've just told them."

"Good. Anything else?"

"I know you're British, but I'm not familiar enough with the various accents to know exactly from where. It's my first time in England. But I do know you have a small dog."

"You're wrong about that I'm afraid."

"Really?"

"You're not accustomed to being wrong, are you?"

"It happens."

"Well, you're not that far off. I'm looking after a colleague's dog this week. Am I giving off an offending canine odor?"

"No, it's nice. Oster flea and tick shampoo."

"And how did you know the dog was small?"

"Mandarin Violet scent. I'm sure there are owners who use that on big dogs, but I've never met one."

He chuckled. "It's a poodle."

"That sounds about right."

He opened a file folder and turned the pages. "So . . . You're nineteen years old?"

"Twenty next week."

"And you've been blind since birth." He spent another moment flipping through the file pages before resuming. "Just so you know, I'm meeting with you as a courtesy. Our pilot program is filled. We had thousands of applicants. If you had called or e-mailed, I could have saved you and your mother an awfully long trip."

20

"My mother called and e-mailed. She already knew it was full."

"Then why are you here?"

"My mother never takes no for an answer."

"I got that impression. I know she wants this, but I'm not sure you want it, Kendra."

"What makes you say that?"

"Your tone. Most people I interviewed for this program practically begged to be part of it. You seem as if it's an inconvenience."

"Wanting it and believing it are two different things. Do you want me to beg? I'll do it, if that's my role in making this work. But don't expect me not to take this with a grain of salt. My entire life I've met a lot of doctors, scientists, and con artists who promised to make me see. My mother has been on a mission."

"How does that make you feel?"

Kendra bit her lower lip.

Waldridge leaned forward, and asked quietly, "Like you're not good enough for her the way you are?"

Kendra recoiled. "No. Why would you think that?"

"I've seen it a lot in the past few months."

"Well, that's not the case here. My mother's just trying to help. She's the one who is going to be hurt the most if she can't pull this off. She doesn't care if she ruffles a few feathers as long as she's doing everything she can for me. Me," she repeated fiercely. "It's all for me. She wants the best for me. Nothing for herself."

"Did your father feel the same way?"

"No. I never knew him. He left before I was two. He wasn't prepared to care for a special-needs child."

"That's also more common than you might think."

"It doesn't matter. My mother and I have always gotten along fine without him."

"I believe that." Waldridge paused. *"I'm not promising anything to anyone. Anyone who does is either a con artist or a fool. I'm neither. But I do think I offer the best hope you've had so far."* He paused. *"If I were standing, I suppose this would be one of those moments where I lean back on my heels for emphasis."*

She found herself smiling. She hadn't expected him to have a sense of humor. Most of the specialists who had examined her before had tended to have a God complex.

He turned more pages of the file. *"You're actually just the type of test subject we were looking for. Your corneas degenerated due to a disease you contracted in the womb. We're experimenting with a technique to help corneas regenerate."*

"How?"

"It's fairly simple. We combine stem cells with cells that we harvest from healthy parts of the subject's own eyes. We implant them in the corneas and we have hopes that the corneas will regenerate themselves based on the genetic blueprint provided by your own cells."

"Cool."

He was silent for a long moment. *"If you participate in our study, you would have to stay here at least two months. No air travel. The pressurized cabin is a variable we don't want to contend with right now."*

She went still. *"You're talking like . . . you might actually let me in your program."*

He closed the file. *"That depends on you, Kendra. Depends if you'd be willing to join us here for the next few months."*

She couldn't breathe. She was suddenly dizzy with hope. She hadn't expected this abrupt turnaround. "Does my mother know?"

"No. If you're not interested, we'll step outside, and I'll incur her wrath by telling her again that the program is full. It's entirely up to you. What do you say, Kendra Michaels? Would you like to join us?"

Kendra smiled shakily even as she felt her throat tighten, surprised into a sudden flood of emotion. "Yeah." Her voice was unsteady. "Sure."

"Good. Then I'll go and discuss details of the procedure with your mother. It was nice to meet you, Kendra." He stood up and leaned toward her. He said softly, "And here's to not taking no for an answer."

"EARTH TO KENDRA?" Olivia said quizzically. "Hello?"

Kendra snapped out of her daze. She and Olivia Moore were on their morning jog on the embarcadero in Marina Park, overlooking San Diego Bay. They had stopped to cool off when Kendra had checked out for a few moments.

"Sorry about that." She grimaced. "I was just thinking about Dr. Waldridge again."

"You haven't thought of anything else since you came back to the condo last night," Olivia said dryly. "And I might as well have been exercising with a sleepwalker this morning."

"I know. I know. It's just that the man I saw last night was so different than the man I remember."

"Different how?"

"He was . . . unsettled. Evasive. I don't know . . . The Waldridge I've always known has always been supremely confident and at the top of his game. Something was definitely wrong."

"You said he was out here for some fund-raising. Maybe it hasn't been going well."

"No, it was more than that. I think he wanted to tell me something, but for some reason he changed his mind. He kept saying it was for my own good."

"That's strange. You know, I've been getting e-mails from him once or twice a year ever since you introduced me to him. Every time he runs across research that he thinks could one day be promising for me, he sends a link." She shook her head. "I think he feels guilty that he couldn't help me with *my* eyesight."

Kendra gazed at her friend and didn't state the obvious, that she felt guilty, too. She and Olivia had met as children at the Woodston School for the Blind in nearby Oceanside, and one of the great pains of Kendra's life had been leaving her friend behind in the darkness. Olivia, who had lost her sight in a childhood auto accident, sustained optic nerve injuries beyond the reach of even Waldridge's revolutionary techniques. He had graciously met with her and reviewed her medical case files and seemed genuinely regretful when he was unable to help her. Kendra wasn't surprised that he'd kept in touch with her even though years had passed. Olivia was a very special person, and he must have recognized that fact. "Maybe not guilty as much as frustrated. He's something of a genius, and he doesn't like to admit defeat."

"Believe me, I would have been ecstatic to be one of his successes." The wind from the bay blew Olivia's long brown hair up and around, gently caressing her beautiful, olive-toned face. Never once had she expressed a single iota of jealousy over Kendra's amazing transformation, but she did harbor hopes of one day regaining the eyesight that had been taken from her.

"He really did want to help you," Kendra said gently.

"I know. He's a good man." She smiled. "You know, the way you always talked about him, I'm surprised nothing ever happened between the two of you."

Kendra's eyes widened. "What? You mean in a romantic sense?"

"Why not?"

"There's twenty years and eight thousand miles between us. I never thought about him that way."

"Are you sure?"

"Yes." Kendra found her tone getting defensive.

"The twenty years wouldn't have bothered me," Olivia said. "Mature men are more experienced, and that makes them sexier. The eight thousand miles are an obstacle that can melt away in a heartbeat. Did you ever hear about jet planes?"

"I've *never* described Waldridge as sexy to you."

"I've heard you describe him as brilliant at least a hundred times. And refer to him as good-looking on at least half a dozen occasions. I know you, Kendra. The intelligence alone is a big draw for you. Put those two descriptions together, and you come up with sexy."

"He *is* good-looking. It doesn't mean I want to jump him. And it doesn't take a schoolgirl crush to know that he's a brilliant guy."

"Of course. It's just a vibe you put off."

"No vibe. The man changed my life in a profound way, so naturally I'm going to feel a certain amount of . . ."

"Awe?"

Trust Olivia to zero in and strike home. How could Kendra help but feel a certain amount of hero worship toward Waldridge, who had not only given her a fantastic gift, but had been the only man in that first year to teach her, work with her, and chase away all the fear and uncertainty. Even Olivia would never realize what he had meant to her during that time. So don't try to explain the unexplainable. "I was going to say gratitude."

"Well, I'd sure feel awe." Olivia felt the face of her Bradley touch-capable wristwatch. "We should start back. I have Reddit online chat in less than an hour."

Olivia's online Web destination, Outasite, featured articles, interviews, and product reviews, all geared to a vision-impaired audience who accessed the content via audio-reader software. Outasite had quickly become a very successful business for Olivia, and she spent many of her waking hours generating material for the site.

"Okay," Kendra said. She looked down the sidewalk. "Clear!"

She had developed a verbal shorthand for guiding Olivia through a variety of terrain and conditions on their frequent runs together.

"Side!"

Olivia ran beside her as they continued their conversation.

"Will you see him again before he leaves?" Olivia asked.

"That may be up to him. I tried to call his cell phone this morning, but he didn't answer."

"Try him again."

"I will." She had no intention of letting Waldridge fly out of her life again and leave her with this feeling of uneasiness. He'd had a reason for contacting her yesterday, then had backed away. She couldn't just let it go. "As soon as we get back."

They ran through the Gaslamp District and cut down Fifth toward the five-story building that housed both of their condominiums. But as they neared the building, Kendra saw a police car double-parked outside with flashers on.

"What the hell?" she murmured.

Two uniformed officers stood on the sidewalk. One of them turned toward Kendra as she put her key in the front door. "Dr. Michaels?"

"Police," she said to Olivia. She looked from one officer to the other. "You're here for me?"

"Yes. Lieutenant Ortiz would like to see you at the station."

"I'm not doing police consulting work right now. He usually calls me."

"He did. There was no answer."

"I never bring my phone with me when I run." She stared at him quizzically. "So he sent a squad car to lasso me in?"

"He was concerned for your safety."

"My safety? Why would he—?" Her brow furrowed. "What's this about?"

"If you'll come with us, Lieutenant Ortiz will—"

"Tell me now," she said flatly. "Or I'm not going anywhere."

The cop sighed and glanced at his partner before turning back. "Do you know a Dr. Charles Waldridge?"

Kendra felt herself tense. "Of course I do. What's happened?"

"He's missing under suspicious circumstances. And you may have been the last person to see him."

"DR. MICHAELS, GLAD you could join us."

Lieutenant Mark Ortiz entered the police-headquarters lobby and gestured toward the detective walking a few paces behind. "Detective Vince Halderman, Kendra Michaels."

Halderman nodded his greeting, but Kendra ignored him and launched immediately into attack mode. "What happened to Charles Waldridge?"

"We were hoping you could help us with that. When was the last time you saw him?"

"We had dinner together last night. At Geoffrey's, in Malibu. We left around 8 P.M., each in our own cars. So what's the story?"

"Be patient. I have a few more questions."

"No. I answer some, then you answer some. That's how this will work. What happened to him?"

Ortiz turned toward his partner with a pained expression that Kendra knew she'd given a lot of other cops in her time. Then he turned back to her. "Dr. Michaels, I'm afraid the answer is that we don't know. He was staying at the Huntley Hotel in Santa Monica. There was some kind of disturbance in his room, a lot of noise. Other guests complained, but by the time security arrived, no one was in the room. The lamp was broken, and the television screen was shattered. But all of Waldridge's belongings, including his phone and wallet, were still there."

Not good. Kendra cursed under her breath. *What have you gotten yourself into, Charles?*

"You were in a relationship with him?"

Kendra shook her head. First Olivia, now this clown. But she knew that the detective was merely fishing, straight out of the cop playbook.

"No, we're good friends. We've known each other a long time. We hadn't seen each other for a while and he met me at Pepperdine, where I was presenting at an academic conference, and we had dinner afterward." She went on the attack. "How did you know I had any connection with him?"

"He had your Pepperdine seminar page still up on his laptop, and we found your name and number in his telephone address book. Google told me a bit more about your medical history together."

She raised her eyebrows in approval. "Wow. Good cop."

"Now it's my turn. He was a long way from home. What brought him to California?"

"He was fund-raising for a project. He's a research scientist."

The detectives shared a quick glance.

Kendra caught that look of doubt between them. "Now what?"

"We've been in touch with his colleagues in England," Halderman said. "They didn't even know he'd left the country. They had no idea why he would have come here."

Kendra let that sink in for a moment. "Are you absolutely certain?"

Ortiz nodded. "As far as they knew, he was just taking a few personal days. What did he say to you?"

"Just what I said. He told me he was raising money for a medical-research project."

"And yet none of his colleagues knew anything about it."

"It doesn't sound right to me, either. But a lot of what he said didn't sound right."

"Like what?"

Kendra told them about Waldridge's evasiveness, general uneasiness, and cryptic statement about wanting to protect her.

Ortiz jotted down some notes in a notebook as she spoke. He glanced up. "Protect you? Were you under the impression that he felt he was in any kind of physical danger?"

"No, I didn't get that vibe from him. I'm not sure what he meant, and he wasn't in any mood to explain himself. I was planning to call him today."

"And you had no idea what he was working on?"

"No." She leaned back in her chair, wishing desperately that she'd pressed Waldridge to talk to her. Then maybe whatever mess he'd managed to get himself into wouldn't have escalated to this degree.

Ortiz pushed a legal pad across the table. "We need a list of Dr. Waldridge's friends and associates in the area."

Kendra pushed the pad back. "There's only one. Me. At least, as far as I know. Waldridge doesn't like California. It's too laid-back for him. The few times he's come here since I've known him, he did his business and got away as quickly as he could. There may be some professional contacts here, but you'd have to ask his colleagues about that."

"We have. They said you were the only one."

"Well, there you go. Have you been to Waldridge's hotel room yourself?"

"No. Santa Monica PD is working the scene."

"Don't let them break it down. I'm going down there right now."

Halderman scowled. "Why? You think you'll see something all those cops missed?"

Ortiz shrugged. "Actually . . . she might. I'll tell you about Dr. Michaels later." He turned back to her, and offered, "I can make a call."

Kendra stood. "Thanks, Ortiz. It might make things easier when I get there."

"You're not even going to wait and see if they're willing to let you in?"

"I'll keep my phone on while I'm driving down. Let me know what they say." She was heading for the door.

"But, one way or another, I'm going to take a look at that room."

SHE DIDN'T WAIT TO HEAR from Ortiz whether he'd been able to get her into the crime scene. She decided it was time to take out insurance.

Before she was even on the I-5 freeway, Kendra voice-dialed a number she hadn't called in months. She had hoped it would be a good while longer. After hurdling the jittery receptionist, she was finally patched through.

"Special Agent Griffin."

"Hello, Griffin."

"Kendra, will you please go easy on my assistant," he said testily. "She's already terrified of you for telling her that her sister married a guy just so he could get a green card."

"Did she disagree? Call me a liar?"

"She's not talking, and to tell you the truth, I don't want to know anything more about it."

"Then tell your assistant she should remove the photo in the lower-right side of her cubicle. I'll leave it at that."

"The lower-right side . . . ?" His voice trailed off. "Never mind. Surely you have something more pertinent to talk to me about."

"I'm on my way to Santa Monica. It's a case the FBI may have some interest in."

He paused for a long moment. "Okaay . . . In that case, perhaps you should be talking to the Bureau's Los Angeles office."

"Not yet. It's about someone I know, Griffin." She told him about Waldridge and his disappearance.

Griffin clicked his tongue. "So what do you want from me?"

"Access. I want to get in there and look around."

"And you want me to grease the wheels for you."

"Yes. Tell them I'm a consultant."

"But you're not. At least not on this case."

"Not yet."

Silence. "Does that mean you're ready to come back and do some more work for us?"

Kendra had known this was coming. "Do this for me, and we'll talk about it. I have to get in that room, Griffin."

"Believe it or not, most big-city police departments employ very competent investigators. Is there anything that leads you to believe they're not doing their jobs?"

"No. But they can always use an extra set of eyes."

"Especially yours?"

"Yes. That's what you always told me when you wanted my help."

"But Santa Monica PD hasn't asked for your help. Or the FBI's help."

Griffin was playing with her, trying to manipulate her as he usually did. He hadn't liked it that she had opted to stay away from the Bureau this long. Put up with it. She needed him at the moment. "Waldridge isn't just a British citizen. He's an internationally renowned medical researcher. We may want to get a head start on this."

"So now it's 'we.' I know this doctor means something to you, Kendra, but you—"

"Then make the call. Get me in there."

Griffin sighed. "Okay, I'll see what I can do. The Huntley Hotel?"

"Yes. Thanks, Griffin."

"Don't thank me yet. And if I do get you in there, do me a favor and don't treat them like they're total idiots. Okay?"

"But what if they are total idiots?"

"Keep it to yourself."

"I'll do my best."

"That's not very comforting. Good-bye, Kendra."

DESPITE A TRAFFIC SNARL-UP in Irvine, Kendra reached the Huntley Hotel in less than two hours. She stepped off the elevator on the eighth floor and immediately spotted a uniformed officer at the end of the corridor. As she walked toward him, he quickly sprang into intercept mode.

"I'm sorry, ma'am. I'll have to ask you to—"

"It's okay, Officer," a voice called from the end of the hall. "Let her through."

Kendra looked up to see a stocky detective with close-cropped blond hair and a bright red face. It wasn't a sunburn, she decided. He was probably just of Irish descent.

She extended her hand. "I'm Kendra Michaels."

"Tommy Shea, Santa Monica PD." He shook her hand. "In the past couple hours, I've heard from both the FBI and the San Diego PD about you, Dr. Michaels. They seemed to think it was extremely important that you take a look at this crime scene."

"I appreciate it."

"I'm the one who helped piece together your connection with Waldridge. After I couldn't get hold of you, just to be safe, I called San Diego PD and had them make contact."

"Which they did. That'll teach me to go running without my phone. Have you found anyone who might have seen him after I did last night?"

"He popped up on security cams in the lobby and parking garage around 9 P.M. After that . . . nothing."

"That's strange. No sign of him leaving?"

"No. And no sign of anyone suspicious around him. I looked at the video myself."

"Is his rental car still here?"

"Yes, but it doesn't appear to have been disturbed. The keys were in the room next to his wallet and phone. We're having it towed in."

She glanced inside the room. "You're not about to break the scene down, are you?"

"Actually, we are. We've got what we needed. Fingerprints, photos . . ."

"DNA?" she asked.

"They took a few swabs, but you probably know what disgusting Petri dishes hotel rooms are."

She grimaced as she recalled the few times she'd seen a hotel-room comforter illuminated by a UV light. "Gotcha."

"Besides, we're not even sure there was a crime committed here. Except maybe a little property damage. So if you want to take a look, knock yourself out. But after that, we're packing up his belongings, and the hotel will send up their handyman to get the place back in circulation. There might be someone else in that bed tonight."

"Great. Well, guess I better get to it before someone else obliterates whatever evidence might be left."

Shea smiled and shook his head. "Naturally, you're assuming there's evidence we've missed. Detective Ortiz told me about you."

"And still you're letting me in."

He gestured toward the open door. "Chalk it up to curiosity."

"Anything that gets me inside."

"Knock yourself out."

She entered and stopped short inside the door. One side of the room looked as if Waldridge had merely stepped out for a bucket of ice, with his wallet, rental-car keys, and hotel-parking-garage ticket on an end table next to the un-made bed.

The other side, however, was a mess. The flat-screen TV was shattered, with weblike cracks emanating from the center. Fresh dings played over the pressed-wood white chest of drawers below, obviously struck by the overturned chair. Kendra looked at the desk, where the smashed phone had been knocked on the floor and a long ethernet cable had been stretched taut, halfway to the bed.

Kendra felt a sickening chill as she looked at the cord. "This cable was used as a weapon."

Shea crossed his arms. "What makes you say that?"

"It's pinched in two places about two feet apart, as if it had been gripped and wrapped around a pair of hands. Then it was stretched. Just the way it would look if had been used to . . ." Her voice trailed off.

"Strangle someone?" Shea finished.

Hearing him say it was like getting a punch to the gut. "Yes," she whispered.

"For the record, I saw it the same way. I've already had it swabbed."

"It probably won't help. Whoever handled it was using gloves."

Shea glanced back at the cable. "How do you figure that?"

"That cable has a soft sheaf. Soft enough to show ridges on the spots where it was gripped. Ridges from hard rubber grips on a pair of gloves. With some time, your forensic people might be able to tell you the brand of gloves. It's worth a shot."

Shea nodded, looking closer at the cable. "That I didn't see. Not that it makes a lot of difference. Hundreds of people probably pawed that cable in the past few weeks. In any case, I'll be bagging it and sending it to the lab."

Kendra turned away. She didn't want to look at that cable any longer. She was having trouble keeping from shaking. *What in hell happened here, Waldridge?*

"Dr. Michaels?"

She forced herself to look back. This was no time to fall apart, not when Waldridge might need her. She cleared her throat. "Was there luggage?"

"Yeah. In the closet. But we checked it, and he'd totally unpacked."

"I'll take a look anyway."

Shea produced a pair of latex evidence gloves from his jacket pocket. "If you wouldn't mind."

"Of course."

Kendra pulled on the gloves and moved to the open closet door. Hanging there were a pair of slacks, three shirts, and the jacket Waldridge had worn the previous night. His rolling suitcase was on the floor.

Kendra knelt beside it. A small blue-and-white tag was affixed to the handle, imprinted with the code L35. She angled the tag toward Shea. "Any idea what this means?"

"No. Only that it wasn't put on here by a bellman. I asked."

She dragged out the suitcase, unzipped it, and looked inside. As Shea had indicated, it was empty.

"Satisfied?" He crossed his arms, watching her.

"No." She shoved the suitcase back into the closet, then stood up and walked into the bathroom. Waldridge's toiletries were neatly arranged on a hand towel next to the sink, perfectly spaced with the same precision that Waldridge demonstrated in everything he said or did.

"A little OCD if you ask me," Shea said.

"He's a surgeon. It's exactly what I'd expect." She looked closer. "There was medication here. Did you or your officers take anything away?"

He gazed at her quizzically. "Medication? No."

"There are two faint impressions on this hand towel. See?" She pointed to a pair of round indentions on the towel's surface. "Most likely put there by low-to-medium-quantity prescription bottles. Did you find bottles this size here or in his car?"

Shea shook his head no.

"People steal meds, but since his wallet wasn't touched, I doubt that's what happened here."

"It could be a good sign."

"Yes. If someone did take him, it might mean that they wanted to keep him alive and well. You should check and see what his prescriptions are."

He was already scribbling in his notebook. "I'm on it. Anything else?"

She looked around the bathroom for a moment longer. "That's all in here."

She followed Shea out of the bathroom. "I'll check the drawers and under the bed, but that's all I'll probably—"

She froze.

He turned toward her. "What is it?"

"I just heard something."

He gestured toward the window. "From outside?"

"No." She looked down at the floor. "Could you please retrace your steps?"

"You're kidding."

"I *don't* kid. It may be important."

He stared at her in disbelief. "Okay. I'm trying to cooperate. Do you want me to retrace my steps since I got here this morning, or—"

"The last six steps you've taken."

He shook his head and stepped backward. Kendra cocked her head and listened as he walked.

Thump. Thump. Thump. *Squish*.

"There." She pointed down. "Did you hear that?"

He stopped and looked around. "Not really."

"Sure you did," she said impatiently. "You heard it, but you didn't listen." She knelt and pressed her gloved hand over the spot where he had just walked. "The carpet is damp here, all the way down to the pad. It squished a bit when you stepped on it. So unless one of your officers spilled something . . ."

"Your faith in my department is overwhelming. No spills."

She sniffed the liquid on her glove. "This needs to be analyzed. It's very faint, almost odorless. That's why I didn't pick up on it before."

Shea rubbed his glove over the spot and sniffed it. "Unusual smell."

She closed her eyes and tried to make some connection with the odor. "It's a little tarry, a bit like citrus . . . But neither, really. I'm sure I've never smelled it before, whatever it is."

Shea dropped a fluorescent yellow evidence tag on the spot. "I'll get forensics back here to sop up a sample."

"Thank you."

Shea nodded. "Just doing my job. You surprised me. I like to be surprised. That FBI guy told me that you were born blind and you'd still probably be that way if it wasn't for Waldridge."

"That's right."

"In that case, I'd be doing everything in my power to

help him, too." He nodded thoughtfully. "He's lucky to have you in his corner, Dr. Michaels."

AFTER A QUICK ONCE-OVER in Waldridge's rental car that turned up absolutely nothing, Kendra gave her card to Shea and walked out to her car on Second Street. She leaned against her car for a long moment.

What now?

Everyone involved would probably prefer that she just sit back and wait for a call.

Dammit, Waldridge deserved better than that. But with no clear sign that a crime had occurred, it would be days before the police treated the case with any kind of urgency.

By then, it could be too late. She had been uneasy as hell at what she'd seen at that crime scene. So what could she do to make sure Waldridge received the same single-minded dedication from her that he'd given her all those years ago? She knew the answer. She'd known it all along. As much as she hated to admit it, she needed help. She needed the big guns.

And she had one of the biggest guns of all on her speed dial.

CHAPTER
3

ADAM LYNCH PICKED HER CALL UP on the first ring. "What a complete pleasure. Though I knew you'd call sooner or later, Kendra. I'm glad it turned out to be sooner."

Kendra gripped her steering wheel harder. It had been two and a half hours since she'd left the hotel, and she'd spent most of the drive wondering if she was really going to make this call.

"Lynch, your smugness is actually radiating through the phone."

Lynch let out a laugh that boomed through her car speakers. "No smugness. Just happy to hear from you. Is that such a surprise? What's going on?"

She hesitated. "Something's come up. I can . . . use your help."

He paused so long that she thought the connection had dropped. "Lynch?"

"I'm still here. I'm just a little stunned. I'm the one who

always has to ask *you* for help. I'm not quite sure how to deal with this."

She mouthed a silent curse. Lynch wasn't going to make it easy for her. They both knew there wasn't anything Lynch couldn't handle and manipulate to suit himself. He was a former FBI agent who now worked freelance for whatever government agency needed his unique abilities. She had teamed with him a few times recently, and she was now violating her own pledge to put some distance between them.

"You'll find a way to deal, Lynch. The question is, are you even in the country right now?"

"It so happens I am. I just got back from Madrid, and I'm sitting here thinking about unpacking. Do you want to meet somewhere?"

"How about your place?"

"Sure, but if you don't feel like driving up here, we could always—"

"I'm looking at your house right now. You wanna open the gate for me?"

"Seriously?"

Kendra looked up at Lynch's beautiful two-story Tudor-style home in an exclusive neighborhood in northern San Diego County. "Yes, I was driving back from Santa Monica and thought I'd give it a try. I just pulled up. Turn off the motion sensor weaponry and let me in, okay?"

As if in response, the tall iron gates silently swung open.

She cut the phone connection and drove up the stone-tiled driveway. As always, the landscaping was garden-club beautiful, and the house's beveled-glass windows twinkled in the late-afternoon sun. She parked in front of the garage. As she climbed out, Lynch stepped out onto the driveway.

"Miss me?" He hit her with his movie-star smile. He wore white cotton slacks and a blue shirt that brought out the intensity of his eyes. And, as usual, he was totally high-impact.

"Should I have?"

"I can but hope. Well, I've certainly missed you."

She raised her brows.

"Stop being so skeptical. I think I've been very considerate giving you your space. But after all you've been through in the last year, you made it clear that you wanted to step back from the FBI, the police, and everything that reminded you of that part of your life." He tapped his chest. "And that evidently included me."

Not included. He was in a class by himself. Lynch managed to dominate both her thoughts and her responses when she was with him.

"Oh, I'm sure your bikini-model girlfriend kept you company." Kendra looked up at the house. "Is she here now?"

"No. No, she's not."

Kendra studied him. Lynch had suddenly become guarded, which was totally out of character for him. "I see. Is there a story there?"

"Well . . . maybe. Ashley moved out of the country."

Kendra's eyes widened. "That's quite a power over women you have. A few months with you, and they run screaming to distant lands."

"Cute. She's been working more and more in Europe, and it seemed whenever she was here, I was gone. Not a great recipe for a relationship. She lives in Rome now."

"I'm sorry to hear that."

He shrugged. "We just spent the weekend together in Marbella while I was over there. We still know how to have a good time together."

Kendra rolled her eyes. "You know, I was almost feeling sorry for you."

His lips turned up at the corners. "Oh, I wouldn't want you to do that."

"You don't deserve it. Ashley is the one I feel sorry for."

"I'm sorry you never got to meet her. You would have liked her."

"I admired the catalogue swimsuit spreads, but I'm not sure it's the same thing."

"It's not. She's very sweet."

"Sweet." She tasted the word. "Ah, I'm sure *that* was the attraction."

He tilted his head. "Did you come here to bust my chops about my ex-girlfriend? Somehow I don't think so."

"No, as enjoyable as that would be, I want you to go with me to the FBI field office."

He stared at her for a long moment. "That may have been the last thing I expected to hear you say."

"Yeah." She made a sour face. "Didn't sound right to me, either."

He motioned toward the front door. "Come inside. I need to hear about this."

She joined him on the curving walkway and followed him inside his home. As he closed the tall door behind her, she glanced around the dark wood fixtures and tile floors. It wasn't her style, but she felt herself oddly comforted by her surroundings. Some of the tension drained from her shoulders.

"You like it here." He smiled. "This is one place you've always been able to relax."

"I can relax lots of places."

"Not like you can here. You know I'm right."

He was right, she realized, even if she didn't like to admit it. "It would be pretty sad if I needed retractable bulletproof shutters, motion sensors, and security cameras to relax."

"Why? That's why I built this place."

"One of the drawbacks of being a government agent for hire. You've made a lot of enemies over the years."

"And you haven't?"

"My enemies are either dead or in prison."

"Lucky you. Still, you have to admit it's nice to have an impenetrable barrier between you and the outside world."

"I can't let myself feel that way."

"You already have. And there's nothing wrong with that, especially after the things you've been through. You deserve some peace."

Peace.

Kendra looked away. She wanted peace, but it wasn't in the cards for her right now. Not while Waldridge might be in trouble.

"But that's not happening with you." Lynch's gaze was searching her face. He leaned closer. "So I think you'd better tell me about it."

She hesitated. This was why she had come, wasn't it? But if she drew Lynch into this, it would be a commitment. A commitment she'd been avoiding for months. Because she never knew where that commitment would lead.

He was looking into her eyes. He said softly, "Tell me."

Do it, before she changed her mind. She quickly told him about Waldridge, his cryptic statements, and his disappearance.

After she was done, Lynch placed his hands on her upper arms. "See that wasn't so bad, was it? Whatever you need, I'm here for you."

"Good." She stepped back and slid out of her jacket.

Lynch's eyes lit up. "Oh, yes. By all means, get comfortable."

She gave him a squelching glance and showed him the jacket sleeve. "There was liquid on the floor of Waldridge's hotel room. Something I couldn't place. I sopped up some on my sleeve."

"Did you tell the cops on the scene?"

"Yes, and they promised to run it by their crime lab. But I don't think—"

"You don't think they'll give it high priority," he finished for her. "And you're probably right."

She held up the jacket sleeve. "I want to take this to the FBI lab and have it tested there."

"I'm surprised you're not there now. Griffin would jump at the chance to get you back in the position of owing him."

"He already thinks I owe him one for getting me in that crime scene to begin with. And I don't want this to get lost in the crime-lab in-box. I want priority."

"Priority over every active FBI investigation?"

"Exactly. I want it done today."

He chuckled. "Of course you do. And you think I can make that happen?"

"I know you can. I've seen how fast things happen when you decide to send a text or two to D.C."

"I've spent years building currency there. Currency that can evaporate if I tap it too much."

"You're the go-to guy for people at every government agency. You replenish your currency with each assignment you do for them."

"Only if I'm successful."

"Which you always are."

"*Almost* always. That's a big distinction. One that can sometimes mean the difference between life and death."

"Are you trying to impress me? Because as much as bikini-model Ashley may swoon when you talk like that—"

"No, I wasn't trying to impress you." He thought for a second. "Well, maybe a little."

"Another day I might have been impressed. A little. But right now, I'm just worried sick about my friend. I owe him, Lynch."

Lynch nodded. "I know. Which is why I'm willing to spend every bit of professional capital I have to help you. Now that should both dazzle and impress you. Okay? We'll leave right now." He walked her toward the garage. "I'll drive."

Kendra stopped in front of a large painting in the hallway. It was a striking portrait of her, one that she and Lynch had actually watched being painted by a suspect in a previous case. Her eyes were closed in the painting, and her lips were slightly curled in a serene smile.

Kendra nodded toward the painting. "Maybe this is why Ashley left. Most women aren't cool with their boyfriends' decorating their houses with pictures of other women."

"Ashley loved this painting. She joked about taking it with her."

"So she could burn it?"

"No. She looked at it a lot. To her, it looked like you were enjoying something that only you could see."

"Even though my eyes are closed?"

"Maybe *because* your eyes are closed. It was very perceptive of her, I thought. I had the exact same impression.

I couldn't get it out of my head after you and I saw it being done. That's why I had to go back and buy it."

"I still think you got taken."

"No, I didn't," he said softly.

She turned to face him.

Lynch was looking at her, not the painting.

And she found she was caught and couldn't tear her gaze away.

After a long moment, he gestured toward the garage door. "Shall we?"

Release.

She nodded. "By all means." She hurriedly followed him to the garage.

FBI Regional Field Office
San Diego

They made record time to the FBI's gleaming, glass-fronted building in Sorrento Valley, home to much of San Diego's high-tech industry. They rode in Lynch's Ferrari, and for once Kendra resisted the urge to tease Lynch about his expensive, overcompensating-for-something wheels.

Her gesture didn't go unnoticed. "No snide remarks about the car?" he said as he parked. "Now I know you're upset. Either that, or you've finally learned to respect my ride."

"There's also the third option."

"And that is?"

"I'm grateful for what you're doing for me. So you get a onetime pass."

"It's my pleasure."

"Although . . . the way you were stroking that gearstick

47

makes me a little uncomfortable. It's really kind of disturbing. I know you have feelings for this car, but should I leave you two alone for a little while?"

Lynch shook his head. "*That's* the Kendra I know. The world still spins on its axis. So much for the free pass."

"You got a pass by my not mentioning the two women you've had in this car in the past week. Young women, probably midtwenties. You liked one of them, the Latina woman, well enough to bring her back to your house."

He shook his head. "Okay, I definitely need to know how you knew that."

"Later." She opened the door. "We have work to do."

SPECIAL AGENT IN CHARGE MICHAEL GRIFFIN stood in the corridor outside the FBI crime lab, staring at the jacket in Kendra's outstretched hand. "You're kidding, right?"

"That's what that LAPD detective asked. I thought you'd know better." She shoved the jacket toward him. "It's on the left sleeve. It could mean nothing or everything, but we won't know until it's tested."

Griffin looked at her, then at Lynch. "You two are tough enough to take when I have to deal with you separately. How did you come to team up on this?"

Lynch scratched the back of his head. "You know, I'm still trying to figure that out myself. I think I was shanghaied."

"Uh-huh. And what if I tell you that our lab is already on a weekslong backlog?"

Lynch crossed his arms and smiled. "I'd say you should expect a call. Soon."

Griffin cursed. "The last time you said that, I got an

extremely unpleasant phone call from the Deputy Director of the Justice Department."

"Good. Then you already have some history together. You'll have something to talk about."

Griffin sighed and took the jacket. "Fine. But even if I bump this to the front of the line, it's not something that can be done in an hour."

"When?" Kendra persisted.

"I'll call you tomorrow. Or I'll have the lab guys call you." Griffin glared at Lynch. "Don't bother to sic your patrons on me. It's the best I can do."

Lynch nodded. "Understood."

Griffin turned to Kendra. "Listen . . . I'll put in a call to Santa Monica PD. I'll make sure they keep us in the loop on their investigation."

She looked at him in surprise. "Thank you."

He shrugged. "I can imagine what this guy means to you, Kendra. I'll let you know if I hear anything." He turned and disappeared through the double doors that led into the lab.

Lynch shook his head. "Damn."

"What?"

"I've practically made a career of disliking that man. Then he goes and pulls a stunt like that."

"You mean being decent."

"Yeah, the nerve of that guy, huh."

"Yeah, some nerve." Kendra smiled and turned to walk back down the hallway.

He fell into step with her. "What now?"

"I guess we wait."

"Like hell. I know you better than that, Kendra. You're not going to twiddle your thumbs while you wait for the lab to do its thing."

"No, I mean . . . You've done what I asked you to do."

He sighed. "And now you're done with me? How cruel."

"I figured you have better things to do than traipsing along with me on a case that may not be a case."

He stepped close to her. "Haven't you noticed I enjoy traipsing with you? It's always an experience. It's the most fun I've had in the past couple of years."

"You have a strange idea of fun."

He flashed that million-dollar smile at her again. Was he trying to be irresistible, or did it just come naturally to him? He was trying, she decided, though he didn't have to try very hard.

"I mean it," he said. "Where do we start?"

"I'm going to the mountains. Big Bear."

"Why?"

"I could tell from Waldridge's shoes and tires that he'd been in snow recently. They were frosted with rock salt. That doesn't leave much of Southern California left. And he had a tag on his suitcase labeled L35."

Lynch nodded. "Big Bear City Airport."

"You knew that off the top of your head? I had to Google it on my phone when we were driving here."

He shrugged. "I get around."

"Anyway, I figure I'll drive up there and ask some questions."

"Now?"

"Like you said, thumb-twiddling isn't my style."

"I don't like the idea of driving. It's getting dark, and the roads are icy and slick up there. I think it would be better if—"

"Ha! You're just afraid of getting that Ferrari dinged up. No problem. Take me home, and I'll get my—"

"I was just going to say, why drive, when we can fly? Especially, if we're going to the airport anyway."

"It's a little late to try and arrange a charter."

"Who said anything about a charter?"

She stared at him for a long moment. "Don't tell me you have your own plane?"

"No, I've done very well for myself, but those things are tens of millions of dollars and I wouldn't use it enough to make it worth my while." He motioned for her to follow him toward the elevators. "I'll borrow one from a friend."

She snorted. "But who's going to fly it? You?"

"Yes. Unless you'd like to take a whack at it. But I'm afraid my friend would insist that your CE-525-license rating be up to date."

"Seriously? You can actually fly a plane?"

"I guess you're about to find out." He pulled out his phone as they walked. "I just need to make a quick call. It's always nicer to have the jet warmed up and waiting when we get there."

She just stared at him. "Warmed up and—?"

He spoke into the phone. "Greetings, Giancarlo. It's Adam. I have a favor to ask . . ."

KENDRA SPENT THE TWENTY-MINUTE drive to Montgomery Field Airport in a state of disbelief that abated only slightly when Lynch drove through a group of small hangars toward a small, low-winged jet with a rear T-tail. A high-pitched whine emanated from the plane's engines.

Lynch parked a few yards away. "Beautiful, isn't it?"

Kendra pointed toward the plane. "You didn't say it was a jet."

"I didn't say it wasn't. It's a Cessna Citation Jet. This one's configured for eight passengers, so the two of us should be very comfortable." He opened his car door. "Shall we?"

She followed him out of his car and across the tarmac to the plane, where Lynch shook hands with a ground mechanic. They boarded the few short steps into the cabin. Kendra ducked into the doorway and froze.

"Is everything all right?" Lynch asked.

She surveyed the main compartment, which was over twenty feet long. With plush leather chairs, a large coffee table, and a sectional sofa, it was decorated more like a sumptuous living room than a corporate jet.

She shook her head in amazement. "This is nicer than my condo."

"My friend hates to fly. This takes the sting out of it for him."

"I guess it would."

He moved toward the cockpit. "My seat is up here. Make yourself comfortable. You'll find the bar stocked with some of the nicest wines you'll ever taste. I recommend the '89 Grand Puy Lacoste."

"Give me a break. Don't pile all this fine living on me at once. Is there room in the cockpit for me?"

Lynch shrugged. "There's a copilot seat, but I guarantee you it's a lot less comfortable than that sofa."

"It's okay. I'll ride shotgun."

They settled in the tiny cockpit and buckled up. Lynch slipped on the headset and after a brief exchange with the tower, he conducted the instrument check. He then piloted the jet onto a runway and took off into the night sky.

Lynch glanced at her and smiled. "You're very quiet.

You look like you've never ridden in a private plane before."

"No, and certainly not piloted by someone I know. But you seem to know what you're doing."

"Thanks." He grimaced. "I guess that's why you wanted to sit up front, so that you could see for yourself. I'm glad I passed the test."

"I'm not qualified to judge your ability. I was just interested in the entire process." She smiled. "And you can never tell when you might be able to use something you watch being done."

He chuckled. "Please, tell me you won't attempt to fly this Cessna without a little more instruction than a visual."

"I wouldn't think of it . . . maybe. When did you find the time to get a pilot's license?"

He shrugged. "I started flying about seven years ago, when I was still on the FBI payroll. I figured it would be a handy skill to acquire. It's actually come in more handy since I left. I'm now rated on several planes and helicopters. When I'm in a tight spot, it's always nice to have extremely fast transportation options."

"I guess that makes sense. But not everybody has a friend with a private jet at his disposal. Who is this man?"

"Giancarlo? Just a guy I helped out once."

"Helped out *how*?"

Lynch paused to check his altitude. "I was sent to find him in Budapest a few years ago. Our government got some intel that he was plotting some terrorist activity against U.S. targets, and they wanted him taken out."

She went still. "They wanted you to kill him?"

"No, they just wanted me to find out where he was." He looked at her quizzically. "Who do you think I am?"

It was a question that she had been trying to solve for all the time that she had known him. She knew how clever he was, she knew he had a genius for manipulation and an experience in black ops that was both dangerous and impressive. She just didn't know how and in what depth he used those skills. And it wasn't something she would ever ask him. "Do I really need to say it?"

"Hmm. Well, they had other people standing by for that. Anyway, I found out we were working with some faulty information. He was being set up. I helped him out of a potentially lethal situation. In the end, I helped clear him and broker a deal with the State Department that brought him here. He's been a grateful friend ever since."

"His gratitude includes the use of this plane?"

"As long as I bring it back in one piece and gas it up when I'm finished."

"Nice."

"Yes, I try not to abuse his generosity, but there are times it's incredibly convenient. Like tonight." He shot her a sly glance. "When it enables me to impress a woman who is exceptionally difficult to impress."

"Who said I was impressed? I'm merely interested in a new experience."

"New experiences," he murmured. "I'll have to remember that's the way to lure you."

"And I wouldn't really worry about abusing your friend's generosity." She looked away from him. "Sometimes the debt is so great that you're willing to put up with anything, do whatever is possible or not possible, just to pay a little toward it."

"I don't think we're still talking about Giancarlo," he said quietly.

"Sure we are." She smiled with an effort. "I was just

reminding you of something that a master manipulator like you should always keep in mind. I'm surprised that you're treading so softly where your friend is concerned."

"The emphasis and key word is friend." He grinned. "That concept can sometimes mess everything up when you're trying to rule the world." He checked a flight map on his tablet computer. "So what do you expect to find in Big Bear?"

She was glad that he had shifted the subject to one that made her feel less vulnerable. "I have no idea. But I know Waldridge was in the area, probably earlier in the day yesterday. He wasn't pleased when I figured out he'd been there, so that's pretty much all the reason I need to check the place out. We'll see what turns up."

"Sounds reasonable. Only another few minutes." He glanced at the snow blowing across the windshield. "You're not dressed for this weather. Look in the closet just outside the cockpit. I think you'll find something to wear."

Big Bear City Airport
Big Bear Lake, California

Fifteen minutes later, Kendra stepped off the plane wearing a Mackage moto jacket, all leather and zippers. She looked down at the snug-fitting garment. "The snow won't be kind to this leather, you know."

"I don't care. I'm positive that jacket has never looked better." Lynch smiled and followed her down to the tarmac. He was wearing a long wool coat he'd grabbed from the same closet. They stopped and looked around the small airport. It was quiet and dark. There were no other planes in operation, and the place was obviously working with a skeleton crew. He motioned toward a brightly lit building at the end of a row of hangars. "That's the administrator's office. We'll start there."

They walked toward the building and glanced through the glass door to see a dimly lit office of three desks. The room's only occupant was a young man peering intently at a laptop. Kendra tried the door. Locked. Lynch rapped on the glass, and the man stood up and came to the door.

He unlocked it and pushed it open. "May I help you?"

Kendra's eyes flicked to the name plaque on his desk. "You can if your name is Matt Paulsen."

"Uh, yeah. That's me."

"Good. I was told you could help us." She pulled out her phone and showed him a photo of Waldridge. "Did you see this man arriving here in the last couple days?"

He squinted at the phone. "I'm not sure. I don't see everyone who comes through here. You might ask some of the ground crew. There's no way to know for certain—"

"He was probably on a charter," she interrupted. "He might have transferred from LAX or another international airport. He has an English accent, and he would have been pulling a brown-and-black rollerboard—"

"Wait." He studied the photo for another moment. "I do think he was here."

"And what makes you think that?"

"I remember the accent. Kind of upper-crust. It was the night before last. Somebody met his plane."

"A limo?" Lynch asked.

"No. It was another English guy, and they seemed like they were friends. The guy picked him up in an SUV."

"What color?" Kendra asked.

"It was dark. Maybe green."

She turned to Lynch. "Sounds like the same car Waldridge was driving. His rental car was a dark green Explorer."

Lynch leaned closer to Paulsen. "What can you tell us about the plane that brought him here?"

The young man hesitated.

"Not sure? You'll probably need to check your files." Lynch pushed past him and strode confidently into his office. "Come on, Kendra. We'll wait inside, out of the cold."

Paulsen frowned uncertainly as he watched Kendra enter the office. "Uh . . . I'm not sure I can talk to you about this. I mean, do you have some kind of warrant?"

Lynch took a step forward, instant dominance and aggression. He must be getting impatient. He was usually much more diplomatic. Kendra raised a hand to stop him. She reached into her pocket and produced Detective Shea's card. "We're working with the Santa Monica Police Department on an investigation. If you have any concerns, please call this number. But we need this information immediately, so if you want to call now, we'll wait."

Paulsen looked at the card for a long moment, giving Kendra time to wonder how Shea would react if he actually decided to phone. Paulsen finally waved the card away. "It's okay." He moved to the front desk and jiggled the trackpad of a laptop to wake it up. "It's all part of the public FAA record. We log all the flights here. It wasn't from any of the charter companies that usually service the airport." He studied the screen. "Hmm."

"What?" Lynch asked.

"It's a tail number. I cut and pasted it into the FAA registration database, but it's not coming up as a valid entry."

"Like it doesn't exist?" Kendra asked slowly.

"Exactly like that." Paulsen tried it again, this time making sure that he had inserted all of the characters. The monitor flashed: NUMBER NOT VALID.

"Could it have been changed?" Kendra asked.

Lynch shook his head. "Even if it had, this registry would still show us every plane that had ever carried this number." He turned to Paulsen. "Are you sure this is correct?"

He shrugged. "There's always the possibility of a mistake, but I doubt that. We check and double-check these things. Homeland Security pretty much demands it. No, I'm sure that's the number on the plane that brought him here."

Lynch turned toward a bank of three monitors mounted high on the office wall. Each camera showed a night-vision image of another part of the tiny airport. "What are chances of one of these capturing the plane's arrival?"

"Not great. Those cameras are more for loss prevention. They might have caught your guys coming or going in the car, though."

Lynch and Kendra exchanged a glance.

Kendra studied the monitors. "How long do your recordings stick?"

"They sit on a hard drive for seven days."

"Good," Lynch said. "Take us forty-eight hours back." Lynch fired it more like an order than a request, but he correctly predicted it would be the surest way to get Paulsen to immediately comply.

"Okay." Paulsen leaned over a computer desk beneath the monitor bank and used a trackpad to move back the surveillance camera's timeline. He stepped back and looked at the screen. "There. Too bad it wasn't during the day, but the night-vision camera helps a bit."

Kendra studied the image, which at the moment only showed the familiar SUV. "That's definitely the vehicle that Waldridge was driving," she said. "Right down to the scrapes on the right-wheel hubs. As if someone had ground them against a tall curb." She pointed as two men stepped into the frame. "That's Waldridge."

"How about the other guy?" Lynch asked.

Kendra studied his pudgy features, bushy eyebrows, and unkempt white hair. "I don't know. I've never seen him before." She turned to Paulsen. "Is this the man you were talking about? The one who also spoke with a British accent?"

"Yep. That's him."

Waldridge loaded his rollerboard suitcase into the hatchback, then climbed into the passenger seat as the white-haired man took his place behind the wheel. After another few moments, the SUV turned around and disappeared through an opening between the hangars.

"I'd like a photo printout of those two men," Lynch said.

Paulsen smiled apologetically. "I'm afraid we're not set up for that."

Lynch pulled out his phone. "No problem. If you'll rewind it, I'll snap a photo right off the monitor."

As Paulsen and Lynch worked on their crude frame grab, Kendra took the opportunity to take a closer look at the man. His suit, with its narrow cut, high arms, and sculpted shoulders, was likely British, as were the leather Cheaney shoes. She couldn't get a read on his spectacles though they were consistent with many European frames she'd seen. His wild hair probably hadn't been cut in three months or more.

"That SUV is over five years old," Lynch said. "Too old to be in the fleet of the major rental car companies. Where could he have gotten it?"

Paulsen shrugged. "Those are popular rentals around here. Easy to throw skis and snowboards in the back." He thought for a moment. "It could be one of Fennel's cars."

"Fennel?" Kendra repeated.

"Yeah, Wally Fennel. He runs a small used-car lot near the hospital, but I think he makes most of his money renting the cars while he tries to sell them. Some of those wrecks have a tough time making it back up the mountain. If anyone's renting five-year-old cars around here, it's probably that guy."

Kendra nodded. "Okay. Good. We'll find out where he lives and see if he—"

"Oh, you won't find him at home. Not for another few hours."

Kendra checked her watch. "It's almost ten. Is his lot still open?"

"Uh, no. He spends most nights at Murray's Saloon on Cottage Lane. He sings karaoke there until he gets too drunk. Then he just drinks."

Lynch smiled. "In that case, we'd better get over there before he goes facedown on the bar."

"You're probably still okay." Paulsen stopped the recording and the current security camera feeds resumed on the monitors. "But you still may have to listen to his really terrifying rendition of 'My Sharona.'"

CHAPTER
4

ONE TEN-MINUTE CAB RIDE LATER, they walked through the front door of Murray's Saloon and Eatery, a bustling bar/restaurant decorated with an uneasy mixture of wood and neon. A pool table was in heavy use by the door, and a small stand served as the karaoke stage, where three drunk young women belted out a song that might have been "Love Shack." A long bar lined the left side of the room, which seemed to be populated by a combination of young snowboarders and older locals.

"I'll talk to the bartender," Lynch said.

Before he could get the bartender's attention, the women finished their song and the DJ introduced the next karaoke singer. "Okay, everybody. Give it up for Wally F."

Kendra and Lynch turned toward the stage, where a bearded man with long, kinky brown hair picked up a wireless microphone. No one applauded.

"Think we're about to hear 'My Sharona?'" Lynch murmured.

She listened to the first few bars of music. "No. God help us, I think we're about to hear 'Copacabana.'"

He flinched. "Please tell me you're joking."

She wasn't joking. Wally performed the song with gusto, making up with enthusiasm whatever he lacked in actual talent. He danced during the extended musical bridge, oblivious to the fact that no one appeared to be watching him.

No one except Kendra and Lynch, that is. They stood next to the bar with stunned expressions. Lynch shook his head. "The guy has cojones, I'll give him that."

"I hope this is worth it."

After the song ended, they walked over to him. "Good job," Kendra lied.

Wally looked them up and down, perhaps registering that they didn't look like the bar's usual clientele. "Thanks. It's a little cheesy, but what the hell?"

"What the hell," Lynch agreed. He raised his phone and showed Wally the picture he'd taken of the security video. "Is this SUV one of yours?"

Wally suddenly appeared a bit guarded. "Who's asking?"

"I am," she said. "My name is Kendra Michaels. One of the men in this picture is a good friend of mine, and he's missing."

"Shit. What about the car?" he asked immediately.

Kendra rolled her eyes. "Your concern is touching."

"Sorry, but I—"

"But you're worried about your car," Lynch interrupted. "It's sitting in a police garage in LA."

"A police garage? Why?"

"We'll get to that," Lynch said. "But you can confirm that this is your car?"

Wally nervously looked from Lynch to Kendra. "Yeah. It's mine. I loaned it to him."

"You mean you *rented* it to him," Kendra said.

"Well . . ."

"Come on," Lynch said. "We're not trying to jam you up for the kind of business license you do or do not have. We know about your side business. Just tell us what we need to know, and we'll be on our way."

Wally hesitated once again. "Okay. Let's step outside. It's kind of noisy in here."

They followed him out the door, making a detour past a large barrel of peanuts so Wally could grab a handful. They exited the bar and stood near the parking lot, out of earshot of a few bar patrons smoking on the sidewalk.

Lynch showed him the photo again. "Do you recognize either of these guys?"

"The shorter one with all the hair. He's the one who rented the car from me."

"What was his name?" Kendra asked.

Wally cracked open a few peanuts and popped them into his mouth. "Mmm. Don't remember."

"Maybe we have to take a ride to your office," Lynch said.

Wally shrugged. "Maybe we would if it was 1998." He pulled his phone from his pocket. "I keep all my docs in the cloud. Doesn't everybody?"

Kendra smiled. "I will now."

Wally thumbed his way through an app and drilled down to a collection of saved documents. "I do know he rented it from me about three weeks ago."

"Three weeks? Was he with anybody?"

"Naw, he was alone. He didn't know how long he'd be in town."

"Did he say why he was here?" Kendra asked.

"No. He did seem kind of nervous, though. Jittery. At first, he wanted to buy an old car from me, but then he changed his mind. I don't think he was too interested in messing with registration and all that. He seemed more comfortable staying under the radar." Wally raised his phone. "Here he is."

Kendra and Lynch moved closer to look at the screen, where there was a photocopied Montana driver's license. Definitely the same man who had picked up Waldridge. She read the name. "Peter Hollister?"

"Yep."

Lynch looked up. "The license is a fake, you know."

"How do you figure that?"

"There should be a strip of microprint on the front right corner. It's extremely hard to reproduce. Whoever made this license didn't even attempt it."

"Damn." Wally looked at the license image. "I didn't know that."

"Most people wouldn't. I'm sure that's why he picked a license for the least populous state in the union. Did he give you a local address?"

"Yeah." Wally swiped his finger across the screen to flip through the rental contract. On the last page, he pinched to zoom in on the signature and handwritten address. "211 Starvation Flats."

Kendra grimaced. "Starvation Flats? That has to be a phony address."

"No, it's a real street. It's just off the main road." Wally popped some more peanuts into his mouth. "You think this guy may have done something to your friend?"

"I don't know. I'm just hoping I can get some answers from him."

"And I'd *really* like to get my car back."

Kendra nodded. "I'm sure you'll be hearing from the Santa Monica Police Department very soon. In any case, I'll pass along your info to them."

Lynch looked down the street. "Is your lot near here?"

"Yeah, just down the street. But I told you, all that info on this is—"

"That's not what I want," Lynch interrupted as he produced a wad of bills. "I'd like to rent one of your cars for a couple of hours. Let's go pick one out."

IN LESS THAN FIFTEEN MINUTES, Kendra and Lynch drove up Big Bear Boulevard in their rented Subaru Outback. Kendra sniffed the interior. "Did you have to pick a car drenched in the aroma of beef tacos?"

"I thought it was cheeseburgers."

"Nope. Taco Bell beef tacos with maximum strength Fire Sauce."

"I'll take your word for it. It was one of the only vehicles with four-wheel drive. So it was either the taco odor or sliding into a ditch."

She wrinkled her nose. "I'm not sure which is worse."

He glanced down at the screen of Kendra's phone on which she was searching the Web. "Any luck finding out who this guy is?"

"No. The name pops up a few times, but it isn't him. It looks like a fake name came with the fake ID. Waldridge was obviously comfortable with him, though. I could see it in his body language."

"On the surveillance video?"

"Yes. Waldridge tends to stick his chest out a bit more when he's around men he doesn't know well."

"Only men?"

"Yes."

"How Cro-Magnon of him."

"It's not all that uncommon. Anyway, he wasn't doing it with this guy. If we don't find him here, a thorough search of all his friends and associates back in England would be a good place to start. But maybe we'll get lucky."

Lynch slowed as they turned onto a street covered with several inches of snow. "The plows haven't been here. We were right to choose four-wheel drive, taco smell and all."

"So you say." She looked at the house numbers. "His place is probably at the end, near the cul-de-sac. Four houses down."

Lynch cut the headlights and pulled to the side of the road. "Let's walk the rest of the way. Agreed?"

"Agreed. No sense in announcing ourselves any sooner than we have to."

They climbed out of the Outback and trudged through the snow, making their way past the mostly deserted vacation cottages. They stopped short of Hollister's house, which was a fanciful Germanic-styled home with yellow-and-blue trim. The house was dark.

"Did we somehow stumble into a Grimm fairy tale?" Lynch asked. "I'm pretty sure this thing is made of gingerbread."

Kendra looked at a single line that cut through the snow and moved around the house. "I don't think this motorcycle tread belongs to Hansel or Gretel," she said as she knelt beside it. "This is fresh."

"How fresh?"

"Last hour or so. No snow has accumulated on top of the tread marks." She used her camera to snap a picture of the tread in the snow.

"Well, he did let Waldridge use his car. Maybe now he's getting around on a bike."

"Maybe." Kendra activated the flash on her phone and shined it up ahead. Just before the tread peeled around the house, there was a footprint on either side, as if the rider had paused for a moment. Kendra stood over the print and inspected it. "It's a SIDI Fusion Lei riding boot, size seven or eight." She looked up. "This was a woman."

He raised his brows. "SIDI Fusion Lei . . . ?"

"In my wild days, a lot of my friends were bikers. This is a hot-looking boot. It's hard to miss."

"Even from just a footprint in the snow?"

Kendra shrugged. "I thought about buying a pair myself once."

Lynch looked up at the front porch. "No footprints up there. No one has come or gone in the last day or so."

"Let's check around back. It looks like that's what the motorcycle rider did."

They circled around back, following the tread to the large expanse of land behind the house. It was darker here, but the snow-covered ground reflected the half-moon with a blue, iridescent glow.

Kendra motioned toward the back of house, where the footprints told the story. "Whoever the motorcycle rider was, she checked the back door and windows. After that, she circled around . . ." Kendra's eyes followed the line of footprints behind her, which appeared to circle a dark object half-covered in snow. "What's that?"

Lynch was already heading toward it. "Wait here."

"No way." She half waded, half hopped, through the snow, but Lynch got there first.

He whirled sharply toward her. "Stay back!"

"What makes you think you can—"

She froze in her tracks, suddenly realizing what he'd seen, what he was trying to keep her from seeing.

A body. A dead body.

Waldridge?

"Oh, God. Is it—?"

He crouched next to the corpse. "I don't know. I'm not sure."

She made herself walk over and kneel next to him. Someone else had already brushed some of the snow off the body's head and chest. But not enough, she couldn't tell—

She reached out, but Lynch stopped her. "I'll do it."

She shook her head. "It should be me."

Don't let it be him, she prayed. Don't let all that brilliance and dedication end like this. Her hand was shaking as she carefully brushed off the rest of the loose snow.

She stopped as she saw the plump features and straggly white hair. It wasn't Waldridge.

Thank God.

"It's Hollister," Lynch said. "Or whatever his name really was. He was shot in the chest. Looks like he's been out here a couple of days, at least."

Kendra nodded. "He may have been dead even before Waldridge came to see me. But why? And why here?"

Then something occurred to her. "The motorcycle tracks . . . Which way did they go?"

Lynch pointed to a clump of trees and brush. "They go in that direction . . ."

Kendra stiffened as her gaze followed where he was pointing. She whispered, "But where does it come out, Lynch?"

A single blinding headlight flooded through the trees and a motorcycle engine roared to life!

Before Kendra could even react, the cycle and its rider burst through the brush and spun its wheels in the snow.

It roared back around the house and hit the street.

Lynch was already running for the car. "Come on!"

They scrambled toward the Outback and piled in. Lynch started the engine and turned the wheel hard left. "Buckle up. I'm not sure what this thing can do."

"There's no way we can catch her."

"We can sure as hell try."

He jammed the accelerator and spun the Outback up the street. The back end fishtailed on the snow and ice.

Kendra glanced over at him. "That's not good. Too slick. How does it feel?"

"We could use some more weight in the rear. Wanna get back there?"

"Seriously?"

"No."

He stepped harder on the gas, getting more traction when they hit the plowed roadway. He pushed a button on the door console, powering down the door windows. Icy wind whipped through the passenger compartment.

"What's *that* for?" Kendra shouted.

"Listen for the motorcycle. Which direction?"

Kendra nodded. Of course. Clever man. She should have thought of that herself, she thought in disgust. She leaned toward her open window and closed her eyes.

Detach. Concentrate.

There it was. That obnoxious motorcycle engine was echoing off buildings in the distance.

She leaned back. "Turn right."

"Are you sure?"

"Yes. You asked me to find it. Now trust me, dammit."

He pulled the wheel hard right and skidded down a well-lit street of small shops.

"It's up ahead now."

Lynch nodded. "I hear it now. It doesn't sound like she's gunning it as hard."

"She isn't. She may not know we're after her."

Lynch stepped harder on the accelerator.

Kendra cocked her head. "I think she veered off to the left."

Lynch cursed. "She's heading down the mountain."

"That's a bad thing."

"Depends on how icy the roads get. Hang on." He spun onto a side road, kicking up snow and rock salt as he raced toward State Route 18.

There was a bend in the road just ahead. They barreled around it.

Flashing lights. A police car up ahead.

They skidded to a stop, narrowly missing the police car parked in front of a blue-and-white barricade. Two uniformed officers approached them with guns drawn.

"Show us your hands!" one of the officers yelled.

Kendra and Lynch immediately complied.

"There's been a murder," Lynch said. "We're pursuing a suspect."

"Hands where we can see them," the officer repeated.

"He's telling the truth," Kendra said. "A man is dead."

"So we've been told," the other officer said. "But right now, the only suspects are you."

"Shit," Kendra whispered. "*She* called the police."

Lynch nodded. "Check and mate."

* * *

IT TOOK OVER NINETY MINUTES of explanations, confirmations, and follow-up calls at the local police station before Kendra and Lynch were able to convince the police who they were and their exact interest in the case. They were finally allowed to drive back to the murder scene, which was by then taped off and lit in every direction by several work lights. It looked like a stadium as they approached.

A young detective bent under the police tape and approached them. "Dr. Michaels, Mr. Lynch?"

Kendra extended her hand toward him. "Yes. Detective . . . ?"

"Sergeant Mark Brantley. I heard my buddies put you through the ringer tonight. They were just doing their jobs, you know."

There was a trace of defensiveness in his tone even as he flashed an appealing, lopsided smile. Brantley projected a more nerdy vibe than most cops that Kendra had met with his prep-school haircut and wire-rimmed glasses. But even through his long winter coat, she could see that he was in phenomenal physical shape with well-defined chest muscles and abs.

Lynch shrugged. "They did an amazingly fast job of getting out there and laying down the roadblock. Too bad they got the wrong people."

"It would have been a different story if *you* had called the police. Then they would have caught the right person."

Kendra looked away. "We already got this lecture from the detectives at your station."

Brantley shrugged. "A lesson for next time, then."

Lynch put a warning hand on her arm as if to hold her back. He knew that Brantley was annoying the hell out of her, and she was literally biting her tongue to keep from retaliating.

Brantley turned to Lynch. "Did they let you hear the 911 recording?"

"Yes. It was a woman's voice, and she was obviously on her motorcycle when she called. She most likely had a headset in her helmet."

"And you think she might have murdered this guy?"

Kendra cut in curtly, "No, I don't think that at all."

"Then why the hot pursuit?"

"We wanted to know why she was here," she said. "We could see from her footprints that she'd scoped the place out before she found him."

Lynch gestured toward the cottage. "From the footprints we saw here, it's obvious she looked in those windows before discovering the body. She brushed away just enough snow to get a read on who it was. It's not the behavior of someone who had murdered him two days before."

"We're inclined to agree," Brantley said. "But it's my understanding you're investigating another case. The disappearance of another man?"

"Yes," she said. "Charles Waldridge. He's from England, just as this man probably was. They knew each other." Kendra told him about the surveillance video at the airport and the rental car."

"Do you have a name?"

"Yes," Lynch said. "But it's probably not the correct one. He rented the car under the name of Peter Hollister, but the driver's license was a phony."

"That's the same name he used to rent this house. We've already been in touch with the property-management company that handles it. They've sent someone over with a key."

"You haven't been inside yet?"

"No, we haven't been here all that long ourselves. I'm guessing you'd like to join the fun?"

"We would," Kendra said.

Brantley nodded. "Since the FBI and half the police departments in Southern California have instructed us to extend you every courtesy, I guess we can make that happen." He looked back at the corpse. "We'll get prints and DNA off the body, and your FBI buddies have already promised to try a facial-recognition match with passport entries. But it would make everybody's job easier if there was something in that house that could ID him."

"Something like a passport?" Kendra asked.

"Dare to dream, Dr. Michaels. Let's go to the front door."

Kendra, Lynch, Brantley, and two uniformed officers walked around front, where another officer was standing with a middle-aged woman who could only have been the property manager. She wore a pink ski jacket and matching boots over a pair of flannel pajamas. An old lift ticket on the jacket identified her as Stacie Liston.

"Thank you for coming so quickly," Brantley said to the woman. "But you really could have taken the time to have gotten dressed."

"I kinda freaked when I got the call." Her hand trembled as she handed him the key. "We had someone O.D. in one of our properties once, but never anything like this."

"Did you ever meet the victim?" Kendra asked.

Stacie shook her head. "No. He arranged the rental a few weeks ago. He paid a month's rent and a security deposit up front with a cashier's check."

"From where?"

"Some English bank . . ." She thought for a moment.

"Barclays. He picked up the key at our after-hours lock-box."

Brantley unlocked the door and handed the key back to her. "We'll be here at least until midmorning. We'll give your office a call when we're about to leave."

Stacie made a face. "You don't think there's anybody else in there, do you? I mean . . . like him?"

"You mean dead?"

She nodded.

"Probably not." Brantley patted her arm. "Go on home. We'll take care of things here."

She nodded uncertainly and headed back up the front walk.

Brantley opened the door, and Kendra took a deep whiff. Pinecones, wood varnish, and mint. Nothing that would indicate another corpse inside.

Thank goodness for small favors.

Or perhaps a gigantic favor. She'd been afraid if they found another corpse, it might be Waldridge.

They moved into the front hallway and looked around. Inside, it looked less like a fairy tale and more like a standard-issue ski lodge with an abundance of wood, shag rugs, and more wood. The furniture was heavy and dark, and ski equipment adorned the walls in such a fashion that Kendra couldn't tell if it was there for storage or decoration.

Lynch glanced around. "There are no personal items here. None."

Kendra nodded. "You're right. The only sign that anyone was even here is that half-empty coffee cup on the end table."

Brantley shrugged. "Maybe upstairs."

They mounted the stairs, which featured twin banister posts carved in the shape of boy and girl skiers. The steps creaked as they made their way up to the second floor. Kendra looked each way as they reached the top. It was basically a long hallway with doors to three bedrooms and a single bathroom. Small prints of snow scenes hung on the hallway walls, punctuating the gaps between rooms.

Kendra opened the door of the first room they passed and paused, staring into the darkness. "Dr. Waldridge stayed in here."

Brantley turned on the wall switch and peered inside at the room. "How do you know?"

"Arlington."

"As in the national cemetery?"

"As in the British-made cologne. Waldridge is the only man I've met who uses it. I'm also smelling a spray-on deodorant he uses. It's called Fogg." She turned toward Lynch. "I saw both bottles in Waldridge's hotel room this morning. He sprayed both in this room recently before he went to Santa Monica."

Brantley stared at her. "How can you possibly—?"

"Long story," Lynch said. "Let's look at the other rooms."

They walked down the hallway to a brightly-colored bedroom with bunk beds.

Brantley turned to Kendra. "Let me guess. The aroma of Play-Doh?"

She shook her head. "Just Ortho Home Defense Max insect spray. I don't think anyone's been in here recently."

The sergeant smiled. "Certainly not any roaches. One room to go."

The master bedroom at the end of the hallway was more than double the size of the others, and it featured a canopy bed that appeared to have been hand-carved. A flat-screen television was mounted to the opposite wall suspended over a rustic set of dresser drawers. An open suitcase was next to it stuffed with wrinkled clothing.

"Someone has gone through this suitcase," Kendra said.

Lynch looked at it. "Are you sure? You should see my bags after I've been out of town for a few weeks."

"It looks like it's been turned upside down onto the floor, and all the contents shoved back in here a piece at a time. It's possible he did it himself, but the rest of the place is so immaculate that it doesn't seem consistent with his fastidious nature."

Lynch looked around. "No computer."

"No computer, no phone. Although he did have an Acer laptop and an iPhone in here. And a computer bag, too. They were taken."

Brantley's brow wrinkled. "How do you figure that?"

"There are two power adapters still plugged in under the table. One's for an Acer laptop, the other has an Apple iPhone connector." She turned back to the open suitcase. "In that jumble of clothes, there's a leather computer-bag carry strap. With a good look and a bit of research, we'll probably even be able to identify the maker and style of the computer bag it goes with."

"You can't tell us off the top of your head?" Brantley joked.

"Don't even say that," Lynch said. "I have a hunch she'll soon know more about laptop-bag carry straps than we ever knew existed."

"Only if it's necessary," Kendra said. "Otherwise, I wouldn't waste my time right now."

Brantley stared at her. "I'm starting to get an idea why the FBI and all those police departments like you so much."

"That's not at all accurate. I don't think any of them will admit to actually liking me." She continued her scan of the room until she spotted his toiletries next to the sink in the connected bathroom. She stepped inside and looked them over. "Nothing unusual here. Though it does help to confirm that he was English. Maclean's toothpaste is a British brand."

Lynch had already begun opening the drawers and closet door. "Nothing here," he said. "Just a jacket in the closet, nothing in the pockets."

Kendra shook her head in frustration. "Unbelievable. Not a thing to let us know who he really was or what he was doing with Waldridge."

"We'll take the whole place apart to make sure there's nothing hidden someplace," Brantley said. "And, of course, we'll photograph and fingerprint the body in the next few hours."

"Good," Lynch said. "We'd appreciate it if you could forward your docs to the FBI field office in San Diego. It might help to find the man we're looking for."

"We can do that."

Kendra stepped back into the hallway. Damn. The trail to Waldridge had come to an abrupt halt, right to that man lying dead in the snow. A man without a name or even a—

She stopped.

What in the hell?

The work lights outside bathed the shadowy hallway in a dim glow, just enough that she could see that something was out of whack in the wood-paneled hallway.

"I know that look of yours," Lynch said quietly from behind her. "What do you see?"

"The pictures in this hallway . . . Can you see it?"

Lynch studied the nature scenes. "Other than they wouldn't be out of place in a cheap hotel room? No."

"It's not the pictures themselves . . . It's the walls. They're slightly faded from the sunlight that streams in here. It's darker where the pictures have been hanging. But it looks like they've been rearranged."

Lynch nodded slowly. "I see what you mean. The walls are slightly darker where the pictures have been, but they don't quite match now."

She stepped closer to the picture nearest to her. "It looks like these have been taken down for some reason, then put up in different places. And it happened recently." She pulled the picture off the wall and stared at the backside.

"What is it?" Lynch asked.

"Nothing, except . . ." She turned the picture around to show that the back of the canvas was covered with several purple splotches.

"Paint?" Brantley asked.

"I don't think so." She dabbed her finger into one of the splotches. "It's still sticky."

Lynch pulled two more pictures from the walls and spun them around. The backsides were covered with splotches that matched the ones on the first. He put them on the floor and continued down the hallway, pulling pictures off and setting them on the floor with their rear sides exposed. All ten pictures had the same markings.

"They're fresh," Lynch said. "All of them."

Brantley picked up one of the pictures and examined it more closely. "I don't get it."

"Join the club," Lynch said.

Kendra picked up the smallest of the pictures. "I want to take this one with us. The FBI lab might be able to tell us what it is."

* * *

KENDRA AND LYNCH DROVE back to the Big Bear Airport, and as arranged, they left the car parked outside the main departure building with the keys in a magnetic box tucked under the rear wheel. Kendra held the picture carefully in front of her as they boarded the plane.

"What do you think you have there?" Lynch asked.

"I have no earthly idea. Just like everything else we've run across . . . Lots of questions, but no answers. And I don't feel like I'm any closer to finding Waldridge."

He placed his hand in the small of her back. "You're closer than anyone else. And at least you're out here asking the questions."

His touch should have felt casual. But somehow it didn't. There was a warm comfort, an intimacy, about the way his palm was—

She stepped away from him. "And you're asking them with me." She put the picture down and settled on the large leather sofa in the plane's main compartment. She smiled wearily. "Thank you, Lynch."

"You're very welcome. We'll find him, Kendra."

There was something so definite about his tone that, for the first time since they'd found that body in the snow, she felt genuine hope. "Sure we will." She leaned back. "I guess I'm tired."

"It's been a long day. We'll get in the air, and I'll take you home."

She suddenly remembered. "My car . . . It's at your place."

"You're welcome to stay with me, and I'd certainly prefer it. But I know you well enough to know that you'll be more comfortable in your own bed."

"You *do* know me well."

"I'll drop you off at your place and pick you up tomorrow. The FBI lab may have some answers about that substance you found in Waldridge's hotel room. And while we're there, we can give them that picture to work on."

"Oh, they'll love that."

"They'll do it. Not because of the pressure I can put on them, but because they owe you. And they're smart enough to know that they'll need your help again sometime. You're the one with the real capital, not me."

"If that's true, I'll use it all if it will help me find Waldridge."

"I know. Waldridge is a lucky man." He picked up a throw blanket and draped it over her. "Get some sleep. I'll have you home in no time."

Intimacy again, she thought drowsily as she watched him go into the cockpit. The way he had tucked the blanket around her, his smile, the comfort that he had managed to instill. He had sensed that slight withdrawal and moved to reassure.

Why?

It didn't matter. Better just to accept the complications that made Lynch the man he was.

Just as she'd learned to accept the complications of Waldridge all those years ago . . .

CHAPTER
5

"*ENJOYING YOUR TIME* in London, Kendra?"

It was Dr. Waldridge's voice, she realized with relief.

It had been almost half an hour since she'd been wheeled into the surgical theater, and she was beginning to wonder if Dr. Waldridge was even going to show. He could have changed his mind, couldn't he? She smiled up from the operating table. "Nice of you to drop by. I hope I'm not cutting into your breakfast time."

"You are, but I'll try not to hold it against you. I'll make up for it at lunch. Did you get a good night's sleep?"

"Good enough, I guess." She was lying. She had been too tense, too aware of what this day could hold for her. But now he was here and, as usual, she felt calmer, more able to cope. "I'm surprised they didn't knock me out. They told me there isn't even an anesthesiologist in the room."

"That's right. No need. You'll be awake the entire time. I don't want you to miss a second of this."

"What kind of surgeon are you anyway?"

"The cunningly brilliant kind. Most of the difficult work has already been done. We've already combined stem-cell cultures with cells from your eyes, and we'll be secreting them back in with a formula we've developed to help your damaged retinas regenerate. Your body will be doing most of the work over the next few weeks, my dear."

"We hope."

"The human body is an amazing thing. You can sew on a severed finger and all those thousands of nerve endings will work furiously to reattach themselves within months. Incredible, isn't it? The body wants so very desperately to make itself whole. In this case, I'm just giving it a helping hand."

"Well, you do your part, and I'll do mine."

"It's a deal."

She cocked her head as she heard more footsteps entering the surgical theater. "But if this is such a simple procedure, why the big production?"

"Production is right. We have video cameras covering this from several angles. We'll be trying this a few different ways in our various subjects, and we need to see what works best."

"As long as mine is the one that works best, I'll be happy."

He chuckled. "So will I. By the way, your mother is watching. She's sitting in the observation booth above us."

"I told her she should go see Stonehenge or something."

"Well, maybe soon you can go see it with her."

Possibles. All those wonderful possibilities teasing her on the horizon.

Kendra smiled. "Aren't you supposed to manage my expectations? You told me yourself this was a long shot."

"And it is. But I have a good feeling about you."

"A 'good feeling'? That's funny talk coming from a research scientist."

"Agreed. And I can guarantee that I will never repeat it in any paper I write on the project. But instinct can be a powerful thing."

"If you say so." Anything he said at this moment was going to be fine with her. She was trying to fight the fear and the excitement and not show him either.

But evidently she hadn't been totally successful. "I say so," he said. "But you're something of a skeptic, so I brought you something to remind you while I give you the benefit of all my cunning brilliance." He took her hand and placed something in her palm. "Shh, don't tell anyone. It's not sterile."

"Are you trying to sabotage me?" Her fingers were probing, exploring. Tiny. Metal. Shaped like a—"Fish."

"Try again."

Then she knew what it was. "The dolphin charm you said your niece gave you. The one you always have on your key chain."

"It's only a loan. I get it back after I prove myself to you."

"Is it supposed to be lucky?"

"No, we make our own luck. But at the time when she gave it to me, I was having a rough time developing this process and was pretty discouraged. But Elswyth was only three, and she was facing years of therapy for cerebral palsy. She smiled up at me, and I knew that she would never surrender, never give up." He squeezed her hand,

and said softly, "So I couldn't either. Never surrender. Never give up."

She could feel the tears sting her eyes. "How is she?"

"Still fighting. Still splendid." He took a step closer. "Now, let's begin." His voice was very gentle. "I understand you brought an iPod loaded with music you'd like to listen to while we work."

"Only if it's okay with you," she said quickly. "You're the one doing the work here. If you want to listen to your classical music or whatever, I'm cool with that."

"Why does everyone think I prefer classical? Is it because I'm English?"

"English and highly educated. Sorry for pigeonholing you. What's your pleasure?"

He paused. "Well, I do have London Symphony Orchestra season tickets at the Barbican."

"Ha! I knew it."

"But pick any music you like. Your iPod's warmed up and waiting on the dock. Once I start work, I'll tune it out anyway."

It was going to start. Together, they were going to begin the adventure of her lifetime. Her hand tightened on the dolphin. Never surrender. Never give up.

She tried to concentrate on what they'd been talking about. Music. She thought for a moment. "How about The Clash? London Calling . . . "

KENDRA WOKE UP TO the sounds of The Clash in her ears though she hadn't set her music alarm. It was a memory echo of an album she hadn't played in years, but it came to her with astonishing clarity.

Then she remembered.

Waldridge.

Damn.

She checked her phone—7:17 A.M. One text from her mother, but nothing from the cops or the FBI. Probably a good thing. Any message from them at this early hour would most likely be bad news.

Nothing from Lynch yet, either. It had been almost 3 A.M. by the time he'd dropped her off at her condo, but she was sure he was already mapping out their day.

She opened the text from her mother. It read:

WAITING WITH BREAKFAST AND A POT OF COFFEE ACROSS THE STREET. COME OVER WHEN YOU WAKE UP.

What?

Kendra checked the time stamp. The text had come less than twenty minutes before.

Well, it was one way to start the day.

She threw off her covers and stepped into a pair of flip-flops. She splashed water in her face, ran a comb through her hair, and did a rudimentary teeth brushing. Then she left her condo, rode the elevator down, and ran across the busy street to Thompson's, a neighborhood restaurant that did a booming breakfast business, but was practically deserted every other hour of the day. Kendra knew just where to look. Her mother was at her usual table in the corner, surrounded by platters of Danish, bagels, waffles, and sausages. The food was competing for space with a tall coffeepot and two newspapers.

Kendra walked toward her. "Jeez, Mom. How many people are you expecting?"

"Just you. I wasn't sure what you would want, so I thought I'd give you a choice." She looked disapprovingly at Kendra's sweatpants and T-shirt. "You look like you just rolled out of bed."

"I *did* just roll out of bed. I knew you were waiting. You could have given me some warning, you know. If you wanted to meet for breakfast, I would have been happy to—"

"I didn't know until this morning. And you never get enough sleep, so I thought it would be best if I did it this way so you could join me whenever you woke up." She cleared a space for Kendra. "Sit down. Eat something."

Kendra took a seat and grabbed a Danish. "Don't you have class today?"

Her mother shook her head. "Finals week." Dr. Dianne Michaels was a history professor at UC San Diego and her skill as a lecturer was matched only by her impatience with students who didn't take her classes seriously. Kendra had no doubt that the kids were frantically preparing themselves for her mother's notoriously challenging final exam.

"So what brings you downtown on a weekday?"

Dianne folded the newspaper in her hands and placed it on the table. The headline read. BRITISH RESEARCHER MISSING, along with a photo of Waldridge.

Kendra stiffened in her seat. Not good. Her mother had been an integral part of both her operation and her relationship with Waldridge. She had a right to know what was going on. Kendra had just hoped to delay it until she had a more concrete idea herself.

"I can see from your expression that this isn't news to you."

"No, it's all I've been thinking about for the past twenty-four hours or so. I saw him the night before last."

"And you didn't tell me? I would have loved to be able to see him and—"

"He surprised me. He just showed up at my Malibu lecture. We had dinner afterward. I could tell something was wrong. He was . . . different."

"What do you mean?"

Kendra brought her mother up to speed on Waldridge, his disappearance, and her visit to Big Bear.

Dianne shook her head. "I should have known you'd be in the middle of this."

"You think I should just sit back and wait for the police to give me progress reports?"

"Believe it or not, that's the way it usually works."

"Not with me. Not when it concerns Waldridge. And you should be happy that I'm not going it alone."

"Maybe I should take some comfort in that." She grimaced. "But there's something about Mr. Lynch that frightens me."

"I can see that. He can be intimidating. Lucky for me, I'm on his good side."

Dianne looked away for a moment. "I know that. It's obvious he cares for you. He's very protective of you."

"So what's the problem?"

Dianne paused to put her thoughts into words. "I guess the problem is that I'm protective of you, too. Kendra . . . He's a dangerous man. Just in your experience with him, you know that. He wouldn't hesitate to kill anyone he thinks might be a threat."

"He wouldn't be alive otherwise. I might not be either."

"But don't you think he helps create the dangerous situations he finds himself in? The man comes on strong like a Mack truck. That kind of force practically demands a forceful response. I just don't want you standing next to him when that response comes."

"I can take care of myself."

"That's exactly the attitude that makes me worry so much about you."

"Hey, I'm your daughter." She smiled gently. "You taught me to take care of myself. Mostly by example."

"Well, now it's come back to bite me. The man has to live in an armored fortress. That should tell you something about him."

"It tells me that he knows how to take care of himself."

Dianne placed her hands on Kendra's. "Let's get the hell out of town. I'm done for the semester. My teaching assistant can administer the final exams. I was supposed to attend a seminar in Denver in a few days, but I'll cancel. Let's go someplace nice. Hawaii. I know what Dr. Waldridge means to you, and you've made sure he's on everyone's radar. Now it's time to let them do their jobs."

"I'll let them do their jobs. But I still need to do everything for him I can. You should know that more than anyone, Mom. You're the one who took me to him because you still believed in miracles. Well, he gave me that miracle. Now I have to do everything I can to give back. And I'm telling you, Lynch is valuable, an asset. He's already been a big help."

"Glad you think so," a familiar voice said. "I can but try."

Kendra and Dianne looked up to see Lynch walking toward the table, smiling broadly. "Good morning, Dianne. Wonderful to see you again." He leaned close and kissed her on the cheek.

Dianne shook off her look of surprise. "Mr. Lynch . . . Kendra didn't tell me that she invited you here."

"She didn't," Lynch said. "I was on my way for a visit, and I glimpsed her dashing across the street. It just took me awhile to find a parking spot." He turned to Kendra. "Well rested?"

"Ha. Very funny."

He shrugged. "When I first saw you on the street, I thought it was a young woman on her walk of shame."

"Flatterer. But when you got closer and saw it was me, you realized . . . ?"

"No, I quickly realized it couldn't be a walk of shame. Not with that sloppy look you're sporting."

"Right," Dianne said.

Kendra rolled her eyes. "Okay, enough about my clothes. This is what I slept in."

"Obviously," Lynch said.

Diane smiled and motioned toward an empty chair. "Mr. Lynch, would you care—"

Before she could finish her thought, Lynch dropped down in the chair and began scooping food onto an empty plate. "Smells delicious. Are these waffles as good as they look?"

"Better," Kendra said, watching him with an amused look. "By all means, help yourself. Don't worry about leaving me any. I'm not very—"

"Okay." He deposited the rest of the waffles on his plate. He looked up. "I take it Kendra has brought you up to speed on the disappearance of Dr. Waldridge?"

Dianne nodded.

"And I'm quite sure you voiced your displeasure with her taking the case, particularly with me?"

Dianne looked flustered, which was most unusual for her. "I—Well, I only . . ."

"It's quite all right. You wouldn't do your duty as a

mother if you didn't say those things." He poured syrup on his waffles. "Just let me assure you that your daughter's safety is always my number one priority."

"I don't doubt your desire to protect her, Mr. Lynch. But there are things you can't always control."

Kendra leaned forward. "Okay, Mom. Enough. You haven't grilled a guy like this since Tommy Schiller took me to my high-school prom."

"Tommy Schiller?" Lynch said. "I think I need to hear about this guy."

"No, you don't," Kendra said firmly. "He was thoughtful and sweet. Qualities that would never interest you."

Lynch made a face. "Ugh, you're right. Definitely anemic. But they apparently didn't interest you either since you now refer to him in the past tense."

She opened her mouth, but she didn't have a response.

Lynch turned to Dianne. "You were probably right to grill him. What tipped you off?"

"I thought he might be a phony." Dianne shrugged. "He was very slick, but there was something about him. She was still blind at the time, and I was afraid that she couldn't sense what I could see."

"You didn't tell me that, Mom," Kendra said. "Why?"

"You were stubborn. I wanted you to trust your instincts, but there was always the chance that you might resent my interference. I had to be careful."

"So careful that somehow Tommy faded into never-never land."

"It's all right," Lynch said. "I'm sure Tommy has gotten over you by now." He glanced at Dianne. "Good job."

Kendra said with exasperation, "Surely you didn't come here to talk about my high-school boyfriends."

"No, but I found it fascinating." Lynch grabbed a pecan

roll and poured himself a cup of coffee. "As much as I enjoy watching you squirm, I wanted to discuss our strategy for today. I thought it would be best if we started camping out at the FBI lab as early as possible. Although we were promised priority, things have a way of slipping down the to-do list if you don't stay in their faces there."

"And you learned that the hard way."

"You don't get very far in the FBI without learning to navigate a bureaucracy."

"Sounds like the best way to navigate that is to leave and just go freelance."

"It works for me."

"Okay. So we make pests of ourselves at the FBI. I have a lot of practice at that. I'll also follow up with Santa Monica PD and the Big Bear police."

Dianne threw up her hands. "I guess Hawaii isn't even on the table. I suppose I'm heading for that seminar in Denver in a couple days."

"Sorry, Mom. I have to do this."

"I know when to accept defeat. So what can I do to help?"

"Nothing."

"Don't say that. If you're going to do this, I have to feel useful somehow. I care about Dr. Waldridge, too." She smiled. "You're right, he was the dream maker. I remember the first time you looked at me after the operation and really saw me. I wanted to get down on my knees to him."

"So did I." Kendra was silent a moment. "Well, you're still fairly well hooked in to the academic scene in London, aren't you?"

"I don't know if I'd call it a 'scene,' but I do have quite a few friends at the universities there."

"Maybe you can ask around about Dr. Waldridge. See

if anybody has any idea what he's been working on, who he's been working with."

She pursed her lips. "Hmm. Sounds like busywork to me."

"It's not. It could really help us."

Dianne thought for a moment. "Okay. I'll see what I can do."

"Thanks, Mom."

She waved her hands. "Now go. Leave. Get out of here, before Mr. Lynch eats the rest of my breakfast."

But there was definite amusement in the remark, Kendra noticed.

"I like your mother," Lynch said as he guided Kendra through the crowded restaurant. "Charming *and* sensible. I'm glad we arranged to have breakfast with her today."

"I didn't arrange to have breakfast with her. You might say I was hijacked." She glanced at him. "Now, *you* might have arranged it. I found it a little too coincidental that you happened to see me flying across the street and decided to join us."

He smiled. "Coincidences do happen."

"And so does that truly amazing skill with electronics and phones that you've used on me before. When you stopped by to pick me up, and I didn't answer the door, did you hack into my phone and read Mom's text?"

"Why, Kendra, you told me never to do that again."

"And when did that ever stop you when you wanted to do something." She tilted her head. "But why did you want to join us? It was almost all attacks on my sloppy clothes and past boyfriends and . . ." She stopped. "Mom. It was all aimed at Mom. You were manipulating her, you bastard. All of it was making sure she considered you both on the same team, fighting the same fight. By the time we left, you'd gotten exactly what you wanted."

"I like her," he repeated. "And I knew she'd be more comfortable about you if she liked me. I enjoyed breakfast, and I found out more about you, and Dianne knows that she can trust me because we both think Tommy Schiller would have been a big mistake. I think it's been a good day so far."

"And I think that Mom was right." She gazed thoughtfully at him. "You're a very dangerous man, Lynch."

"Without doubt." He nodded. "But not to you. Never to you, Kendra. And now Dianne knows that whatever threat I am is aimed at protecting you from the Tommy Schillers of the world. We just won't mention all the other serial killers and scumbags you might stumble across. Okay?" He took her elbow and guided her across the busy street. "Now, let's get you out of those sloppy sweatpants and into something more alluring to impress the lab boys."

FBI Regional Field Office
San Diego

Kendra and Lynch arrived at FBI field-office main lobby and approached the reception desk. Kendra spoke brusquely to the thick-necked young man behind the counter. "Kendra Michaels and Adam Lynch to see Special Agent in Charge Michael Griffin."

She expected a blank look and at least two phone calls before they would be admitted since no one had any idea they were coming. Instead, the guard immediately slapped two badges on the counter, each preprinted with their names.

"The lab's on the eighth floor. Do you know where you're going?"

Kendra stared at him in disbelief. This circumventing of bureaucracy was mind-boggling in her experience. "Uh, yes. Of course."

The man glanced down at the small nature print that Lynch was holding in his left hand. "Nice painting."

"It really isn't." Lynch scooped the badges up and steered Kendra toward the elevator. "Thank you."

After the elevator doors closed, Kendra shook her head as she clipped on the badge. "What just happened? Did you tell them we were coming?"

"No. Not at all. I guess I didn't have to. Griffin knows us too well."

"He sure does."

"And this way, we're the lab's problem. Appearances to the contrary, Griffin is no fool."

The elevator opened almost directly in front of the white double doors of the forensics lab. A slender, ponytailed young man in a white lab coat walked past. Kendra remembered him from another case.

"Dustin Freen?"

Freen turned around and smiled. "Hi, guys. What took you so long? I thought you would have been here awhile ago."

"Apparently everyone knew that but us," Kendra said.

Lynch immediately got down to business. "Do you have something for us?"

"Actually, I do. I came in early today. Way early. Griffin authorized overtime for this."

"Nice of him," Kendra said.

Lynch smiled. "He probably wants to clear the lab and get us out of his hair as quickly as possible."

Freen spoke to Kendra. "You say that fluid transfer came from the floor in Dr. Waldridge's hotel room?"

"Yes," Kendra said. "I couldn't quite identify the odor."

"Come in. I may have some answers for you."

He led them through the double doors into the lab. They walked past several aisles of scientific equipment and lab tables before reaching a series of cubicles that wouldn't have been out of place in any office in corporate America.

But instead of Dilbert cartoons, most were decorated with gruesome crime-scene photos.

Freen leaned into his cubicle and picked up a printout. "It appears to be a combination of some fairly typical household products."

"Like what?" Kendra asked.

"Like sodium metabisulfite and sodium hydrosulfite."

"Common in *your* household, maybe."

"They're the principal ingredients of a rust-stain remover. The trade name is Iron-Out. It was mixed with a smaller amount of hydrogen peroxide."

Lynch clicked his tongue. "That's not good news."

Kendra looked from one to the other. "What am I missing?"

Lynch took a deep breath. "If someone tried to clean up blood from a crime scene, it almost always shows up under Luminol and an ultraviolet light. But there are ways of obscuring it."

"Like bleach?" Kendra asked.

"That's one way," Freen said. "But bleach stinks and totally discolors any carpeting and many hard surfaces it comes into contact with. If you're trying to cover up a crime, that's not a very stealthy way of doing it."

Kendra glanced at the report in Freen's hands. "I don't think I like where this is headed."

Lynch spoke gently. "Iron-Out and hydrogen peroxide can be sprayed over an area to obliterate any bloodstains that might show up under Luminol and a UV light. It doesn't have a strong odor and doesn't cause discoloration. There are other chemicals that may be more effective, but these products are easier to get."

"Shit," she whispered. "Someone's trying to hide a bloodstain."

Freen nodded. "That's the way it looks. You probably wouldn't have even known if the liquid hadn't pooled where you found it. Maybe there was a spill, or it was over-sprayed in one area. Santa Monica PD has already been in touch with us about it. They say they probably wouldn't even know about it if you hadn't picked up on it, Kendra."

Someone's trying to hide a bloodstain.

She could still see the horrified look on the face of that dead man lying in the snow. Did the same thing happen to Waldridge?"

"He could still be okay," Lynch said.

"But it just got a hell of a lot less likely," she said jerkily. "But I'm not giving up."

"I know," Lynch said softly.

Kendra grabbed the framed print from Lynch's hand and displayed the backside to Freen. "I need you to do something else for me."

"Okay," Freen said doubtfully.

"We found this at the murder scene in Big Bear. We discovered this and nine others, all with fresh splotches on the back. I need to know what this purple stuff is."

Freen took it from her and held it up, letting the overhead fluorescent light play across the rear surface. "Where did this come from?"

"No idea. But it was placed there and put back on the wall, along with the other prints."

Freen nodded. "I can take a look, but I'll have to get approval from Griffin."

"Please do," Lynch said. "And tell him to call me if he'd like to discuss it."

KENDRA SLUMPED DOWN IN the seat of Lynch's car, trying to fight off the depression. They had just left the FBI building parking lot, and she had been too lost in thought to even speak as they left the building.

"Talk to me," Lynch said.

"Not much to say. It's not what I was hoping for, but after seeing that body in the snow last night, I've been preparing for the worst."

"Well, it's better to know. The police can start testing the floor to see if they can get DNA match off any of the blood residue. And it's likely they'll now allocate more manpower and resources to the case."

She nodded. Okay, think on the positive side. "Yes. And we do have a lot of things set in motion. We have the FBI testing the material from the back of the picture, and hopefully we'll be able to ID Waldridge's associate before too long."

Lynch reached under his seat and pulled out his tablet computer. "I have something that may help."

She tried to smile. "Sorry, but your skill at Angry Birds isn't going to be much use to us right now."

"I don't like computer games. You should know that by now."

"Of course. When you've mowed down dozens of armed assailants in real life, an online game can't compare."

"I wish I was half as interesting as you make me out to be."

"Are you denying it?"

"I can neither confirm nor deny any operations in which—"

"Blah-blah-blah."

He flipped back the tablet cover and showed her a close-cropped photo of a man's head and shoulders. "Look familiar?"

She took the tablet and stared at the photo for a moment. "That's the dead man we found . . . But he's alive here. Where did you get this?"

"He's not alive here. This is the picture I took with my phone last night. After I got home, I e-mailed it to a friend who's a wizard with Photoshop. I had her alter the picture to show how he might have looked when he was alive."

"This is amazing . . . How did she get the eye color?"

"She just guessed. I didn't think to lift his lids when we were out there last night, so she inserted a pair of eyes she found online. They're actually Robert Redford's eyes."

"Really?" Kendra looked for some sign that the picture had been altered, but the effect was seamless.

"I also sent her a photo I took off the airport security video. The camera was too far away to be of much help, but it did give her an idea of how he set his jaw and eyeline when he was alive."

"I'm impressed." She handed the tablet back. "Who is this wizard? One of your government photography experts?"

"No. Actually . . ." he paused a long moment before finishing, ". . . it was Ashley."

"Your supposed ex-girlfriend?"

"My *definite* ex-girlfriend."

"Whose photography skill obviously goes beyond merely standing in front of a camera."

"It's her career. She's made it her business to know everything about the process."

"The process. Making a dead guy look like he's alive."

"This was a first for her. She enjoyed the challenge."

"If one of my exes e-mailed a picture of a dead guy to me, I might not be so understanding."

"Sure you would. And then you'd solve the case yourself."

She shrugged. "You might be right about that."

"I know I am."

"Incredible. It's not enough that every city bus had a larger-than-life ad with Ashley's beautiful Asian face and magnificent bikini-clad body, she can also toss this off on command."

"Time is of the essence. I wanted it done quickly, so I asked her. She was happy to do it. It could help us to identify him. People get a little . . . disturbed when you flash them a picture of a corpse, and it often doesn't look like the person they knew. This is probably a more accurate picture of him."

"I agree." Kendra gestured toward the picture. "She even neatened his hair."

"And the photo will come in handy for an idea I have."

"What's that?"

"You gave it to me when you were talking your mother this morning. It's a very good idea to approach this from the London angle. What Waldridge was working on, who he was working with . . ."

"I'm not going to London."

"That's not what I'm suggesting. I know someone there. We should contact him."

Kendra checked her watch. "I have some appointments today. Two at the studio and one new referral. I really can't miss them."

"Do you still have a teleconferencing setup at your studio?"

"Yes."

He started up the car. "We'll use it to get in touch with my friend. It will only take a few minutes."

CHAPTER
6

AFTER A QUICK DETOUR TO Kendra's condo, so she could pick up her car, they met at her office, situated on the ground floor of a medical building. Most of her space was dedicated to a large, carpeted studio where she conducted her music-therapy sessions. The room was filled with an assortment of musical instruments, an adjacent observation area, and a seventy-inch television monitor.

Lynch looked at the monitor. "Do you use your teleconferencing equipment often?"

"Occasionally. Music therapy is a new discipline, and we're still feeling our way with new techniques. It's a good way for me and my colleagues to share our sessions and compare results."

"Well, I think it would be an excellent way for you and my friend to meet each other."

"Really? Why? And just who is this guy?"

"His name is Ryan Malone, but he'll take serious offense

if you call him anything but Rye. He's a good man, extraordinarily competent at what he does."

"What, exactly, does he do?"

"A little difficult to explain. He's kind of like me."

"I already don't like him."

"Rude. Very rude. And not truthful. You will like him. He's Oxford-educated and spent his first several years out of college writing reports and doing research for the various intelligence agencies. Then he got restless and started taking assignments out in the field. Turned out he was good at it. He saved my bacon a couple of times."

"Do you think he'll help us?"

"I would think so." Lynch gave her a sideways glance. "I've also saved his bacon. And he's usually available. He really doesn't like to work. He relaxes in his house in the English countryside, drinking wine and reading French literature. When he runs out of money, he just takes another assignment."

Kendra smiled. "Sounds like he has it figured out."

"He does. He's probably the happiest person I know." Lynch held up his phone. "I've already traded texts with him. He's expecting our call. His address is right here."

Kendra glanced at the address on Lynch's phone and picked up her teleconferencing remote. She keyed in the address and looked at the screen, which glowed blue with the manufacturer's logo. The screen flickered and, finally, an image appeared. It was a large brown leather chair in what looked like a study. A moment later, a fiftyish man dropped into the chair. As he smiled, his thick moustache jumped high on his round face. "What in the bloody hell have you gotten yourself into now, Lynch." His tone was playful, with a thick British accent.

"Nothing you can't get me out of, Rye."

"Tell me something I don't know. Who's your pretty friend?"

"This is Kendra Michaels. I've told you about her."

His eyes widened. "Ah, yes. The blind girl who now isn't."

Kendra smiled. "I hope there's more to me than that."

"Of course there is, my dear. I've heard of your remarkable achievements. But surely you understand why I would be so fascinated by the wonderful gift you've been given."

"I do understand. And it is wonderful."

"But there's something I've wondered ever since I heard your story, if you'll indulge me . . . When you finally got your sight, was there anything that . . . *disappointed* you?"

She thought for a moment. "Something I saw that didn't live up to my expectations?"

"Exactly."

"Well, disappointment is a strong word. Almost everything I saw was beautiful to me. Still is. But there was something that was . . . disturbing."

"Yes?"

"Noses."

He looked at her in disbelief, then roared with laughter. "Really?"

She nodded. "Obviously, I've always been able to feel them, so I knew they stuck out and had nostrils on the underside. But there was something about actually seeing them . . . They looked strange to me. I was really kind of freaked-out for a while."

He laughed again. "That's fantastic. I love it."

"You just reminded me of another one."

"What's that?"

"The facial expressions people make when they laugh."

"Seriously?"

"Yes. The wide-open mouth, closed eyes, the red face . . . It was strange at first. But now it may be my favorite thing in the world."

"Mine, too, my dear." He wiped his eyes. "Thank you for tolerating my rude curiosity. I hope I can make it up to you."

"You can," Lynch said.

Rye chuckled. "Somehow I thought I might. What's going on?"

Lynch stepped toward the monitor, getting down to business. "We've been working on a missing-persons investigation. He's a resident of the UK, but it happened while he was here visiting Southern California. His name is Charles Waldridge, he's a surgeon and medical researcher."

"Who changed my life," Kendra added quietly. "Dr. Waldridge gave me my sight."

"Ah, then I understand." Rye jotted notes on a small pad resting on his chair arm. "How long has he been missing?"

"Less than forty-eight hours," Lynch said. "We found the body of an associate of his last night. He'd been murdered. We haven't ID'd him yet."

"Hmm. You don't think Waldridge killed him and went on the lam?"

Kendra shook her head. She'd had an instant of fierce protective defensiveness before she'd smothered it. Rye was the first to say it, but she was sure others had begun to mull that possibility. "No," she said flatly. "No way."

"Where did Waldridge work?"

"He was vague when we spoke about it the other night," Kendra said. "But he worked with the Night Watch Project for years. It's based there in London. You can find a lot about it online."

Rye jotted down some more notes. "And about you, I'm sure. I'll take a look."

"I'll send you an e-mail with all the details of the case so far," Lynch said. "The FBI and the local police are helping us locally, but we could use some help on the London angle. I thought that with your research and investigative background . . ."

"And a willingness to get my hands dirty," Rye interrupted.

"That shouldn't be necessary."

"One man's missing and another is dead." Rye put down the pen and leaned forward in his chair. "Not a promising situation. There could be something very dark at the bottom of this. You should both be careful."

Kendra smiled. "You're the second person to say that to me today. The other was my mother."

Rye groaned. "That's a new low. I meet a beautiful woman, and she says I remind her of her mother."

"I've heard women say much worse to you," Lynch said.

"You're right." Rye sighed. "Often accompanied by a hard slap across the face. I guess I should consider myself lucky."

"Will you help us?" Kendra asked.

"Why not?" Rye gestured around the room. "It's about time I got out for a while. I've made this place far too comfortable for myself. Send me the info, and I'll see what I can find out."

Lynch bowed his head and gave a mock salute. "Thanks, Rye. You're the best."

Rye cut the connection.

Lynch turned to Kendra. "Well, that's another front we've covered. Rye is extremely thorough. If there's anything to be found out there, he'll uncover it."

"I hope so." The moment of distraction and optimism that Rye had brought was fading fast. "Thank you, Lynch."

He caught the change immediately, and his eyes narrowed. "Sure. Anything wrong?"

At that moment, the studio door opened, and Selena Motter entered with her eight-year-old twin sons. One of the boys suffered from depression, and Kendra had been successfully using duo sessions to draw him out.

Kendra nodded. "I think work is just what I need right now."

"Good. I'll go home and send Rye the photograph and everything else I have." He reached out and gave her hand a quick squeeze. "We'll touch base tonight."

He leaned close to her, but pulled away as the two boys bounded closer.

Lynch smiled at them. "Go easy on her, guys."

He turned and walked out of the room.

KENDRA'S BACK-TO-BACK afternoon sessions were just the jolt she needed. Her anxiety didn't completely dissipate, but it felt good to focus on something other than Waldridge. It didn't hurt that both clients appeared to be success stories.

Finally, a few rays of light to scatter the oppressive darkness.

She checked her phone for the e-mail that had come in early that morning. A psychologist in Mission Valley wanted her to meet with a young autistic girl who might benefit from her techniques. After an hour-long evaluation at her psychologist's office, Kendra would decide if she'd take her on or not. Not everyone responded to music therapy, and it would serve no one's best interest to waste time on techniques that would have little chance of succeeding with this particular patient.

Kendra drove the twenty minutes to Mission Valley and found her way to the smallish, two-story medical building that bordered the Riverwalk Golf Course. The medical building was new. So new, in fact, that there were still pallets of ceiling tiles sitting in the lobby, and the lone elevator had yet to be activated.

No problem, she thought as she started up the freshly tiled stairs. She needed the exercise anyway. She climbed to the second floor, then the third.

She left the staircase and stepped into the hallway. It was dimly lit, as if all the offices had closed for the day, and everybody had gone home.

She checked her watch—5:15 P.M., right on schedule.

So where the hell was everybody?

She glanced down at the floor, where long boxes of molding lined the corridor. The air was thick with the odor of paint and new carpeting.

She approached Suite 316, where she was supposed to meet her prospective new client.

She stopped.

No name on the door. The frosted-glass panels next to it were dark, indicating no life or activity beyond.

She tried the handle. Locked.

What the hell?

She checked her phone to make sure they hadn't canceled.

Nope.

She scrolled through her old messages to make sure she was at the right place.

Yep.

But the entire floor appeared to be empty. Just like the entire building, for that matter.

Someone was yanking her chain.

But why? Why in the hell would anyone—?

Footsteps echoed behind her.

She turned. They were coming up the stairs. Good. Maybe she could get some answers.

The footsteps suddenly stopped.

Then a moment later, they resumed. But slower. And quieter. It was like . . .

Like someone who was trying not to be heard as they approached this floor.

Tap. Tap. Tap. Tap.

They were getting closer.

Tap. Tap.

Kendra spun around.

These were coming from the other side of the hall.

Tap. Tap.

Another person trying not to be heard.

Whispers behind her.

Then in front of her.

They were talking to each other.

She wasn't just being paranoid. She was sure they were on their phones or some other devices engaged in a hushed conversation.

And they were both still moving toward her.

She could feel her heart start to pound.

Tap. Tap.

Shit!

The lights had shut off. She couldn't see her hand in front of her face.

That was okay. *More* than okay.

Did they even know who they were dealing with here? She was at home in the dark.

She crouched low against one of the closed office doors. Stay calm. Focus.

Neither of these people, whoever they were, knew that exactly twenty-six steps separated her from the stairs. They weren't aware of the two cartons of molding, box of nails, and the large fire extinguisher in their path. She could make the darkness work for her.

She looked up. Two green eyes glowed at the end of the hallway.

Her heart sank. Oh, no.

Night-vision goggles.

She turned back. Another pair of goggles glowing in the darkness. They could see everything clear as day.

And they were moving toward her.

Her eyes flicked between the two. Judging from the height of the goggles, she was dealing with two large men between six feet and six-foot-two. If she waited, it would be two against one.

Can't let that happen.

She leaped to her feet and ran back toward the stairs, zeroing in on the glowing eyes.

Gotta do this just right . . .

The assailant appeared to be frozen in place, stunned by her frontal assault.

Or had he just stopped to aim a weapon at her?

Can't think about that. Play it smart . . .

She ducked and weaved at the last moment, never breaking stride as she reached out with her outstretched hand.

She clawed upward and ripped the goggles from his face.

She felt his skin fly beneath her fingernails. She whirled around and landed a direct kick to what she thought were his kidneys. The man grunted and fell to the floor.

She spun around and ran for the stairs. Just another few—

Pain. Horrible, excruciating pain between her shoulder blades.

Can't breathe. Can't move.

Her legs weakened, and she felt the floor rushing toward her. Two strong arms grabbed her before she landed. She looked up.

Two glowing green eyes. The other man now had her in his grip. He dragged her to one of the offices and threw open the door. The early-evening twilight flooded in through the bare windows.

At last she could see, but the only sight that greeted her was a nightmare. There, in the middle of the bare office, was a roll of duct tape, a large fifty-five gallon drum, a handcart, and a hypodermic needle.

Great. A psychopath's standard-issue abduction kit.

She could feel her legs again, but they were weak. Rubbery. She was in no condition to fight this man, but if she didn't do something fast, she knew she was going into that damn barrel. She dug her nails into his hand, but that was the only resistance she could summon.

The other man moaned in the hallway as she found herself dragged toward the hypodermic needle.

In an instant, the man's low moan gave way to a shriek. Then silence.

The man holding her called out to his partner. "She's not easy. Stop whining and get in here. Now!"

Silence.

The man grunted a curse word and threw her to the

ground. He placed a knee on her back and picked up the needle.

Kendra's eyes darted around the room. She couldn't move, but there had to be some way, somehow that . . .

Zzzzot!

She heard an electrified crackling, and in the next instant, her attacker was facedown next to her.

What the hell?

She rolled over. The man was twitching and gurgling, and the sudden acrid odor let her know that he was wetting his pants. Then a familiar pair of boots strode into view.

SIDI Fusion Lei motorcycle riding boots. Size seven or eight.

She looked up. A woman stood over her, wearing a motorcycle helmet with tinted visor so as to entirely obscure her face. She wore tight jeans and a brown leather jacket, and she held a still-sparking Taser before her.

"You're hurt. Can you stand?" The woman's voice echoed from behind the visor.

Kendra shook her head to clear it. "I think so . . . yes."

"Then get the hell out of here. You have about three minutes before this wears off." The woman placed the Taser on the back of the man's neck and hit him with another blast of electricity. He screamed and twitched again.

The woman turned to Kendra and shrugged. "Maybe a little longer than three minutes."

"Who—Who are you?"

She ignored the question. "Let me see you stand."

Slowly and gingerly, Kendra pulled herself up. She struggled to maintain her balance.

"Walk." She nodded as Kendra took a faltering step. "Now *go*. Don't waste time."

"Who are you," she repeated.

"For God's sake." She was plainly disgusted. "You sound like someone from a Marvel comic book. I've heard a lot about you, but nobody told me you were stupid. Well, I may be awesome, but I'm no superhero. I just want to get you the hell out of here before I have to stick around to give this guy another zot. Get *moving*."

"I want to know—"

But the woman was already out the door. She paused only long enough to hit the man in the hallway with another jolt from her Taser.

Kendra tried to run to catch up with her, but her wobbly legs and back weren't allowing it. "Wait!"

The woman was gone.

Kendra looked back at the still-twitching thug in the hall. Probably not a good idea to stick around. She could still remember the sense of panic she had felt when she had been helpless, unable to move.

She moved toward the stairs, gripped the railing, and moved down one step at a time. By the time she reached the second floor, she felt herself getting stronger.

She heard a motorcycle rev outside and roar down the street. Thank you, whoever you are. You may be rude as hell, but I owe you big-time.

She looked up.

There was a sound above her. Her attackers were obviously recovering . . .

Get out!

She hurried down the rest of the stairs and moved quickly out the front door. She glanced around the parking lot. No one else there as far as she could tell.

She slid into her car and started it.

She could still hear the woman's voice ringing in her ears. *Get the hell out of here . . .*

She got the hell out of there.

She drove a few blocks, and when she was sure that she wasn't being followed, she voice-dialed Lynch. He answered immediately.

"What's up?"

She drew a deep breath. "More than I'd like. Two guys just tried to grab me."

"What?"

"My afternoon consult was a total setup. It was an empty building. They came prepared, complete with hypodermic and barrel for removal."

Lynch muttered a curse. "Dammit, you could have been killed."

"They didn't want to kill me. That would have been easy for them. They wanted to drug me and carry me out of there. I'm telling you, they had it all set up."

"How did you get away?"

"You're not going to believe this. I had help from our motorcycle-riding friend from Big Bear."

He was silent for a long moment. "You're right. I don't believe it."

"I'm still having a tough time believing it myself. Though it was a dose of cold reality when she accused me of being stupid when I started asking her questions instead of doing what she told me to do. She came out of nowhere and laid them out with a stun gun."

"How long has it been?"

"Just a few minutes."

"Okay, I'm calling Griffin and the cops and have them go there. Give me the address."

Kendra gave him the building's street address. "It was the third floor. I'll meet them there when they—"

"No. Get someplace safe. Maybe your mother's house."

That sounded exactly like what she wanted to do, she thought. And then maybe curl up in bed and put her head under the covers. She couldn't do it. "I'm going back there."

"The hell you are."

"I was there. It happened to *me*. I can help." Kendra turned down a side street and pulled up to the curb. "I just pulled over. I'll wait fifteen minutes before I go back. I'll hang back from a safe distance, and I won't go in until I see the squad cars."

"Just this once, I wish you would—"

"I'll see you there, Lynch."

She cut the connection.

"I'M NOT SURE ALL THIS WAS really necessary," Kendra said as she eyed the four cruisers and two unmarked police cars in the office-building parking lot. She stepped toward Special Agent Roland Metcalf who was waiting for her in the parking lot.

Metcalf smiled. "When Kendra Michaels snaps her fingers . . ."

"Not funny. Cut the sarcasm. Anybody inside?"

"No. Two uniformed officers were first on the scene. They did a sweep, but the men who attacked you had already left." He shrugged. "*Dancing with the Stars* is on tonight. How could you compete? Can't really blame 'em."

She managed a smile. She could always count on Metcalf to try to defuse any tense situation. He was a tall, good-looking man in his midtwenties, and Lynch was sure he had a major crush on her.

Metcalf didn't return her smile. "Hey, you look pretty rough. Are you okay?"

"Yes. Fine. One of the guys got a solid punch between my shoulders and literally struck a nerve, but I'm feeling better now."

He nodded. "Good. Adam Lynch filled us in, but I'm going to need a full statement from you. San Diego PD will want one, too."

"No problem. As soon as I get a look up there."

Two strong arms suddenly wrapped around her from behind. Kendra jumped and let out a startled yelp.

She turned to see that it was Lynch and drew a relieved breath. She backed away from him with her hand to her chest. "I'm sorry," she said. "Guess I'm still jumpy."

"Shit." Lynch shook his head. "I'm an ass. I'm the one who should apologize. I don't know what I was thinking after what you've just gone through. I saw you standing there and I just wanted to—" He repeated, "I'm an ass. I'm sorry, Kendra."

"That's okay." She was as much surprised by Lynch's action as her own case of nerves. Lynch was always cool and contained and seldom displayed any emotion but mockery. "It might not have been your fault. My back took a hit."

"Did it?" His lips tightened. "I'll have to remember . . ."

"Do you still want to go up?" Metcalf was frowning. He was obviously surprised and uneasy with Lynch's show of protectiveness. "Maybe you should—"

"I want to go," she interrupted. "Let's do it."

Kendra led them into the building and up the stairs, giving them a step-by-step description of her visit there only minutes before. As she drew closer to the scene of her confrontation, she found her slight nervousness giving away to anger.

Anger at those bastards for making her feel helpless and unsafe.

Anger at herself for showing fear in front of Metcalf, Lynch, and those cops in the parking lot.

She was practically steaming by the time she stepped onto the third floor.

Lynch squeezed her arm. "I'm sensing a bit of tension or more likely gale-force winds. Are you okay?"

"Yes." She clenched her jaw. "I'm sure as hell not letting them get into my head."

"Good."

She pointed ahead. "I put one of them down right there, but the other struck me in the middle of the back and dragged me into that office." She led them through the open door, where three uniformed officers were standing around the green fifty-five-gallon drum.

Kendra glanced around. "This is all you found?"

"Yes, ma'am," one of the officers replied. "Not sure what this barrel is for."

"It was for me." She gestured to the floor. "There was duct tape, a hypodermic needle, and a gray handcart, but they obviously picked those up on the way out. They also took the night-vision goggles that I knocked off the man in the hallway. I guess they were in too much of a hurry to take this thing."

Metcalf crouched next to the drum. "They knew it would have been a giant marker identifying them as the people we're looking for. We might be able to get some prints off it."

"Well, we do have DNA for both of them."

Lynch slanted a glance toward her. "How do you figure that?"

Kendra stepped toward the uniformed cops. "Officers, I need two plastic, evidence-collection bags. Can you help me out?"

The police officers pulled clear plastic bags from their pockets and gave them to Kendra. She placed her hands inside each one and pulled the adhesive seal taut around her wrists.

She held up her plastic-wrapped hands. "I scratched the hell out of both of those guys. I have their skin under my fingernails. Attacker A with the right hand, attacker B with the left."

Metcalf nodded approvingly. "If either of them has been in jail in the last decade or so, their DNA should be in the CODIS database."

"Exactly what I was thinking."

"Well done," Lynch said quietly.

She grimaced. "Not pleasant. But my options were limited. I was feeling pretty helpless. It's all I had."

Metcalf pulled out his phone. "Tell you what. Suppose I get some forensics people out here so that you won't have to walk around with those bags on your hands for the rest of the evening."

"Great idea," Kendra said grimly. "I don't need any reminders. I have more than enough."

AS PROMISED, A CRIME-SCENE tech arrived within thirty minutes and scraped the skin from Kendra's fingernails. After giving a statement to Metcalf and the police officers on the scene, Kendra left with Lynch.

Metcalf appeared clearly disappointed when she refused

IRIS JOHANSEN & ROY JOHANSEN

his offer of a lift to her home. But he smiled back at Kendra and waved as they walked away from him.

"See?" Lynch said as they walked across the parking lot. "The guy has a major crush on you. Even you can't be so socially impaired that you don't see it."

She smiled. "Okay, you may be right about him."

"Of course I'm right. The only question is, what are you going to do with that information?"

"Nothing. Metcalf is intelligent and handsome, and I'm sure he has his choice of women."

"Not the one he wants." Lynch leaned closer to her as they reached their cars. "So what are you waiting for? *Who* are you waiting for?"

The heat of his body was radiating, touching her own. She had to hold her ground against his sudden intrusion into her personal space. She wouldn't let him know it disturbed her. "What business is it of yours?"

"Consider me a concerned bystander."

"That doesn't answer the question. It's your business because—?"

"I care. Isn't that enough?"

That could be a barbed or enigmatic question coming from Lynch. But she wasn't going to be anything but honest. "Sure it's a good reason. Fine. Those years after I got my sight, the wild days, I was with a lot of guys just because I cared enough about them to do it."

"Even with our funny-looking noses?"

"Yes."

"Just out of curiosity, what would constitute 'a lot'?"

She gazed at him in disbelief. "If you really think I'm giving you numbers . . ."

"Sorry. Go on."

"I was so determined to experience everything and

everyone I could that I don't think I ever stopped to truly appreciate any of it. Then, somewhere along the way, I realized it's important to have a good *reason* to experience the things in my life. Not just because they're there."

"It was good enough for Sir Edmund Hillary."

"It's not good enough for me. Not anymore."

"Makes sense. Come home with me."

"What?"

He leaned even closer. "It's the one place you can be safe. Somebody went to a lot of trouble to lure you out here and try to grab you. They're not going to just give up. Especially when it's painfully easy to find out where you live and work."

"You're inviting me to your house for my personal safety?"

"Yes."

"Kind of an abrupt segue."

"Was it?"

"By design, I suspect. In any case, I'm not going to your house."

"It worked for you before."

"I can't run to your suburban fortress every time things get a little dicey."

He chuckled. "You would classify attempted kidnapping as a little dicey?"

"No, it was flat-out terrifying. Which makes me even more determined not to run away."

"Sometimes running is the smartest thing to do. Running, regrouping, plotting your next move . . ."

"I'm going home. *My* home."

"Fine. Then I'm going with you."

"Like hell."

"I'm not joking. After what happened tonight, I'm

sticking close. At least until we can figure out what the hell is going on. I think we'd be a lot more comfortable at my house, and you might even find it less intimate. Plus we both know it can withstand a military bombardment. But if you insist on going back to your condo, I'll be there with you."

"My spare room is filled with boxes and junk. There's no place for you to sleep."

He tilted his head. "Oh, we can work something out."

"Really?" she said sarcastically.

"I was referring to your living-room sofa. It's a stronger line of defense than anyplace else in your condo."

"I really don't think—"

"I'm an excellent house guest. Magnificent, I've been told." He started back toward his car. "I'll follow you."

"We need to discuss this."

"We already have. You're just too tired and beat-up to realize it. I'll order Chinese on the way."

She was clearly going to lose this one. "Don't you even want to pack a bag?"

He pointed at his car. "I keep a suitcase packed in the trunk. I can never tell when I'll be called to Lisbon or Shanghai on a moment's notice."

"You think you're impressing me again."

"Not really. Traveling sounds glamorous, but it almost never is. I do have an unbelievable number of frequent flyer miles, though. Want to go to Dubai tonight?"

"No."

"Chinese food it is. See you at your place."

He climbed into his Ferrari and started the engine.

"YOU DIDN'T STOP FOR CHINESE," Kendra said as she watched Lynch set his leather suitcase down in the corner of her living room.

"They're going to deliver." He checked his watch. "In about fifty minutes. Which should give us just enough time."

"Enough time for what?" she asked warily.

"For me to get you taken care of." He slipped off his jacket. "Take off your shirt."

"I beg your pardon?"

"You heard me." He was heading for the kitchen. "That son of a bitch hurt you. You jumped when I touched your back at the parking lot. Then, when you got in your car, you flinched again. I'm going to take a look at it and see what I can do."

"It's a bruise. It will go away."

"I'll take a look at it," he repeated as he opened the freezer. "I've had my share of wounds and bruises. I know how to get by with as little pain and discomfort as possible. Take off your shirt."

She hesitated, then unbuttoned her shirt and took it off. The painful motion caused her to flinch again.

"See?" He was coming toward her with a large bag of frozen green beans in his hand. "He hurt you. Sit down on the couch and let me take a look at it." He sat down beside her and gently turned her so that he was facing her back. "Shit," he muttered. "You've got a bruise back here that's almost a foot long. Nasty." He undid her bra fastening and pushed it off so that it fell on her lap. "It's going to hurt."

He gently pressed the frozen bag to her back and held it there.

She inhaled sharply.

Ice-cold plastic on top of that bruised flesh.

"It will get better in a minute. Hang in there."

It did get better. The ice was causing a numbness to spread over the inflamed bruise.

"Why ice and not heat?" she asked.

"Ice is better for the first twenty-four hours. Heat tomorrow." He was carefully moving the ice bag around the bruised area. "Do you have any Arnica?"

"Don't think so. Should I?"

"It might help. I'll call a drugstore and have them send a bottle."

"You *do* know about bruises."

He chuckled. "Did you doubt me? Hell, yes. I remember one time I was beaten so badly by a tribal leader in Nairobi that I could barely walk. But the next day I knew I had to escape, or it wasn't going happen. So I learned very fast how to lessen the pain and make it bearable."

"How long do you have to do this ice therapy?"

"Another five minutes or so. Then I'll massage it for another fifteen."

"Massage it?" The idea of rubbing that painful area made her shudder. "I don't think so."

"Trust me. I'll make it work for you."

She was silent, letting the numbness grip and take the pain away. "Why was that tribal leader beating you?"

"His daughter decided she couldn't do without me, and he didn't like the idea of me as a son-in-law."

"Lynch."

"I thought that sounded pretty good. Much better than his wanting to know where I'd hidden a cache of diamonds he'd stolen that we were planning to use to ransom hostages being held by pirates from his village. Boring."

"It depends on how you look at it."

"True." The ice was gone, and she heard him move away from her. "Lie down flat on your stomach now, and I'll get to the massage."

She stiffened.

"Do it, Kendra. I won't say I'll never hurt you. But I won't do it if it's not necessary. And it's not what you're thinking it's going to be."

She hesitated, then slowly stretched out on her stomach. "It just seems weird and definitely not medically approved."

"I won't touch the bruise itself. I'll just go around the edges in gentle circular motions." He was doing it even as he spoke. "Breathe deep and relax. Massage helps your body's normal lymphatic process to clear it away."

"This better not be bullshit, Lynch."

He chuckled. "Suspicious woman. You do have a fantastic back, but this isn't my idea of foreplay."

And it wasn't hers either, but his fingers were skilled and gentle and infinitely soothing. She felt . . . treasured.

But she was beginning to feel something else, too, that was not at all soothing. She was acutely aware of her naked breasts pressed against the soft pillows of the couch, his warmth above her, the sound of his breathing.

"How . . . long?"

He went still. "A few more minutes." Then he continued to massage. "I'm not stopping while I know it's helping. You wouldn't want that."

"No." Her voice was muffled in the pillow.

But that few minutes was a long time.

Then his hands were gone. "That should do it. Now go get cleaned up while I set the table. It's almost time for the food to get here."

"Right." She grabbed her bra and shirt, jumped up from the couch, and hurried across the room. "Thanks. You must have done a good job. I hardly felt a thing."

IRIS JOHANSEN & ROY JOHANSEN

"Didn't you? I did." His quiet voice followed her. "And if I can make a suggestion? When you change for dinner, why don't you put on that sloppy sweatshirt you wore at breakfast. I believe we both might be more comfortable."

124

CHAPTER
7

"CHINESE FOOD" WAS A VERITABLE feast whipped up by the Szechuan chef who owned one of the most popular restaurants in the city. He delivered the food himself and even insisted on cooking part of it in Kendra's small kitchen.

After he left, Kendra stared in amazement at the spread on her dining-room table. Dry-fried chicken with chiles, hot glass noodles, Fei Teng fish, and multiple other delicacies she couldn't even identify. "This is astonishing. I'm stunned that you were able to get him to do this. I once saw that chef's picture on the cover of *San Diego* magazine."

"He's one of the best."

"Okay, so how did you get him to do it? Let me guess . . . You once rescued him from the clutches of a Macau crime syndicate?"

"No."

"You sprung a family member from one of China's notorious 'black jails?'"

Lynch laughed. "Afraid not. I got Huang here the old-fashioned way. I offered him an obscene amount of money."

"You didn't have to do that."

"You've been through a lot today. I figured you deserved it."

She eyed his leather suitcase in the corner. "You're serious about staying here."

"I am. Unless I can change your mind about coming to my place."

Kendra thought for a moment, then nodded toward the living room. "The couch isn't so bad."

Lynch smiled. "It's a nice night. Let's load up our plates and take these up to the roof. There's a sundeck up there, isn't there?"

She nodded. "It was one of the perks that made me buy the condo."

They toted their dinners and a bottle of wine to the table on the rooftop deck, which was illuminated only by the downtown city lights. After eating a plate of the most delicious Mapo doufu she had ever tasted, Kendra leaned back contentedly with her glass of wine. It was good to gaze out at the lights and just let herself relax. Lynch was always disturbing, but tonight he had turned down that high-powered appeal to low voltage, and she felt almost comfortable with him.

"This feels wonderful. I can almost think." She paused. "You know, I was pretty scared today."

His lips tightened. "I know you were."

"And I'm still trying to understand what happened." She took a sip of wine. "And why."

"Are you working on anything else?" Lynch asked. "Any other open cases?"

"No, it's been months. I have to think it's related to what happened to Waldridge."

"I can't disagree. And it's significant that they wanted you alive. In my experience, people only do that if they think you have something they want."

"Like what?"

"Information."

"*What* information? I'm still trying to figure out what the hell is going on."

"Those men might not know that. And you were the last person to see Waldridge. Maybe they think he told you something or gave you something."

"But he *didn't*."

"If they don't know that . . ." He leaned forward, gazing down at the wine in his glass. "We might be able to use it."

"What do you have in mind?"

"Nothing at the moment, but it's always good to keep our eyes peeled for any kind of leverage we can exert."

She smiled. "And it's always interesting to see how the Puppetmaster's mind works." She amended, "When it's not being used to manipulate me."

He quickly veered away from dangerous waters. "It's not half as interesting as watching yours at work. What are you thinking about all this?"

She shrugged. "Right now I'm wondering about my Fusion-Lei-boots-wearing savior."

"So am I." He grinned. "I'm a little peeved. Swooping in for last-minute heroics is *my* job."

"Yeah, sure. Not likely. Well, maybe on occasion." Kendra stood up and looked out at the shimmering, twinkling lights of the city. "Was she following me or them? Or did she somehow know about their plan in advance? She said something about things she'd heard about me." She made a face. "It wasn't complimentary. But right now, she's the one I want to talk to."

"And you're sure she's the same person we were chasing in Big Bear last night."

"Positive. Designer riding boots aside. I recognized her voice from the 911 tape we heard at the Big Bear police station. It was definitely the same woman."

"But no one you've ever met before?"

"Never. I'm sure of that even though I couldn't see her face behind that helmet visor."

Lynch stood up and came over to stand beside her. "But I'm sure that hasn't stopped you from picking up some useful information about her. Am I right?"

Kendra shrugged. "I'm pretty sure she's from California. Maybe up in the Central Valley around Bakersfield. She's around thirty, but she's already traveled a lot in Western Europe. Maybe even lived there for a while. She's ex-military."

Lynch's lips quirked. "You couldn't tell which branch?"

"Sorry. She was riding the same motorcycle as she was last night. She didn't ride far, though. She's either staying nearby or more likely she's driving a truck or van that she uses to tote the motorcycle around."

"Really?"

Kendra nodded.

"Okay, curiosity won't be denied. I'm not letting one more second pass without some explanations. I'm assuming the geographic data came from her speech patterns."

"Simple linguistics."

"Not so simple, but go ahead."

"Central Valley residents have a slight but unmistakable twang. It's a carryover from the Dust Bowl migrant days. I'd say she's from north of Bakersfield. She's picked up a few vowel suppressions that are associated with exposure to Romance languages. It can be acquired from a relative or spouse, but more likely to come from longer-term travels."

"Very good. But what about the military background? Was she wearing her dog tags?"

"No. When she came at the guy who had me, she had a distinct forward fighting stance. Front knee bent, weight evenly distributed on the balls of her feet. She probably had military training. She's in great shape, but she's no kid. There's a maturity in her movements. She's at least thirty, but almost surely under forty."

"How about the motorcycle?"

"Her odor. Or her *lack* of odor. Anyone riding for any length of time on a warm, sunny day like today should be giving off a distinctive smell . . . Perspiration evaporated by the sun and wind leaves behind a stale scent. Add automobile exhaust fumes, and it's a recognizable combo. I didn't pick up anything like that from her although I recognized the sound of her motorcycle starting up on the street and leaving. She either lives close by or transported the bike here using another vehicle, probably one where she could hide it. That's why the police weren't able to find it on any of the roads out of Big Bear."

Lynch smiled. "Excellent, as usual. This may be better than a composite sketch."

"I'm not sure about that. It's as close as I can come. But I'm thankful for her, whoever she is."

"So am I."

She turned to see that Lynch was staring intently at her and had moved even closer. Almost unbearably close.

He lowered his voice. "You scared the hell out of me today, you know that? When you called and told me you were going back to that place . . . I couldn't get over there fast enough."

"Not necessary. I'm a careful girl."

"Not always. One of the most fascinating things about you is that you've made mistakes, and you've learned from every one. Yet there's still that streak of recklessness in you that makes me wonder what would happen if we ever came together. I believe it could be . . . mind shattering." He moved still nearer. "What do you think?"

She wasn't thinking at all. She could only stare up at him and *feel*. "I don't know where you're going with this, Lynch. I don't believe you do either."

"Maybe. I'm acting purely on impulse. I've been doing that all day ever since you called me. But I do know where I'm going. And I know I'll never get there if you don't stay alive." He reached out and took the wineglass from her hand and placed it on a planter at the rooftop's edge.

"What are you doing? I wasn't—"

He pulled her close and kissed her.

Hot. Wet. Erotic.

Full-impact. Just like everything else Lynch did.

She went still. Then she realized that she was kissing him, too.

Not enough . . .

She pressed forward against him, opened her mouth, and took his tongue.

She couldn't breathe. So close . . . She felt full of him . . . But not full enough. Her entire body was aching, readying to take more of him. This was Lynch. The center of how many moments of sexual tension that she'd ignored or pushed away? There was no way she could ignore it now. She felt as if she'd been starved, the hunger growing so intense that it had to break free.

His hands were cupping her buttocks, bringing her into him.

She arched and cried out as she felt him against her. Then she was frantically rubbing against him, making sounds deep in her throat.

"*Yes.*" His eyes were glittering wildly. "Kendra . . . It's going to be—" His hands were on her sweatshirt, pulling it up, then off her. "Let's get downstairs. You won't like it if your neighbors decide to—"

"I don't care." All she cared about was his hands, which were now on her breasts. "Why should I? This is all that matters. Just *do* it."

"Oh, I will." His mouth was on her nipple, his teeth tugging. "I don't know why it took me this long. I've been crazy to do this since I first saw you. Things kept . . . getting . . . in the way."

She knew that, and she'd been the one putting up barriers against Lynch. Crazy. There didn't have to be reasons when there could be this pure eroticism, when she could have him inside her.

Reasons.

She'd told Lynch she had to have reasons. That anything else wasn't good enough for her anymore.

That was crazy, too. Not when they could have this moment. Sex was everything, wasn't it?

"You're backing off," Lynch muttered. "Stop it. Dammit, I can *feel* it."

"No, I'm not."

"You *are*." He pushed her away. He was breathing hard, and his eyes were blazing. "You're thinking, and you're wondering about what happens next. Do you think I don't know you by now?"

"I know you're not screwing me," she said fiercely. "And I know I want you to do it."

"*Shit!*" He whirled away from her. "I've got to be the stupidest son of a bitch on the face of the Earth."

"Come *back* here."

"No, I'm *not* screwing you." He was breathing hard. "Because when you woke up in the morning, you'd still be wondering if you'd made a mistake. You're comfortable with what we have now. You don't know who the hell I am, and I intimidate you a little."

She couldn't believe this, she thought desperately. She wanted him to shut up and *touch* her, to come inside her. She took a step closer. "No, you don't."

"Oh, yes. And I knew you'd be vulnerable tonight because you felt frightened and helpless. I even tried to back off. But I still moved too fast. Because I wanted it too damn much. Because I know it's going to be fantastic." He violently jerked open the door that led downstairs. "Shall I tell you what would happen if I screwed you tonight?"

"You don't have to tell me. Just do it. I'd love it. I'd want it."

"Don't *say* that. And then afterward you'd feel uneasy about having me with you as a friend and partner, and you'd end up not calling me if you needed me. And I could find you dead in a fifty-gallon drum someday. You *like* the status quo, Kendra. The fastest way to lose you and everything we have right now would be to drag you down on this roof and fuck you."

He slammed the door behind him.

SHE STOOD THERE SHAKING, looking after him. What the hell had happened? She had never seen Lynch that explosive. He had wanted her. She knew he had wanted her.

And, my God, how she had wanted him. It had been crazy and sexual and pure need. How long had she been feeling that way about him and not letting herself recognize the intensity?

Too long.

But then she couldn't remember ever feeling like that about any man. It had been bewildering and a little frightening. Not that she had shown him those emotions. She had been more aggressive than she'd ever been in her life. She had almost jumped him, dammit.

She sank down to the floor and linked her legs in her arms and rocked back and forth. Her body was still feeling hot and ready and aching.

And what would she have felt if she'd actually had him inside her?

Too much.

Lynch was always too much, always kept her on edge, always made her uncertain that she could handle him.

That was the man himself, not the sex with him.

But what if they were bonded together?

It could be mind shattering. What do you think?

He had said that, and she had instinctively shied away from answering. Because she had thought that he was right, and she was terrified of that lack of control.

She was now afraid that he had been right about a lot of things. Why not? she thought bitterly. He was the one who was so good at pulling the strings, who studied people and situations and developed them to suit himself. Who had studied Kendra's thought processes and could guess what the aftereffects would be if she allowed herself to let their situation change.

She *wasn't* a puppet. She would make her own decisions.

She wouldn't let herself be controlled by anyone. She would do what she wished.

And she would sit up here on this damn roof and not get near Lynch again until she made up her mind exactly what that was.

THE LIVING ROOM WAS in a shambles when Kendra came back down to the condo two hours later.

Boxes everywhere. Lamps and folded clothes on the floor and stacked against the far wall.

And Lynch moving back and forth, carrying more boxes from the spare bedroom.

Kendra frowned. "What are you doing?"

"Clearing out my bedroom. I decided the couch isn't going to do the job." He set the box down with the others. "You'll have to find another place for all this stuff."

"That's *my* bedroom."

"Not right now. It's either giving me this spare bedroom or sharing yours. Since I decided that's not going to happen at the moment, you'll have to cooperate."

"Will I? You've decided that the couch won't do?"

"Yes, I'd be uncomfortable, and you'd be much closer to me. I'm not fond of self-sacrifice. I'd give it two nights."

"Was that what you'd have given it when you first came?"

"No, but then I hadn't realized how hot you are." He met her eyes. "I'd lie there and think about it, then I'd go in and screw your brains out."

She felt a wave of heat ripple through her as she looked at him. She'd thought when she'd come down from the roof that she had that erotic craving firmly under control. Evidently it was still vibrantly alive and ready to break free.

He shook his head as if he'd read her thoughts. "Uh-uh. Too soon, Kendra. It's going to take awhile."

"I think the sensible thing would be for you to go home," she said steadily. "I've been thinking about what you said . . . what we did, and it's probably best that we don't see too much of each other for a few weeks or months. I'm really not the kind of woman that appeals to you and, you're right, the way you live your life is very . . . foreign to me. It was just a random sexual moment that was—"

"Shut up, Kendra," he said roughly. "I'm still aching, and I'm within a heartbeat of coming over there and starting it all again. I know that for the last two hours you were up there analyzing the situation, trying to put the pieces together in your usual brilliant fashion. Now you're thinking that caution is best, and caution tells you to run away from me. It isn't going to happen."

"That's really up to me, isn't it?"

"No, it's up to both of us. But I'm the one who is going to make the decision because I messed up, and I have to straighten it out."

"By having me stumble over you every time I turn around? Go home, Lynch."

"No, I'm staying here and keeping you safe. That goes without argument."

"The hell it does."

"No argument," he repeated. "There's no way that I'm going to let anything happen to you because I lost control tonight." He added through set teeth, "I don't lose control. That's not how I run my life."

"Or run everybody else's life?"

"Maybe. Right now, I'm sure you choose to interpret it that way. At any rate, it's true, and you should feel comforted that I've no intention of having it happen again."

135

"I don't need comfort. I need my house and my life back."

"And you'll get it. When it's safe for you."

Her hands clenched. "Lynch."

"Ready to slug me? I wouldn't advise it. Any close contact could lead to even closer contact." He suddenly smiled. "And I'm sure that you're worried where that would take us. You like to be in control, too. Those hours on the roof probably made you think twice about losing it in even the most pleasant manner. I could see how stiff and wary you were when you came into the condo tonight. Admit it. I was right."

"I told you that you were."

"But you didn't come up with the right solution. You wanted to run. That wouldn't solve anything." He leaned back against the couch. "Here's how it's going to play out. You're uneasy with anything but the status quo, so that's what we're going to step back to. There's no way we're going to be able to go all the way back, but we'll do our damnedest. If we're careful, we'll only have a few episodes that could turn marginal."

She remembered those explosive moments on the roof. "It won't work."

"Sure it will. Because we're smart, and we want it to work. We spark off each other, we like each other, we respect each other, we have a good time being with each other. Neither of us wants to blow that to hell because we haven't worked this out." His voice was suddenly softly persuasive. "Tomorrow, when you get up, we'll pretend tonight never happened. It didn't, you know. Nothing irrevocable. It will be a little stilted at first, but as time goes on, we'll fall into the rhythm. Then it will feel natural and right. Doesn't that sound like what you really want?"

She could feel the relief pour through her. Not to have

to lose Lynch, not to have to have face a massive adjustment or decision that might compromise her independence. "It sounds like a reasonable solution," she said slowly. "But is that what you want?"

"Yes, partly. But you'd never believe me if I told you that would satisfy me. I'm an extremely selfish and horny bastard." He smiled. "I want it all. And I'll get it eventually, when the time is right." He straightened. "But don't think I'm going to be pining for you and make you uncomfortable. As I said, I have a voracious appetite. There will be other women who are less interesting, but also less complicated than you." He added softly, "Status quo, Kendra."

She nodded. She found she didn't want to think of that particular aspect of status quo. "Of course, that's reasonable. It's not as if we— We're both free to—" She moistened her lips. "I don't know how this is all going to work out. I don't know why you'd want it to."

"Think about it. I hate to lose. I'd particularly hate to lose someone in whom I've invested so much time and effort. I'd lose a friend, a companion, a potential lover. It would be foolish not to make the effort."

"I guess it would." She found herself smiling. "And no one could ever call you a fool, Lynch."

"Wrong. If you remember, I was calling myself that on the roof tonight." He turned away. "Go to bed, Kendra. I have just a few more things to clear out of the bedroom. I'll try not to make too much noise."

"Do you want any help?"

"No, I think distance is a good idea." He headed for the bedroom. "By tomorrow, I'll be ready. See you in the morning."

She hesitated, then turned and went to her bedroom and closed the door.

It hadn't turned out as she'd thought it would when she'd come down to talk to Lynch. She had lost both control of the situation and focus the minute she'd seen him. What had she expected? He always knew what he wanted and how to go about getting it. She had always regarded that as an invaluable asset in him.

And now was she the target?

No, she would have been incredibly easy for him tonight if that was true. He was the one who had rejected her.

I want it all.

And what did Lynch consider as all?

Well, she was too tired and spent with emotion to try to guess or analyze what a complicated man like Lynch would want from her. It was time to get some sleep and forget about Lynch until she saw him in the morning.

EGGS. PEPPER. CHICKEN.

Kendra was aware of the odors emanating from her kitchen before she was even fully awake. It had been a restless night for her, and she wondered if Lynch had fared any better. As she tried to decide if his cooking breakfast for her was the result of more or less sleep, she caught a whiff of chili sauce.

She knew that recipe. It wasn't Lynch cooking.

She tore off the covers and bounded into her living room. Olivia was standing over her kitchen stove.

"Olivia, what on earth are you doing?" she asked.

"Omelets," she said matter-of-factly.

Lynch emerged from the spare room, smelling of aftershave. "I invited her. I knew Olivia was an early riser, so I gave her a call. I thought she'd be concerned about what was going on with you. It was her idea to make breakfast for us all."

Kendra nodded. Smart. Lynch had obviously brought Olivia in as a buffer. And it was working. Any awkwardness between them was rapidly dissipating with her friend's presence there.

"Great," Kendra said. "Olivia's a better cook than I'll ever be."

Olivia turned from the stove. "Well, Lynch helped identify the ingredients for me. Your gift of sight has made you terribly lazy about organizing your pantry and refrigerator."

"Many apologies," Kendra said. "I guess he filled you in on everything that's going on."

"Oh, yes. And so has your mother. I got an e-mail from her yesterday."

"Naturally."

"She said that if I can talk you into going to Hawaii with her, she'll bring me along, too."

"I'm not going to Hawaii."

"She knows that. She's just covering her bases."

Kendra turned to Lynch. "Sleep well?"

"As well as I thought I would," he said noncommittally. "You?"

"The same. But at least I put my time to good use."

"You've taken up scrapbooking."

"No." She picked up her tablet and flipped open the cover. "Something occurred to me before I went to sleep. The products used in Waldridge's hotel room to make any blood invisible to Luminol. They were household products, easily obtainable at a moment's notice. But you said there were better chemical solutions available."

"There are, and they're also available to anyone. You would just have to order them online or go to a chemical-supply store."

139

"Exactly. So maybe they had to settle on this Iron-Out and hydrogen peroxide mix because they hadn't planned ahead of time. Maybe they had to go out and get it the night after Waldridge was taken."

"Like at Home Depot?"

"All the Home Depots were closed at that time." Kendra raised her tablet and showed a city map on which she had used a stylus to circle two destinations. "But there are two twenty-four-hour Walmart stores within an easy drive of the hotel, and they carry these products. What if we get the FBI to request that these stores check and see if someone purchased these items from them that night?"

"And pray they used a credit card?"

"It's worth a shot."

Lynch nodded. "Good idea. Put all that in an e-mail to Griffin."

"I already did. Before I went to sleep. You really think I'd wait to run it past you?"

"In my dreams." He smiled. "What a team."

Yes they were, and the reminder was probably deliberate. Regardless, it was oddly comforting at this moment. "I haven't heard back from Griffin yet either to say he'll do it or for me to go to hell."

"He'll do it." Lynch checked his watch. "It's only seven-thirty. We'll call him at nine and harass him." He turned toward Olivia, and said lightly, "Until then, we'll occupy ourselves with what promises to be the best breakfast I've had in a while."

GRIFFIN CALLED TWENTY MINUTES LATER, just as they were finishing Olivia's delicious chicken-pepper omelets. Kendra put him on speaker.

"It's early, Griffin. You're working long hours for a government worker."

"Blame it on the lunatic who tasks me with silly errands in the middle of the night."

"So . . . I'm the lunatic?"

"Yes."

"Just checking."

"I should have trashed your e-mail after that ping woke me up, but you happened to make sense. So I forwarded your request just a few minutes after I got it. The office reached out to both stores."

"In the middle of the night?"

"As you pointed out, those stores are twenty-four-hour operations. So's the FBI. But I guess you're aware of that since you saw fit to disturb my well-earned sleep."

She thought it best to veer away from that last sarcastic comment. "Good. Any idea when we'll hear back?"

"We already have. We got a hit."

Kendra and Lynch exchanged a glance.

"Where?" Kendra asked.

"The Walmart at Baldwin Hills. Someone came in and purchased Iron-Out, hydrogen peroxide, sponges, and cleaning cloths at 10:16 P.M. that very day."

"How did they pay?"

"Cash."

Damn.

"I know," Griffin said, as if reading her mind. "But they promised me they have razor-sharp security cameras there. They've scanning for the footage as we speak."

"Okay. Good. Lynch and I will drive up to L.A. It shouldn't take us more than—"

"Don't bother. "They'll be e-mailing the video to my office."

"We'll be there at 8:30."

"I'll be there at 9:15. Unless you like those benches in the building foyer, I wouldn't arrive before then."

FBI Regional Field Office
San Diego

"We're doing very well, don't you think?" Lynch murmured, as he and Kendra crossed the parking lot toward the front entrance. "Easy conversation, very little tension. I told you we'd get through this. Every day it will get better."

She couldn't deny it. That easiness had been mainly Lynch's doing. Even on the trip here in his car with no Olivia as a buffer, he had not let her be aware of any disturbing sexuality. He'd been friendly, amusing, mocking, the Lynch she had known and bonded with for all these months. "I can almost believe you."

He smiled. "Told you so. We're back on track." He opened the door for her. "Just relax and enjoy it."

It was 9:25 by the time Kendra and Lynch were escorted to the fourth-floor A/V Lab by Griffin's assistant. Griffin was already there, with Special Agent Metcalf standing behind a tech who gripped a jog shuttle control wheel at the console.

"Anything?" Kendra asked.

Metcalf, smiling broadly, gestured toward the large wall-mounted monitor. "It just came in. Fantastic video. If this is the guy who cleaned up Dr. Waldridge's hotel room, he might as well have sat for a portrait."

Griffin pointed at the screen. "Here he is at the checkout stand. They matched it up with the time stamp and register number of his purchase. It's more of a profile shot here, but in a few seconds you'll see footage they pulled of him entering the store."

The screen flickered and they saw the dark-suited man walking through the store's main entrance. The tech froze the image.

Lynch stiffened. He leaned toward the screen. "My God, isn't that—" He whirled toward Kendra. "Kendra?"

"Yes." She slowly nodded. She was stunned, still not believing what she was seeing. "It's him. That man is Dr. Charles Waldridge."

CHAPTER
8

KENDRA STARED AT THE MONITOR for another long moment, still not believing her eyes.

What the hell, Charles?

"You're positive that's Dr. Waldridge?" Griffin asked.

"Yes. That's literally the last person on Earth I thought I'd see here." She shook her head. "Keep it going. Let's see the rest."

The tech punched the PLAY button. "There isn't much more. They sent the clips that would give us the clearest image of him."

"Tell them to pull up everything. They have security cameras all over the place, right? In the aisles, in front of every exit, in the parking lot . . . I want to see him every minute he was in that store from the moment he walked in the door to the moment he walked out. I want to see the car he came in. If he was with anyone. I want to see them, too."

Kendra heard her voice crack slightly as she spoke. It didn't surprise her. She felt as if a boa constrictor were crushing her throat.

"Don't worry. We'll get everything they have," Lynch said quietly.

She turned to Griffin. "Tell them to pull every frame of video they have during the time that Waldridge was there. Even if he wasn't in the shot."

"I know how this works," Griffin said testily. "It's what we do, Kendra."

He was annoyed. Too bad. She ignored it. "I'm going up there right now. I want to talk to that clerk and anyone else Waldridge might have spoken to that night. Can you have them meet me at the store?"

Griffin thought for a moment. "Metcalf, go up there with her. I'll have to let Santa Monica PD in on this, so don't step on any local toes. Got it?"

Metcalf was trying to look cool, but Kendra could see his eyes brighten. "Sure." He nodded toward her. "I'll call them on the way up there, so they can pull everything—and everybody—we need."

"Thanks, Metcalf."

"We'll take my car. I'll dash off a couple quick e-mails, then we'll get on the road and—"

"Kendra and I will go in my car," Lynch interrupted.

Metcalf shrugged. "I just thought—"

"In case she and I need to stay and follow up on anything," Lynch said. "Call us when you get on the road. We'll meet in the store parking lot."

"Sure, no problem." Metcalf looked disappointed. "I'll meet you there."

*   *   *

"I HATED TO CRUSH THAT poor guy's spirit," Lynch said as he drove north on the I-5 freeway. "But this makes more sense."

Kendra leaned back in her seat. "You enjoyed the hell out of it. By the way, I seriously doubt his spirit was crushed."

"Well, I also thought you might like some time to process what you just saw back there." He glanced at her. "Are you okay?"

"I'm relieved he's still alive, but I'm no less worried about him. Charles Waldridge is the last man on Earth I'd expect to be scrambling to hide blood evidence on the carpet of his hotel room."

"It does seem out of character for a world-renowned research scientist."

"It's crazy," she said flatly. "He needs help, and I think he was on the verge of asking me for it. He backed off at something I said." She shook her head. "Or maybe everything I said. Anyway, he changed his mind. But I have to find him."

"It's looking very much like he doesn't want to be found."

"Tough. I'm still going to do it."

THEY ARRIVED AT THE BALDWIN HILLS Walmart store just a few minutes ahead of Metcalf. The three of them walked in together and were taken through a maze of corridors to the spartan office of the store manager, a trim African-American man dressed in a crisp white shirt and a striped tie.

"Derek Collins," he said as he stood and shook hands with each of them. He gestured for them to walk with him down the concrete-floored corridor. "We've been pulling all the video we have from that night. Our security manager has compiled and ordered video from the different camera feeds and burned them to a DVD for you guys."

"Thank you," Kendra said. "I didn't realize you were set up for that kind of thing."

"We're not, really. You'll also get the raw video. Our guy just happened to be handy with laptop and editing software." He smiled. "Like a lot of people under thirty."

He turned into the security office, where a bank of monitors lined the far wall. A stocky young man looked up from his laptop. "Hi, I'm almost done."

"This is Larry Delmos," Collins said. "Larry's the assistant security manager and he pretty much runs the surveillance camera system for us."

"It doesn't have to be a polished Hollywood production," Kendra said as she walked over to his laptop.

Delmos flashed a toothy grin. "Too late. I stitched the feeds together into chronological order. I thought it would be more helpful to you that way."

He spun the laptop around for them to see. The first image showed a man walking through the parking lot. "Here he is approaching the entrance."

"Did you get the car?" Lynch asked.

"Afraid not. He either came to the center on foot or parked next door to stay out of range of our parking-lot cameras. But here, look. He walked in through the front doors and goes immediately back toward the hardware section."

Kendra watched as the various angles showed Waldridge's journey past a soda display, stacks of Rubbermaid storage containers, and finally to the hardware aisles, where he spent a few moments looking over the shelves. He fumbled as he picked up a red-and-white bottle."

"Is that Iron-Out?" Kendra asked.

The manager squinted at the screen. "Yes."

They watched as he made his way through the store, picking up the cleaning supplies, and finally to the pharmaceuticals, where he picked up a large brown bottle that had to be the hydrogen peroxide. He then took his purchases to the checkout stand, where they saw the same footage they had watched at the FBI field office. After that he exited the store and a parking-lot camera captured him walking out of camera range with his purchases.

"Scan back," Kendra said. "Take us back to where he first entered the store."

The video clips sped back to Waldridge's entrance. Just as he was about to leave the frame, Kendra pointed, and called out, "Stop!"

The image froze and she pointed to the doors, where a man in a long jacket and a baseball cap had entered. "See?"

Lynch nodded. "Yes, but he doesn't seem to be with Waldridge."

"Just wait," she murmured.

As they watched the other shots of Waldridge in the store, the other man followed from a distance, stopping and appearing to look at items every time Waldridge paused.

"Waldridge was being followed," Metcalf said.

"It's more than that," Kendra said. "They make brief eye contact several times. Watch."

Waldridge appeared to glance at the man as he picked up the hydrogen peroxide bottle.

"You're right," Lynch said. "They *were* together. And

notice how this guy uses his hat to keep his face from the camera."

"He doesn't want to be seen, yet he needs to be there," Kendra said.

"He could be keeping a leash on Waldridge," Metcalf said. "Maybe making sure he doesn't talk to anyone."

Kendra watched for another moment. "Scan back to the hardware aisle. I want to see something."

Delmos scanned back to the hardware section, where Waldridge fumbled as he picked up the Iron-Out.

"'That moment there," she said. "See how his hand hesitated and makes a couple grabs at that bottle? He's usually very precise with his movements. He's a surgeon. This is unusual for him."

"He could have just been nervous," Metcalf said.

"Maybe." Kendra stepped closer to the monitor before turning to face the manager. "Take me there."

"Sure. This way."

They followed the manager out of the office and back onto the sales floor, where they made their way to the aisle they had just viewed on the video. The manager stopped and pointed to the bottles of Iron-Out. "Here's where he was standing. The camera was inside that dome on the ceiling, and the other guy you were looking at was standing about three aisles to the right."

Kendra glanced around to get her bearings. "Thank you. Waldridge was here, and he reached toward this shelf . . ."

The red-and-white bottles were displayed two across and a half a dozen deep. Kendra moved aside the first two bottles and peered into the back of the shelf. She squinted, trying to see deeper. There was a small glittering object back there . . . She reached in and pulled out a small silver charm.

"What is it?" Lynch asked.

She stared at it a long moment before showing the others. "A dolphin."

"Is that supposed to have some special significance?" Metcalf asked.

"It belongs to Waldridge. He's been carrying it ever since I've known him."

She turned it gently over in her fingers. *Message received, Charles.*

"So . . . He put it here for you to find? Kind of a leap, isn't it?" Metcalf asked.

She shook her head. "No. He's always had faith in me, even when it seemed no one else did." She spoke softly as she continued to stare at the charm, "Never surrender . . . Never give up . . ."

"What?" Lynch asked.

"He knew I'd see this. He knew I'd track him here, even if no one else did. This charm is a symbol of perseverance . . . of never giving up. It's what he had to remind himself for his entire career. And now . . ."

". . . now it's his message to you," Lynch finished for her.

She closed her hand around the charm. "Yes. He knew I'd be on his trail. He's telling me not to give up."

KENDRA WAS STILL HOLDING the charm as she, Lynch, and Metcalf walked out into the parking lot. She looked down at it in her hand. Its once-shiny surface was now dull, and the sharp features had been worn down by the years. But its meaning had never been more vivid, more startlingly clear.

Metcalf awkwardly produced a Ziploc evidence bag

from his inside jacket pocket. "Uh, I should probably take that as evidence."

Kendra nodded. "Sure."

Metcalf opened the bag. She looked at the charm for a moment longer before dropping it inside.

"Thanks," he said. "I'll take good care of it."

"You'd better. Waldridge will want that back."

"Do you have a copy of all the security video?" Lynch asked.

Metcalf patted his pocket. "Right here. The whole thing is on one USB drive."

"I'd like a copy of that," Lynch said.

"Sure. After I get back to the office, I'll—"

"I mean right now." Lynch pulled out his phone and plugged a small adapter into the jack on its underside. "If you don't mind."

Metcalf shrugged and fished the thumb drive from his pocket. Lynch inserted it into his adapter and opened an app to upload the drive's contents to his phone.

"This will be just a couple of minutes."

Kendra looked around. "Maybe we can get some traffic-cam footage from that night. If we can track a vehicle going from the hotel to here at this exact time—"

"Griffin is on it," Metcalf said. "They probably hit a dozen cameras between there and here. There's a good chance that—"

Metcalf's phone rang. He glanced at the screen. "Speak of the devil."

Metcalf answered, and after a terse few words, he cut the connection.

"Quick call," Kendra said.

He nodded. "Griffin wants us all to get back to the office."

"Why?" Lynch asked. "What has he heard?"

Metcalf snapped his fingers impatiently. "Can I have the flash drive back?"

"Another fourteen seconds. What has Griffin heard?"

Metcalf looked between Lynch and Kendra, then shrugged. "We have an ID on the Big Bear murder victim you found last night."

"Who was he?" Kendra asked.

"His name was Porter Shaw. From London." Metcalf glanced at Lynch. "Facial-recognition software matched your photo reconstruction with his passport picture."

"Score one for Ashley," Kendra said.

"Who was he?" Lynch asked.

"They're building a file on him right now. We should know more by the time we get back." He looked at Kendra. "Does his name mean anything at all to you?"

"Porter Shaw?" She shook her head. "No. Should it?"

"I thought it might." He turned away and headed for his car. "Shaw was part of the Night Watch Project."

KENDRA'S FINGERS FLEW OVER Lynch's tablet for most of their ride back, but she was able to glean only small nuggets of information about Dr. Porter Shaw, former professor of human physiology at Cambridge University. It was only after their arrival at Griffin's office that she discovered any further evidence of his association with Waldridge.

Griffin handed her a file of documents and photos still warm from the printer. "We'll probably have more before you leave here, but this is what we have so far. I thought the Night Watch angle would intrigue you."

"I don't remember him," Kendra said. "I thought I'd met everyone connected with the project."

"You probably did. He only joined Night Watch in the past six years."

She wrinkled her brow. "That doesn't seem right."

"Why not?"

"Waldridge stepped away from it long before then. He told me he had moved on to other projects."

"Projects he wouldn't tell you about?" Griffin asked.

"Yes. Honestly, I thought Night Watch ended years ago, when Waldridge departed."

"Apparently it didn't. There have been a couple mentions of it in recent medical journals."

Kendra stopped at a photo of Shaw and Waldridge, standing together at a Cambridge alumni event. Her gaze narrowed on the date. "This was just last April."

"What was his specialty?" Lynch asked.

Kendra raised a copy of an eleven-year-old journal article. "Internal medicine. According to his bio, he won several awards."

Griffin leaned back in his chair. "He entered the country just eleven days ago. London to Vancouver, then into LAX."

"Then to Big Bear," Kendra said. "But why there?"

"Maybe he thought it would be a place he wouldn't be found," Lynch said.

Griffin clicked his tongue. "Well, that didn't work out well for him."

Kendra gazed at the pudgy face in another photo. It was a kind face, an intelligent face. And amazingly similar to the photographic reconstruction whipped up by Lynch's ex.

She looked up. "Did he have a family?"

"Yes, a wife, married for over thirty years. No children. He also had a sister. London police will be notifying the wife anytime now."

"I'd like that contact info," Lynch said.

"Why?" Griffin said. "Thinking of paying her visit?"

"Not personally, no. But we have a man helping out there."

"*What* man?"

Lynch started to reply, but Griffin raised his hand to silence him.

"On second thought, never mind. I don't want to know. Your circle of acquaintances has the potential to cause me a good deal of trouble with the director. I'll make sure you get an address and phone number."

Lynch grinned cheerfully. "Thanks, Griffin. You're always so understanding."

A JET PLANE.

No traffic.

Coyotes.

Dr. Charles Waldridge lifted his head in the dark room that had become his home for the past few days. He'd been sleeping, and his dreams had once again echoed the only sounds he could hear, that of the jets and coyotes outside.

Coyotes? There were plenty of coyotes in L.A., but this sounded like a pack. Probably a sign he was no longer in Los Angeles. And the sounds of jets were too infrequent to indicate he was anywhere in the vicinity of the airport. Maybe a military base. Not much information, he thought wryly. If Kendra were here, she'd probably have been able to figure out a lot more. There were no windows here, just four walls and a bathroom no larger than one might find in a recreational vehicle.

"Ready to work, Dr. Waldridge?"

That mocking voice again. It was probably what had wakened him, he realized.

"Why don't you come and face me?" he called out into the darkness. "It's not as if I don't know exactly who you are. Come here, and I'll tell you in person that I'm not going to do it."

"I hope that's not really the case. I've been trying to be patient with you."

Waldridge sat up on his cot as fluorescent lights flickered on high above. He was situated at the end of a long room, forty by fifteen feet. Long workbenches lined each side of the room to form a makeshift laboratory, packed with glassware, test tubes, heating elements, and half a dozen centrifuges.

The voice blared again from a small webcam over his cot. "Look around you. See how generous we're being? Everything you could possibly need. How could you ask for anything else?"

"Very easily. You know what I need," Waldridge said. "Agree to it, and we might start over. Without that, we're just wasting our time."

"And I don't intend to waste any more time. I *will* come there to see you, and you won't find it pleasant." The voice lowered to menace. "I suggest you start working before I get there."

CHAPTER
9

London
Nine Years Earlier

KENDRA POSITIONED THE OVERSIZED sport sunglasses over her face as she rounded the corner. It was past 9 P.M., but the sidewalks were still crowded with holiday shoppers. There was a distinct energy at this time of year; the groups were bigger and much more varied in ages. She could hear the voices of children, thirtysomethings, and the elderly walking together in numbers she seldom heard at any other time of year. It was nice . . .

She tightened the sweep of her cane as the crowd thickened. She was trembling, she realized. Not from the cold, though there was a stiff breeze in the air, but from the realization that her life might be about to change.

Might. Remember that word. In spite of what anyone had told her, she must not let herself fly too high.

Because, in just a few minutes, for the first time in her life, she might be going to see.

She hoped.

Hoping was okay, it was in the same category as that "might" word. It wasn't taking miracles for granted.

She knew it wasn't supposed to happen this way. She had an appointment the next morning at St. Bartholomew's Hospital, where Dr. Waldridge, her mother, and dozens of researchers would witness the removal of the bandages she'd worn since her procedure five weeks before.

She'd spent countless hours imagining what that moment would be like; Dr. Waldridge would certainly be calm and reassuring as he removed the bandages and waxed eye patches, and her mother's voice would be dripping with tension, terrified that a failure might crush her daughter's spirit.

If it was a success, there would be cheers and champagne; for failure, there would only be apologies and empty words of encouragement. Either way, Kendra would be forced to mask what she felt to give everyone around her what they needed from her.

No thanks.

She'd decided to make the story her own. Maybe she was being selfish, but she had been the one living in the dark all these years. She'd earned the right to do this alone on her own terms.

Two blocks and a right turn later, she found herself right where she wanted to be.

Piccadilly Circus.

She'd visited the area several times during her stay in London and she enjoyed the gasps and squeals of delight it elicited from tourists and children seeing it for the first time. It was the junction of several streets in the heart of this large shopping and entertainment district, and from what she understood, it's already-spectacular lighting was even more breathtaking with the seasonal decorations.

Not a bad place to take her first steps into a new world.

She stopped in the pedestrian plaza and felt the cool breeze on her face. She took a deep breath. Engine exhaust, perfume, and baked goods from a nearby market.

It was noisy. Cars and buses roared by on the criss-crossing streets that surrounded her, shoppers talked and laughed, and a brass quartet played Christmas carols nearby.

She stood motionless for a long moment. A moment which became one full minute, then five.

What in the hell was she waiting for?

It was time to rip off the Band-Aid. So to speak.

Are you ready for me, world?

Because I'm ready for you.

She pulled off her large sunglasses and reached toward the bandages glued between her forehead and upper cheekbones. She tugged, the bandages barely moved. Hmm. The hospital staff probably had a solution that would dissolve the adhesive. This wasn't going to be easy.

She peeled back the bandages, feeling her skin stretch and pull. She felt no pain, just an unbearable excitement that sent her heart leaping into her throat.

Was she really doing this?

The bandages fluttered to the sidewalk. She peeled off the thick pads that covered her eye sockets.

She held her breath.

There was . . . something.

Her eyes were still closed, but there was a sensation she'd never experienced.

Was this . . . light?

She opened her eyes.

She gasped.

In that instant, she stood in another world.

No words. No words to describe what she was suddenly experiencing. There was simply no frame of reference, nothing she could possibly compare this with.

The sounds were the same, but they were now paired with these . . . things.

Lights. Colors. People.

Oh, the people . . .

Did noses really look like that? And those ears . . .

So this is how everyone saw each other. How arbitrary it was that some would be considered more attractive than any others . . . At this moment, they all looked beautiful to her.

One of them was staring at her. A woman with shoulder-length hair whose face was twisted in what Kendra realized was a smile. Could this person see the amazement, the wonder, the awe?

"*Kendra, baby,*" *the woman whispered.*

Kendra gasped. It must be . . . For the first time in her life, she was looking at the face she'd wanted to see more than any other.

"*Mom?*"

The woman's head bobbed up and down. "*You can see?*"

"*Yes.*"

"*Everything?*"

"*I . . . think so.*"

Her mother laughed even as tears rolled down her cheeks. She took Kendra in her arms and hugged her.

Kendra squeezed her tight. "*You followed me?*"

"*I had a feeling. I know my little girl.*" *She laughed shakily.* "*And you know me. I had to keep my distance. I knew you'd realize it was me if I didn't.*"

"*I'm sorry, Mom.*"

"No, don't be. As I said, I know how you think. I—I just needed to be here."

"I'm glad you are." Kendra spun around and faced the multicolored lights. She wanted to reach out, embrace them all. She was brimming with wild exhilaration. She felt as if she were part of those brilliant lights, that they were shining out of her. "You have to tell me what those colors are. It's incredible. I just want to soak in every detail."

"There's so much more to see . . . The Grand Canyon, the Mediterranean Sea at sunrise, the canals of Venice . . ."

"I want to see it all. Every single bit of it. Tonight!"

Her mother laughed. "Soon. First there's someone else you need to see. Someone who deserves to be here with you."

Kendra nodded. "I know."

"Should you call him, or should I?"

"I'll do it." Kendra pulled her phone from her pocket. She started to tap out the number, but realized that the illuminated buttons were disorienting her. She closed her eyes to finish entering the digits.

He answered on the first ring. "Hello."

Kendra could barely contain the joy in her voice. "Dr. Waldridge . . . It's me, Kendra. Sorry to bother you, but I really think you should get yourself here to Piccadilly Circus . . ."

Old Town San Diego
Present Day

Lynch held his phone between him and Kendra on a quiet side street on the bustling tourist and entertainment area of Old Town. He had Rye on speaker, and they had just given him the info on Dr. Porter Shaw and his involvement in the Night Watch Project.

"Night Watch," Rye said. "Interesting."

"How so?" Lynch asked.

"I've started asking around about Waldridge, and the Night Watch Project has been mentioned a few times. But when I try to dig in about it, people tend to clam up fast."

"Do they not know or do they just not *want* to talk?" Kendra asked.

"Probably both, depending on the person with whom I'm talking. Don't worry. I already have an idea how to find out what's going on there. I promise I won't leave London until I find out."

"Keep us posted," Lynch said. "We'll check in when we hear more."

He cut the connection and looked at Kendra. "I have faith in him. If anyone can figure out what's going on there, it's Rye."

"I believe you."

Lynch gestured for her to follow him around the corner, where they stood in front of a bar emblazoned with the words CAFÉ COYOTE high on a neon sign.

Kendra shook her head. "I can't believe you took me to another bar. Did you suddenly acquire a taste for bad karaoke?"

"You don't know bad karaoke. You haven't heard *me* try to sing yet."

"Ooh, now I'm intrigued. What's your pleasure? 'New York, New York'? Or maybe 'The Gambler'?"

"That would take a lot more tequila shots than this place could possibly stock."

"Oh, I'd gladly make a run to the liquor wholesaler to make it happen."

"I bet you would. It'll have to wait for another night. This isn't a karaoke bar." Lynch gestured for Kendra to precede him through the open door.

She entered to find herself in a rowdy bar largely populated by college-age patrons. In addition to a long bar, there was a dozen or so high-top cocktail tables, four dartboards, and a small stage elevated only a few inches above the rest of the floor. The stage held a guitar and keyboard duo of male vocalists who were covering Hall & Oates' "You Make My Dreams Come True."

"See?" Lynch said. "No karaoke."

"Well, this is a close cousin. But these guys are pretty good." She turned to Lynch. "So what lead are we following here?"

"No lead. No lead at all."

She frowned. "Then why the hell are we here?"

"To allow you to decompress for a bit."

She turned toward the door. "I don't have time for this."

He grabbed her arm. "Make time. You need it." He met her eyes. "I've watched you since this began, and you're at the point where you're pulled taut and ready to break. Waldridge means too much to you. You're losing perspective." He gave a half shrug. "Added to the fact that it bothers the hell out of me to see you like this."

"I'm fine. I'm not losing—" She stopped. She didn't like to admit it, but she couldn't lie about being on edge. At the FBI office today, she'd had trouble keeping it together. She asked sarcastically, "You think drinks at an Old Town bar are what I need to decompress?"

"Absolutely not."

"Then explain to me why we're here."

"For some music therapy."

She pointed to the stage. "And you think listening to these guys will give me what I need?"

"Actually, no. The guitarist is a friend of mine, but I seriously doubt his talents have the rehabilitative power to soothe your nerves and restore a sense of calm and focus to your psyche."

"You have a lot of friends in this town, you know that?"

"I can't help it if I'm a popular guy. It's the cross I bear."

"So who is this music-therapy wizard you have in mind?"

"You."

Her eyes widened as she stepped closer to him. "Are you crazy? You want me to practice music therapy on myself?"

"You do it all the time. I've seen it."

"You've seen nothing of the sort."

"Of course I have. Every time I've seen you with one of your clients. You come away invigorated, but at the same time a sense of calm comes over you. And that razor-sharp focus of yours is never more acute than it is after one of your sessions. Do you deny it?"

Kendra thought for a moment. She couldn't deny it, but she hadn't realized that Lynch had studied that aspect of her life enough to know that basic and very intimate force that drove her. But she should have realized it; anyone as controlling as Lynch would probe and watch until he did know everything. "Okay, music has always been a big part of my life. When I couldn't see, it was one way I could connect with anyone else. It was one experience I could share completely." She suddenly felt uncomfortable. "But you make it sound like I'm doing my sessions for myself instead of my clients."

"Of course not. I know you're doing it for them," he said quietly. "It's just a fortunate side benefit that it also helps you."

"And just how am I supposed to treat myself here?"

To Kendra's surprise, Lynch suddenly hopped onto the small stage. He whispered to the guitarist, who nodded. Lynch stepped back toward Kendra.

"What the hell did you just do?" she said with ice in her voice.

Lynch smiled, but didn't answer.

The musicians finished their song, and the guitarist spoke to the crowd. "Okay, we're going to have a smoke break, but while we're gone, we'll leave you in some very capable hands. Be back in a few."

He stepped off the stage, handed Kendra his acoustic guitar, and clasped hands with Lynch. She watched in amazement as the musicians disappeared into a back hallway.

She held up the guitar. "What am I supposed to do with *this*?"

"What you always do. Play it. Connect."

"*You* play it."

"This is how you used to earn your living, wasn't it? Playing clubs during your so-called wild days?"

"I wouldn't call that a living. Scraping by is more like it,"

"Okay, then scrape on up to that stage. Your public is waiting."

Kendra glanced around the crowded bar, where several patrons were indeed looking at her. It still would have been a simple matter to place the guitar on its stand next to the stage microphone and walk away.

She turned back. Lynch was wearing a borderline-cheesy, self-satisfied smile. The bastard was practically daring her to do it.

Fine.

She gripped the guitar and stepped behind the microphone. She leaned toward the mike to make an introduction, but she stopped.

Not necessary. The music would speak for itself.

She leaned back and strummed the guitar, feeling the pull of the strings beneath her fingers. Nice.

She closed her eyes, as she often did while playing any musical instrument she'd mastered during her years in the dark. She played a few chords, still not knowing what song she'd play. She had an instinct for what chord progressions would work in this bar, on this night, and she knew the right song would soon follow.

That song was James Taylor's "Fire and Rain."

She wasn't sure she'd actually sing it, but again, it felt *right*. She let herself feel the words and music, allowing them to become extensions of *her* as her voice warmed to the soulful lyrics.

When she finished, she opened her eyes. Most of the bar's patrons were now staring at her, having put their beers, darts, and conversations on hold.

They erupted into cheers and wild applause. She merely nodded her appreciation, put her guitar down, and left the stage. The crowd was still applauding as Lynch mouthed a single word.

"Wow."

She walked toward him and stopped just inches away.

A long moment of silence.

She kissed him squarely on the mouth.

Again, not something she'd planned. It just felt right.

He smiled. "What was *that* for?"

"For knowing what I need. Before I even knew it myself."

He nodded. "My pleasure. You want to get out of here?"

"Yes."

They moved through the bar and stepped out onto the street, which had become busier in the short time they were inside.

"Are you okay?" Lynch asked. "You seem a little . . ."

"Buzzed?" Kendra finished for him.

"I was going to say woozy."

"Definitely buzzed. And I mean in the best possible way. It felt wonderful." And all the jagged edges of anxiety that had been lacerating her were magically smoothed away. She knew it was temporary, but she'd take it. "I've never had any desire to perform in front of people again. And it may be years before I do it again. But right now, it's just what I needed to—"

She froze.

"What is it?" Lynch asked.

"Keep walking. Act normal."

His brows rose. "That's exactly what I was doing before you stopped dead in your tracks."

They continued down the busy sidewalk.

"She's here," Kendra said in a low voice.

"Who?"

"Motorcycle woman. I think she followed us into the bar."

"Did you see her?"

"No. But I'm willing to bet she's following us right now. Don't look back."

"That's probably the most insulting thing you've ever said to me."

"Sorry."

"What makes you think she's here?"

Kendra nodded toward the strip of fine dirt running between the sidewalk and the street. "Those damn Fusion Lei riding boots again. I just spotted a relatively undisturbed footprint heading in the direction of the bar."

"Other people wear those boots, right?"

"Of course. But they're rare enough that I'm willing to bet that it's more than just a coincidence. She's here."

Lynch thought for a moment. "Okay. I want you to walk four blocks down, just past the Western wear store. Then take a left and keep walking."

"And what exactly will you be doing?"

"I'll be nearby. Right now I'll duck into this restaurant and out through the back. Make a big show of saying goodbye to me."

"How do I do that?"

He kissed her. "That's how. See you around the corner."

She was so surprised by the gesture that she could only summon a limp wave as he ducked into the restaurant and moved toward the back.

She continued down the street. Motorcycle woman, whoever the hell she was, had saved her from those two thugs in the building. Why not turn around and confront her? Difficult, she decided, because the woman could be tailing her from blocks behind. She'd been studying reflections in the shop windows and knew the no one in the immediate vicinity was following her.

Kendra turned, walked past the Western wear store and turned left as instructed. She stole a glance back as she made the turn. There were several people on the sidewalk some distance away, among them at least two females with roughly the same body type as Motorcycle woman.

What in the hell did she want?

If, indeed, one of those women was her. She hadn't been able to catch a look at the shoes.

Keep walking. Stay alert. Don't look back.

Where the hell was Lynch? If he was somewhere on this street, he was damned good. She sure couldn't spot him.

She walked an entire block, then another. Did Lynch expect her to just keep walking until she reached the—

A sharp yell behind her!

Kendra whirled around. Lynch was there, and he had a woman in a hold.

She had short dark hair in a pixie cut and wore jeans and a long black coat that looked somewhat like a duster. And Fusion Lei riding boots.

She used one of those boots to kick backward and strike Lynch's knee. He winced in pain, and she seized the opportunity to drop out of his grip. She spun around and pummeled him with half a dozen lightning blows to his kidneys. He was obviously in agony, but he snapped his hands over her wrists and twisted her around with her own left arm pulled taut over her throat.

The woman was still struggling as Kendra ran toward them. "Enough," Lynch said, gritting his teeth. "Keep it up, and I promise you'll be unconscious in seconds."

She muttered something Kendra couldn't understand, but was probably obscene.

Kendra studied the woman. "It's definitely her. Same body type, exact same boots with a light blue scuff mark on the right heel."

Lynch readjusted his grip on the woman. "It feels like there's a wallet of some kind on the left inside pocket of her coat. Pull it out."

Kendra carefully reached inside the coat and pulled out

a thin leather wallet. She opened it and studied the ID card behind a plastic window. "It's a private investigator's license."

Lynch loosened his grip. "A private detective?"

Kendra showed him the license. "Her name is Jessie Mercado. She's from L.A."

The woman finally spoke through set teeth. "And I saved your ass yesterday. Don't leave that part out." She jerked her head back at Lynch. "Does this ape follow your commands? If so, please tell him to let me go."

Kendra closed the wallet and shrugged. "Lynch, let go of her."

Jessie Mercado stepped away from Lynch and rubbed her shoulder as she glared at him. "Just so that you know, I could have put you down. I was going easy on you."

"Got it." He placed his hand on his side. "I'll be pissing blood for days, but you were going easy on me."

Jessie was now rubbing her arm. She was a pretty woman of medium height, about thirty, slender, with tanned skin, huge dark eyes, and delicate features that belied the obvious toughness in her attitude and bearing. She said grudgingly, "Well, I think you dislocated my shoulder, so I guess we're even."

"Not really," Kendra said. "Why are you following me?"

"How do you know I was?" Jessie shrugged. "You're nothing to me."

"Why don't I believe you?"

"Believe me, don't believe me, I don't really care." She hesitated. "I'm on a case for a client."

"What client?" Lynch asked.

"Have you ever heard of a thing called professional confidentiality?"

"Heard of it. I don't give a damn about it," Kendra said. "I need answers. A friend of mine is missing. He's my only priority."

"Well, that's something we have in common." She met her eyes. "Because my client happens to be Dr. Charles Waldridge. He's my priority, too."

Kendra wondered if her face was showing the shock she felt. "Waldridge hired you?"

Jessie nodded.

"Where is he?"

Jessie grimaced. "I wish I knew."

"How could he be your client if you don't—"

"I met him the day he disappeared. A satisfied former client referred him to me. He hired me on the spot."

"Hired you for what?"

She shook her head. "Confidential. He swore me to secrecy. That's why I didn't come forward as soon as he disappeared."

"Something's happened to him," Lynch said. "May I say your priorities are a little screwed-up? You might hold information that can save his life."

She stiffened defensively. "Don't think I haven't been weighing that."

"Must have been torture for you," Lynch said caustically. "How about if I put my thumb on the scale by taking you to the police?"

"Just try it," she said softly.

"Hey," Kendra said. "Let's just table this for a minute. I'm tired of watching the two of you bristle at each other. Let's talk about why you're following me."

Jessie thought for a moment. "I guess *that* we can talk about." She glanced around. "But not here."

"Where?" Kendra demanded.

She smiled faintly. "I'd invite you to my office, but it's a bit far to L.A."

"No problem. I happen to have an office nearby. It's at—"

"I know where it is. I've been there." Jessie reached out and snatched her license from Kendra's hand. "I'll meet you there in fifteen minutes."

"How do we know you'll show?" Kendra asked.

Jessie shrugged. "How do I know you won't have a squad car there waiting to take me in for questioning? I guess we'll just have to trust each other." She gave a mock shiver. "What a truly bizarre thought."

FIFTEEN MINUTES LATER, Kendra and Lynch drove into the office parking lot to find Jessie standing next to her motorcycle, checking her e-mail.

"Anything interesting?" Kendra asked.

"Like an e-mail from Dr. Waldridge? Afraid not. But three different companies want to sell me penis-enlargement tools." Jessie put away her phone. "It comes with owning a motorcycle. I'll read those later."

Kendra smiled. Lynch seemed annoyed with her, but she was enjoying Jessie's dry sense of humor.

Kendra led her and Lynch to her office studio, where she and Lynch had teleconferenced with Rye only the day before.

Jessie looked around with interest at the musical instruments. "Nice job with the song at the bar, by the way. You pretty much nailed it."

"You were there?" Lynch asked.

"She was standing near the dartboards," Kendra said. "I couldn't see her boots; otherwise, I would have ID'd her in a second."

171

Jessie rolled her eyes. "The *boots*. Is that how you made me?"

"They leave a very distinctive footprint. In the snow up in Big Bear, in the fine dirt outside the bar."

"Freaky. I guess the stories about you are true."

"Depends on where the stories came from."

"True-crime blogs, police discussion boards, places like that."

"Any special reason why you've been reading up on me?"

"Homework."

Kendra waited for her to say more, but Jessie was silent, perusing the music-themed laminated posters on the wall.

"Waldridge hired you to follow me?" Kendra finally asked.

"No. He didn't even mention you to me."

"Then why the hell have you been on my tail?"

"For the record, I've been doing more with my time than just following you. Remember, I found my way to Big Bear before you did."

Lynch crossed his arms and leaned against the piano. "Yes, and you led us quite a chase."

"Not much of a chase. I'm guessing that the San Bernardino County PD stopped you long before you even got off the mountain."

Lynch nodded. "You guessed right. But what brought you up there in the first place?"

"The same thing that brought you. The corpse in the snow, Dr. Porter Shaw."

Kendra and Lynch exchanged a glance.

"You knew who he was?" Kendra asked.

"Not immediately. When did you figure it out?"

"A few hours ago. You?"

"Last night. I ran the pictures I took of the body against photos of Waldridge's known associates that I grabbed off the Web. A facial-recognition program did most of the work."

"Smart," Kendra said. "The FBI did something similar."

"I just happened to do it faster. Not that I'm bragging or anything."

"Oh, of course not," Lynch said. "Are you going to help us out, or did you just come here to jerk our chains."

Jessie smiled. "Chain-jerking does have its appeal, but no. You asked why I'm following you. You were one of the last people to see Waldridge, and I knew you were on the case."

"*How* did you know?" Kendra asked.

"Santa Monica PD. I have friends on the inside over there. I heard you were getting FBI help, which is a hell of lot more than I've been getting. Every time I got stalled, I decided to see what you were doing."

"Why did Waldridge hire you?"

Jessie didn't answer.

"I have to *know*."

"Confidential territory again," she said quietly. "I have an obligation."

"Bullshit. Your obligation is keeping your client alive."

Jessie hesitated, thinking.

"Please," Kendra said. "Tell us. I only want to keep him alive."

Jessie stared ruefully at Kendra. "I hope I don't regret this."

"Regret what? Trusting me?"

Jessie nodded. "I'm not big on trust."

"Neither am I. But there are times when you have to

173

take the chance. You won't regret it," Kendra said. "If your friends at the Santa Monica PD are keeping you in the loop, then you know I've done more to try to find Waldridge than anyone."

"I do know that."

"Then what's the problem? I guarantee you, Waldridge would want me to have every bit of information that might help me find him."

Jessie dropped down on a chair. "Okay, I'll tell you what I know, but I need you to reciprocate. Deal?"

"Sure," Kendra said.

Jessie glanced at Lynch. "I know that *he* won't be co-operative. From what I've been able to gather about him, I don't know if I'd want to deal with him anyway."

"Very wise," Lynch said. "But do be aware that I don't like Kendra's being lied to. It tends to upset me."

Jessie shrugged, and her gaze shifted back to Kendra. "I haven't found out much. I'm not sure what good it will do you."

"It has to be better than stumbling around in the dark," Lynch said.

"Sounds exactly like what I've been doing," Jessie said. "Anyway, I met Waldridge when he came to my office in West L.A. He was on edge. There was a certain . . . desperation."

Kendra sat down across from her. "About what?"

"He was concerned about a colleague of his."

"Shaw?"

"No. Another man. His name is Hayden Biers. Waldridge told me that this guy had come to L.A. from England late last month. They'd been in touch, but Biers had suddenly dropped off the face of the Earth."

"Sounds familiar," Kendra said. "What did Waldridge tell you about him?"

"He's a medical doctor. More into research than treating patients."

"Also familiar," Lynch said. "But why was he in L.A.?"

"Waldridge couldn't say."

"Couldn't or wouldn't?"

Jessie's lips twisted. "Funny you should ask that. For someone who was so obviously concerned for his colleague, he was extremely cagey. I had to pry information out of him."

"I feel your pain," Kendra said. "I went through the exact same thing when I saw him that night. But he didn't tell me about this at all."

"He was extremely concerned about confidentiality at all costs. His words. That's why I haven't talked to anyone about it."

"So what did he tell you?"

"He gave me an address down in Redondo Beach. Biers had been renting a furnished house there month to month. Waldridge went there as soon as he hit town, but there was no sign of Biers."

"Did you go there?" Lynch asked.

She was clearly annoyed at his question. "Uh, yeah. I *am* a real private investigator. No sign of a struggle. There were some clothes and a few things in the fridge, but that was about it. So I slipped in a couple webcams and moved on."

"Any local contacts?" Lynch asked.

"None that Waldridge knew of."

"And he didn't give you any clue why Biers might have come from England to L.A.?"

"Just some B.S. about him having a high-stress job and needing to get away from it all. I didn't buy it, and I even called him on it. But Waldridge wouldn't tell me any more."

"What was Biers's job? Did he tell you that?"

"Only in the most general terms. I had to dig around myself to find out, and it wasn't easy. But you'll be interested in this, though."

Kendra leaned forward. "Let me guess. He was involved in the Night Watch Project."

Jessie looked at her in surprise. "You got it. Looks like someone else has been doing her homework."

"It's a common thread between these three men. And now one is dead, and the other two are missing."

"Did Waldridge tell you anything else?" Lynch asked.

"Not much. I got Biers's cell-phone number, but there's been no activity on the line since he disappeared."

"How do you know?" Kendra asked.

"The next morning, when Waldridge disappeared, I'd taken his money to find his associate, so it wasn't a stretch to figure there was a connection between what happened to those two guys. Biers's trail stalled pretty quickly, so I began to look into Waldridge's case. That's when I found out that you were on it. I tracked him back to Big Bear, and—"

"How?" Lynch asked.

She gave him another annoyed look. "Again, I'm a licensed private investigator. I know how to do my job. But if you must know, he paid me using a prepaid Visa credit card, so I had the number. I have credit-agency contacts, too. He'd used the card a few times in Big Bear. I went up there and asked around. It wasn't too hard to find the house that Shaw rented."

"Why a prepaid card?" Kendra asked. "Why not his own?"

Jessie shrugged. "He was visiting from England. Some people like to use those in lieu of traveler's checks. Only later did I think that he was trying to avoid being tracked."

"Like *you* tracked him?"

"Exactly. If that's what he was trying to do, he should have hired me to help him stay invisible. I'm pretty good at that. Anyway, I found Shaw's body, just a few minutes before you came along that night. I tried to hide, but my damned footprints in the snow made that impossible."

"When did you start following me?" Kendra asked.

"The next day. I knew you were getting FBI help that I couldn't tap, so I started following you to see where it led. Good thing because that's why I was there when those thugs tried to bottle you up and cart you away."

"You have no idea who those men were?"

"No idea. They came out of their van wearing those ski masks." She mockingly inclined her head. "You're welcome, by the way."

Kendra smiled. "Thank you."

"You must have seen the vehicle they were driving," Lynch said. "You should have reported it to the police."

"I put a tracker on their van on my way in, but they must have found it and given it a toss."

"Plates?" Lynch asked.

"Stolen. They were pros, whoever they were. I'm sure they ditched the vehicle within minutes."

"Probably," he murmured.

"So what did you find out today?" Jessie asked.

"Your crackerjack sources didn't tell you?" Lynch asked mockingly.

"There's a bit of a time lag. The FBI has been pretty

good about keeping Santa Monica PD posted on the status of the investigation, but they aren't always timely. Find out anything interesting?"

Kendra turned to Lynch. "I want to tell her."

"Your choice. This is your show."

Kendra turned back to Jessie. Everything she'd told them lined up with the truth as they knew it. She found herself wanting to trust her.

"First things first," Kendra said. "How long have you been following me today?"

"Since an hour or so ago, when you left the FBI field office."

"Okay. We'll start there." Kendra told her about Waldridge's appearance on the security video and their visit to the Baldwin Hills Walmart store.

Jessie was silent for a long moment. "Well, at least we know Waldridge is alive, or he was at that time."

Kendra nodded. "We just need to find him."

Jessie's brow wrinkled in thought. "Maybe it's just a matter of drawing him out."

"That's assuming he has his freedom. Someone was sure keeping close tabs on him at the store."

"I'd like a frame grab of the person you saw watching him."

"We can get you that."

"Good." Jessie hesitated, looking between Kendra and Lynch as if something had suddenly occurred to her. "Just out of curiosity, how much do you know about me?"

Kendra shrugged. "What could we know? Only what you've told us."

"That's not really true, is it?"

"What do you mean?"

Jessie got to her feet. Her entire body language spoke

of wariness and defensiveness. "I told you I've done my research on you. If what I've read is true, I bet you knew quite a bit about me even before today."

"I may have picked up a few things."

"Like?"

She might as well tell her. In spite of Jessie's toughness and wariness, that defensive attitude reflected a certain vulnerability. If she thought Kendra was hiding anything, it might get in the way. "I did think you were ex-military from your attack stance the other day, and now I'm sure of it."

Lynch painfully touched his side. "My kidneys are also sure of it."

Kendra stood up and slowly walked around Jessie. "You were in Afghanistan. Your father was also in the military. Your family moved with him, including quite a bit of your childhood in Western Europe. You were probably born in Bakersfield, where you spent your early years."

Jessie smiled. "Tehachapi. About forty miles southeast of Bakersfield."

"And I was doing so well. At least I think I was."

"You definitely were. And still are. Anything else?"

"You're a marathoner. You've done the Bay to Breakers run in San Francisco and the Honolulu Marathon. But for exercise you usually just go to Gold's Gym, I'm guessing the one in Venice."

Jessie nodded. "Wow. If I knew you better, I'd high-five you right now. And I usually think high fives are idiotic."

"Then I take that as a compliment. Oh, you vacationed in Fiji a few years ago."

Jessie gave a low whistle.

"And you or someone you know has been in Bermuda fairly recently."

"My then-boyfriend about eight months ago."

"It was clearly an amicable breakup."

Jessie nodded in amazement. "Holy shit."

Lynch leaned back and crossed his arms. "I keep waiting for this to get old, but it never does."

Jessie bit her lip. "I can't see it getting old, but something about this is *really* pissing me off."

"You asked for it," Kendra said.

"You're right, I did. I guess I'm just uncomfortable being such an open book."

"You aren't," Lynch said. "At least not to anybody except her."

She was staring directly into Kendra's eyes. "I consider myself a fairly private person. I think I'd feel better if you told me how you know all this."

"You won't feel better," Lynch said. "But at least you won't drive yourself crazy all night trying to figure it out. Trust me, I've been there."

"As I said, I have trouble trusting anyone but myself." Jessie stepped closer to Kendra. "How about where I'm from, and the places I've lived?"

"Linguistics."

"You're a linguist, too?"

"Amateur. When you're denied the opportunity to form an impression of people by looking at them, how they speak becomes very important. After your kind rescue the other day, I told Lynch I could hear a Central Valley twang in your voice. Add in some subtle continental Europe vowel suppressions, and you have someone who spent a lot of time overseas in their younger years."

"I didn't have to be a military brat, though. What if one of my parents worked for an international company that moved them around a lot?"

"True, and that was certainly possible. But your fighting style made me think you had a military background, which significantly raised the chances that one of your parents had served."

"But how did you know about Afghanistan?"

Kendra grabbed Jessie's wrist and pushed up her sleeve. "You have a tan line here. You often wear a bracelet that's fairly representative of Afghan tribal jewelry with beads and little bells. I'm thinking you bought that there."

Jessie nodded. "Chicken Street in Kabul. I did two tours in Afghanistan."

"That's impressive."

"Is it? I guess some people would call it that. What about my marathons?"

"I saw your motorcycle, remember? You have a Bay to Breakers water bottle tethered to your drink holder and a Honolulu Marathon license-plate frame. I also saw a Gold's Gym bar-code tag on your key ring. It was easy to spot because I have one on mine. I guessed the Venice location because it's close to the mailing address on your private investigator's license. I've meant to go there every time I've attended symposiums at UCLA." She made a face. "Somehow, I've always found an excuse not to go."

"Probably the same excuses I often seem to find." Jessie thought for a moment. "My key ring also told you about Fiji, didn't it?"

"Hard to miss with that red-and-yellow tiki-mask pendant. It shows a lot of wear, so it's something you've probably been carrying for years."

"Wait one minute. How the *hell* did you recognize that mask as Fijian? You've only had your sight for what, ten years?"

"Nine."

"Most people go their whole lives without being able to recognize things like that."

"Most people have probably seen that mask dozens of times in different places. They just don't remember. Sight is such a gift to me that I try to take nothing for granted."

"I got that. But there's nothing to see on me or my motorcycle that could tell you that I or someone I know has been to Bermuda."

"You're right, but there is something to *smell*. You're wearing a perfume called Easter Lily. It's very distinctive, but the only time I've smelled it on anyone is when they or a loved one brought it back from Bermuda themselves. I haven't investigated this, but my guess is that you only buy it there."

"Which is what my ex-boyfriend did. He bought it for me at the perfumery."

"The fact that you're still wearing it tells me that it wasn't an unpleasant breakup. Otherwise, that bottle would probably be buried in a landfill by now."

"Right again."

"Feeling less violated now?"

"Oh, no." She deadpanned, "More violated than ever."

"Like I said, a normal reaction," Lynch said.

"And that remark makes me feel even more violated. People don't usually accuse me of being normal."

"This really isn't your day, is it?"

Kendra frowned. "All my parlor tricks aren't worth a damn if they don't help to get Waldridge back."

"We'll find him," Lynch said softly. "We got closer today."

"Not close enough." She turned to face him. "All roads lead to Night Watch. It's the one thing these three medical researchers had in common."

Jessie nodded. "Agreed. I haven't been able to find out much about the Night Watch Project. There was a fair amount written about it when you got your sight, both in scientific literature and the mainstream media. But here's been almost nothing in the last few years."

"We found that out," Lynch said. "We have someone in England working on it."

"Someone good?"

"The best." Lynch checked his phone. "I'll text him about what you've told us concerning Hayden Biers. If you can give me his cell-phone number and any other info Waldridge provided you about him, it may help."

"It's not much, but I'll give you what I have."

"Thank you. My contact information is now in your phone's address book. Adam Lynch."

"What do you mean?" she asked warily.

"Check your phone."

Jessie fished her phone out of her pocket and scrolled through her contacts. "Cute. Now *that's* a violation. This is what you've been doing with your phone since we've been here . . . Hacking into mine?"

"Hacking is a word with such unpleasant connotations. I was merely exchanging contact info. I have yours, and you have mine."

"Uh-huh. My life is on this thing. What else did you grab?"

"Nothing else. I promise."

She held down her phone's power button. "I'm turning my phone off now. Our partnership is getting off to a rocky start."

"A partnership?" Kendra repeated. "Is that what this is?"

Jessie shrugged. "Makes sense. We're both working

183

toward the same end. Waldridge is still my client. He paid me up front."

"What happens when his retainer runs out?"

Jessie headed for the door. "We'll see when that time comes. Until then, I'm on this case whether we work together or not." She stopped and turned at the door. "It's been . . . interesting." She gazed at Kendra. "I think I can trust you, but you make me damn uneasy." Her eyes shifted to Lynch. "And you're definitely an unknown factor, but if we're going to work together, I think I should be honest with you. I wasn't telling the truth about being able to put you down this time. You were good. Very good. But now I've fought you, and I've learned you. *Next* time I'll be able to take you down."

She turned and left the studio.

After a long moment of silence, Kendra turned to Lynch. "What do you think?"

"Other than that she's smart as a whip and fires on all cylinders? And the fact that I think there's so much beneath that surface that it would take years to uncover it all?" He shrugged. "I'll run a background check, but I'm inclined, in this case, to believe her."

"So am I." She smiled. "And there's nothing wrong with hidden depths. Sometimes it shows character."

"And sometime it hides land mines." He smiled back at her. "You're prejudiced because she saved your neck. That's okay, I'm prejudiced, too. That neck has great value to me. I'll just keep an eye out to make sure she doesn't circle around and attack from the rear."

Warmth. That damn charisma. It had come out of nowhere, and she was having trouble looking away from him.

But his smile was fading, and he was shaking his head.

"Uh-uh, we're doing too well." He reached for his phone and started to punch in a number.

Relief. Disappointment. Frustration. Curiosity. "What are you doing?" Kendra asked.

"I'm sure it has a name and purpose other than the one that I'm cursing at the moment. Ah, yes, that's it. I got a text from Rye while Jessie was here. He might have some news for us."

CHAPTER
10

RYE STOOD IN THE EMPTY LOT, staring at the acres of paved crumbling concrete. The air was damp from the predawn mist, and the sky was beginning to lighten in the east.

His phone vibrated in his pocket. He tapped his Bluetooth earpiece to answer.

"Lynch?"

"Yes. Sorry I couldn't pick up before, Rye. I was talking to someone. You're up awful late . . . or is it early?"

"I couldn't sleep. Something was bothering me. The more I looked into Waldridge's work history, the less it added up."

"What do you mean?"

"He's given the same work address on at least three official documents in the past couple of years. Hyperion Laboratories, Limited."

"Hyperion?"

"Yes. The late Mr. Shaw also listed it as his place of

employment at an academic conference last year. It's somehow related to the Night Watch Project."

"Okay . . . So why doesn't it add up?"

"I'm at the address right now . . . and it's a vacant lot."

"What?"

Rye stepped over a clump of weeds that had burst through a crack in the concrete. "There was a building here once, but it's probably been twenty years or more. No one's worked here for decades."

"What does it mean?"

"Don't know yet. I looked it up on Google Earth, and I thought it must be some kind of mistake. So I came down to see for myself. Not much to see."

"I hate to repeat myself, but I don't understand what the hell that means."

"Me neither. I just thought it was curious, and you might want to be informed. I'll talk to some more people and try to get it sorted out."

"Good. While you're at it, I have another name for you to check out. Hayden Biers. Yet another colleague of Waldridge's. He also came here to California, and it seems as if all three men may have come here to hide out."

"Hide from what?"

"As soon as you find out, let me know."

"Pressure, again." He sighed. "I'll do my best. I'm not going to find it in this vacant lot, that's for sure."

"What's your next move?"

Rye checked his watch. "A fine breakfast and a cup of tea. After that, Shaw's widow lives in Covent Garden. If she hasn't been notified already, she should get the news of her husband's death in the next couple of hours. I'll go over and talk to her around the time she should be getting up."

"Seriously? Sure you don't want to wait on that?"

"Positive. She'll be numb. In shock. Not quite sure which way is up. In my experience, people can be very forthcoming when they've been knocked off-balance."

"And people call *me*, the Puppetmaster. Go easy on her, Rye."

"Worry not, my friend. I can be quite a comforting presence when the occasion demands it. I'll let you know what I find out." Rye cut the connection.

Lynch could be something of an enigma, he thought. Considering his background, he hadn't expected him to caution him about hurting that woman. He usually displayed no emotion and just got the job done. It just went to show that it was a vast world filled with multifaceted people. Which, except for his books, made it the only thing bearable.

Together with the unique puzzles that occasionally were brought for him to solve. He must not forget that spur, and Lynch was adept at furnishing him with that particular stimulation.

He would have to be very clever and innovative and give Lynch something for his trouble . . .

"MAY I HELP YOU?"

The sixtyish woman stood in the front doorway of a charming flat on Monmouth Street. She was attractive, well dressed, and didn't seem to have a care in the world aside from the stranger on her front stoop.

Rye studied her face. Her eyes weren't red, and the mascara wasn't running. This wasn't right.

"Madeleine Shaw?"

"Yes."

"Wife of Dr. Porter Shaw?"

"Yes."

She appeared almost . . . chipper.

Had she not been notified yet? Awkward.

He hesitated. "Has someone . . . spoken to you this morning?"

"About what?"

Oh, Lord. He was going to be stuck with giving her the news.

"My husband?" she offered.

"Yes. You received some notification this morning?"

For the first time, a bit of stress lined her face. But only a bit. "Yes. He passed away."

"Were you told of the circumstances?"

"I was." Her expression still wasn't troubled. Curious, but not troubled. "And may I ask what business it is of yours?"

"My name is Ryan Malone. I'm working with the American authorities on the case. Two of your husband's colleagues were also in California. They've gone missing. I know it's a devastating time for you, but I wondered if I might—"

"Of course. Come in." The chipper voice and attitude were back. She opened the door wide for him to enter. "I was just having tea. Would you like some?"

"Thank you."

So much for not knowing which way was up.

He followed her through the narrow but tastefully decorated home back to a sunroom. She gestured for him to sit in one of the two white wooden chairs. She had already started pouring his tea by the time he was seated.

"I'm very sorry for your loss," he said. "You and your husband made a beautiful home for yourselves."

"He had nothing to do with it. I think he liked our home

189

well enough, when he cared to notice. But it's certainly nothing he ever cared to weigh in on."

"I see." This was going down a far-too-static path. Time to stir it up a little. "Pardon me for saying so, but you seem to be taking your husband's demise incredibly well."

She picked up her teacup and gazed at the garden outside. "I can see it does seem that way." She shrugged. "He left me a long time ago in spirit. It's the old cliché, I suppose. The man whose passion was his work."

"Really? And how long has it been that way?"

"Always, if I'm honest with myself. Even when we met, it's what attracted me to him. I thought it would be enough if just a little bit of that fire and intensity was thrown in my direction. It never was, not really." She looked up. "I'm sorry. You're not really interested in all this. It's been a confusing morning. I guess I'm still in shock. I haven't even told anyone yet. He has a sister in Leeds who really needs to know, but I'm still . . . processing."

"I understand."

"So how can I help you?"

Rye leaned forward in his chair. "Tell me why your husband was in the United States."

"Work. He was always traveling someplace. And even when he was here, he wasn't here, if you know what I mean."

"Was there anything unusual about this particular trip?"

She nodded. "Actually, yes. For one thing, he'd told me he was going to Chicago. He never mentioned California."

"Odd. Are you certain?"

"Positive. I didn't know he was there until this morning, when I was told that he was dead. But there was something even stranger . . . He left his phone here."

"He forgot it?"

"I thought so at first. But he never went anywhere without it, not even the corner store." She shook her head. "Who does in this day and age? We all live with our phones. He called twice in the three weeks he was gone, each time from a different disposable phone he'd purchased. I offered to send him his own phone, but he didn't want it. He was very specific. He didn't want me to power it on or even charge it."

"Interesting."

"I handle all the finances, and I can tell you he didn't use a credit card or cash-machine card since he's been gone. He withdrew several thousand pounds before he left, and I suppose he'd been getting by on that." She grimaced. "Which also kept me from knowing where he was."

"And kept anyone else from knowing," Rye said. "Tell me, what exactly was your husband working on?"

"To be honest, I have no idea. He wasn't very forthcoming. He'd been very excited, but his mood had soured in the past couple of months." She shook her head. "And heaven forbid he explain himself to me. I was only his wife."

"In what way had his mood soured?"

"In almost every way you can imagine. Sometimes depressed, sometimes angry, sometimes frustrated. Not an unusual range of emotions for a researcher struggling to solve a problem, but this has been worse. Much worse."

"Hmm. Can you tell me anything about his colleagues? People he might have been working with in the last months of his life?"

"Well, there was Charles Waldridge. Porter worshipped him. He thought the man was a genius. I should probably try to contact him."

Rye hesitated, wondering if he should tell her about

Waldridge's disappearance. He decided against it. "Anyone else?"

Her lips twisted. "No one he ever discussed with me."

"Did you ever visit his lab?"

"Heavens, no. It was in the Docklands near the fish market, I think."

"Near Canary Wharf?"

"Yes."

"I was just there. It's a vacant lot."

"What?"

"No lab. Just an empty lot. It's been that way for quite some time. Could there have been someplace else?"

Her face was frozen in utter bewilderment. She shook her head.

"Did he drive to work?"

She nodded.

"I wonder if you might let me look in his car. Is it here?"

She motioned out the sunroom windows toward a freestanding garage on the other side of the small backyard. "It's in there. It hasn't been driven since he left."

"Would you mind? It could be very helpful."

She didn't speak for a moment. "Isn't it silly? I think I'm dreading looking at it. I'm used to thinking of him in this house. It will be different with the car, perhaps a bit jarring . . ." She finally put down her teacup. "Certainly. I'll get the keys."

After a few moments rustling through an overstuffed kitchen drawer, Madeleine found her husband's spare keys and led Rye out to the detached garage, where a silver Mercedes SL shared space with an MG Mini.

"The Mercedes is his. *Was* his." She paused. Her voice

was the slightest bit unsteady as she added, "Still doesn't feel right to say it that way. I guess I'll get better at it."

He held out his hand for the key. "May I?"

She used the key's remote button to unlock the car, then she handed it to him.

Rye slid behind the wheel and surveyed the vehicle's interior. Immaculate.

He started the car. The engine roared to life, and the touch screen lit up the dark interior. Rye tapped the screen and cycled through the GPS map screens until he found the navigation app's driving history.

The passenger door opened, and Madeleine leaned in. "Any luck?"

"Maybe." He pointed toward the screen. "Do you recognize this address? It's on Scarbrook Road in Croyden. Looks like he went there almost every day."

Madeleine's eyes narrowed on the screen. "Croyden? No. Not at all. It's not a place he ever mentioned going."

Rye took a photo of the screen with his phone. "I don't like to ask this, especially in light what's happened today . . ." There was no delicate way to ask this question. "But I can't help but wonder, since your husband was regularly going someplace without your knowledge, if perhaps . . ."

"You want to know if my husband was having an affair," she said quietly.

"Yes."

"The answer is no." She swallowed hard and looked away from him. "Among other reasons, I honestly don't think he would've made that kind of time for it. Believe me, this was about his work."

"I do believe you." He avoided looking at her as he

cycled through several more destinations on the touch screen. He snapped photos of a few of the other recurring entries, but none appeared with anything near the frequency of the Croyden address.

He cut the engine and turned toward Madeleine.

Tears were now running down her cheeks.

The mask was off.

"I'm very sorry," he whispered.

"So am I." Her eyes were glittering tears. "I loved him, you know. I wanted to make him happy. All these years of loneliness . . . I didn't take my first lover for over fifteen years. I was careful. I didn't want to hurt Porter." Her lips twisted. "I didn't have to worry. He wasn't interested." She met his eyes. "But in the end, I realized it's what I felt, not what he felt. If you truly love someone, then you accept who they are and still want the best for them." Her voice was low and uneven, but rang with sincerity. "And I wish with my whole heart that Croyden address belonged to a woman who could give him what I couldn't."

"You're a very wise and generous woman," he said gently. "I'll find out what happened to your husband, I promise."

"Thank you. I believe it will help to know."

She took the key and slammed the door closed.

San Diego
6:50 A.M.

THIS IS YOUR WOULD-BE KIDNAPPER.

Kendra had been jolted wide awake by her buzzing phone. It signaled a one-sentence text message from Griffin.

The phone buzzed again.

LOOK FAMILIAR?

She scrolled to see that he'd included a photo. It was a man with a broad face, close-cropped brown hair, and penetrating eyes.

Those eyes . . .

MEET WALLACE DEAN POWERS.

Her bedroom door flew open. Lynch, wearing only a pair of black lounge shorts, held his phone in front of him. "Griffin included me on the text. They must have gotten a DNA hit on the skin cells from under your fingernails."

Her phone rang and the caller ID screen lit up with a most unflattering picture of Griffin. Kendra had gleefully snapped it when he was scratching his lip, but it looked more like he was picking his nose. She swiped to answer, leaving it in front of her in speaker mode. "That's one of the guys, Griffin. He tried to grab me. I know those eyes."

"Good. Unfortunately, we didn't get a hit off the other guy you mauled."

"I *wish* I'd mauled them. This man's skin was under my left nails, wasn't it?"

After a clicking of keyboard keys, he replied. "Yes, left."

"I knew it. That's the second man. Deeper voice, maybe from the Midwest."

"Very good. He did some jail time for a domestic abuse charge about four years ago, committed in Missouri. That's why his DNA was in the system."

Kendra looked at the man's photo on her phone. "And his name is Wallace Dean Powers . . . Anything else?"

"He lives in Downey. He's an unemployed high-school physical education instructor."

"He's a *gym coach*?" Lynch asked.

"That's our best information."

"Well, I guess thugs have to come from somewhere," Kendra said. "It's not like you can pick up the phone and call Henchmen-R-Us."

"Hmm, you've just given me an excellent idea what to do with my retirement years," Lynch said. "Griffin, do we know anything else about this wife-beating jock?"

"Very little. No prior associations, no clue who he might be working with now. But I'm hoping that we can ask him ourselves in the next couple hours."

"You're bringing him in?"

"Yes. We're coordinating with Downey PD as I speak. I'll text you directions to our staging area in the neighborhood. If you want in, meet us there at 9:15 A.M."

"We want in," Kendra said as she jumped out of bed. "See you there."

Downey, California
9:15 A.M.

Kendra and Lynch arrived at the large office parking lot adjacent to the Downey Pizza Co. restaurant on Florence Avenue, where three squad cars were waiting with flashers on.

FBI Special Agent Metcalf climbed out of his car a few feet away. "Damnedest way to ID a suspect I've ever seen."

Kendra wriggled her fingers. "Your lab deserves all the credit. I just collected the samples."

"Remind me to keep my distance from those talons of yours, okay?"

"What's the plan?" Lynch asked.

Metcalf folded his arms in front of him. "We just placed a call to his residence, posing as a solar-panel company. He's home. Two detectives are keeping an eye on the house while we prepare to move in. We need you to keep your distance until we have him. Then maybe you can come over, look at his build, listen to his voice, and see if you can confirm."

"I've seen his eyes in the photo. That plus his DNA is confirmation enough. But I'll check him out to make sure."

Metcalf nodded to a uniformed officer who was obviously in charge, who in turn signaled to the officers in the patrol cars. He turned to Kendra and Lynch. "Okay, follow us. I'll signal you at the top of his block to pull over."

Lynch nodded. "Got it."

They caravanned to a residential street just three blocks south of the staging area. Metcalf, riding behind the squad cars, stopped just long enough to signal Kendra and Lynch before continuing.

Lynch pulled over, and they watched the three squad cars and Metcalf's vehicle continue down the block.

Kendra glanced over at Lynch. "It's killing you, isn't it?"

"What?"

"Not being down there in the thick of it."

Lynch stared at the cars speeding down the block. "One reason I prefer to work alone. I'm much more comfortable when I get to make the rules."

"That makes two of us even though I don't have a strong desire to break down doors with an automatic weapon in my hand." She added, "That must be a guy thing."

"You're taunting me. Now I *need* to be down there."

"They'll have him in just a couple of minutes," she said soothingly.

Lynch leaned back in his seat. "It's just as well. After what that guy tried to do to you, I probably would have beaten him senseless. That would have been most counterproductive."

"You think?"

Lynch pointed to the cars spinning to a stop in front of a house halfway down the block. "They're moving in."

Kendra found herself holding her breath as she waited for some sign that they had the man who had tried to abduct her.

Could he lead them to Waldridge?

Chill out. One step at a time.

Get him first, then worry about—

Buzzz!

She lifted her phone. It was a text from Metcalf.

NO GO. HOUSE EMPTY.

"Shit."

Before she even knew Lynch had seen the message, the car roared to life and the wheels spun on the pavement.

"What are you doing?"

Lynch shifted gears and sped down the street. "He slipped out after they called. He knew they were onto him."

"But there were detectives watching the house."

"He might have crawled through a neighbor's yard.

198

Who knows? However he gave them the slip, we don't have time to poke around and figure it out right now. Keep your eyes peeled. He's got to be close by."

They roared by the police cars and turned at the corner to circle the block. There were few people to be seen; two kids playing, a landscape crew cutting grass, a man in a track suit jogging with his dog.

"He might have had a car parked on the street," Kendra said.

"In which case he could be miles away by now. But let's exhaust all of our other possibilities while we still can. He might be in one of these backyards, in a toolshed, or a barbecue island."

". . . or pretending to be a landscape worker," Kendra said.

"What?"

"Turn around!"

Lynch spun out and gunned the engine as they faced the direction from which they'd just come. Kendra pointed to the landscape crew. "Check out the guy kneeling by the gardenia bushes. The one in the white shirt and baseball cap."

"I see him. He looks like pretty much everyone else on the crew."

"His jeans are the only ones that aren't grass-stained. Also, no perspiration on the back of his shirt."

The man looked up and locked eyes with her.

"That's him!" Kendra said.

Powers jumped to his feet and bolted toward the backyard.

Kendra unbuckled her seat belt and opened her door. "Stop the car!"

"For what?"

"I'm going after him. You circle the block and try to cut him off."

Lynch hit the brakes. "And if you catch him?"

"We'll beat the hell out of each other until the cavalry arrives. You're the cavalry. So get your ass in gear."

Before he could object, she jumped out of the car and took off running.

The landscape crew stopped their work and stared as she ran past them and bolted down the side of the house. She bent over and grabbed a shovel as she ran, barely breaking stride.

Powers had pushed through the gate and was making for the back fence. He was a big man, probably not the most agile. Maybe she could catch him before he made it over.

He gripped the top of the wrought-iron fence and swung his leg up. A miss. He tried again. Another miss.

She extended the shovel before her, aiming the blade for his lower back.

This is going to hurt, buddy.

But with a burst of energy, he managed to swing his leg up and catapult himself over the fence.

Dammit.

He landed on his feet and was already running through the opposite yard by the time she got within striking distance. She threw down the shovel and climbed up and over the fence.

By the time she made it over, he was already sprinting down the side yard toward the street beyond.

Good. With any luck, Lynch and maybe half the Downey PD would soon be on top of him.

She ran down the side yard and emerged on the street beyond.

What the hell . . .

The man had vanished.

She glanced around. She suddenly felt extremely vulnerable. He could strike from any direction, especially since he now knew she was alone.

Where the hell could he be?

Maybe on one of the porches.

In the tall shrubs to her right.

In between some cars on the street.

He was *inside* one of the cars, she realized. Which one?

Powers's head bobbed up in the driver-side window of a Dodge SUV. Either he owned it or he'd just completed the fastest hotwire job she'd ever seen.

The tires spun hard against the pavement, and the SUV rocketed down the street.

Shit!

She heard a familiar roar and turned to see Lynch's Ferrari rounding the corner. The cavalry was here. She yelled and pointed at the SUV. "That's him!"

He nodded and sped after Powers.

She stared dumbfounded at his Ferrari as it roared away. She'd expected Lynch to stop long enough for her to jump in, but of course it made more sense to stay on Powers's tail and not risk losing him.

Fine. She'd make her way back to Powers's house and see if there was anything there she could—

Another familiar roar. Behind her.

Jessie Mercado's motorcycle rolled up and screeched to a stop just inches away. Jessie flipped up her visor to reveal those huge dark eyes and a broad smile. "Need a lift?"

"Seriously?"

"Seriously. Even though I'm a little annoyed with you right now. I thought we were working together."

"I really didn't know that—"

"Relax. Just kidding. There's a helmet strapped to the back. Take it and hop on. Hurry!"

Kendra put on the helmet and threw her leg over the seat of Jessie's motorcycle.

"Ready?" Jessie asked.

Before Kendra could reply, Jessie squeezed back the throttle and rocketed down the street.

Kendra leaned around Jessie to see that Lynch's and Powers's cars were still within sight.

Jessie shouted over her engine. "Are we chasing one of the guys I put down the other night?"

Kendra shouted back. "Yes, the one who dragged me into the office."

"He pissed his pants, right?"

"Yes."

"Good! I'd love another crack at him." Jessie put on another burst of speed.

Up ahead, Powers turned right, almost taking out a streetlight pole as he went wide on the busy cross street. They were heading deep into a congested retail district, with four lanes of traffic and traffic lights stretching to infinity.

"Hang on!" Jessie shouted.

She took a hard right turn into the intersection. Lynch was now only a few yards ahead. Powers was half a block beyond him, weaving in and out of traffic.

"Wave to your friend," Jessie shouted.

While Kendra was still trying to figure out what she meant, Jessie passed Lynch on the left. Kendra smiled. She didn't have to be a skilled lip-reader to pick up the curses tumbling out of Lynch's mouth.

With another burst of speed, Lynch was behind them.

Kendra looked forward. They were now nimbly weaving between the few cars that separated them from Powers.

Almost there . . .

Dozens of taillights flashed, and Kendra realized they were approaching a stoplight. Powers turned left into the lanes of oncoming traffic, where he narrowly missed a pickup truck and a Lexus convertible.

To Kendra's horror, Jessie stayed on his tail, dodging the same vehicles. Kendra wanted to look away, but she felt compelled to watch as if that would somehow stave off a deadly collision.

Powers turned left at the next intersection, where Jessie hurtled through and shortened the gap.

"What's your plan?" Kendra gasped.

"Keep the pressure on until he crashes," she said calmly. "Or until we do."

"I'm way better than he is."

"Modest. I like it . . . I think."

"Hang tight. I'm going to try something."

Jessie gunned the engine and drew alongside Powers's car.

Powers glared at them. His knuckles were white on the steering wheel and sweat poured from his face. Jessie was right, Kendra realized. The man wasn't comfortable in a high-speed pursuit. He abruptly pulled the wheel, in an attempt to hit them, but Jessie sped past and cut in front of the SUV.

He bore down on them. Kendra could hear his engine roaring in her ears.

"Uh, Jessie . . ."

"I see him. I need you to reach into my right jacket pocket."

"What?"

"I have some ball bearings in there. Reach in and grab a few."

Kendra reached into the pocket of Jessie's leather jacket and pulled out a handful of shiny little orbs. "Who rides around town with ball bearings in their pockets?"

"I do. Now throw them at his windshield as hard as you can. Aim for the driver's side. Do it!"

Kendra hurled the metal balls with all the force she could muster.

Contact!

Kendra glanced back to see that three of the ball bearings had made contact with the windshield, creating webs of cracked glass in Powers's field of vision.

The car swerved erratically.

Jessie fell back alongside the SUV long enough to grab another ball bearing from her pocket and hurl it into the driver's side window, shattering it completely. Again the SUV swerved crazily.

They dropped farther back until they were once again following the SUV. Kendra looked behind her to see that Lynch had caught up. He was talking, she realized, communicating their location to the police.

Jessie beeped her high-pitched horn several times. Powers glanced back, and Kendra could see that he had a fine mist of blood on the side of his face. Likely a casualty of the shattered driver's side window.

Jessie beeped again.

Kendra thought she was doing it to rattle Powers, but she quickly saw that it was a warning for a supermarket delivery truck slowly pulling out of the alleyway ahead.

Powers saw it an instant later. He swerved to avoid the truck, but overcompensated and jumped onto the sidewalk.

He tried to correct his course, but it was too late. He plowed into the brick wall of a diaper factory.

Jessie winced. "That's gotta hurt."

They circled the smoldering wreck as Lynch stopped and climbed out of his car.

He looked at the wreck. "How is he?"

"Still breathing," Jessie said. She and Kendra dismounted the cycle. Powers was slumped in his smashed car, partially covered by an airbag. He moaned in pain.

Jessie reached in and pulled the airbag forward, revealing Powers's swollen and bloody face. "He's not going to be winning any beauty contests anytime soon, but he'll survive."

Police sirens wailed in the distance.

"I called them in," Lynch said. "They'll be here in under a minute."

Jessie leaned down to face Powers. "Where's Waldridge?"

He wrinkled his brow. "Who?"

"Dr. Charles Waldridge. Thin British guy, late forties. Where is he?"

"Can't help you."

Jessie jerked her thumb toward Kendra. "Then why did you try to kidnap her the other night?"

He glanced at Kendra before looking away. "Didn't . . . have a choice."

"What the hell is that supposed to mean?"

He closed his eyes. "I'm not saying another damn word."

Lynch stepped forward and placed his hand gently on Powers's shoulder. "You're pretty beat-up. Where does it hurt. Here?"

"Yeah."

Lynch squeezed his shoulder.

"Aaah!" Powers cried out.

Lynch squeezed harder. "I suggest you tell these ladies what they need to know."

"I . . . can't . . ."

"Sure you can." He applied more pressure on the shoulder.

"Aaah! Shit!"

Kendra flinched at the sheer agony in his voice. She braced herself, tensed, then leaned in closer. "We know it was you who tried to take me the other night. Why?"

He gasped. "I can't say any more."

Lynch squeezed his shoulder again.

"Owww!" Powers grimaced. "Keep it up, and I'm gonna pass out. Then you won't get anything from me."

"We're not getting anything from you now," Kendra said. "And I have to say, I'm really enjoying this," she lied.

"I'll bet you are, you b—owww!" He looked up at Lynch. "I'll have you brought up on police brutality charges."

Lynch smiled malevolently. "I'm not the police. Just a concerned citizen who's extremely annoyed with you for what you did to my friend." He slowly increased the pressure on Powers's shoulder. "And if you think you're hurting now, what do you think of this? It's all in the fingers . . ."

Powers eyes bulged, and he let out a bloodcurdling scream.

Lynch released his shoulder. "Just a little sample. So tell us why you tried to kidnap my friend here."

Sweat rained down Powers's face. "We weren't going to hurt her. We just had to bring her there. They told us they needed her. I promise."

"Where were you taking her?" Lynch asked.

He shook his head. "Do whatever you want, but I can't say any more. My life is at stake here."

"Your life?" Kendra said.

"Yeah." He was pale and shaking. "Excuse me, if I don't feel like dying."

Kendra's eyes narrowed on him. "Who are you working for?"

He stared at her for a long moment. "For your sake, I hope you never have to find out. But you probably will, they want you real bad."

"Who? What's that supposed to mean?"

"Not another word." He looked at Lynch. "Do whatever you want with me." He breathed a sigh of relief as he saw squad cars coming down the street. "I'm not talking."

"No?" Lynch smiled. "I'd barely started. Those time restraints really hampered me. Oh, well, there will be another time."

Behind them, the four squad cars and Metcalf's car rolled up. The police cars cut their sirens, but the flashers stayed on.

Lynch called out to them. "Get a paramedic unit out here. This man needs a hospital."

Metcalf jumped out of his car and ran up to them. "Is it him?"

Kendra nodded. "Yes, but he's not overly talkative. I need to know everything about him we can find out."

"We have cops swarming through his house, and we'll subpoena phone records."

"Good." She turned back to Powers. She tensed, her hands clenching into fists at her sides. "One last question. Is Dr. Waldridge still alive?"

Powers didn't answer. He closed his eyes and slowly leaned back against the headrest.

No use, she realized in frustration as she turned away from him.

Fifteen minutes later Kendra and Lynch watched the ambulance drive off down the street.

"I'm out of here." Jessie strode toward her bike. "I'll see you at Powers's place." She glanced over her shoulder at Kendra with a mischievous grin. "I suppose you're going to opt for riding with Lynch in that opulent jalopy, but you're welcome to come with me. I bet you'd have more fun."

"But I wouldn't," Lynch said firmly. "I've had enough for one day of wondering whether I'm going to have to peel her remains off a truck or light pole." He took Kendra's elbow and led her firmly toward the Ferrari. "She might have fun, but it will take me the entire trip to Powers's to recover."

"Poor Lynch. I can see what a delicate creature you are." Jessie laughed and roared off.

Lynch waited until they were back on the freeway before he glanced at Kendra. "I didn't think. Did I offend your precious independence?"

"If you had, I wouldn't have let you push me into this car. I was ready for your 'opulent jalopy.' I need to get my breath." She leaned back against the leather headrest. "In more ways than one."

He nodded. "That was a wild ride. Jessie is . . . unique." His gaze narrowed on her face. "Was it 'fun?' "

"Yes. And exciting. And scary. It brought back a lot of memories."

"What kind of memories?"

"Back to the time when I took as many chances as Jessie. In all kinds of ways." She smiled. "But I was never as good as she is on that motorcycle. Of course, I could go back to it and see if—"

"No!" He paused. "You'll do what you please, of course. But I'd appreciate it if you don't do it around me. It was an experience I prefer not to repeat." He smiled. "Jessie's right. I'm such a delicate creature."

"Yeah, sure." She looked away from him. "So delicate that you're one of the reasons I have to get my breath and recover."

"Powers? I had to get the information, and we didn't have much time." He paused. "He hurt you. He might have been planning to kill you."

"That's not what he said. But he could have been lying. I don't know what reason anyone would hire someone to kidnap me."

"We'll find out. What's important was that I wasn't there to help you that day. But I was here today."

"Oh yes, you were here all right."

"Look at me." When her gaze shifted to meet his own, he said, "You know what I am. What I do. Any way I can. I'll never say I'm sorry. I'd do it again."

"Do you think I'm blaming you? I don't have the right to ask you to say you're sorry. I didn't stop you. I didn't even try." She moistened her lips. "I even helped you. What does that make me? There's so much damn pain in the world. I *hate* it."

"I know you do," he said quietly. "And I knew there would be a payoff after today. You . . . surprised me."

"He knows where Waldridge is. We *have* to find him, Lynch."

He nodded. "Anything for the good doctor. I could almost envy him."

"Envy? We'll be lucky to find him before they kill him."

"I misspoke." He covered her hand with his own. "We won't be lucky, we'll be smart. And we'll be fast." He pulled off the freeway. "But right now we'll stop by Starbucks and pick up a couple of cups of coffee. You could probably use the caffeine now that you don't have Jessie here to cause your adrenaline to spike . . ."

CHAPTER
11

HALF AN HOUR LATER, Kendra, Lynch, and Jessie
stood in the living room of Powers's house watching as the
police searched every drawer and surface. Metcalf emerged
from a back room with an expression that was far from
encouraging.

"Anything?" Kendra asked.

"Not yet." Metcalf shook his head. "No ski mask, no
night-vision goggles, nothing that you saw him wearing the
other night."

"The guy knows how to clean up after himself," Jessie
said.

Metcalf extended his hand to Jessie. "I'm Special Agent
Roland Metcalf. FBI. Your motorcycle makes me think
you might be the person who lent a timely assist to Kendra the other night."

She shook his hand. "I'm Jessie Mercado. I guess I was
just in the right place at the right time."

"Uh-huh. Something tells me there's more to it than that."

"There is," Kendra said. "I'll explain it to you later, Metcalf."

"Sure." Metcalf's eyes were narrowed on Jessie's face. "Have we ever met? I have a nagging feeling that I've seen you before."

She smiled. "I don't think so."

He was still staring. "I'm pretty sure I have."

"I think I just have one of those faces."

"No, you don't. It'll come to me."

She shrugged. "If it does, let me in on the secret. Because I'm sure we haven't met."

"Okay. I'll think about it." He pulled his gaze away and finally turned to Kendra. "As for our search of the house, we've only come up with one interesting thing so far."

"What's that?"

He placed a business card on the table in front of them.

Kendra leaned over and read the card aloud. "Peter Hutchinson, Attorney at Law."

Lynch chuckled. "That *is* interesting."

Kendra looked up. "Why? Other than the fact that we're supposed to be impressed by his willingness to spend big bucks on silk-laminated business cards."

"He can afford them," Jessie said. "Peter Hutchinson is probably the highest-priced lawyer in the city." She glanced around the living room. "Too high-priced for anyone who lives here, for damned sure."

Lynch turned to Kendra. "Does anything here catch your eye?"

Kendra scanned the foyer, living room, and small kitchen. "Not much. He makes his living as a manual laborer of some kind. There are work boots in the foyer, construction gloves tucked inside. He owns an RV. It's probably stored in a facility nearby, so it might be worth checking out."

"How do you figure that?" Jessie asked.

Kendra pointed toward a hook in the kitchen where a ring of keys hung. "Fleetwood ignition and rear-compartment keys, plus a Medeco security key cut on a slant that most likely goes to a storage unit." She glanced at Metcalf. "Did you find any medication?"

He looked surprised. "Yes, actually. In the bathroom."

"Injectable?"

"How did you know?"

"There are two sterile syringe wrappers in the waste can next to the computer desk." She thought for a moment. "Are they prescription?"

"The vials look commercial, but there wasn't a prescription label."

"Hmm. Let me take a look."

Kendra and Metcalf walked back through a messy bedroom to the master bath. Metcalf pointed to two small vials next to the sink. "Here they are. The labels have no product name and no manufacturer name, just a series of numbers. Maybe batch and sorting ID codes."

Kendra knelt, and her gaze narrowed on the bottles. "I don't know what they mean." She raised her phone and snapped a picture of both labels. "Can you bag these and take them to the lab?"

"Any special reason?"

Kendra stood up. "I saw two bottle impressions on a hand towel in Waldridge's hotel bathroom. They were the exact same size as these. It might mean nothing, but we should check it out."

"Oh, I agree." He smiled. "You've been racking up some major lab time. Griffin isn't going to like it."

"He can take it out of my pay."

"What pay?"

"Exactly." She turned toward the doorway where Lynch and Jessie were standing. "I think we've gotten what we can from here for now. What do you say we go to the hospital and continue our conversation with Powers? He should be out of ER by now."

"THERE WILL BE NO CONVERSATION with Wallace Powers."

Kendra, Lynch, and Jessie stood in the hospital corridor, gazing at the tall, broad-chested man blocking their way. He wore a charcoal-gray Brioni twill suit that had to have cost him thousands, Kendra thought.

The man handed each of them a business card identical to the one they had seen at Powers's house. "My name is Peter Hutchinson. Any communication you wish to have with Mr. Powers must be conducted through me."

"You're his attorney?" Kendra asked.

"I am."

Lynch pocketed the card. "I just spoke with the officers on duty here. They told me Powers hasn't made any phone calls."

"I'm sure he hasn't."

"Then how did you know he was here?"

Hutchinson's plump, pouty, lips smiled. "It's my job to be attuned to the needs of my clients, Mr. . . ."

"Lynch. Adam Lynch. You didn't answer my question. How did you know he was here?"

"I'm afraid you'll have to accept my seemingly glib response, Mr. Lynch. May I ask, what is your official capacity in this matter?"

"No you may not. But you can ask me," Kendra said. "My official capacity is victim. Your client attacked me."

"Allegedly. We have slander laws in this state, Miss . . ."

"If you want her name, ask your client," Lynch said. "He knows. And while you're at it, ask him why he did it. Unless you know already."

"Why would I have knowledge of such a thing?"

Kendra smiled. "Whoever is paying you may have told you. By the way, who is paying you? I have a feeling it isn't Powers."

"Financial matters are between me and my client."

"Right." Jessie stepped forward. "But are you really representing Powers's best interests? We already have some rock-solid evidence against him, so unless he gets cooperative very soon, he's going to jail. That may be okay with whoever's paying your bills, but I have a hunch it won't be okay with the man in that room. Even if he isn't willing to talk, you can't keep a cop from coming and telling what is or is not his best interest."

"They're certainly welcome. But I'm willing to put my powers of persuasion against those of a local police detective, any day of the week."

"Maybe they'll let me in the room," Lynch said. "I've been known to be very persuasive."

Hutchinson smiled. "Ah. So you can get in a few more licks on an injured man? Trust me, I'll do everything in my power to make sure you stay as far from him as possible."

Time to throw out another bit of bait and see if he'd take it. "Your client may be involved in another abduction," Kendra said. "A man named Dr. Charles Waldridge."

IRIS JOHANSEN & ROY JOHANSEN

He didn't change expression. "Your proof?"

"We'll have it. I promise you, if anything happens to him, we'll find all the proof we need to nail everyone responsible."

Lynch added softly, "*Everyone*."

"More threats, Mr. Lynch."

"Call it a warning. In my line of work, I've always found threats a waste of time. You just make a decision, then you act."

"Call it whatever you like. I've instructed my client not to speak to anyone about this case. Go look elsewhere for your proof."

Hutchinson crossed his arms in front of him, assuming the pose of a thuggish bouncer guarding the door of a college-town bar. Something that didn't quite work in this setting, Kendra thought. Maybe it was the six-thousand-dollar suit.

"Oh, we will," Kendra said as she turned away. "But expect us to be back."

AS THEY STEPPED OUT of the hospital parking garage, Jessie held up Hutchinson's business card and snapped a picture of it.

"Think you can get his client list?" Kendra asked.

Jessie put away her phone. "Maybe. I can search some databases and scan online court records for filings. But good attorneys usually keep their clients from going anywhere near a courtroom."

"I'll look into it, too," Lynch said. "It would help if we could find out who's paying for Powers's defense."

Jessie had stopped at her motorcycle. "I'll look into it right now." She looked at Kendra and slowly nodded in approval. "By the way, you handled yourself pretty well on the back of this bike."

"I've ridden a few motorcycles in my time." Kendra smiled. "But tell me, do you always travel with a pocket full of ball bearings?"

Jessie smiled back at her and pulled a few of the little silver balls from her pocket. "Pretty much. I got the idea a few years ago, when smash-and-grab thieves were using them to break car windows and steal purses on passenger seats. No one thinks of these as weapons, so even if I'm searched, I can go anywhere with them. I've gotten very accurate, and can inflict pretty heavy damage if the occasion demands it."

"*How* accurate?" she asked curiously.

In response, Jessie swung her arm in a lightning arc and released one of the ball bearings. The motion was followed by a metallic *ting* behind them.

Kendra whirled around. "What did you do?"

Lynch chuckled. "I'll show you what she did." He walked twenty feet to a steel lamppost, where a cardboard sign advertising a local band had been taped. Lynch tore off the sign and brought it back to Kendra.

She took the sign. A hole had been punched cleanly through the head of the band's lead singer.

"Wow," Kendra said. "Very good. Are you some kind of ninja?"

Jessie gave her a peculiar look. "What makes you say that?"

"I'm just . . . impressed. You nailed this all the way from over here."

"Oh. Well, I'm no ninja. I've just picked up a few things along the way."

Yet that response had been a little strange, Kendra thought. "I meant it as a compliment."

"Then that's how I'll take it." Jessie threw her leg over the bike and started it. "Stay in touch. I accepted that you might have not had time to contact me this time. Next time remember we're working together."

Jessie revved the bike and roared away.

HUTCHINSON ENTERED THE HOSPITAL room and closed the door behind him. He walked over to the bed, where the extremely banged-up and bruised Powers was handcuffed to the side rail.

"We don't have much time," Hutchinson said. "They've gone, but the police will be here anytime now."

Powers nervously adjusted himself on the bed. "So what's the play? I don't think they have any real proof."

"They say they have DNA."

"No way. I was careful. Incredibly careful. I did just as I was told."

"DNA can be left behind in many ways. A finger on a touch screen. Perspiration on a shirt. A sneeze on a window. Or . . ." Hutchinson placed his fingertips on Powers's left temple and turned his head to reveal the scratches on his neck. ". . . skin under a fingernail. Did Michaels give you those scratches?"

"Shit," Powers whispered.

"This clearly puts you in that building as her attacker. So you see, there's careful, then there's *careful*." Hutchinson moved Powers's head back with slightly more force than was necessary. "You have the right to remain silent. You're going to avail yourself of that right, do you understand me? When the police come, don't say a word."

"What if they—"

"Not a word. You mustn't even listen to them. Everything that comes out of their mouths will be only to trick you. Understand? When they begin talking, you just think of your favorite song and mentally sing it to yourself over and over again. Don't try to strategize. That's my job, and I guarantee I'm a hell of a lot better at it than you could ever be. Not one word must pass your lips, do you understand?"

"Okay, I got it. You didn't have to tell me this. I've already gone through a hell of a lot of pain and didn't tell them anything."

"That's good. Because you and the others were incredibly clumsy, and Jaden is not pleased."

Powers's eyes widened in alarm. "You're not sending Jaden after me?"

"That's not my call. I just take orders like you do. I'm only telling you that Jaden is a perfectionist and would be happy to clean up loose ends." He stared him in the eye. "If you prove to be a problem."

"I won't be a problem," Powers said quickly. "We did everything we were told. It should have gone smooth as glass."

"But it didn't, and now we're faced with a very delicate situation we have to solve."

"Not by using Jaden."

Hutchinson shook his head. "That would cause ripples. Ripples are discouraged in this matter. Which is your good fortune. Our mutual employer appreciates your cooperation. He has at great expense employed one of the world's greatest legal minds—that's me—to fight on your behalf. If he senses that you do not appreciate the extent of his concern, he will cut off all contact, all assistance. Do you understand what that means?"

Powers turned and stared out the window. "It means I'll die."

"I'm accustomed to a fair bit of melodrama from my clients, but in your case, your concern is warranted." Hutchinson reached into his jacket and produced two foil packets.

Powers tensed. "What are those?"

"A token of appreciation." Hutchinson grabbed two plastic cups from a countertop and set them on the small serving table next to the bed. He tore open the packets and emptied their gooey contents into the cups. He then picked up a pitcher, filled both cups with water, then stirred each with a straw.

Powers stared at the cups. "Is that what I think it is?"

"Yes. It's your medicine. Something that no hospital can provide you. You need it, don't you? Less efficient than the type you inject, but I've been told it's just as effective. The officer on duty searched me before I came in and I never would have been allowed to bring a syringe and needle in here. Drink the one on the right first, then the left."

Powers picked up the right cup and examined it for a long moment. "No offense, but . . . how do I know this isn't poison?"

Hutchinson smiled. "Poison? Is that why you think I came here?"

"I think you came here to make sure I keep my mouth shut. Okay, you won't use Jaden. But two packets of fast-acting poison would do the job, wouldn't it?"

"If that's what they really wanted, then all they had to do was absolutely nothing. Correct?" His voice lowered. "Why are you being difficult? It's a little incentive to keep you doing what we want you to do. You know you need it."

Powers looked at the cup for a moment longer, then downed it.

Hutchinson tapped the other cup. "Now this one. I'm not to leave until I've seen you drink both."

Powers drank the other one in one long gulp. He wiped his lips. "Sour."

Hutchinson folded the foil packets and placed them back into his pocket. "Now remember our discussion. Co-operation is everything. Not one single word."

"I won't forget." His lips twisted bitterly. "How could I? I'm just wondering something." Powers leaned back in his bed. "Would you have given me those packets if I hadn't agreed to keep quiet?"

Hutchinson brushed his hands together and straightened his jacket. "See you soon, Mr. Powers."

He left the hospital room and closed the door behind him.

"POWERS IS SCARED SHITLESS and he's not talking," Hutchinson said when Jaden answered the phone. "You won't be needed . . . yet."

Jaden muttered a curse. "And when you make that call, it might be too late. It should be done now."

"The job was fumbled. Michaels got away, and now we have a situation. I'm not going to have to answer for it. It's in your court."

"I set it up, but you sent inefficient bumblers to grab her. I should have done it myself. I won't make that mistake again," he said. "He should have let me take care of her a long time ago."

"I don't advise you to tell him that." He hung up.

Jaden took a deep breath and tried to smother his rage. Hutchinson wasn't important. He was only a high-priced mouthpiece who was afraid to get his hands dirty. But he didn't mind relaying orders to him to do it. But this time Jaden would have welcomed that order. He'd only remained safe during his career by leaving no evidence of his passing. Now the Michaels woman was starting to shine a spotlight on Powers, and Powers might be a weak link that might lead to him.

Not to be tolerated.

So find a way to stop Kendra Michaels once and for all.

Croyden, England
Middlesex Lane

Rye walked down the main drag of the depressed industrial town sixty-five kilometers north of London. He had no reason to go there since he was a boy, and it looked almost nothing like how he remembered it. More than half of the shops had been shuttered, and those that remained were mostly secondhand stores, pawnshops, and the occasional Laundromat. At the end of the street he saw the reason for the financial despair—the closed clothing factory, which he'd just learned had supplied many of England's military uniforms for two world wars. Now, however, the gray brick buildings towered above the wrought-iron gates, silently taunting the town that had once so depended on it.

He walked to the factory entrance and looked through the gate's iron bars. It looked as if no one had been there in years.

Except . . .

High on the stone flanking, there was a relatively new opening mechanism with an articulated arm attached to the gate. A tiny red light beamed down from the apparatus, indicating that it was on and receiving power.

Nothing else about the grounds indicated that anyone had been there in years. No sound emanated from the factory and no exhaust was emitted from the twin smokestacks and numerous vents.

He turned back toward the street. Dapper Dan's Pub was on the corner next to the tiny sundries store that probably made most of its sales from lottery tickets. He crossed the street and walked into the dark pub.

A curling match, of all things, was on all three televisions above the narrow bar. Two elderly men, obviously regulars, stared absently at their beers.

The bartender, a plump woman in her seventies, was wiping off the stools. She didn't acknowledge him even after he sat down on one of them.

"A pint of Pride," he said.

Still no acknowledgment.

After a few moments, she walked behind the bar and pulled his beer from a well-worn tap. She placed it in front of him.

"Appreciate it," he said. "It's been a long time since I've been here. My uncle used to work at that factory."

The bartender snorted. "*Everybody's* uncle used to work at that factory. At least around here."

Rye smiled. "How long's it been shut down?"

A patron with a Santa Claus beard spoke up. "Twenty-three years last March. But most of the workers were let go five or six years before that."

"And the place has been empty ever since?"

The bartender nodded. "There was talk about building computers there, but it never came to anything. The local government bent over backward to make it happen, but the company went to Taiwan instead."

He shrugged. "Well, someone's been going in and out of there lately."

The bartender and her patrons stared at him. He'd tried to make it sound casual, but his tone had probably been a bit too insistent, he realized. "I mean, the gates look like they've been automated. Recently. I thought it might mean the factory was opening again."

The second bar patron shook his head. "No such luck. There have been some people coming and going from there, but no one local."

"I don't think they're workers," the bartender said. "The cars are too nice. A couple Bentleys, a Mercedes, Range Rovers, those kind."

"I think they're stripping the place for parts," the Santa Claus look-alike offered. "Or maybe there's a crew in there designing a remodel."

The bartender shook her head. "The only remodeling that's gonna be done there is to level it to the ground."

"Those cars come every day?" Rye asked.

"Yeah," the bartender said. "Saturday and Sunday, too."

"Huh. Just cars? No trucks or construction equipment?"

"A few trucks last year. Lately, just cars."

Rye turned in his stool and looked out the front windows toward the factory. "It's right across the street. I'm sure they must stop in for a pint once in a while."

"Never, and they don't go next door for chewing gum or a pack of smokes. Me and Alfie, the owner there, were just talking about it. Those people are too snooty to bother with the locals."

"Huh." Rye stared at the factory for a moment longer. "They're there right now?"

"Sure. I'm pretty sure there are always people there around the clock."

"Strange." He downed the rest of his beer and stood. "Well, good day to you all."

He'd just the reached the door when he was aware that the bartender had followed him.

"Drug dealers or spies?" she suddenly asked.

"I beg your pardon?"

"You ask too many questions. I figured you're maybe Scotland Yard or maybe Mi6." Her cheeks were flushed, her eyes sparkling with eagerness. "We're not fools here, you know."

He smiled. "I'm sure you're not. But I assure you that I don't belong to either of those august organizations. I'm only guilty of having an insatiable curiosity."

"You wouldn't admit it if you were." But she still looked disappointed. "I was getting excited. You saw how boring it is in this town. Like I was telling Alfie, it's pretty sad when it takes people running back and forth into an old factory to cause us to perk up and have something to talk about. It wasn't like that when we were younger. Maybe our minds are going as dead and rotting as this town."

"I believe you have a very sharp mind," he said gently. "You just made a bad guess."

She shrugged. "You still asked too many questions. I could be on the right track." She turned away. "By the way, my name is Dorothy Jenkins. Drop in anytime. I'll keep my eyes and ears open, and maybe we'll have another chat."

"Ryan Malone." He nodded and smiled as he opened the door. "And maybe we will, Dorothy."

"AN OLD UNIFORM FACTORY?" Lynch's voice was incredulous on the phone.

Rye climbed into his car and closed the door. "Yes. According to Dr. Porter Shaw's vehicle navigation system, this was one of his most frequent destinations."

"No hint of what's going on there?"

"None. The locals are clueless. I traced ownership records for the factory, and it was purchased by an overseas holding company, a couple of years ago."

"What holding company?"

Rye glanced at his tablet computer. "An outfit called Schyler Investments, Ltd."

"A brokerage firm?"

"You'd think so from the name, but the entity seems to have had no business other than owning this one abandoned factory."

"Sounds like a cover."

"Definitely a cover. I already have someone tracing ownership. Following the money, as they say."

"Good. That's also what we're doing on this end. We found one of the thugs who tried to snatch Kendra the other night."

"Excellent. I hope you gave him a good punch in the gut from me."

"Don't worry, I made sure he felt some pain. So what's your next move?"

Rye put down his tablet. "As much value as I place on old-fashioned research, sometimes you just have to get your hands dirty. Filthy dirty."

Lynch chuckled. "That sounds ominous, Rye."

"Come now. It's why you called me, isn't it?"

"Of course it is."

"Then let me do what I do best."

"You mean cause trouble, raise hell, and make the world safe for democracy?"

"Something like that. But I have to call your attention to the fact that I'm a Socialist. Parliament would much prefer I choose to make our little corner of the world safe. Say hello to beautiful Kendra for me."

"Will do, Rye. Thanks."

11:40 P.M.

Rye crouched next to the factory's east wall, which he'd identified as the spot least likely to be equipped with cameras or motion sensors.

He looked around. The town was dead. The pub was the last of the businesses to close for the evening, and he hadn't seen a soul in over an hour.

He unzipped his black canvas duffel and pulled out a grappling hook and twenty-five feet of canvas rope. He'd sprayed the rope with adhesive that afternoon, and it was reassuringly tacky to the touch.

One . . . Two . . . Three!

Rye tossed the hook over the wall and it took hold immediately. He climbed hand over hand over the twenty-foot wall, and it was difficult enough that he was reminded how long it had been since he'd been in the field. Damn. Need to get out more often.

He straddled the top of the wall, reversed the hook, and surveyed the factory yard. Quiet, like any other sad, old factory that had been closed for decades. Had those people at the bar been pulling his leg?

Only one way to tell.

Rye rappelled down the inside of the wall, finally letting go and dropping the last few feet. He adjusted his black turtleneck shirt and slacks. He'd felt slightly silly

227

when he donned the outfit—this wasn't the Kremlin, after all—but he was now happy to be as invisible as humanly possible.

He crept around the side of the building until he approached a cracked, peeling wooden door that had practically rotted off its hinges. Close enough to the target area. Might as well give it a shot.

He slid his fingers behind the hinges and tugged on the crumbling door. It pulled away easily. He slid in through the opening and switched on his tiny flashlight. He was in a machinist's work area, where oily, dusty assembly-line parts littered the floor. He took a photo. He'd take photos throughout the entire factory and examine them later. You could never tell when the ordinary could become extraordinary on close inspection. He stepped over the gear and made his way to a door on the far side. He opened it and peered out.

Darkness.

Silence.

Not completely dark, he realized. There was something down the corridor to the right.

Exactly where the heat signature had shown up in his scan.

He took another photo. Then he moved toward the dim glow, keeping his eyes and ears peeled for any sign of activity.

The light was coming from a doorway at the end of the hallway. As he drew closer, he was aware of a low hum coming from the same place.

He stopped and listened. Still no sounds of footsteps or other movements.

He moved through the doorway, amazed that the dark,

dusty factory abruptly gave way to an antiseptic, white-tiled room bathed in purple-tinged light.

What in the bloody hell . . .

Two modern, tripod-mounted cameras leaned against a wall on the other side of four desks equipped with laptop computers. The room faced a glass door and a wall of double-paned windows that looked into a much larger room illuminated by the same purplish glow.

He stepped past the desks and looked through the windows. More antiseptic white walls and white tile. But this room was outfitted with row upon row of small stations, approximately three feet wide. Each station was in use, but he wasn't entirely sure how. It looked almost as if . . .

Holy shit.

The stations were topped by glass domes. Underneath the glass, something appeared to undulate in the purplish glow.

Could this be . . . ?

He stared, squinted at the stations. As if that would suddenly help it to make sense.

There was no sense to be made here. None.

Holy shit.

He pulled his phone from his pocket and squeezed off a series of photos. Now to transmit them to Lynch and Kendra. He hoped they would know what to do with them once they arrived in their—

Pfffft.

He heard the sound an instant before he felt an icy chill. He looked down.

A long silver blade was protruding from his chest. It was coated with blood. *His* blood.

Only then did he hear the breathing of his attacker behind him.

Darkness.

KENDRA DRUMMED HER FINGERS as she sat in the passenger seat of Lynch's car. They'd been on the way to the FBI offices when Lynch's phone rang with an insistent tone she'd only heard twice before. Each time, Lynch had stepped away and took the call someplace where she couldn't hear him. Classified stuff, she'd been told. Not that she really cared.

This time Lynch abruptly pulled his car over on Fifth Street and spent the first minutes pacing back and forth on the sidewalk next to her with the phone pressed to his ear. Then he leaned against the brick wall of the restaurant where he'd parked. His posture slumped, and he was frozen in place for a long moment even after he ended the call.

This wasn't high-impact Lynch. Something was wrong. Very wrong.

She climbed out of the car and walked over to him. "What's going on?"

His face was tense, his lips tight. "I have to go to England."

"Another one of your assignments?"

"No, it's just . . ." He looked away. "Rye is dead."

Her breath left her. "What?"

"His body was found in a landfill a hundred kilometers outside of London. It so happened there were cadaver dogs on-site for another investigation. It's the only reason they found him. They think he was bagged and tossed into a Dumpster."

The words didn't sound real to her as they tumbled from Lynch's mouth. Neither the words nor the terrible vision of that amusing, lively man just tossed away like so much garbage. Lynch was obviously having trouble believing them, too.

Kendra placed her hand on his. "I'm so sorry. I really liked him."

"And Rye liked you."

"I feel guilty," she said unsteadily.

"For what?"

"For pulling him into this. He didn't know what we were getting him into."

"We didn't know much ourselves." Lynch took a deep breath. "Rye never did anything he didn't want to do. I feel bad ten different ways right now, but guilt doesn't enter into it. Rye loved living on the edge. He almost died on three separate occasions in the years since I met him. It's who he was."

"I feel bad that he was doing it for us."

Lynch nodded. "I guess I am feeling some guilt there. If I hadn't called him, he'd be in his cottage reading and drinking wine right now."

"What was he doing the last time you spoke to him?"

"He was tracking a lead from the auto investigation system of our Big Bear corpse, Dr. Porter Shaw. Shaw's supposed workplace didn't exist, but Rye found an old factory where he'd been going."

"That was the last time you talked to him?"

"Yes. He texted me the address. It may be nothing, but as far as I know, it's the last place he went. I have to go there."

She nodded. "But can't the local police handle it?"

"They *are* handling it. I was just talking to a mutual friend of mine and Rye's. He's with the National Crime Agency. I told him what I knew, but I still need to go there."

"Of course."

Regret flashed across his face. "I *have* to do this, Kendra."

"I told you, I know you do. I'm just sorry I can't go with you. As long as Waldridge is missing, there's no way I can leave here."

"I wouldn't ask you to." He looked away from her. "Damn. A world without Rye Malone is a sadder place. I'm already missing him."

"Did he have family?"

"An ex-wife who was happily married to him when he was an intelligence-agency desk jockey. When he was in the field, she just couldn't take it."

"I guess she never wanted to receive a call like the one you just got."

"I guess she didn't." His lips twisted. "Maybe she's a very smart woman."

CHAPTER
12

LYNCH DROVE KENDRA BACK to her condo, where he threw together his belongings and packed with astonishing efficiency.

Kendra smiled. "Something tells me you've spent a lot of time living out of that suitcase."

"Too much time." He zipped his Eagle Creek duffel and rested it on the floor. "When a piece of luggage feels more like home than my actual house, I know I've been doing something seriously wrong."

"It cost Rye his marriage, and it sounds like it cost you Ashley."

He stepped closer to her. "I'm not thinking about Ashley."

She felt herself tense. "Out of sight, out of mind?"

"No. That was a relationship that had run its course." His face was only inches from hers. "But this . . . This has been nice. You and me, here, under the same roof. I had the same feeling when you were at my place. There's something very . . . *right* about it."

He was too close. She was having trouble breathing. "I seem to remember a few moments when it felt anything *but* right."

He smiled. "There are a few awkward moments in any new relationship. I told you that we'd get through it, and we did."

"Relationship? I think we're getting a little ahead of ourselves."

"No. You just need to catch up."

Kendra was about to toss off a flip rejoinder, but she saw Lynch was no longer smiling. "You're still shell-shocked from losing your friend. I'm not going to take anything you say seriously."

"I'm more serious than I've ever been. If Rye's death tells me anything, it's that it's foolish to waste time."

"Is that we've been doing? I thought that we were assessing which way we wanted to go and what was wise. At least, that's what you—"

He'd pulled her close and was kissing her. "Assessed, hell. I'm done with that game." He kissed her again. A hot rush surged through her, and once again she felt overwhelmed by everything that was Adam Lynch. The whiff of his scent, the feel of his facial stubble, and the heat of his deep, almost animalistic breathing.

He finally pulled away. "I'm not waiting anymore. When I get back, I want to see what this can be. What *we* can be. Together."

"Really?" She was having trouble putting words together when all she wanted to do was go back into his arms, then the nearest bed. "Don't I get a say?"

"Not at the moment. You're still too edgy about committing to anything, and you'll just annoy the hell out of me. I'm too aware right now that at any time a ten-ton truck could come barreling around a corner and smash one or both of us into the hereafter. Not to mention those sons of bitches who killed Rye and are still out there."

"I told you that you were shell-shocked."

"Yeah, maybe. Besides, it's not necessary that you have your say." He picked up his suitcase. "You're not the only one who knows how to read people."

"Is that right?"

"Yes. Of course, you make it easy for me. You have a terrible poker face, at least as far as this subject goes." His eyes were suddenly glinting with mischief. "You keep pushing me away, but I realize how irresistible I am."

That damn smile *was* irresistible.

And he was going away, and might face fatal ten-ton trucks and those men who'd killed Rye without her.

She found herself smiling back at him. "And so very modest, Lynch."

"False modesty is no virtue. Like I said, I'm tired of wasting time." He walked to the door, opened it, and turned around. "I hate doing this, you know. I'll call you from England. I'm going to find out what happened, but you need to be careful. If they got Rye, they can get any one of us."

She nodded soberly. "I know. You be careful, too."

"Hey, I guarantee nothing's going to happen to me." He said grimly, "I'm mad as hell, and I have an agenda. Both of those factors can move mountains."

He turned and left the condo.

KENDRA WAS JUST ABOUT to leave the condo again when the front door buzzed. She punched her wall-mounted intercom unit's talk button and spoke into it. "Let me guess, Lynch. You forgot your toothbrush. Or was it your semiautomatic?"

Jessie Mercado's voice blared from the speaker. "Neither. But it sounds like he left behind some good memories."

Shit.

"Jessie?"

"Yes. I can come back if you want to spend more time lolling in the rosy glow of your night with Adam Lynch."

"No lolling. No rosy glow. Come on up."

"If you insist."

Kendra pushed the button that unlocked her building's front door. Jessie entered her condo a minute later. "Sorry to drop by unannounced. I was nearby and decided to take a chance." She slipped out of her leather jacket. "Where's Lynch?"

"On his way to England."

Jessie's eyes widened in surprise. "Was there a break in the case?"

"Not exactly. We told you we had someone working the case from there . . ."

"Yeah?"

"He was murdered. They found his body early this morning."

Jessie flinched. "God, I'm sorry."

"It hit Lynch pretty hard. They were old friends."

"That begs the question . . . Is Lynch going there to kick ass, or is he going to pick up the trail and actually work the case?"

"Hopefully both. His friend was investigating an abandoned factory that had something to do with Dr. Shaw."

"And with Night Watch?"

"That's what we're trying to find out."

"Well, I've been investigating your pants-pissing kidnapper."

"My pants-pissing *attempted* kidnapper, thanks to you."

"Yeah, that guy. I decided to see what I could find out about him."

"Between last night and this morning?"

"Sure. Hospitals don't close."

Kendra's eyes widened. "What did you do?"

"There's one nice thing about large health conglomerates . . . The minute Wallace Powers's social security number went into the system, his entire medical history could be accessed from any computer in their network. Even if that computer happens to be in a fairly quiet, twenty-four-hour urgent-care location."

"Don't you need a key card and a password?"

"A pretty smile and a couple hundred bucks will go a long way in a place like that at three in the morning."

"Did it tell you anything other than that Powers once sprained his ankle playing beach volleyball?"

Jessie smiled. "He *did* do that. How did you know?"

"A framed photograph in his house, signed by his teammates. It was between the front door and the bathroom."

"I missed that. In my experience, these medical histories are more useful to get a sense of the employment history, emergency contacts, addresses where he lived, that kind of stuff."

"Well?"

Jessie pulled a sheaf of papers from her inside jacket pocket. "I got all that. But there was something else here."

"I hate to think of how many laws you'd just broken."

"Then don't think about it. Just think of him trying to drug you and carry you off in a barrel."

"Since you put it that way . . ."

Jessie looked down at the papers. "Our friend was diagnosed with stage-four liver cancer. He was given eight weeks to live."

"Eight weeks . . . That's horrible."

"The diagnosis was made over three years ago."

"What?" Kendra took the pages and looked at them. "What kind of treatment did he have?"

"No treatment. At least none that appears in his records. The next time anyone in the network saw him, seven months later, he was completely cured."

Kendra looked up from the pages. "Are you sure?"

"I had a doctor friend look these over, and he says his levels went from death's door to perfectly healthy in a matter of months."

"How is that possible?"

"It isn't. As least not according to my doctor friend." Jessie took the printouts back. "You have no idea what kind of work your Dr. Waldridge was doing?"

"No. I told you, he was incredibly coy about it. It wasn't something that made him happy, though. I didn't get the impression he'd come up with some all-powerful miracle disease cure."

"He performed a miracle on you."

"And he and the Night Watch Project made sure the whole world knew about it. They didn't keep their miracle under wraps for years on end." She frowned, and said slowly, "No, there's something else going on here."

"It was a long time ago, wasn't it? Maybe you don't remember it the way it was. That happens sometimes."

"I haven't forgotten one thing connected to Charles Waldridge. And I wouldn't be confused or mistaken just because a little time has passed."

"Aren't you being defensive? A *little* time?"

Jessie was right to call her on it, she thought. It had been more than a little time since that day in Monterrey when everything had changed for her . . .

Monterey, California
Eight Years Earlier

Kendra paced alone in a back corridor of the Monterey Conference Center listening to the din of the crowd seated in the adjacent five-hundred-seat theater. She was a featured speaker at the TED Conference, an annual event which gathered interesting people to share their experiences and insights with attendees and eventually worldwide audiences on the Web.

She glanced at the exit sign, which glowed red in the dim hallway.

Tempting.

Damned tempting.

"Those doors open to the parking lot," a voice said from the darkness. "You can make a clean break for it."

She turned to face Dr. Waldridge as he stepped toward her. She smiled with an effort. "I could make the Santa Cruz boardwalk by sunset."

He smiled. "What's in Santa Cruz?"

She sighed wistfully. "The ocean. A basket of fried shrimp. A cold bottle of beer."

"I can see your conundrum. But what about all the disappointed people you'll leave behind?"

"They can come with me. There's enough beer and fried shrimp for all. My treat."

"I don't really think that will work," he said gently.

"No? Oh, well." She brushed a strand of her hair behind her ear. "It was a solution. I'm having trouble forcing myself to go out there today."

"Nervous?"

"Are you joking? I've done a hundred of these in the last year. Academic conferences, press events, fundraisers . . ."

"Then what's the problem?"

"Maybe I'm burned-out." She rubbed the tense muscles at the back of her neck. "I've been thinking that I can't do it anymore."

"Of course you can."

She shook her head. "Burned-out is probably the wrong term. It's hard to describe. Ever since I got my sight, I feel like . . . I'm living in someone else's body. Every minute of every day is a different experience. So much has changed for me."

His lips turned up at the corners. "I don't believe you're telling me that you'd rather still be blind."

"Of course not." She turned to him and her voice was suddenly passionate. "Do you know how grateful I am to you? Every day I wake up, and I tell myself how lucky I am that Charles Waldridge agreed to see me that day in London and decided to perform a miracle."

He chuckled. "Hardly a miracle. Pure science and medicine."

"I know all the explanations, but when it's all said and done, it was a miracle for me."

"But you've suddenly become uncomfortable with your miracle?" His gaze was narrowed on her face. "Or maybe not so suddenly. I can't say that I haven't seen a few signs emerging in the past few weeks."

She'd known he'd probably been aware of the way she

was feeling. He was the most brilliant person she'd ever met, and he'd grown to know her so well. She was only surprised that he'd waited for her to confront him with it instead of stepping in and dealing with the problem as he had all the rest of the obstacles they'd overcome together. "It's not that I'm ungrateful, but it's been an adjustment. And when I'm still trying to figure out what my new life is going to be like, I'm having to jump through hoops. The same speeches, the same questions, the travel, the hotels . . . I'm looking for normal, and I'm wondering if I'll ever find it."

"You will."

"When?"

"Give it time." He was suddenly beside her, gazing into her eyes. "Don't you realize that you may never be what people call 'normal?' I knew the moment I met you that even if the operation didn't work, you'd always be extraordinary. You had a disability, but you were still working to become all that you possibly could be." He lifted her chin, and said quietly, "And that result would have been far from ordinary. Miracles don't always happen in an operating room, Kendra."

She couldn't look away from him. He seemed to be trying to tell her something that had nothing to do with conferences and cold beer and everything to do with . . .

What?

But he'd stepped back and was turning away. "So protect that miracle. Let yourself have time to get priorities in order before you jump into the fray. Life out there can be scary, even terrifying."

"Terrifying?" It was a strange thing for him to say. "I'm not afraid of terrifying. It's only the unknown. It's what people who aren't protected by people like my mom

and you face every day. It's called life." She turned toward
the doorway to the auditorium, where a stage manager
appeared. He spoke into his wireless headset and flashed
his index finger, indicating one minute until showtime.

One minute, and she'd once more be drawn into that
smothering darkness. One minute, and she'd feel the
chains reaching out for her again.

Kendra whirled back to Waldridge. *"I've given it all the
time I can. This needs to stop."*

He tilted his head. *"That sounds very defensive. No
one's making you do this, Kendra."*

"I know it." She moistened her lips. *"But sometimes it
sure feels like it."*

"No." Waldridge glanced toward the end of the corridor, where a tall, lanky man stood. Was that coincidence?
Kendra wondered. The man wore a black suit and a crisp
white shirt, and his appearance vaguely reminded Kendra of a Secret Service man . . . or an undertaker.

"Who is he?" Kendra asked.

"A supporter of the project."

*"I've seen you with him before. In Dallas and New
York."*

"Yes."

She frowned. *"You speak differently to him than you
do everyone else."*

Waldridge looked at her in surprise. *"What do you
mean?"*

*"With everyone else, with all your colleagues, you're
the main man. You're the boss. Everyone is always trying
to impress you. But not this guy. For some reason, you
defer to him."*

"That's not true."

"Yes, it is."

He stared at her for an instant and smiled. "Those eyes have become very sharp in these last months. He's a very important supporter. Everyone has to defer to someone in this world."

"Not you. You shouldn't have to do that. Why hasn't he ever introduced himself to me?"

"Perhaps he's shy."

"I don't believe that." She studied the man at the far end of the corridor. He stiffened and turned toward her as if he'd felt her looking at him. He stood there gazing at her for a long moment. Then he abruptly walked away, disappearing into the darkness. Kendra's gaze shifted back to Waldridge. "I don't like your 'supporter.' He wants me to keep on doing these dog-and-pony shows, doesn't he?"

"It doesn't matter to him. Not at all."

"I believe it does. Why else would he be going to all these conferences? I'm not that fascinating."

"Oh, but you are. You just haven't found it out yet."

"I haven't found out a lot of things. That's what I've been trying to tell you. I know you think my appearance at these conferences help promote what you're doing, and that's why I've been on board for it." She stared down the corridor at the spot where the lanky man had stood. "But I don't like anyone thinking they're so important that they can tell a man who works miracles what to do. And I don't like the politics, and I don't like the publicity. So you're going to have to find another poster child. I'm bowing out. This is the last speech I'm giving for you guys."

"Could we talk about this later?"

"No. This is later as far as I'm concerned."

"Kendra . . ."

"You said I might never be normal, and that's all right. I'll be what I'm meant to be because I'm going to get to know who that is." She stepped closer to him. He was so important to her. She had to make him see what she was seeing. She was willing him to understand with all her heart. "I'm going to experience everything that comes my way. I'm going to drink the wine. I'm going to reach out to people. I'm going to understand how they think and why they think it. I'm going drown myself in music. I'm going to sing and not mind if I'm not perfect at it. I'm going to live."

She drew a deep breath, staring desperately up at him. "You mean so much to me. I'll listen to you. I don't know if you can convince me, but if you tell me that I'm wrong, I'll listen, and I'll think about it."

He slowly shook his head. "I refuse to lose credibility in your eyes. I value your respect far too much." He smiled ruefully. "Besides, you've already made up your mind. I stood here watching you, and you almost swept me away with you."

"You understand?" she insisted. "It's not because I don't realize what I owe you."

"You don't owe me anything. I was paid in full when I watched your face that day you took off the bandages."

"Bullshit."

"I'll accept the correction. Perhaps you owe me a bit more, but you have to accept that I received a huge gift that day, too." His smile vanished. "So I refuse to collect any more compensation from you in any form. Get the hell out of here. Right now."

She shook her head. "I'm going to do this one last speech. I won't leave you to make awkward explanations."

"I'm told that I'm capable of handling situations like

that." He tilted his head. "But you appear to have a plan in mind."

She nodded. "I'll do this speech, and when I'm done, I'll walk off the stage and step through those doors to the parking lot. And that's the last I want to hear about the Night Watch Project for a long, long while."

"A fine plan." He leaned forward and brushed a kiss across her brow. "And I hope it works out for you. I'll miss you, Kendra."

And she'd miss him. She wanted to reach out and touch him, keep him with her. Tell him once again how much she cared that he'd come into her life. But he'd stepped back, and the moment was gone.

She turned to go onstage.

"I want you to promise you'll do everything that you told me you were going to do just now," he said softly. "It will mean a good deal to me if I can look back and think of you joyously tearing full tilt through life."

She looked back at him. "I promise. Everything I said and more."

She went another few steps and stopped and turned to face him. From where she stood he was only a shadow-silhouette against the light, but it was a strong, purposeful silhouette. The silhouette of a man who had changed her life and made her believe she could conquer the world. "This all sounds so . . . permanent. I told you I want to live. But that doesn't mean I want to do it without you. I won't have it." She smiled as she felt the blood pumping through her veins, the excitement of the adventures to come bringing a flush to her cheeks. "Tonight my first stop is going to be Santa Cruz. If you don't have anything better to do, then come and have one of those ice-cold beers with me. You can toast my new life." She turned and *walked toward the stage. "And I'll toast the existence of miracles."*

BUT WALDRIDGE HAD NEVER shown up that night in Santa Cruz. And she had been so absorbed in tasting everything that life had to offer that she had let him slip away when she should have kept him close to her.

"Hey, are you okay?" Jessie was gazing quizzically at her, and Kendra realized her silence had become noticeable. "I didn't mean to insult that super-duper memory. I'm just trying to put things together. Nothing makes much sense."

"It's not super-duper. I only tend to apply myself and try to retain what I've learned." She shrugged. "But I don't have to try with Charles Waldridge. You don't forget someone who changed your life the way he did mine." She got to her feet. "So what are we going to do? Go back to the hospital and talk to Powers?"

"If we can get past that lawyer."

"It was like battering against a wall talking to Powers last time. We need something to use to break through that wall." She headed for her bedroom. "I'm wondering if I may have that battering ram and didn't even know it. Give me ten minutes to wash my face and get my thoughts together. It's been quite a morning. You might make us a cup of coffee."

"Just a kitchen slave," Jessie said as she strolled toward the kitchen. "Did you use Lynch like this? No wonder he ran out without his gun or his toothbrush."

"I think you'll both survive," Kendra said dryly. "And I'm certain Lynch had a spare for anything he left behind."

"Including you?" Jessie asked over her shoulder. "I'm

not too sure about that. You may be one of those irreplaceable items."

Kendra gazed at her in surprise. The tone was flip, but the remark was more personal than she would have thought Jessie would toss out. "Irreplaceable?" she asked.

"Yeah, you know." Jessie was suddenly grinning. "Like my motorcycle." She disappeared into the kitchen.

Kendra was smiling as she went into her bathroom. She should have known that Jessie would never venture close enough to be accused of intimacy. She might be amusing and brimming with vitality, but she kept her distance, and any approach had to be initiated by her.

Kendra gazed in the mirror as she washed her face and hands. Actually, she looked better than Jessie's motorcycle. However, she could have used some of its power right now. She was feeling sad about Rye, disturbed about Lynch, and frustrated and worried about Waldridge. But at least she wasn't alone, and Jessie had made her smile. So maybe it wasn't the worst day she'd lived through.

But Jessie might not want to compare her to her beloved bike after she ran what she had in mind past her. The only thing she could do was talk to her and see if she would be on board. If not, she had worked alone before. She wasn't going to stop if she had no Lynch or Jessie to go down that path with her. She tossed the towel on the vanity, turned, and headed for the kitchen.

"I like these automatic coffeemakers," Jessie said as she turned away from the Keurig and handed Kendra a cup of coffee. "It's called Black Magic. It sounded like the kind of brew you'd need today."

"Thanks." Kendra dropped down in the kitchen chair and cradled the cup in her two hands. "You're not having anything?"

"Nah, I was at Starbucks when I had the idea that I should drop in on you. Maybe I'll have something later." She sat down opposite her. "Talk to me about battering rams."

"When we were talking earlier about how Charles Waldridge and Night Watch always made sure everyone knew what a terrific advancement this stem-cell surgery was for the world, I remembered something from that last conference I attended in Monterey."

"And that was?"

"There was a man who followed me on the tour. I saw him in at least three cities. I never met him, but Waldridge said he was an important supporter of Night Watch."

"Why would he be following you?"

"I don't know. I assumed it was part of the publicity and other financial support they were trying to generate." She made a face. "I wasn't being very gracious after the first six months. The man was just part of the wallpaper that was making me very impatient. I wanted out."

"But he was noticeable enough that you remembered him even though you were never introduced?"

"Not him personally. At least I don't think so. It was the way Waldridge deferred to him. I even remarked on it that night in Monterey. He was important to Waldridge. It annoyed me. Charles Waldridge was the most significant person in my world at the time. He was that essential to a hell of a lot of people, and he shouldn't have had to take a backseat to anyone."

"Whew, do I detect a case of king-size hero worship?"

"Maybe." She was tired of denying it even to herself. "He deserves it. You only met him once. You'd have to know him, Jessie."

"I look forward to it." Her gaze was narrowed on Kendra's face. "How does Lynch take all this?"

"He understands. He's an intelligent man after all."

"Yes, intelligence is important, and Lynch impresses me as being way above the ordinary in that department. I'm sure that he understands quite a bit more than you might want him to about Waldridge." She waved a dismissing hand. "Anyway, you were uneasy about this man who appeared to have some kind of authority over Waldridge. Why?"

She shrugged. "I thought that he might have something to do with sending me all over the country to show off Night Watch's wonder operation. I was feeling kind of used."

"And you wouldn't let yourself blame Waldridge."

"He wouldn't have done it." She grimaced. "Okay, he might have persuaded me to do a few speeches and public appearances, but he wouldn't have made me do anything that would make me unhappy. There had to be pressure."

"Did he know you were unhappy?"

"I didn't hide it."

"But you didn't discuss it. Because you didn't want to disappoint him."

"Sharp." She took a swallow of coffee. "Are you grilling me, Jessie?"

"It's how I make my living. I'm a P.I. who's trained to look below the surface. I'd say most of the time you're very clear and honest with yourself and everyone around you. This time, you're doing a cover-up because you're not certain you want to see." She leaned back in her chair. "If Waldridge is as brilliant as you say, then he knew what you were feeling and was avoiding a confrontation. Why would he do that?"

"I don't know."

"Honestly?"

"Look, there was no way that Charles Waldridge would feel the same gratitude and emotion that I felt for him. I was the one receiving gifts. But he liked me, he felt pride in me. He's a decent human being, and he wouldn't want me to be unhappy. So I can only guess that Night Watch was putting pressure on him to keep me on that lecture circuit. It was important to them, and I have no idea why." Her lips twisted. "Perhaps if I'd been a little more mature, I'd have probed or noticed more about what was going on around me. I was just a kid who wanted my freedom and a chance to go out and explore the whole damn world."

Jessie nodded slowly. "I've been there."

"I'm sure you have." She looked down into the coffee in her cup. "But I've been thinking that maybe I should have stuck around and—" She shook her head. "The ever-alluring what-might-have-beens. You can't go back. You just have to go forward."

"And I've been there, too," Jessie said. "So how are you taking this battering ram into the future? I'm guessing that you're talking about this Night Watch supporter who you think had Waldridge under his thumb?"

"I thought it might be a place to start. It looked like he was lording over Waldridge, and making him do something he didn't want to do." She was remembering more about that night with every passing moment. "And when I finally convinced Waldridge I wanted to go, he told me to get the hell out of the auditorium. To go right now." She added, "It was almost as if he was afraid someone would stop me. Or as if *he* would be forced to stop me."

"Forced?"

"I don't know. Maybe not."

"And maybe so," Jessie said. "Night Watch is very much involved from what we can find out. The word force might be significant in the scheme of things. You don't have any idea of this man's name?"

She shook her head. "No idea. Waldridge didn't mention it."

"I suppose we could go back to paperwork about your tour and see if we can find anything."

"Eight years ago, Jessie."

"Difficult, but not impossible. We might even find some candid photos." She wrinkled her nose. "Though it might be time-consuming."

"Particularly since the tour was sponsored by Night Watch for publicity purposes. It's not as if anyone from Night Watch would have to sign up for the lectures."

"I could still go for it."

Kendra was silent. "Yes, but so can I."

Jessie tilted her head, studying her expression. "What's that supposed to mean?"

"You're right, we need a photo. To show Powers as a point of strength. To give to the FBI and see if they pull anything from facial recognition. To see if he was anywhere near Big Bear or Waldridge's hotel."

"And where can we get this photo?"

"You check your sources. I'll check mine."

"And what are your sources?"

She tapped her temple. "The one that I told you that I didn't have. Super-duper memory. I remember what he looked like. I remember everything about him."

"After eight years?"

"It was a very strange and special night. I felt as if I were exploding inside, and everything around me was caught, held forever. I was looking into a crystal ball and

251

seeing my life ahead of me. He was only on the edge of that crystal ball, but he was caught in it, too."

"And how are you going to bring him out of that crystal ball?"

"I know a wonderful sketch artist, Bill Dillingham. He's helped me on cases before. If anyone can do it, he will."

"Some sketch artists are terrific. But they're only as good as the witness who gives them the description."

"Are you doubting me?"

"Yep. Eight years, no prolonged exposure to the subject, emotional involvement. It's a long shot."

Kendra nodded. "I know it is. But we haven't gotten lucky so far. I'm figuring that it's time. As I said, I don't have a perfect memory, but it's pretty darn good. And that night was so special for me, it might give me the edge I need." She paused. "I'm going to call Bill Dillingham now and see if he'll see me. Do you want to go along?"

"I wouldn't miss it."

"So that you can laugh at me later?"

"No way. If anyone can pull it off, I think it could be you. And, if you really fall on your face, then I'll be there to sympathize." She grinned. "And *then* tell you I-told-you-so."

WHEN KENDRA HUNG UP from talking to Bill Dillingham, she was frowning. The conversation had made her very uneasy, and so had Bill's voice on the phone.

"Something wrong?" Jessie asked curiously.

"I hope not. He didn't want to do the sketch. He told me he'd give me the name of someone else." She shook her head. "I told him that I only wanted him, and I'd see him in an hour."

"Pushy."

"I didn't like the way he sounded. Bill has to be almost eighty-five now, and he was kind of frail the last time I worked with him. I don't think he has family. Or, if he does, he's still something of a loner." She got to her feet. "This may be a waste of time for you. You probably won't be able to meet him. He doesn't even want me to come."

"Then I'll wait outside." She shrugged. "I don't think a man that old is going to try to take you down, but a little moral support might do you some good."

"Take me down?" She looked at her in disbelief. "That's why you were going with me?"

"Of course not. I was interested, and I wanted to see how talented he was. I'm just accustomed to thinking in terms of protection." She headed for the door. "Want to take my bike? It will be more fun."

"I do not. All I'd need is to have Bill have a heart attack when we come roaring up his driveway. We'll take my Toyota."

"May I drive? I promise not to roar."

"I don't believe you could help yourself." She headed for the front door. "I think it's in your genes."

"Actually, I had to work on it. I think the roar started about my second year in Afghanistan." She followed her out the door. "I'll tell you what. Let's flip for it . . ."

CHAPTER
13

BILL DILLINGHAM LOOKED TERRIBLY FRAGILE, and Kendra's eyes widened with shock when he opened the front door of his small house in a subdivision in south San Diego. He was at least fifteen pounds thinner than he'd been the last time she'd worked with him, his faded blue eyes lacked the spark of former days. What was most troubling was the lack of vitality in his face.

"What arc you looking at?" he asked sourly. "I never invited you here, Kendra. I know what I see in the mirror. I don't have to see it reflected on your face. Why don't you go away?"

She quickly recovered. "Because I need you to do this sketch for me. It's very important that it be done right since your witness is questionable."

"I don't need to work with witnesses who are going to give me headaches before I even begin. Go away."

"No. May I come in? I haven't seen you for a couple years, but you're just as rude as you've always been." She smiled. "I've never seen your home." She was peering over his shoulder. "I see an interesting painting of a little girl in a sun bonnet on that far wall. Is it yours? I've only seen your sketches."

"Because that's how I make my money," he said dryly. "And are you trying to flatter your way into my house?"

"Yes. Though I would like to see that painting. If you don't let me in, then I'll stay out here on your doorstep." She met his eyes. "Because when I knew I had to have this sketch done, I knew it had to be you, Bill."

He was silent. "I'm not the same artist I was two years ago, Kendra." He held up his hand, and she saw a slight quiver. "I had a bad case of pneumonia, and I didn't bounce back. It seems unfair that when you age, every little illness seems to take its toll. Or maybe it's the depression afterward. Anyway, I don't do sketches anymore."

She could see that depression was still a living presence in every line of his face. "But you could, Bill. I've seen you work." She looked at the painting of the child. "That's quite wonderful and I'm sure you enjoyed doing it. But it didn't give you the same creative excitement as doing those sketches, did it?"

"I'm retired, Kendra."

"Bullshit. I *need* this, Bill. It's important to me. It might save a good man from being killed." She took a step closer. "I *know* you. If you're retired, then that's probably what's wrong with you. You need a reason to get up in the morning. Well, I'll give it to you. It will only be a start, and you'll have to take it from there. But you'll do this sketch, and it will be good because you can't be anything else." She took another step. "Now, may I come in?"

He stood looking at her for a long moment. "I guess I'd better let you, or you'll run me down like a bulldozer."

He stepped aside and gestured for her to enter. "But it's not going to do you any good. You'll see when I start to sketch."

"Yes, I will." She looked around the living room and saw three really fine paintings besides the one of the child in the foyer. "Wonderful. By all means, keep on doing them when you don't have anything else to do. But you're a true genius about translating words and vague thoughts into real faces, Bill. No one else can do it like you can."

"I'm glad you're going to permit me to continue my choice of art endeavor," he said sarcastically. "Who is this questionable witness?"

"Me." She smiled. "Eight years ago, Bill. But I remember him as if it were yesterday."

He made a rude sound. "Tell me another one."

"I can't. I can only tell you the truth. I can't even promise that it's going to help to have his face. But it's a chance, and I've got to take it."

His gaze was searching her face. "It means something to you."

"Yes, it means a good deal to me."

"Personal."

"Very personal."

He went to the bookshelf and took down his sketchbook. "You see?" he said roughly. "Look at my hand. It's shaking. What do you think that you're doing to me?"

"I hope I'm waking you up. What do you think?"

He didn't move, looking down at the sketchbook. "We'll have to see, won't we?" He jerked his head to a chair on the other side of the desk. "Sit your ass down and start talking to me." He flipped open the sketchbook. "How old was he?"

"About forty-five then. Eight years ago."

"Face shape?

"Sort of triangular. Pointed chin.

His pencil was slow, a little shaky.

"Eyebrows?"

"Thick. A little bushy."

Stronger, faster strokes.

"Shape of the eyes?

"Round. Deep-set."

The pencil flew over the page.

Demands.

Answers.

The pencil.

Always the pencil.

Drawing. Going back. Changing.

Drawing again.

"Lips?"

"Full bottom lip. Upper lip, thinner."

"Jaw?"

"Thin. A little flat toward the ear."

"Like this?"

"Maybe thinner."

"Like this?"

"Yes."

"Hairline?"

"Receding at the forehead. But the rest of the hair looked healthy, shiny."

"Dark? Light?"

"Dark. Latin-looking."

"What's that supposed to mean?"

"Just an impression."

"I don't sketch impressions."

But he did, and the hair of the man suddenly had longer sideburns.

The pencil flew. The words flew. The image on the page changed, became something, then changed again.

Kendra didn't know how much time had passed, but she knew that Bill had turned on the lamp sometime during the session.

"Best I can do." He finally handed her the sketch. "Considering that you don't know what the hell you're doing, either."

She looked at the sketch. "It's a very good best," she said softly. "It's the man I saw that day at the auditorium. You've *got* him, Bill."

"Providing he doesn't have wrinkles or scars that he's developed since you saw him. Time doesn't stand still, Kendra."

"It did for you today, Bill."

"Yeah, maybe." He looked at the sketch. "When you find him, will you let me know? Maybe take a photo of him. I want to know how close I came."

"I'll get you proof." She hoped she was telling the truth. "I'll even get you a name."

"Do that." He looked away from the sketch. "That doesn't mean I'm going to do any more sketches."

"It doesn't mean that you're not." She got to her feet. "You're too young to be wandering around this house when you could be doing something interesting. I'm going to call Griffin at the FBI and tell him that if he has something really challenging, you're here, ready and waiting."

"The hell you will."

She nodded. "I'm going to do it. Though I'm still going to insist on being first on your preferred list." She looked down at the sketch. "Thank you," she said quietly. "This means a lot to me, Bill."

"I thought it did. That's why I let you harass me." He

stood up and walked with her to the door. "And I *might* let you get away with it again. If I get bored enough."

She grinned. "Griffin won't let that happen." She reached out and shook his hand. "I'll let you know as soon as I locate our mystery subject. It's been good seeing you again."

"Do you expect me to say the same?" he asked wryly. "It's been interesting. I'll have to see after the fallout if I'm going to say that your coming here was a good experience or just memorable."

"I can't wait for your report." She turned and waved. "But give it a little while to make a decision. Bye."

"Kendra."

She looked back over her shoulder.

"Maybe you've got a few more smarts other than the ones that are connected to all that brainy stuff you manage to pull out of your hat." He smiled. "I guess it wasn't such a bad afternoon."

He turned away and closed the door.

No, it hadn't been a bad afternoon at all, she thought as she went down the driveway to where Jessie was waiting in passenger seat of the car.

Jessie got out of the car and came around to the driver's seat. "I get to drive now. You owe me, after keeping me waiting out here all afternoon. I've been going crazy." She glanced down at the rolled-up sketch Kendra was carrying. "You got what you needed?"

Kendra nodded. "And it's really good. It's *him*, Jessie."

Jessie unrolled it and studied the sketch. "Not bad-looking. Don't like the eyes." She handed the sketch back to her. "You can take some photos of it while I'm driving us to the hospital."

"You're being very demanding."

"I was bored. I hate to be bored. I sat here twiddling my thumbs and wondering if I should break in and see if you needed help with Dillingham."

"With Bill?" She stared at her in astonishment. "Whatever for? You must have seen him when he opened the door. Unless you meant convincing him to do the sketch?"

"No, I knew you had that covered. But I've seen some old guys that were more spry than you might think and almost put me down." She grimaced. "But I could tell Dillingham wasn't one of them. So that left me with no job to do and bored mindless."

That protective instinct again, Kendra thought. "No, the only problem I had with Bill was convincing him that he had to jar himself back to the land of the living. I think he's alone too much. Depression can be pure hell."

"Yeah, I know. I had a few buddies who came back from Afghanistan with wounds that could be healed except the ones in their minds."

"How about you? You said you'd done two tours in Afghanistan."

"I had my own nightmares." She held out her hand. "So can I drive?"

Kendra dropped the car keys into her palm. "No roaring."

"Okay." She jumped into the driver's seat. "This car isn't suited for roaring anyway. Too sedate. Now if I had Lynch's Ferrari . . ."

FORTY-FIVE MINUTES LATER, Kendra and Jessie approached the police officer standing watch outside Powers's hospital room. The cop held up his beefy hands to stop them.

"Whoa. Can I help you?"

Kendra took the lead. "I hope you can. We're here to see Wallace Powers."

"Sorry, ladies. He's in police custody."

"I'm Kendra Michaels. I'm on the list."

The cop pointed to a clipboard hanging on the wall. "It's a very short list, and you're not on it."

"It's been updated."

"Since when?"

"Since a few minutes ago. Call and check."

The cop frowned with annoyance as he pulled out his phone and called his station. After a minute or so of conversation, he pocketed his phone. "I'll be damned. You're on it."

Kendra uttered a silent thanks to Griffin for so speedily greasing those wheels for her.

The cop had obviously done hospital prisoner duty before. He easily slipped into his rote visitor speech. He informed them that no purses, bags, or packages would be allowed in the room, even though neither of them were carrying anything other than Bill's rolled-up sketch. No weapons of any kind were allowed in the room, and a quick frisk was necessary. "If you request it, I can have a female officer come here and conduct the search," he said.

"How long would that take?" Jessie asked.

"Anywhere from ten minutes to two hours."

Jessie raised her arms. "Just curious. Knock yourself out."

The cop did a perfunctory frisk that Kendra thought would have allowed them to smuggle Uzis under their jackets without his detecting them. Then he opened the door. "For the protection of you and the prisoner, I must be present at all times during your visit. But I have to tell you, he hasn't been seeing anyone without his attorney present."

261

Jessie smiled. "You couldn't have told us that before you frisked us?"

The cop became momentarily tongue-tied.

Jessie waved him off. "Just giving you a little grief. Let's go inside and see what happens."

The officer preceded them into the room. At first, Kendra wasn't sure they were looking at the right person. Powers's face was now several shades of purple and swollen in ways that didn't seem physically possible.

His puffy eyes widened at the sight of Kendra and Jessie. "What in the hell are you doing here?" His speech wasn't altogether clear.

"You're slurring your words," Jessie said. "Is it your swollen tongue or is it the painkillers? Or both?"

"I'm not talking to you," he said. "You got something to say, talk to my lawyer."

"We already have," Jessie said. "He'll be billing you for that five-minute conversation, I'm sure. It's more than you make in a week."

"How do you know what I make?"

"We do our homework," Kendra said. "Enough to know that someone else is paying for that lawyer. The question is, how much do you trust whoever is paying the bill?"

"I'm not saying shit."

"Then just listen," Jessie said. "That lawyer told you not to talk. Who do you think that advice helps more, you or the people paying him?"

Powers didn't respond.

Kendra stepped toward him. "If it's a question of incriminating yourself, that train has left the station. We have your DNA, which puts you there. It was under my fingernails."

"And in the pee in the carpet," Jessie said. "I've Tased

a lot of guys in my time, but I've never seen anyone piss his pants like that. That was a new one."

Powers lunged angrily toward her, but the handcuff held him to the bed rail.

Jessie smiled. "Aw, come on. Was I being indelicate? No reason to be embarrassed. You're among friends here. And you need all the friends you can get right now."

"You're not my friends."

"You're right," Kendra said. "Especially considering how we met. But we can help each other."

"Still not talking . . ."

"Which is exactly what that lawyer and his employer want. But if we already have all the evidence we need to put you away for assault, battery, and attempted kidnapping, what good is your silence really doing for you?"

Powers's jaw clenched, and he looked away.

Jessie moved closer. "Maybe you're thinking your lawyer is some kind of miracle worker, that he can magically make all this disappear. He's good, but he can't make DNA evidence vanish. But maybe that isn't his concern. Maybe he just wants to protect whoever is paying him. Maybe to protect whoever paid you to grab my friend here. Don't you think that's more likely? Do you really feel so valued that you think that lawyer is on the case for *you*?"

Powers turned back. He looked as if he was about to say something, but then caught himself.

Kendra shook her head. "You know what else isn't going to disappear? The fact that you knocked your ex-wife around. You did some jail time for that, didn't you? How is it going to play at your sentencing hearing after you've been convicted of attacking another woman? Come on, Powers," she said softly. "The smartest thing you can do for yourself is tell us who hired you. If you had a lawyer who was really representing *you*, he would tell you the same thing."

Powers's resolve was obviously weakening. "Shit," he muttered.

Jessie nodded. "Do yourself a favor. Get a new lawyer, any lawyer. Make sure he or she is working for you and no one else."

Kendra pulled the rubber band from the rolled-up sketch and unfurled it in front of Powers's face.

Instant recognition.

The look that flashed across his face made it obvious that he knew the man in the sketch. Kendra couldn't miss the reaction, and she tried to read his expression.

Fear?

Maybe. Or perhaps he was just nervous that they'd made a link between him and this man.

Jessie had obviously read his reaction, too. "You *know* him."

"The hell I do."

"You have the worst poker face in the history of the world," Kendra said. "Give us a name to go with this picture."

"I can't help you."

"Sure you can," Jessie said. "Just a name. We'll try to leave you out of it."

"Is this the man you're protecting?" Kendra asked. "It's time that you started protecting yourself."

"That's what I'm doing." Powers was sweating, and the bedside heart monitor showed that his pulse had quickened.

"You're a lucky man," Kendra said. "Your liver was failing a few years ago. You were handed a death sentence."

He moistened his lips. "I beat it."

"You had help," Jessie said.

"Clean living. Diet and exercise."

"Bullshit," Jessie said.

Kendra shook the sketch. "Just a name. It's information that can't be traced back to you."

He scowled. "Why should I help you?"

Kendra shrugged. "As the victim of your attack, my testimony can help you or hurt you. You can be seen as a woman-hating monster or someone who was acting under duress. It could mean the difference between years of your life in prison."

There was sudden panic in his face. "You don't understand. I'd never survive prison."

"Really? Because that's where you'll end up. And are you sure you'd survive even if you didn't go to prison? A man who knows what you know will never be safe. You have big problems."

He moistened his lips. "And you're saying you'd promise to help me with them?"

It was a break in the wall. "Give me a chance," Kendra said. "I'll help you any way I can, if you'll just give me a name. You're not the one we're after."

"Look, I told you. I never meant to really hurt you. I was just supposed to deliver you. He *needed* you for something."

Kendra leaned forward. "He?"

Powers was frowning, his gaze clinging desperately to her face. "If I help you . . . How do I know you'll really—"

The door flew open, and attorney Peter Hutchinson strode quickly into the room. "This conversation is over. Ladies, I must ask you to leave."

"Just a friendly chat," Kendra said.

Hutchinson stepped between them and his client. "I'm afraid it was nothing of the sort."

"Too bad you can't muzzle us the way you do your client," Jessie said.

"I don't believe I've been altogether successful in impressing upon my client the need for absolute silence." He glanced back at Powers. "That *was* your voice I heard as I walked in here, wasn't it?"

Powers's hand was shaking as he reached for a tomato-juice box on the table next to him. "I was telling them to get the hell out."

Hutchinson gave him a skeptical look. "From now on, I'll do all the talking for you. Understand?"

Powers played with his straw, stirring the thick juice, avoiding looking at them. "Sure."

"No problem," Kendra said. "We'd rather talk to your real client anyway. You know, the one pulling your strings?"

Hutchinson flashed his toothy smile. "My loyalties lie exclusively with Mr. Powers. And I must ask you to respect his wishes by staying away."

"His wishes . . . Or yours?"

"Mr. Powers," Hutchinson prompted his client. "Tell her."

Powers glanced up from toying with his straw to meet Kendra's eyes. "*My* wishes."

"You see?" Hutchinson said. "Good day, Ms. Michaels."

Powers lifted his hand and gave Kendra a weak wave. "You heard the man. Don't bother coming back."

Kendra studied him for a moment. "Fine. See you at your trial."

Kendra and Jessie left the room and started down the corridor toward the elevator.

"Well, *that* was a bust," Jessie muttered. "I thought we were damn close."

Kendra smiled. "I don't think it was a bust."

"What do you mean?"

"I think we got through to him."

"What makes you say that?"

"Dyle."

"What?"

Kendra stepped on the elevator and punched the DOWN button. "Powers used his juice straw to write the name on his hand. Four letters. Barely discernable. He showed me his palm, and it was there, written in red tomato juice. He didn't want his lawyer to know."

"But who is Dyle?"

Kendra was already typing furiously on her phone. "I'm searching for the name right now. If we're lucky, it may actually be the man who—" She froze. "It's him. The man in the sketch. The guy I saw all those years ago."

She turned the phone around to show Jessie a photo. "Meet Ted Dyle."

"You Googled him?" Jessie's eyes widened as she studied the man in a gray pin-striped suit smiling out of the photo. "Oh, that's the guy in the sketch all right." She took the phone and was reading the biography as she and Kendra left the hospital and walked across the parking lot. "Venture capitalist, owns a pharmaceutical company and two corporations that fund hospitals. Has interests in several hedge funds. Multi-investments in research projects at three universities. Something of a power broker and was said to be behind the scenes in electing the last two senators from California." She handed Kendra's phone back to her. "That's all they have on him. Pretty scanty." She frowned. "But he's based in L.A. That's my town. Why haven't I heard of him?"

"Because he probably pays to stay out of the limelight," Kendra said. "Thank God for Google. At least we were able to get this much information." She could feel the excitement zinging through her. "He has to be connected to Night Watch."

"And probably that attack on you, or Powers wouldn't have recognized him." She smiled. "A giant step closer, Kendra."

"I know." She couldn't stop smiling. "And a step closer to Waldridge. I've felt like we've been going down blind alleys, but this is so damn promising."

"Yes, it is." She was gazing with amusement at Kendra's face. "You look as if you're on top of the world. We've still got a long way to go."

"Don't rain on my parade," Kendra said. "Tomorrow, I'll worry about all the bad things that could happen. Tonight, I want to think good thoughts and be happy. Do you think it's too late to drive up to L.A. and try to see Dyle?"

"Yes." She chuckled. "It would be midnight, and he'd have his staff toss us out. He might do it anyway. But we'd have a better shot in the morning." They'd reached Kendra's Toyota. "So let me worry about all the bad things that could happen tomorrow, and you try to keep your grand parade intact for the rest of the evening. Deal?"

"Deal." Kendra didn't know if she could do it, but right now, it seemed a wonderful idea.

"Well, now that we've settled that important detail. I'd

like to announce that I'm hungry. You haven't eaten either. Want to stop for a late supper?"

"Maybe." Kendra watched with rueful amusement as Jessie jumped into the driver's seat . . . again. "I'm a little hungry. It's been a long day."

"So where do you want to stop?" She started the car. "We could go to a pancake house. Or fast food . . ." She didn't look at her as she backed out of the parking space. "Or I saw a Thai restaurant in your neighborhood. Is it any good? We could get takeout and go back to your place and eat it. I have to get my bike anyway."

"It's very good."

"I thought it might be. It had people lined up at the door even this morning." She smiled. "So where do you want to go? Your choice. I'm just your humble chauffeur."

"Definitely the chauffeur. You won't have it any other way. Humble? Not so much." She laughed. "The Thai place sounds the most practical. We can take it up on the roof to eat it. It's nice up there."

"Whatever you say. Just as long as I get food and a chance to stretch out and move. I'm not accustomed to being this inactive."

Kendra could see that it bothered her. She'd been aware of the other woman's restlessness all day. She was surprised Jessie hadn't opted out of sitting patiently in that car and waiting at Bill Dillingham's. Ever since she'd met Jessie, she had been a dynamo of energy and activity. Yet their time together today had still been productive and amusing, and she found she was genuinely fascinated and curious about Jessie Mercado.

"Okay. Then we'll stop at the Thai place. On the way there, I'll text Griffin the photos I made of the sketch and ask him to check and report on Dyle." She went around the car and got into the passenger seat. "And I'll tell him he should use Dillingham more for his sketches and use muscle with the local police to have them do it, too."

"Will he pay attention?"

"Sometimes. If it suits him. I'll stress what an asset Dillingham is. He likes assets." She was looking at the sketch again. "It's not a lie. I think I'll text a photo to Lynch, too. Along with the Google biography."

"That sounds like a plan. Lynch doesn't impress me as a man who likes to be kept out of the loop. Control, all the way . . ."

THE LIGHTS OF SAN DIEGO were sparkling, glowing in the darkness. There was a strong wind whipping occasionally over the rooftop, which was vacant except for Kendra and Jessie.

"We could go down to the condo if the wind's bothering you." Kendra grinned as she righted one of the cartons of Thai food on the table between their chairs. "But you did say you wanted movement."

"No, I like this," Jessie said. "For Pete's sake, I own a motorcycle." She lifted her face to the wind that was blowing her hair wildly back. "Wind is clean and strong. Both good things."

"Except if it comes packaged in a tornado," Kendra said dryly as she lifted her wine to her lips. "I think I'd choose to go inside if it escalated to that point." She smiled. "But I like it, too."

"Do you come up here often?"

"Not often." The last time she had come up here was that night with Lynch, when everything had blown up both sexually and emotionally. Those memories were suddenly bombarding her, and she could feel her body readying, tightening at the thought of him.

Back off. Everything about her relationship with Lynch was full of pitfalls and uncertainties, including what she wanted from him.

Except sex. That was very clear at this moment.

"Did you ever come up here with Lynch?" Jessie's gaze was narrowed on Kendra's face.

Jessie was very perceptive, and she had probably been able to read Kendra's response. "Yes," Kendra said as she took another bite of Thai pepper steak. "This is really very good, isn't it? How is yours?"

Jessie immediately took the hint. "Delicious. Some of the best Thai I've had since Delilah had a box of it flown in special from Bangkok." She leaned back and lifted her wine to her lips. "But in that case, anticipation was a heady sauce, and that might have made it seem better."

"Delilah?"

"Delilah Winter. I worked for her for a while." She shot a glance at Kendra. "She's a pop star. Have you ever heard of her? She probably doesn't produce the kind of music that you teach your kids, but she's pretty famous."

"I'd have to live in a cave not to have heard of her," Kendra said. "She won a Grammy last year, didn't she?"

"Yes, she deserved it. That new song she wrote rocks."

"*She* rocks," Kendra said. "And I do use her in my therapy sessions. The kids don't live in a cave either, and her rhythms are wonderful."

"She'd be glad to hear you say that. Delilah is like a lot of teenage kids who made it big too early. She's still not sure whether she has the talent or that she's just fooling everyone."

"Sad." She asked curiously, "How did you come to work for her?"

"It's a long story."

"You don't want to talk about it?"

She shrugged. "It's not something I'm particularly proud of, nor am I ashamed. It was just a job. I took it because the opportunity was there, and I needed the money. I'd just gotten my degree in criminal justice, but that was during the downturn in the economy, and there were no decent jobs to be had. I got work as a bartender and part-time as a stuntwoman. Then I heard about that TV show *American Ninja*, and I trained and competed for it. I won first place and got a decent amount of money and a little fame thrown in. The notoriety attracted Delilah, and she hired me to head her security." She smiled. "She was just a kid who thought that if there was a star beside the name, the person had to be a star, too." Her smile faded. "She made a lot of mistakes like that. You have no idea how many jams I had to get her out of before she finally grew up."

"But it must have been exciting."

"And exhausting, like living in Disneyland without the rules that Disney enforces about smiles and the customer is always right." She took another sip of wine. "But the money was terrific, and I made sure that I earned every dollar before I turned in my resignation. I left her safe and with good people before I bowed out."

"You sound as if you feel guilty."

She made a face. "It was like kicking a puppy when I told her that I was leaving. As I said, she's insecure, and she felt safe with me. She still calls me sometimes when she needs to talk, or she gets into trouble."

"But you felt you couldn't stay with her?"

"Everyone has to grow up sometime. I'd made enough money to open my own P.I. office. It was time I moved on with my life."

"And you have," Kendra said. "No regrets?"

"Of course there were regrets. Delilah offered me a million dollars a year to stay on. I like money."

"And you wanted to make certain she was safe," Kendra said softly. "I've noticed that you have that instinct."

"It's over." She looked out at the lights. "Time passes. People come and go. But I guess I was brought up to believe that when I did go, it wasn't a bad idea to make sure no one was worse off than when I came."

"That's a good philosophy."

She chuckled. "Actually, it's a little too deep for me right now. It must be the wine talking." She yawned. "How many have I had?"

"Two. No, maybe three."

"Oops. I never have more than two. Cops love to stop bikers and test. They tend to think we have a reckless mind-set and endanger the general public." She glanced at Kendra. "Would you mind if I bunk at your place tonight? Maybe on the couch? We have to get out early anyway."

Kendra blinked. She hadn't been expecting this from Jessie. "Sure. No problem. You can have the guest room if you like. But Lynch might have left it in a mess. He left for the airport early."

"He did, didn't he?" Jessie was picking up cartons and putting them in the trash container. "I promise you that I won't leave my toothbrush like he did . . ."

"Do you have one with you?"

"I always travel with an overnight duffel in my bike kit. I'll just go down to the garage and get it." She smiled at Kendra. "Thanks, I promise I won't be any trouble. You won't know I'm here." The next moment she was across the roof and opening the door leading downstairs.

Kendra believed her. Jessie was self-sufficient and totally responsible, or she wouldn't be so concerned about the possibility of being picked up on a violation.

But if she was so aware and responsible, why had she taken that extra glass of wine?

A slip?

But did Jessie make slips? She was beginning to know the woman now, and what she knew was that Jessie was one of the smartest people she'd ever met. She knew exactly what she was doing and how it would affect the people around her.

For heaven's sake, why was she even questioning Jessie over this one mistake in what Kendra thought her character dictated? Forget it.

Only it was more than one anomaly in her behavior today.

Why had she opted to go to Bill Dillingham's place today when Kendra had told her that she probably wouldn't even be able to meet with him? Why hadn't she just gotten on her bike and taken off on her own business? Why had she stayed all those hours waiting? Then she had gone with her to the hospital and stayed until she had left there, too.

Yes, she had been helpful, but Kendra had still had that feeling of being . . . What?

And she had made that weird remark about not having to worry about Dillingham's being a threat.

Jessie was completely independent, and yet she had stayed with Kendra all day, hovering like a friendly gargoyle. Not a flattering comparison, but Kendra was not feeling like being flattering at the moment.

She was feeling pissed off.

Son of a bitch!

She was on her feet and running down the steps to her condo.

She slammed the door and headed for her bedroom.

She slammed that door, too.

She pulled out her phone and dialed quickly.

Answer, damn you.

Lynch answered immediately. "I received Dyle's photo. Good work."

"Yes, it was."

He caught the barely contained tension in her voice. "But something's wrong?"

"Yes. Plenty is wrong." The words were spitting out. "What gave you the right to call Jessie Mercado and ask her to babysit me while you were gone? Do you know how humiliating it is to have someone treating me as if I'm helpless?"

Silence. "I think she's too smart to treat you like that. I'm sure she made it very pleasant and unobtrusive."

"Oh, she did. She only made a couple mistakes, and that was because all of the subterfuge was going against her basic instincts." She said furiously, "She was so clever that she's now in my guest room, complete with toothbrush."

"Good. But she has to get out when I come back. Unless you let me share your bed."

"I can't imagine that's happening right now."

"I can. But I can also see that you're having problems because I had to keep you safe. We'll discuss that later."

"Oh, yes, I'm definitely having problems. When did you call Jessie? She was here in practically no time after you left. And did you *actually* hire her to protect me?"

"I called when I got to the street after I left you. And I

didn't hire her. I offered, but she said that she'd consider it a debt owed, which had more value to her."

Kendra could see that. Having Adam Lynch owe you a debt was beyond price. "Why, Lynch?"

"You know why. Why was I occupying that guest room myself? You were a target, and I was going across the Atlantic, where I couldn't protect you. I had to have someone there who was watching your back."

"I can take care of *myself*."

"So could Rye, better than you. He's dead. You're not going to be dead, Kendra. You fire Jessie, and I'll hire someone else who will probably scare the hell out of you because you won't know who it is. Just put up with her until I can get back there to you." He paused. "I need to be here for Rye, but if you give me trouble, I'll fly back there. As I said, he's dead. I won't allow that to happen to you."

"You can't fly back here," she said through set teeth. "You have a job to do."

"And I'll do it. I'll find out who murdered Rye. I'll try to find out what happened to Waldridge. Just give me a break. Let me keep you safe."

"I'm not going to give you a break. Do you know why I didn't pick up on those slips that Jessie made? It's because I couldn't believe you'd ever do something like this to me. It's beyond belief." She pronounced every word with precision. "I'm very angry with you, Lynch."

"I know you are. I'll give a damn some other time. Let me keep you safe."

"I'm going to hang up now."

"No, you aren't. Not until you tell me that you're going to let Jessie do her job."

"Her job is Waldridge."

"And you. *Tell* me."

"I'll discuss it with her. It might not be a pleasant discussion."

"Then she'll call me, and I'll take the first flight back."

"Damn you." She hung up.

She stood there breathing hard, trying to regain control.

He would do exactly what he'd said he'd do. Stop what he was investigating and fly back here.

Was her anger and hurt pride worth losing what Lynch might learn in London?

She had felt like a child when she had guessed what he'd done. She was *not* a child. She was an intelligent woman who was capable of taking care of herself.

Lynch had just had that Rye scare and couldn't think beyond it.

But that scare might affect finding Waldridge if she couldn't find a way to get beyond it.

Okay, she would go get a glass of water and spend a little time thinking and regaining her control. Then she would go and have that discussion with Jessie she'd told Lynch she would have.

She was not looking forward to it.

Or maybe she was, she amended. She wanted to strike out, and not from thousands of miles away as she'd had to do with Lynch.

"THE DOOR'S OPEN," Jessie called out when she heard Kendra coming across the living room toward the guest room. "Come in. I went upstairs on the roof and liberated that bottle of wine after Lynch called me. I figured we might need it."

"The wine you used to try to con me?" Kendra pushed

277

open the door to see Jessie sitting cross-legged on the bed. She was barefoot and dressed in a sleep shirt and had two wineglasses in her hand. "I'm not in the mood, Jessie."

"I know." She put the wineglasses on the nightstand. "You're pissed off, and you feel humiliated, and you want to kick someone."

"That about covers it."

"I can't help that you're pissed. I would be, too. I'd want to kill Lynch. He might have meant well, but that doesn't mean he had a right to do it. You shouldn't feel humiliated because he hired the best when he hired me." She smiled. "It's not as if he didn't have respect for you. As far as kicking someone, be my guest. I can take it. I was captured by the Taliban on my last tour, and nothing you could do would be any worse."

"Was that supposed to deflate my anger with both of you? It doesn't. He shouldn't have hired you. You shouldn't have taken the job."

"He has an excuse. He cares about you. I don't have an excuse. I like you, but I don't know you well enough to use it as a reason why I'd violate your independence." She met her eyes. "Independence is important to me. So the only excuse I'll give you is that I believe you have a chance of getting killed if I don't stick around and keep it from happening. Hell, it might have happened the day that I kept them from tossing you into that barrel. But I don't think so. I believed Powers when he said he was hired to deliver you. But if this Dyle hired him because he found you necessary for some reason, that need remains. But after it's fulfilled, you might very well be expendable."

"You can't know I'm still a target. The fact that Powers has been arrested might have scared them off."

"Lynch doesn't think so, or I wouldn't be here." She

lifted her shoulder in a half shrug. "And while you were with Dillingham today, a black paneled van cruised by once, slowed, then, when he saw me in the Toyota, sped up and took off. So I'm beginning to think that they're not finished with you, either."

Kendra gazed at her in shock. "Why didn't you go after them?"

"And leave you alone? That wasn't my job. They could have been trying to draw me away from you." She made a face. "Though I was tempted."

"Did you see the van later?"

She shook her head. "I was on the lookout, but I didn't notice anyone following. But if they were good, I might not. I can manage to follow almost anyone and not be detected."

"And maybe that van was just looking for an address."

Jessie just raised her brows skeptically.

Kendra's hands clenched. "It's never made any sense to me why they would try to snatch me."

"Maybe they don't have Waldridge and think you do? Or maybe you're looking too hard for your old friend, and they want to discourage you? Maybe they believe you have something they want? A few less benign reasons are occurring to me, but I won't go into them. At any rate, neither Lynch nor I want to find out until we have the upper hand."

That last sentence struck her wrong. They were clearly leaving her out of any decision making. "Lynch and you. What about me?"

"You're smart, and you're able to take care of yourself under most circumstances." Jessie tapped her own chest. "I'm equipped to take care of people under *any* circumstances. That's why Lynch made that call to me. I know

279

he's been checking me out, and that's fine. But you should let me do my job. It will help you and Lynch, and it might even save Waldridge." She shrugged. "But that's your decision. If you want me to get out, just say the word."

Kendra stared at her in exasperation. "And if I say that word, it might be the wrong thing to do. You're damn right it's my decision, but I'm in a corner, and I'm not going to be forced to make mistakes. So I'll tell you what we're going to do." She looked her in the eye. "I can't trust Lynch not to fly back here, so you stay on the job. I'd be stupid to not pay attention to your expertise, so I *will* take advantage of it. But you'll never lie to me or pretend to be something you're not. I want honesty and integrity, and I intend to use you to find Waldridge. Tomorrow we're going to go to L.A., and we'll squeeze answers out of Dyle. You'll work your ass off, and Waldridge is going to come out of this alive. We're going to do that *together*, Jessie."

"No problem." Jessie smiled. "Can we have that wine now?"

"No. It's going to take awhile before I'll be able to be on drinking terms with you again."

"It will come. Actually, we do like each other."

"Don't be too sure. It wasn't long ago that I was thinking of you as a friendly gargoyle."

Jessie laughed. "Really? That visual is priceless." She humped over in a gargoyle-like pose, waving her arms like a monkey. Then she reached over and turned out the lamp. "Good night, Kendra. I'm glad the air is cleared now. I'm lousy at deception . . ."

"You should have told that to Lynch." She closed the door behind her.

She was still upset, but some of it had ebbed away. It was difficult being angry with Jessie. It was really all

Lynch's fault, and Jessie was only a tool. She found herself smiling grimly at that description. Jessie would never let herself be a tool for anyone. It was almost like calling her a friendly gargoyle.

The memory of Jessie bent over in that ridiculous gargoyle pose was suddenly before Kendra.

Do *not* smile.

CHAPTER
14

STEVEN KINCAID, THE OFFICER from the Serious Organized Crime Agency, had not arrived when Lynch reached the factory, and he felt both impatience and frustration. Too much time had already passed since Rye's death, and he didn't need bureaucratic red tape and heel dragging to add to the problem.

Calm down. Kincaid was only twenty minutes late. If Lynch weren't so on edge, he wouldn't be making a major thing of it.

He glanced down at his phone. No text from either Kendra or Jessie this morning. He hadn't really expected one from Kendra. It was going to take some time to persuade her that he'd only done what he'd felt he had to do. And it was probably good that Jessie hadn't texted him. She was too professional to leave Kendra without informing him. He could only hope they were working things out.

"There's nobody here, you know."

He looked up from his phone to see a seventysomething

woman with gray hair and wearing a green plaid jacket coming toward him. He smiled. "No, I didn't know. I heard that there might be. And you are?"

"Dorothy Jenkins." She nodded at Dapper Dan's Pub across the street. "I'm the bartender and manager." She cocked her head. "You're American, aren't you? I can tell. Americans always sound so flat. I thought you might be Scotland Yard or something like that." She paused as she had another thought. "Maybe FBI?"

"No. But if I were, why do you think I'd be interested in whether there was someone here at the factory?"

"Cagey." She smiled. "That's fine. I understand. Mr. Malone was like that."

He stiffened. "Ryan Malone?"

"You know him? I've been waiting for him to come back." Her expression was eager. "I wanted to tell him about everything that happened right after he came to the pub and started asking his questions. I told him I'd keep an eye on things for him."

"I'm sure he appreciated it. Would you care to tell me instead?"

She hesitated. "I don't know if I can trust you. You might be one of them."

"Them?"

"Drug dealers, spies, whatever."

"I assure you that I'm not one of 'them.'" He met her eyes. "And Ryan Malone would want you to tell me anything you knew. Believe me. We worked closely together."

She studied him. "Yeah, and you weren't one of those men bustling all around and moving cars and trucks and stuff a couple days ago. And if you were one of the bad guys, what would you be doing standing out here like a hungry orphan, looking through those bars?"

IRIS JOHANSEN & ROY JOHANSEN

"You're very descriptive, if not complimentary," he said wryly. "I never thought of myself in quite that way before. So that's what happened? A complete cleanup and general abandonment?"

"As far as I could tell."

He dialed up the photo that Kendra had sent him of Ted Dyle on his phone. "Did you see him?"

"I don't think so. But most everyone who was here was wearing caps and jackets. Not suits, like this guy." She shrugged. "And I decided not to walk over here and ask questions while it was going on. If Mr. Malone had given me his phone number, I might have called and told him." She smiled. "He was a real gent. I could tell that he didn't think that I could help him, but he was polite to me."

"You were right not to try to do anything yourself. I'm certain he would have told you that himself." It was like Rye to have been able to reach out and touch this woman, he thought. Even in the last hours of his life, he had done his job with kindness and dignity. He looked back at the factory. The chances of their finding anything were very slim now, but he had to try. "And he'd thank you if he were here."

Her eyes widened and her smile faded. "Past tense," she said jerkily. "You're talking as if he—" She moistened her lips. "He's dead?"

Lynch didn't answer.

She looked back at the factory. "It was like a game to me. Or a puzzle. I never thought— But it's not a game, is it?"

"No, it's not a game."

"I liked him." She drew her coat closer about her as if warding off the cold. "But he was part of the game, too." She looked back at Lynch. "Maybe if I'd paid more atten-

284

tion, if I'd been able to tell him more, he wouldn't have died?"

"You had nothing to do with it. I'm certain that you only helped him."

"Maybe." She shook her head. "But it's a terrible world when a nice man like that can die in the blink of an eye because he was just doing his job." She turned away from the factory. "I'm going back to the pub. I don't feel so good."

"I'm sorry."

"So am I." She glanced over her shoulder, and she looked years older than that first moment when she'd so eagerly approached him. "You take care of yourself. If you need something, just ask. Or just come over and have a pint on the house, and we'll drink to your friend."

"I believe he might like that."

He watched her cross the street and go into the pub. Another life touched by Rye. He'd not even known about Dorothy Jenkins. Rye had only spoken about the "locals."

"Sorry I'm late." Stephen Kincaid had pulled up to the curb and jumped out of his car. "Traffic was hideous." He shook Lynch's hand. "Glad to see you. Not glad that it's on this occasion." He added grimly, "Rye was a good friend. Let's go see if we can find something to nail those bastards."

Maybe he wasn't going to have to worry about bureaucracy in motion, Lynch thought. Kincaid seemed sincere, and the SOCA could be efficient if motivated. "I'm not sure if we'll find anything. I've had a recent report that there was a cleanup about the time of Rye's death." He turned to the gate. "And this gate looks different from the photo Rye sent me on that last day. The newer apparatus, like the automatic gates and cameras, have been removed.

I imagine that's a sign of what we're going to find inside, too."

"Well, I can take care of getting us in." Kincaid went back to his car and pulled out a pair of bolt cutters from the trunk. "Always prepared." He clipped one of the chains and swung the gate open. He turned to throw the cutter back into his trunk. "After you, Lynch."

From the moment Lynch walked into the factory yard, he was aware of immaculate cleanliness . . . and emptiness. Only a few spots of motor oil on the concrete that had probably come from the vehicles, but there was no other sign of the cars and trucks Rye had been told about by the locals.

"You're sure this was the place?" Kincaid asked.

"This is the place." He was gazing at the photos on his phone and letting them lead them on the same course that Rye had taken.

"What is this place?" Kincaid asked, puzzled, as they reached a bright, pristine-clean area that had transitioned from the older part of the factory. "It looks new . . ."

But it was as empty as the rest of the factory. Though there were signs that there might have been shelves or other pieces of furniture or equipment in that section. "I don't know what it is. Rye didn't send me any photos of this area."

And he would have sent them, Lynch knew. He'd been documenting the entire factory, as was his custom.

And that meant that something had stopped him before he had been able to transmit them.

Was this the point where Rye was captured or killed?

No blood.

Of course not; it would have been cleaned and sterilized, like the rest of the factory.

"Do we go on?" Kincaid asked quietly.

Lynch nodded. "Sure." He left the sterling-clean area where he was almost certain his friend had died and went out to a loading dock, then through several other areas. Nothing struck him as powerfully as that one bright place in all the darkness. He made his way back to the clean room, where Kincaid joined him.

"Have you seen enough?" Kincaid asked. "We'll have a forensic team in to check for blood and fiber throughout the place."

"They might not find anything. Night Watch has some of the finest doctors and scientists in the world. It's reasonable to expect they'd be able to cover their tracks if needed." He stood there gazing at the bright, sterile room. "Scientists. A lab?"

"Reasonable enough."

"Nothing is reasonable about any of this." He started back toward the main gate. "What about Rye's car? Have you located it yet?"

"Not yet." Kincaid opened the gate. "We've checked out his home and the area around the landfill." He gazed at Lynch. "But you think that was a waste of time, don't you? You think he was killed here."

"He should have sent me photos of that last area of the factory, and he didn't do it." He looked back at the brick building. "He was . . . interrupted."

"And the car?"

"He would have had to drive here. It's possible that whoever killed him searched for his car, found it, and any other evidence Rye had discovered." He shrugged. "And the vehicle might be found in the Thames in six months."

"Possible?"

"You know how sharp and professional Rye always was.

287

He never just left his vehicle on the street when he went on a job like this. He'd park it close, but it would be out of sight and not easy to spot. There's a chance that it's still out there somewhere." He was on the street now. "So let's go find it."

Kincaid nodded. "Where do we start?"

He hesitated, then started across the street toward the pub. "We start with a new friend of Rye's . . ."

"I NEVER NOTICED HIS CAR at all," Dorothy Jenkins said as she gazed out the back window of Lynch's rental car. "I guess I was too excited and interested in what was happening at the factory." They had driven slowly up and down the four streets of the town directly before the factory, with Kincaid following behind. But they hadn't seen anything that appeared promising. "What kind of car did you say it was?"

"A gray Aston-Martin," Lynch said. He pulled over to the curb and got out. "I think I need a closer look." He started to go house to house, peering into backyards and garages.

"You'll get knocked on the head if someone sees you doing that." Dorothy was suddenly beside him. "They'll think you're casing the joint. If someone comes out of the house, let me talk. Most of these people know me."

"I'll leave it entirely up to you. That's why I asked you to come along. I'm relying on you to protect me." But so far, there had been no sign of Rye's car, and Dorothy was right, he'd be lucky if he didn't get arrested or assaulted before this was over. As they reached the end of the block, he turned to Dorothy. "Any ideas? It's your town."

She blinked. "Yes, it is." She thought about it and smiled. "Turn the next corner and go down that block. It has a bunch of deserted homes that people just left when they lost their jobs. That might be a good place to look."

"Right." He turned at the corner and strode down the street. Nothing in the first three houses. The fourth house was almost falling down. No garage.

The fifth house had heavy shrubbery and a garage.

And a gray Aston-Martin.

"*Yes.*" He phoned Kincaid. "Get over here. I've got it."

Dorothy had run up beside him, her cheeks flushed with excitement. "We found it? I helped?"

"You were magnificent," Lynch said. "You did it all, Dorothy." His hand squeezed her shoulder. "And now you'd better get out of here because I'm going to break into my old friend's car, and I don't want you to be an accomplice."

She looked a bit disappointed. "But it's not really a crime. You're one of the good guys?"

"In this case, I'm definitely a good guy. But it gets complicated."

"Like James Bond."

He grinned. "Something like Bond."

She nodded. "Then I'll go back to the pub." She started down the street. "You'll let me know if I can help again?"

"I certainly will. Many thanks, Dorothy."

"No, thank you. It made me feel good to help." She called back over her shoulder, "And I promise I won't tell them you broke into the car . . ."

When she'd disappeared around the corner, he turned back to the Aston-Martin. It took him three minutes to break into the car, and by that time, Kincaid was beside him.

"You know we should wait for forensics before we search the car," he said. "We might destroy evidence."

"No crime was committed in this car. Don't be a dick."

"Well, when you put it like that. What are we looking for?"

"Anything that could help." He was inside the car. "I have no idea. Maybe Rye's tablet. He had his phone with him when he was killed, and that was never found. But he probably wouldn't have had his tablet. It's not portable enough when he had to travel really light." He opened the glove box. He saw a gleam of gray lying beneath piles of receipts and envelopes. "And here it is," he said softly as he took the iPad out and opened it. "Come on, baby. Talk to me . . ."

"Who are you talking to?" Kincaid asked, his gaze on Lynch's flying fingers on the keyboard.

"The cloud. The magic cloud," Lynch murmured. "Rye had a private cloud account connected to his devices. I'm hoping that there might be something on it that he didn't manage to transmit to me."

"Do you think he could—"

"*Yes.*" Lynch had managed to bring up those first photos he'd received from Rye. He flipped through them quickly, and then froze. His gaze was on the last photo, one that he had never received on the night Rye had died. "*Holy shit.*"

Kincaid moved closer, staring at the photo. "It's that lab at the factory."

Lynch nodded. There was no doubt that area was a lab now. In this photo, the space was no longer empty but filled with equipment and workstations with over a dozen incubators.

He stiffened, his gaze narrowed on those incubators. He enlarged the picture, zeroing in on close-ups of what those incubators contained. He gave a low whistle. "My God."

There were human organs in those incubators—hearts, livers, kidneys . . .

Kincaid swallowed. "What the hell was going on there?" he asked hoarsely. "Were those sons of bitches harvesting organs?"

That had been Lynch's first thought, too. But it didn't feel right with what he and Kendra had pieced together about what was going on. So now his eyes were narrowed intently on the photo, and he was studying it more carefully. "I don't think so," he said slowly. "I think this is something else entirely . . ."

Los Angeles
Figuroa Street

Kendra and Jessie arrived at Ted Dyle's downtown office building after a customarily hellish weekday morning drive up the I-5 freeway. For most of the trip, Jessie used her iPad to read aloud about several news stories and blog posts about Dyle's history of backing ideas that had made him billions of dollars. None of the stories made any mention of the Night Watch Project, but Dyle apparently functioned as a silent investor on many of his endeavors.

At one point in the journey, Jessie cast a quick glance back.

Kendra tensed. "See something?"

"No black panel van. That doesn't mean they aren't switching vehicles." She paused. "I did see a white utility truck a block from your condo. And I caught sight of one about four miles back on the freeway."

"Utility trucks are all over the place in Southern California."

"Which would be an excellent reason to use them. But if you're still being followed, they're very, very good."

Kendra smiled. "You know, there's a thin line between protectiveness and out-and-out paranoia."

"Paranoia is good. If I'm wrong, we take a few precautions we don't really need to. But if I'm right, it can mean the difference between life and death."

Kendra couldn't argue with that. Particularly since that life was her own.

Jessie glanced at her and nodded. "I guarantee Lynch would approve."

"At the moment, I don't give a damn what Lynch would or would not approve."

"Oops. You were a little less antagonistic toward me this morning. But I gather Lynch is taking the full brunt?"

"You're not out of the woods yet," she said coolly.

Jessie nodded. "Well, you didn't let me drive. I figured that was a punishment."

Kendra looked at her in exasperation. "It's my car, dammit."

Jessie held up her hand. "It's okay," she said soothingly. "We would have just gotten to L.A. a lot sooner if you'd let me behind the wheel."

"Or ended up in traffic court." She paused. "Are you trying to distract me? You glanced in that rearview mirror twice."

She grinned. "I should have known you'd notice. I didn't think I should worry you. There just appear to be a lot of utility trucks out this morning. But that one got off at the last exit."

"Jessie, since it involves my life and well-being, I do think I should worry, don't you?"

"I stand corrected. In your bad books, but not as deep shit as Lynch. That cover it?"

"That covers it."

"Well, we can get over that." She looked back down at her iPad. "Still no reference to Night Watch on any of these blogs. We need to ask him questions about why he was that secretive. For some reason, he buried his association with them very deep . . ."

After parking on a Figuroa lot, Kendra and Jessie strode through the Dyle Pacific Building's cavernous lobby. It featured three large fountains continuously exchanging short bursts of water that leaped with the intensity of salmon leaping upstream to spawn.

They took the elevator to the nineteenth floor, which was occupied entirely by Dyle's offices. A young man in an elegant brown suit and horn-rimmed glasses lorded over the reception desk, slightly elevated from the rest of the room.

He smiled. "May I help you?"

"We're here to see Ted Dyle," Kendra said.

"Your name?"

"Kendra Michaels."

He checked the screen. "I don't see an appointment for you."

"No appointment. Tell him we have a mutual friend. Dr. Charles Waldridge."

"Mr. Dyle is an extremely busy man. There's no way he can possibly see you unless you have a—"

"Kendra Michaels. Dr. Charles Waldridge. Say those two names to him, and I'll wait right here."

The receptionist didn't like it, but he nodded and spoke into his headset. After a minute or so, he looked up at Kendra and Jessie. "Mr. Dyle may be able to fit you in. If you'll have a seat . . ."

Kendra and Jessie sat in the minimalist waiting area on padded cubes with no backs.

Fifteen minutes passed. Then thirty. Then an hour. Finally, the receptionist leaned toward them. "I'm very sorry. Mr. Dyle will be unable to see you today."

Jessie stood. "You're joking."

Kendra joined her at the reception desk looking toward the hall of offices. "Where is he? Which direction?"

"It won't do any good."

"I'll find out that for myself."

The receptionist said quickly, "He's left the building."

Jessie looked around. "How? The stairs? That's nineteen floors. He must really not to have wanted to see us."

"He has a private elevator. I recommend that you call his assistant next time. I can't guarantee that he'll see you, but at least you won't waste your time."

Jessie's gaze narrowed on his face. "You didn't receive a call telling you that he was unable to see us after an hour's wait. It just came out of the blue. You were told when you contacted him to keep us here for an hour while he left his offices and made his getaway."

"Getaway? Ridiculous. Mr. Dyle is an important businessman, not a hoodlum." But he did not meet her eyes and tapped his headset and turned slightly away. His body language signaled the end of his involvement with them in no uncertain terms.

It was obvious that they weren't going to get anywhere here. Kendra whirled and headed for the elevator. "Great," she said. "Total waste of time. The only thing we learned was that he definitely doesn't want to talk to us about Waldridge. You said you were having trouble finding his home address. It looks like you're going to have to dig deeper. We can't let Dyle skip out on us like—"

"Later." Jessie was looking at her phone as she nudged Kendra onto the elevator and pressed the button. "He may not be first on our agenda right now."

There was something in Jessie's tone that caused her gaze to fly to her face. Jessie's usually impassive expression was still in place, but her eyes were glittering. Excitement? "Later?" Kendra repeated. "You have somewhere else to be?"

"We both do." She was still looking down at her phone. "We'll talk outside." She glanced around as they exited the elevator. "There may be prying eyes and ears here."

Once outside, they walked toward the parking lot in a direction that took them past Pershing Square, an outdoor park outfitted with brightly colored sculptures.

"So where are we going?"

"Back to the car."

"I noticed that. Then where?"

Jessie raised her phone and showed Kendra the screen. "Here."

Kendra looked at her phone. There was a still shot of a man in a half-empty apartment. She looked closer. Could it be . . . ? She stopped, her eyes widening. "Biers?" she said. "This looks like Dr. Hayden Biers."

"That's because it is. Keep moving. We have to get there before he flies the coop."

Kendra hurried after her. "What coop?"

"I planted a couple motion-activated webcams in his apartment in case he showed up. I got a text alert while we were talking to that receptionist upstairs. It looks like he's gathering some of his stuff. Let's see if we can catch him." She held her hands out for the keys. "And I drive."

"You think I can't get us there in a hurry?"

"I'm sure you can. But not fast enough. I can do it faster and in a way that won't get us killed. Trust me."

Kendra was remembering that ride on Jessie's motorcycle that had both terrified her and filled her with admiration. She dropped the keys in Jessie's palm. "A street race may be in order someday."

"I don't believe so." Jessie jumped into the driver's seat. "You have a thing about humiliation."

"Okay, now it's definitely on the books," she said as she buckled the safety belt on her passenger seat.

"You're on. But right now, the only place I'm racing is to Redondo Beach. Get ready to hold on."

True to Jessie's word, it was a wild and woolly ride to Redondo Beach. Jessie whipped through a rear alley just in time to block a blue pickup truck roaring through. The truck braked to a screeching stop.

Before Kendra even realized what was happening, Jessie had thrown open her door and was in the alley, staring down the driver. "Dr. Biers. I need to talk to you."

The man behind the wheel glanced to the rear, as if he might try to back out of the alley.

"No, don't move," Jessie said. "I'm here to help you. Dr. Waldridge hired me to find you."

The man froze. "You know Charles Waldridge?"

Jessie nodded. "I told you, he hired me to find you. He was worried about you."

Biers moistened his lips. "I heard Charles Waldridge is missing."

"And you heard right. He hired me *before* he went missing."

Biers looked at her doubtfully. He then glanced around as if still planning his escape route.

Kendra climbed out of the car. "Dr. Biers . . . Do you know who I am?"

He studied her, then nodded. "Kendra Michaels?"

She nodded. "Were you on my medical team?"

"No. I joined Night Watch a couple of years later. But of course I studied you and your case. To meet you under these circumstances is . . ."

She stepped closer to him. "I'm trying to find Charles. I'm terribly worried about him. We could really use your help."

"It's all I can do to help myself." Biers slumped in his seat. He was in his early forties with a full head of red hair and a matching, close-cropped beard. Kendra was surprised that he didn't speak with a British accent. Canadian, she guessed, probably near Vancouver. "I'm not good at this running. I knew I was taking a chance by coming back here."

"We can help you," Jessie said.

"Help me wind up like Shaw? Or maybe Waldridge?"

Kendra felt a bolt of panic that he'd linked the dead man with Waldridge. "Of course not. We just need to talk to you."

He glanced around again. "Whatever we do, we can't stay here. If you found me, so can they."

"Who's 'they?' " Kendra asked.

"Not here."

"How about my office?" Jessie said. "It's just a few miles down the Pacific Coast Highway in Santa Monica."

Biers thought about it and shook his head. "No offense to either of you, but I'd prefer to stay in slightly more public locations right now."

"No offense taken," Kendra said. "Name a spot where you'd feel comfortable. We'll talk there."

"How about . . . the Redondo Beach Pier. You can't get much more public than that."

Jessie nodded. "Fine. You lead the way."

"WHAT THE HELL IS GOING ON, Dr. Biers?" Jessie asked with her customary bluntness.

Jessie had only waited until she, Kendra, and Biers had staked out a relatively quiet spot toward the end of the pier before she had turned to confront the doctor.

"It's a long story."

Jessie shrugged. "It's why we're here. Start with where you've been."

"Hiding."

"That I figured. But where? And why?"

"I've been in San Clemente. I was sure I'd been found out here, so I immediately took off. I destroyed the disposable phone I'd been using and left without even going back to my apartment. Then when Waldridge disappeared, and Shaw turned up dead, I knew I'd done the right thing."

"But you came back anyway," Kendra said.

"There are some things in my apartment I really wanted to get my hands on. I left with barely the clothes on my back. I broke in through a back window. I thought I could get in and out without anyone's knowing about it. I really didn't think anyone would have twenty-four-hour surveillance on that place."

Jessie smiled. "Two hundred dollars at Best Buy will get you all the surveillance you need. I stashed some motion-activated webcams there. I received a texted photo the second you walked in there."

Biers looked out at the ocean. "Of course. Technology

is making us both safer and less safe at the same time. I'm glad I insisted on getting out of there quickly. Someone else might have done the same thing."

"Possibly. But it hadn't been done when I installed my webcams."

"Please. We need to know what's going on, Doctor," Kendra said.

He turned back toward her. "I'm sorry, but it's hard to know whom to trust. Shaw died trying to protect this project."

"But you know who I am," Kendra said. "You can trust me."

Biers stared at her for a long moment. "Charles Waldridge does think the world of you."

"I feel the same about him. But I can't help him unless I get some answers."

Biers hesitated, then nodded. "How much did Waldridge tell you?"

That Waldridge hadn't trusted her with information would only make him less likely to do so. "I need to hear it from you."

"Everything," Jessie said. "We can't help you if we're stumbling around in the dark."

Biers took a deep breath. "But you'll find a way to keep me safe?"

"I give you my word," Jessie said.

He was silent. "Okay. As you know, the Night Watch Project began with Waldridge and his cornea-regeneration treatment. It was wildly successful, obviously, but the team was soon exploring new frontiers, pushing even more exciting boundaries."

"I don't know, getting my eyesight was pretty exciting for me," Kendra said.

"Of course it was. And it's something that has always been a constant source of inspiration to Waldridge and the team. But just imagine . . . if we could replace any organ in the body at any time. Not just transplants, but perfect genetic replacements."

"Spare parts?" Jessie said.

"To put it crudely, yes. When vital organs are lost to disease, infection, cancer . . . It's often a death sentence. But every cell in your body contains a genetic blueprint to create exact copies of each of your organs. If your liver is dying, what if we could grow a new one exactly like the original? What if we could do the same with your heart? Your kidneys?"

Kendra shook her head. "Sounds like science fiction."

"So did your procedure twenty years ago. This is merely an extension of what Night Watch did with you. It's much more complicated, though, and required more time and resources. Waldridge and Shaw were part of the team from the start, and I joined them later. My specialty was lab-based cellular reproduction."

Kendra couldn't believe it. Yet, if Charles Waldridge was involved, how could she not believe it? "Were you successful?"

"Not at first. There were a lot of hurdles to overcome, not just scientific, but social and moral. There was some question if we should be doing this at all. It was something that never really came up when Night Watch regenerated your corneas. Somehow, that was okay, but the higher-ups got squeamish when it came to generating entire organs. Playing God and all that bullshit. We were just using the blueprint already in the body, but there was still too much controversy. The British government withdrew its support, so Waldridge quietly went elsewhere for financing."

"Ted Dyle," Kendra said.

Biers looked at her in surprise. "Waldridge told you more than I thought."

"Please, go on."

He shifted uneasily. "We weren't the only group working on this. There were—and are—others all over the world, so secrecy was vitally important. We had a lot of failures in the early years, but we eventually got there. Our success rate skyrocketed to well over 98 percent."

"Then why haven't we heard of it?" Jessie asked.

"Well, soon a problem presented itself. The donor recipients were rejecting these organs we felt were an exact match for their originals. Dr. Shaw developed a pair of medications that seemed to solve that problem, but in all likelihood, the patients would have to continue taking those medications for the rest of their lives."

"Seems like a small price to pay," Jessie said.

"Depends on how much the medications' owner decided to charge. Night Watch would own the patent on the medication as well as the original procedure as soon as Waldridge released it to them. Suddenly, the project's investors realized that the real money to be made could come from selling the patients medication for the rest of their lives. If they don't take it, they die. It's the very definition of a captive market."

"Waldridge would never accept that," Kendra said positively. "Not in a million years."

"None of us liked it. We kept working on a way to solve the problem even as it became more and more apparent the project's backers didn't want us to succeed. The Night Watch directors, headed by Dyle, were getting more and more paranoid about security, so they let most of the staff go and put Waldridge, Shaw, and me in an old factory about an hour outside of London. They started requesting more and more documentation, and it became apparent that they were going to move forward with their own plans for the project even though we were very close to finding a solution that would totally negate the need for medication."

"Nice guys," Jessie said.

"They're not, trust me. Not with potentially billions of dollars at stake. They were making veiled threats, so that's when Waldridge, Shaw, and I decided to leave the country on separate planes and hide here in Southern California. The plan was to complete our work here on our own. Waldridge has a fair amount of money from his other patents, so he was going to bankroll us until we licked the problem. Unfortunately, we never got that far."

Kendra nodded. "We know Shaw is dead." She had to ask it. "What about Waldridge?"

"I'm fairly certain he's still alive."

She let out the breath she had been holding as relief soared through her. "Why?"

"Because he has something they need. They would be reluctant to kill him without having it."

"What does he have?"

Biers was silent, then he bent closer to them. "He has the biochemical key that made the whole procedure work in the first place."

Jessie looked at him incredulously. "Nobody else has it?"

"Waldridge developed it. I didn't have it. Shaw didn't have it, and the Night Watch directors certainly didn't have it. They kept demanding we give it to them. Waldridge never trusted them. At first, his fear was corporate espionage, but he later became suspicious of people within our own organization. Good thing, because it may be the only thing keeping him alive right now. If they caught me, I might not last five seconds."

Kendra was starting to shake as she realized what Biers was saying. "Billions of dollars. And they can't touch it without Waldridge. They may be keeping him alive, but there's no doubt they'll be trying to get that information. They'll be torturing him, won't they?"

Biers nodded soberly. "They're probably using every physical and psychological trick in the book to get what they need out of him."

"I *know* him. He's a strong, principled man. He'll die first."

"That's what worries me," Biers said quietly.

"Every physical and psychological trick," Kendra repeated numbly. "Psychological. That's why they tried to take me. They must be having trouble getting him to talk. The threat of violence might not work on him, but they think it might if it was directed at someone he cares about."

He nodded. "Possibly. From what I've heard, there are few people on Earth he cares for more than you, Kendra. You became the symbol of everything he wanted to accomplish in his career, then you became his friend and ally in the fight."

Kendra dug her nails into the railing. "This can't be happening. We have to do something."

"We're doing it," Jessie said. "Everything we can."

"How can you say that? We don't even know where Dyle is keeping him. What they're doing to him right at this minute."

"We'll find out," Jessie said gently. "I can see what this is doing to you. But at least we know what's happening. We can call Griffin and ask him to go after Dyle."

"And what if Dyle stalls him? What's Waldridge going to go through while Dyle tries to get that information from him? He could die."

Jessie turned back to Biers. "But we do have time, right? This all means that they have to keep Waldridge alive."

"Not exactly."

Kendra whirled on him. "What in hell does that mean?"

"There are years of documentation, formulas, and result reports. If they have to reverse-engineer our process, they might be able to do it with enough time and money. They'd probably prefer not to do it, I'm sure. But it could possibly be done. If they decide Waldridge is too much of a liability or just a pain in the ass, they might go that route."

Kendra stared at him, stunned. "So if torture doesn't work, they might kill him. This keeps getting better and better."

"I know," he said sympathetically. "I wish I could give you better news. But you want the truth."

"Yes." But this truth was sending her spiraling into terror.

Detach. Concentrate. She couldn't let her emotions rule her now. Not when Waldridge might need her most.

"I'll call Lynch and tell him what's happening," Jessie said. "This all started in London, so maybe he can find something or someone there to get a lead to Dyle."

"No, I'll call him." Kendra took out her phone and moved down the pier. She could feel the panic rising through the haze of bewilderment surrounding her after listening to Biers's incredible words. "Someone's got to do something. *We've* got to do something. We can't let him die. I won't let that happen."

CHAPTER
15

"IT'S PRETTY MUCH WHAT I thought could be happening," Lynch said slowly when Kendra had finished. "After I found photos in Rye's cloud account that showed incubators with organs in a lab at that factory. It could have been harvesting, and I don't have the medical knowledge to prove that it wasn't. But that wouldn't have been in keeping with the man you believed Waldridge to be, so I had to trust your judgment." He added ruefully, "Which meant I had to discard what seemed the obvious answer and look in another direction. You thought Waldridge was a miracle man, so I had to take a wild leap and start looking for miracles."

She stiffened. "You didn't tell me about any other photos."

"The situation is a little dicey here with SOCA. They're pretty skeptical of miracle cures and wanted to issue warrants for harvesting. I was having trouble convincing them to hold off until I could find some kind of proof one way or the other."

"We still don't have proof. We just have Biers's story. I've been pushing Griffin, but he's not been able to pull up anything on Dyle that's not clean as the proverbial whistle." She shivered. "Harvesting. It's the furthest thing from what Waldridge would ever do. For God's sake, he was trying to *save* lives. Yes, I thought it was a miracle what he did for me. But this is in an entire different class."

"No, just on a bigger scale." He paused. "But I can see how it would increase your hero worship to match that scale. Hell, *I'm* impressed."

"Then find a way to get those British authorities to stop trying to build a case against him." Her mind was leaping forward to scenarios that were far from pleasant. "All he needs is to have Dyle decide he needs a scapegoat, preferably one that permanently disappears, so that Dyle can bring out the Night Watch Project a few years down the road as his own creation."

"Easy. I knew you'd be this upset. That's why I didn't call you until I could give you something concrete that was positive."

"I could use positive at the moment."

"It won't be this moment. But I enlarged the photos of those incubators at the factory lab, and there were minute ID numbers on the sides. I traced the numbers to Cartwright Plastics in Brighton. It's a small company, and there can't be too many orders of the magnitude that Night Watch would need. But they're not real efficient, and they're dragging their feet. I'm driving down there as soon as they open in the morning and applying a little pressure to get them moving."

"You're trying to find out where they delivered them," Kendra said. "And if there might be another lab."

"When they took that equipment from the Croyden factory, they had to put it somewhere. And those organs could be worth millions to Dyle."

"But not the billions he'd net if he gets the answers he wants from Waldridge."

"If I can locate Dyle's employees here, I might be able to get information that would help to find Waldridge," Lynch said quietly. "And the first step is to find where they put those damn incubators. I'll get back to you as soon as I know, Kendra."

"I know you will." She also knew he would be fast and smart and probably come up with all the right answers.

But it might not be in time.

"I can practically hear that mind of yours clicking away, and I'm not liking what it's saying," Lynch said. "Once I locate any of Dyle's people here, that will be the end of it. I'll see that they tell me anything I need to know."

"You'll hurt them," she said dully.

"Yes, if they don't cooperate. Are you going to tell me I shouldn't?"

"No." She swallowed. She had to ask it. "Biers said that Dyle is probably torturing Waldridge. And he said that he might kill him unless he gets what he wants. Do you think that's the truth?"

He was silent.

"Lynch."

"Considering the stakes, it's more than likely the route Dyle will take."

She had known that would be his answer because he was usually honest with her. But she still felt the panic race through her. "Considering the stakes," she repeated unsteadily. "That's all that's important, isn't it? Millions of people suffer or die, a good man who can save them suffers or dies. All because the stakes are so high that it makes it worthwhile to a man who wants to have enough power to rule the whole damn world."

"Did you want me to lie to you? I'll never do that, Kendra. What I will do is knock Dyle down, so that he'll never pick up those stakes. That's all either of us can do right now."

"Of course I don't want you to tell me stories and pat me on the head." She was trying to think through the haze of panic and bewilderment she'd been in since she'd listened to Biers. "But we can't let this happen. Dyle has had it all his own way. He's killed and tortured, and he's made his plans to ruin the lives of all those people whom Waldridge wants to save. And he'll do it if we don't stop him."

"Then we'll stop him," Lynch said. "I'll call Griffin and see if I can put a fire under him. While I'm in Brighton, you go to the FBI field office and ask Metcalf to go with you to question everyone in Dyle's organization to get any idea where he might have gone."

But, again, that would take time.

"Kendra, I know how upset you are. I can *feel* it, dammit." His voice was intense, urgent. "I'll be there as soon as I can. You know that, don't you?"

"I know that, Lynch." She cleared her throat to ease it of the tightness. "Once, a long time ago, I told Waldridge that we'd go have a beer, and I'd toast the existence of miracles. I think this might be the time we might need one." She hung up.

She sat there for a moment, trying to get control. She still felt as if she was in the same shock into which she'd been thrown when Biers had told all the details of Night Watch and what was happening to Charles Waldridge. Speaking to Lynch had not really changed anything. Yes, he had a good lead. Yes, he would follow through with it and probably come up with something that could help them.

But that would not be in an hour or even a day, and she desperately wanted to find Waldridge *now*. She had been so frightened at Biers's words. He had already been missing too long. There was no telling what he was going through now.

But, as she'd told Lynch, it seemed as if it would take a miracle to make that happen.

But miracles could happen. She was a prime example. The blind had been made to see.

She just had to find a way to make this miracle become reality.

She turned and walked back down the pier toward Jessie and Biers.

Detach.

Concentrate.

"DID LYNCH THINK HE COULD HELP?" Jessie's gaze was on her face. "You seem more . . . together." She shook her head. "I don't know. What did he say?"

"I filled him in on everything. He's been following a lead he picked up from Rye's photographs at the old factory. It was a group of incubating organs."

"It was our last group before we left," Biers said.

"The incubators were moved. He's trying to track them to Dyle's men who took them. Can you help him? Was there another facility where the incubators were delivered before they came to you?"

He frowned, thinking. "We never dealt with any of the equipment details. We placed our orders through Dyle, and anything we needed showed up on the loading dock. We were only concerned if it worked properly."

"So the answer's no."

He nodded. "Sorry."

"So am I. Because that means Lynch is going to take too long to see if this search is another blind alley." She turned to Jessie. "And that we can't wait for him to do it. Dyle can't be allowed to do anything more to Charles. We're going to find him right away."

Jessie stiffened. "I don't like this, Kendra. What the hell do you mean?"

"Oh, I knew you weren't going to like it. And I know Lynch would definitely go ballistic."

"I'm under the distinct impression you're about to unload some crazy shit on me."

"You might be right." She smiled mirthlessly. "Desperate times, desperate measures and all that. I can think of only one way to quickly find Waldridge. I have to let them find me."

Jessie's blank expression froze on her face. "Wow. Crazy shit is right. Do you mean what I think you mean? You're going to set yourself up for them to take you?"

"Abduction?" Biers was gazing at her in disbelief. "I thought I'd made it clear what that could mean."

"You also made it pretty clear what it could mean to Charles if we don't get him away from Dyle as soon as possible. It's the only way I can think of to do that."

"Then think again," Jessie said bluntly. "I promised Lynch I'd keep you safe. This could be a suicide mission."

"It's the only way," Kendra repeated. "And I have no intention of doing anything suicidal. They won't hurt me.

They can't if they want to use me as leverage against Waldridge. They need to put me in the same room with him and show that they're willing to hurt me unless he gives them what they want."

"There's no guarantee of that," Jessie said. "They could Skype you in a video call."

"True. But if they're holding him in a secure location, why wouldn't they just take me there, too? It's easier than guarding two people in two different places. The odds are on my side here. And if they're going to inflict some kind of torture on me, it'll have a much greater effect on Waldridge if I'm right there with him."

"Are you listening to yourself?" Jessie asked.

"I did just then." Kendra tried to smile. "Kind of scary."

"Terrifying. And kind of batshit crazy."

"It's not like I'm going in without a net. You'll be tracking me."

"How?"

"You're the private eye. I was hoping you could tell me."

"I'm supposed to help you with this madness? No way."

"I'll do it anyway." She met Jessie's eyes. "Only I might not do it as well without you."

Jessie stared at her in frustration. "You're actually going through with it." She looked away from her. "They'll take your phone and any device that looks like a GPS radio."

"Can't I swallow something or hide one in my hair?"

"Amateur hour for anything electronic." Jessie bit her lip. "When I was Delilah Winter's security director, there was a tech startup in Orange County that was trying to get me to buy their GPS tracker. It goes underneath the skin."

"Does it work?" Kendra asked.

"It seemed to, but power was a problem. It took a special

battery that needed to be taken out and recharged every day or two. I didn't think it was ready for prime time."

"But it could be just what we need," Kendra said.

"No. What we *need* is to get a grip. This is not the answer, Kendra."

"It's the only answer I have." She grimaced. "Believe me, I'm not crazy about it either. If there was any other way, I'd—"

"There is," Jessie said. "We take Dr. Biers here and go talk to the FBI. We let them look for Waldridge."

"We've already discussed all the other options. There's not enough time. If Dyle thinks we might be closing in on him, he might get desperate . . . and reckless. Charles could die."

"So could you."

Biers put his hands on Kendra's upper arms. "Think about it this way. Would Waldridge want you to take this kind of chance on his account? Kendra . . . if he were here, what would he say?"

Kendra gazed at him in disbelief. She was clearly not getting through to him if he thought she was going to be influenced. "What else? He'd say the same thing that Lynch would say. The same thing as Griffin. Stay the hell away."

"Exactly."

Kendra turned back to Jessie. "But why should I start listening to any of them now? I've told you that I'm going to do this one way or another. I could really use your help. If I'm taken, I'll need you to track me and coordinate any rescue with the FBI. I can't tell them about this before it happens. They'd never go for it."

Jessie looked away. "I shouldn't go for it either."

"But you will. Because you know how important this is." She stared her in the eye. "How important *he* is. If not because he's a decent, caring human being, then for what he can give to everyone."

"And maybe because it may be a little important that you get through this alive?"

Kendra smiled. "That's a good reason, too."

Jessie muttered a curse before finally nodding. "Yeah. I'll help."

"Thank you."

"Don't thank me yet. If it gets out that I helped Kendra Michaels get herself killed, it's going to be really bad for business." She added, "And I take it you're not going to let Lynch know about this? That's a mistake. We'll need him."

"We do without him. He'd get in my way."

"That's the truth. He'd never let it happen."

"And that's why you want him here."

"Right."

"We do without Lynch. You don't communicate with him. If he calls you, you don't tell him anything."

"When he finds out, he'll break my neck."

"If you tell him, I'll cross you off and go my own way."

Jessie drew a deep breath. "Shit."

"I agree. But that's the way it has to be." She turned to Biers. "We need to keep you safe. Jessie, can you find a safe house for him?"

"He can stay at my place." She added grimly, "I can't see my being there for the next couple days."

"I can't either," Kendra said. "You need to drop me off at my condo, then get hold of that GPS device."

"You want to go back to San Diego?"

"I want everything to appear normal. I'll go to my studio, take my appointments, and wait." She added, "And after you get me that device, you back off. I don't want anyone to see you near me."

"Kendra."

"Back off."

"Dr. Michaels, this isn't wise," Biers said. "Please. Reconsider."

She shook her head and started down the pier. "I can't reconsider. I won't let this go on."

JESSIE ARRIVED AT KENDRA'S CONDO a little after nine that night. She was carrying a worn leather satchel over her shoulder.

"Did you get it?" Kendra asked.

"I got it." She patted the satchel. "And now I know more about subepidermal tracking devices than I ever wanted to know in my life. They think there could be a big market for parents tagging their children. Those guys are very proud of their gadget."

Jessie rested the satchel on Kendra's dining table and reached into it to produce a small velour box of the size and type one might expect to hold earrings or cuff links. She flipped up the hinged lid and revealed a flat, flesh-toned disk about the size of a quarter.

Kendra picked it up. "This is it?"

"Yes. It goes under your skin, sort of like a pet ID chip. But this is much better. It connects with GPS satellites and continuously transmits your location."

Kendra rested the tiny device on her forearm. "How am I going to get this inside me?"

"I'll make an incision in your hip and slide it in."

"*You're* going to do it?"

"Yes. When they bring it to market, doctors will be doing it. But they showed me some instructional videos. I can do this."

"If you say so."

"I do." Jessie pulled a vial from her bag. "They also gave me a topical solution that numbs the skin and a cover-up to blend it so that it will be completely indiscernible. It shouldn't hurt."

"You don't sound all that certain."

"You're about to go into the lion's den, and you're worried about *this*?"

Kendra made a face. "You're right. Let's get this over with."

Jessie glanced around. "We need a firm surface. Lie on your stomach on the floor."

Kendra stretched out on her rug. Jessie pulled down the edge of Kendra's waistband and rubbed on the topical solution.

"Okay. Do you feel this?" Jessie asked.

"Feel what?"

"You just answered my question. I'm going to just break the surface of the skin with this scalpel and make a small pocket. I guess I should be wearing gloves."

"Now you tell me. I have some latex evidence gloves in the top drawer of my—"

"Too late. I just made the cut."

"Seriously?"

"Yes. And I just slid in the tracker. Now I'm applying something like superglue with antibiotics to close it without stitches."

Kendra looked over her shoulder and saw Jessie peeling off the backing of a square bandage. She applied it and leaned back. "All done. You should be able to take off the bandage tomorrow morning."

"Wow, that was incredible. You missed your calling as a surgeon."

"Nah, I'm just a quick study."

They stood up, and Jessie pulled her iPad from the satchel. She launched an app and stared at the screen. After a moment, a tone sounded, and a green dot pulsed on a map overlay. Jessie pointed at the dot. "This is you. I'll keep checking today and tomorrow to make sure it's working the way it should. It's set to notify me every time you move to a new location."

Kendra studied the screen. "Thanks, Jessie. This makes me feel a lot better."

"It shouldn't. I don't want you to feel better. It's still risky as hell."

And it had been difficult for Jessie to go against her every instinct to help her, Kendra realized. "But then, some people are just worth the risk." She met Jessie's eyes. "Aren't they?"

Jessie opened her lips to reply and closed them again. Then she nodded wearily. "Yeah, they are." She turned and moved back across the room and sat down at the dining-room table. "Okay, come over here and sit down. If I can't talk you out of this, I'm going to go over possibilities you might face in captivity and your best method of overcoming them. I learned a lot while I was being held by the Taliban. Some of it works. Some of it doesn't. But I came prepared tonight if I couldn't talk you out of this. None of what I'm going to say is going to be pleasant, but you're going to listen. And I'm giving you everything I can think of to help you come out of this alive."

Kendra slowly came toward her. Sharing those terrible experiences was going to be painful for Jessie. It would not only stir memories, but reveal her vulnerabilities. It just showed how remarkable a woman she was that she would offer to share them. Kendra sat down opposite her at the table. "I'm listening." She folded her hands on the table and braced herself. "Tell me what I have to know."

JESSIE CALLED KENDRA AT NOON the next day. "The tracking device is operating loud and clear. You're still at your studio?"

"Yes, I'll be here all day and keep my normal appointments. I'll leave at the usual time to go back to my condo."

Silence. "We can still do this some other way, Kendra. Let me, at least, come and stake out your studio. I swear no one will know I'm there."

"And if they do, then they may not come after me. I can't take that chance. This needs to be over."

"I'm good. They'd never know. I swear that—"

"No," she said sharply. "You heard Biers. He said they're probably torturing Charles. He's trying to do something that's going to save the lives of millions of people, and they're *hurting* him."

"I realize that," Jessie said. "And I know how much that's hurting you. But we can go about it another way. Let's scrap all we talked about. Just give me a little time." She paused. "Or let me call Lynch."

"No way. Don't keep bringing it up. I'm not waiting. I can't wait. Monitor that device. When you see where they take me, bring in the troops."

"And what if we're too late?" Her voice was suddenly rough. "For God's sake, you could *die* today, Kendra."

"Then you'd better make sure you're not too late." She drew a deep breath. "But if you are, none of it will be your fault, Jessie. I know you're right. I know that what you're saying is reasonable, but I can't be reasonable right now.

317

I owe Charles too much. I can't stand the thought of their hurting him, perhaps even killing him, because I waited too long."

Jessie was silent. "Crazy." She cleared her throat. "But I see where you're coming from. I just hate it. Call me if you change your mind." She hung up.

Yes, Jessie would understand, Kendra thought as she hung up. She came from a military background and was aware of the duties to family and comrades. And Charles Waldridge was so much more than a comrade to Kendra.

You could die today, Kendra.

That was also true. One faced possible death every day from accidents or illness, but it wasn't often that you knew that you might be seeking it out.

Rye had not known he would find death that night, but he must have realized it might come. Yet he had faced it alone, with no good-byes, like a drop of rainwater merging into a great ocean.

She did not want to be that drop of rainwater. She would do everything she could to stay alive, but she would not leave the people she loved with no good-byes.

She had two hours before her next therapy appointment. Make them count. She sat down at her desk and pulled out a piece of stationary. She started to write.

My dear Olivia,
I hope we'll sit down and laugh when I pull this let-
ter out of the drawer in a week or so. You'll proba-
bly make fun of me, then you'll get angry that I did
something that I thought this might be necessary.
But just in case, my friend, I wanted to tell you how
much you've meant to me through all these years.

*You were the light in my darkness, the warmth when
I was cold, the humor when I took myself too seriously. And so many other things that made my life
worth living . . .*

It was almost twilight.

All the therapy sessions completed. Everything she'd
planned to do was done. Time to close up the studio for
the day.

Only one more thing to do before she left the studio.
No letter for her mother. Kendra wanted to hear her voice.

She dialed the number at the hotel in Denver where her
mother was attending her seminar.

Noise.

Voices.

Then Dianne came on the line. "Kendra, I meant to call
you, but things are so busy here. No one I called at the universities in England know anything about Waldridge, but
I'll still keep—"

"It's okay, Mom. Lynch is over there now, and he'll take
care of it."

"Have you heard from Waldridge?"

"Not yet. I just wanted to ask how things were going at
the seminar."

Silence. "What difference does it make how things are
going here?" Dianne asked. "Why are you even asking? I
know you must be sick with worry about Waldridge. No
progress at all?"

"We've found out a few things that might be promising. And your seminar *is* important, everything you do is
important to me." She tried to keep her voice light. "Why
shouldn't it be? When I should have been the bane of your

life, you made me feel that I was always special and loved. You said you remembered that day that I first saw your face, Mom. I remember it, too." That day was suddenly with her once again, and she could see Dianne walking toward her at Piccadilly Circus. "I don't think I told you, but I thought, 'This must be what love looks like.' Pretty soppy, huh?"

"Kendra, what the *hell* is wrong?"

She'd better get off the phone quickly. Dianne was too smart not to pick up on any false notes, and Kendra was dropping them right and left. "And then you told me I had to call Waldridge and let him join us. I'll always remember we were there together. He was almost as important to you as he was to me."

"Why do you sound like this? Has something happened to Waldridge?"

"I don't think so. I hope not." She was completely blowing it. "I believe everything will be fine. Look, I have to hang up. I have somewhere I have to go. I love you, Mom." She hung up.

A complete disaster, she thought, as she got to her feet. She'd probably sent her mother into a panic. She should have written her a letter as she had Olivia. So much for leaving a memory behind for the people you love.

Maybe a drop of rainwater in a great ocean wasn't so bad.

But it would have been for her, and it might have been for her mother and Olivia.

And now it was time to forget about memories and good-byes and concentrate on life. That call had probably been foolishness anyway. She had no intention of letting Dyle kill either her or Waldridge. Charles Waldridge was too important to the world and, dammit, she was important to her own world, too.

A moment later, she was locking up the studio and facing the deserted parking lot. All the tenants had left for the day, and there was only silence and shadows.

Last night she had told herself that she would face the fear and shadows today, and here they were.

She felt her heart beating hard in her throat. Logically, she knew this was the quickest way to find Waldridge, but she knew the odds weren't wonderful and could always get worse. What if Dyle turned out to be some nut job who now thought the most effective means of persuasion would be to present Charles with her head? The possibility certainly existed.

You could die today.

But she wasn't going to die. She was going to find Charles Waldridge, the man who had given her so much. She was going to pay back just a little of that debt today. She started across the parking lot.

Her gaze searched the shadows as she approached her car. *Come on, you assholes. Come and get me.*

She opened her car door. She looked around the parking lot again. It obviously wasn't happening. Not here, not now.

She was depressed and relieved at the same time.

Damn.

She started the car and drove out of the parking lot.

As she made her way through the city streets, she was tense, her eyes searching. There was no sign of any of the vehicles that had been following her in the past few days. No black panel van. No white utility truck.

She felt a chill.

Maybe it was because they didn't need her anymore.

The thought brought immediate panic.

Maybe they had already gotten what they wanted from Waldridge . . . Or for a much worse reason. She didn't even want to consider that possibility.

She turned down Fourteenth Street to cut over toward her condo. Orange construction cones narrowed the one-way street to one lane, not an unusual occurrence in downtown San Diego. Just before she reached F Street, a large truck backed up from an alley, blocking her way.

Damn.

She checked her rearview. It was a one-way street, but maybe she could still—

Another truck blocked the street immediately behind her.

"What in the . . ."

Crash.

Her driver and passenger windows smashed open simultaneously, and before she could register the twin events, gloved hands reached in and gripped the inside door handles with well-rehearsed precision. They threw open the doors, and two masked, black-clad men jumped inside.

She tried to scream, but there was something over her mouth. She instinctively fought, her fists striking out hard as one of the men was suddenly on top of her. Her hand clawed at his mask, and she tore it off. White hair, gray eyes . . . "Bad move, Kendra," he murmured. "I've been eager to meet you, too. But now isn't the time. That's for later." Then the cover over her mouth was drawn higher, over her nose, then her eyes, then her entire head. A hood, she realized.

She struggled to breathe. She kicked and clawed at the darkness until something pricked at her right forearm.

Suddenly, she couldn't move. It was as if the darkness had become solid, totally encasing her, burying her.

For a moment, she felt sheer panic as she struggled against her tomb.

Then she felt nothing at all.

CHAPTER
16

WHAT THE HELL?

Lynch glanced down at the caller ID on his phone, and he was not liking what he saw.

Dr. Dianne Michaels.

Any way he looked at it, this was not good.

"Hello, Dianne. This is a surprise. I don't even recall your having my number. What's the—"

"I didn't." Kendra's mother's voice was angry, strained, and brimming with tension. "I've spent the last two hours talking to those idiots at the FBI and trying to find someone there who had it. They acted as if I were some kind of threat to you. I finally reached Griffin and made him give it to me."

"Made? Griffin seldom permits himself to be made to do anything. You must have been—"

"Shut up. Let me talk. Why the hell are you in London when you should be here taking care of Kendra? I've never thought it a good idea for you to be anywhere near her, but she says that you're valuable. Well, you're *not* valuable if you're thousands of miles away from her."

"It was necessary that I come here to—" He broke off as the underlying reason for Dianne's call became clear to him, and he cut to the chase. "And why should I be there taking care of Kendra, Dianne?"

"Because she phoned me two hours ago, and now she won't pick up my calls."

"And why are you so concerned about it that you caused an uproar at the FBI?"

"It was a good-bye call, dammit. She was telling me good-bye."

Lynch froze. Don't panic. "Is that what she said?"

"No, she asked me about my damn seminar. She told me how much I'd meant to her over the years. She was loving and awkward, and it was a good-bye."

"You could be mistaken."

"I know my daughter. Good-bye. She thought there could be a reason that she might not get another chance to say it. Now why the hell did she make that call? Why is she in so much trouble, and you don't even know about it? Or do you know and don't give a damn?"

"I give a damn. What else did she tell you?"

"Just that you were in London. And something about how Waldridge had been so important to both of us. She tried to keep it light, but there was no way. She's never been any good at pretending." She paused. "And she said that she loved me." She cleared her throat. "That's what it was mostly about. She didn't want to leave me without a good-bye. Now, dammit, tell me what's happening."

"I don't know." But she was frantic, and he had to tell her something. "Waldridge is being held somewhere, and we haven't found out where. She was concerned."

"She's still concerned," Dianne said. "It's tearing her apart. And I'm not sure that she hasn't found out where he is."

That's what Lynch feared, and it was bringing up a nightmare scenario. "It's a possibility."

"Screw possibilities." Her voice was shaking. "It was good-bye. And why in hell are you still over there?"

"Because she didn't call *me* to say good-bye. She left me completely in the dark. I don't know what's happening. I'll call you back as soon as I do." He hung up.

He took a deep breath. He'd like to think that Kendra's mother was reacting emotionally but without reason. But he was scared to death that wasn't true. Dianne was not only brilliant, she had strength and good common sense. And the bond between her and Kendra was so close that she would recognize and identify what Kendra was attempting to do in any given situation.

Good-bye.

"Shit." He reached for his phone and called Kendra.

No answer.

He hadn't thought there would be. She'd evidently wanted to be off radar after she'd talked to her mother.

He dialed Jessie Mercado.

No answer.

He dialed her again.

She picked up the phone on the sixth ring. "You've heard from Kendra's mom, too? I just got off the phone with Griffin. That's why I didn't pick up right away. He'd evidently taken a lot of abuse from her and wanted to know what the hell Kendra was doing." She paused. "It took a little while to tell him. I had to let him know everything, so he'd realize that he'd have to pull out all the stops to work with us. He didn't like my answer."

"I probably won't either."

"No, you won't. You were first on Kendra's list of those I couldn't talk to about it."

"Kendra's mother was almost hysterical. Why did Kendra call her?"

"I didn't know Kendra intended to phone her, but I can see it. Kendra knew exactly what she was getting into. Maybe she wanted to prepare her."

"Prepare her for what?"

"Kendra staked herself out so that Dyle's men would find it easy to take her. She had me place a transmitter under her skin, so we'd be able to track her location."

Lynch began to curse. "I might just strangle you. Why did you let her do it?"

"I couldn't stop her. Do you think I didn't try? She was afraid Waldridge would die. She kept saying that we had to move faster."

"And you couldn't call me and let me try?"

"Not if I wanted her to not walk away from me and do it by herself. Waldridge means a lot to her."

"I know. What's happening? How much time do I have to get hold of her and persuade her to—"

"It's already gone down, Lynch."

He froze. "What are you saying?"

"An hour ago, her car was involved in an accident near her condo. When the police got to the scene, Kendra was gone and so were the passengers of the truck. A witness said that the woman in the Toyota was removed from the scene by two masked men who took her away in the truck."

"My God, Jessie."

"I know," Jessie said harshly. "Do you think I don't know that I should have been able to stop this somehow? I risked having her find out that I was keeping an eye on the studio. But she would have realized that I was following her car. She was on the alert and watching. She was ready for it."

"And she got it," he said grimly. "I'll catch the first flight out of Heathrow and be there asap. You've brought Griffin on board? When did you get the first GPS transmission after the accident?"

"We had a steady reading for thirty minutes after she was taken. They were heading east. Out of the city."

He tensed. "Only thirty minutes?"

Jessie didn't answer.

"Jessie."

"We didn't receive anything after that." Jessie paused. "The device doesn't appear to be functioning anymore."

WALDRIDGE WAS SITTING BESIDE Kendra when she opened her eyes.

"Hello," he said softly. "This is not how I wanted us to meet again." His hand reached out to gently stroke her hair back from her forehead. "Believe me, I did everything I could to prevent it, Kendra."

He was *alive*.

Through the dizziness that was still clouding her mind, that was the only thing that was clear and important. His face looked leaner, there were circles beneath his eyes, his lower lip was split. But she reached up to touch his hand, and it was warm and strong and *alive*. "Are you okay?"

"Shh." His lips tightened. "That's what I should be asking you. You were out longer than you should have been from that shot those gorillas gave you. It was beginning to worry me. It was too much to hope that they knew what they were doing. If they'd overdosed, they could have killed you."

The truck. The two men running toward her, the smothering black hood. "Well, evidently they didn't do that." She tried to sit up, but another wave of dizziness swept over her. "Bathroom," she gasped. "I have to throw up." She struggled to get to her feet.

"It's across the lab." Charles was beside her, holding her as he hurried her across the room. "Damn, I knew they'd screw up the injection."

She'd reached the bathroom, and she slammed the door and headed for the toilet. When she'd finished, she splashed water in her face, grabbed the glass on the vanity, and rinsed her mouth.

"Kendra. Open this door. I'm a doctor, for God's sake. Are you okay?"

She opened the door. "No, but better. Still dizzy." She was weaving her way back across the lab toward the cot. He slipped his arm around her waist until she reached the cot and he got her settled. She closed her eyes for an instant. "Do you know what they gave me?"

"Yes. Pentobarbital. Ted Dyle gave me a blow-by-blow description of how they intended to take you." His lips curled bitterly. "He wanted to make sure I knew how helpless I was to stop anything he chose to do. That's been his latest game plan." He added harshly, "I was praying that he wouldn't be able to pull it off. You're so damn smart, you had to know there would be a threat to you. I knew there wasn't a chance that you wouldn't be searching for me. I was just hoping that you'd realize you'd have to watch out for yourself."

"You're right, there wasn't one single chance in the universe I wouldn't try to find you." She shook her head to clear it and looked around. She'd been aware they were in a lab of some sort. Now she saw that it was a large laboratory, with long worktables containing test tubes, incubators, instruments, and other equipment. A desk with a computer occupied the far wall. No other furniture except the cot on which she was lying. "And I do watch out for myself." Her gaze was still scanning her surroundings. "Dyle didn't give you very luxurious quarters, did he?"

"He considered the cot a luxury. He didn't want me to do anything but work."

"Do you know if this room is bugged?"

"It's not. I checked it when I first got here. No reason. Dyle wanted me to perform, demonstrate, step by step. He wanted to film and document so that it could be repeated." He grimaced. "And I guarantee he knew that the formulas I'd created were too complicated for me to mutter them in my sleep."

She nodded. "Okay, then I guess we're safe to talk here." She looked at the teak door closest to them. "How long do you think they'll leave us alone?"

"I have no idea. You've been unconscious for hours, much longer than they expected. One of the guards came in ten minutes ago to check on you." His lips twisted. "And Dyle might want me to sit here for a while and worry a bit about you. A softening process. That's what this is all about, you know. Nothing else has worked for him, so he thinks that I might cave if he uses some of his charming methods on you." His hand tightened on hers. "God, I didn't want you here."

"But here I am." She tried to smile. "And Dyle is a fool if he believes that you'd give up all you've worked for to keep me safe. You've always known what's important and how to balance that against the risks you had to take."

"And you're just another risk?" He shook his head. "I might have a problem with this particular risk. And Dyle knows it. He knew that night I let you slip away from the program in Monterey. Why do you think that I didn't contact you for all those years? You were a potential weapon he could use against me. I've known for years that Night Watch could become a monster." His gaze was holding her own. "But, Kendra, the *potential*. It could also become a God that could save lives. I could see it shining and, with every advance I made, it became stronger, brighter. I couldn't let it go."

"I know you couldn't. No one would want you to give it up." She smiled. "Miracles, Charles."

"Which are now being hijacked by the monster. And you may be one of the victims."

"Then we have to make certain the hijack doesn't come off. Which means that we have to get you out of this place. That's why I had to be here."

"What?" He was gazing at her with horror. "Shit. Don't tell me that you deliberately let yourself be taken. I don't want to hear it."

"You *will* hear it. You'd been gone too long, and it was getting increasingly dangerous for you. Biers said that you could be killed and were probably being tortured. We had to get you out."

"Biers? You talked to Biers? When?"

"Yesterday. Jessie Mercado finally located him. He'd been in hiding since he reached California and found Shaw was dead."

"He's safe? I thought he might be dead, too. Dyle kept telling me how he'd gotten rid of all the scientists on the project except me. It was another way to isolate me."

"He's safe. Jessie stashed him in her apartment. After he told us what was going on with Night Watch . . . and you. He said he could only make guesses, but he assumed that you might still be alive since you were the linchpin of the project." She gazed searchingly at him. "He also thought you were probably being . . . hurt." She lifted her hand and touched his cut lip. "He was right?"

"That was just a little initiation to show me possibilities." He made a face. "Dyle got much more innovative after the first session. He got someone who knew about the chemical injections used on prisoners in Iran. Extremely painful, like pure fire in the veins and able to be repeated frequently without danger of heart attack or brain damage. Dyle particularly didn't want to risk brain damage."

"My God. How could you stand it?"

"Oh, I was a complete coward." He smiled wryly. "No stalwart Navy-SEAL attitude for me. I'm a scientist, for God's sake. They had me crying like a baby."

"But you didn't give in to him."

"Maybe I got used to it."

"Yeah, sure." She repeated softly, "Coward? And you wouldn't have told him what he wanted to know no matter what he did to you."

"Well, it helped that I thought that after he got what he wanted, he'd kill me anyway. You're making me out to be some kind of hero." He smiled faintly. "You always made that mistake. I'm only a man who has a skill and sometimes a dream. I'm flawed in so many ways. I'm driven, and sometimes I can be ruthless. I've never been able to maintain relationships unless they were connected to my work. I'm a workaholic, and I expect everyone around me to be as—"

"I always knew you were no hero," she interrupted. "I wasn't that blind. But I learned who and what you were, and that was always enough for me. And I'm learning more all the time, so stop treating me as if I'm a gullible child.

Yes, I came because I owe you. But I also came because you're one of the good guys. There aren't that many left in the world. We have to make sure that they don't become extinct. So stop lecturing me on why I shouldn't have come to help you, and let's think of a way to do it. You said you don't know how much time we have."

He was silent; and then he nodded. "Point taken." Another pause. "And if you decided to bust me out of this place, I trust you have a plan or assistance?"

"I thought I had." Now that the haziness was dissipating, she realized that she was experiencing a dull throbbing ache in her left side. Not good. There had been no pain after the first few hours when Jessie had inserted the device. She shifted and pulled her shirt out of her pants.

A bandage was taped over the incision formerly containing the device. "Shit!" She ripped it off and looked down at the neatly stitched wound. "A GPS device was inserted under the skin that should be sending out a message to Jessie and the FBI. It looks as if it was found and removed."

"Let me take a look." He moved closer and examined the wound. "At least, it looks clean and professionally stitched. As I said, those goons Dyle has working for him aren't usually this careful."

"Jessie made it almost impossible to detect. I was hoping that . . ." She shook her head. "We'll just have to find another way."

"So you're caught, too. Dyle is always careful. He must have run a test and found that signal. You're lucky he didn't have his men just rip it out. As I said, some of them are gorillas."

Yes, she was caught. The only ace in the hole she'd possessed was no longer available. So find another way to go.

And that other way was sitting in front of her.

Charles Waldridge.

"I'm sure you've not just been sitting here waiting for someone to rescue you, Charles. You were here, observing, paying attention to routine. What were you going to try as soon as you got the opportunity?"

His lips tilted up at the corners. "No, I wasn't just sitting around waiting. Dyle managed to keep me fairly occupied in the last few days."

Torture. She didn't want to think about that right now. It made her too upset. "That wouldn't have stopped you from thinking of ways and means. What can we use?"

"I do love the way you discard inessentials and go for the jugular." He shrugged. "I've played over a dozen escape scenarios in my mind, but unfortunately most of them result in my violent death."

"Okay, we can immediately eliminate those. What about the ones that *don't* end with your dying?"

"Still problematic. But there are some things in our favor. This facility seems to be operating on a skeleton crew. At any given time, there are only perhaps four armed guards present."

"Only?"

"Dyle could afford an army, but I'm guessing he wants to minimize the number of people who know about this operation. They're probably private security officers he uses in his riskier overseas trouble spots. As far as I can tell, John Jaden runs the entire team. White hair, tan, gray eyes, about forty. He has a special place in Dyle's organization."

Kendra stiffened. "I think he must have been one of the men who took me. I recognize the description. What kind of special place?"

"He's a combination of enforcer and executive trouble-shooter. I only knew him in the latter role when I was in London. It was only when Dyle decided he needed more firepower after we took off for California that Jaden showed his true spots. He's quiet, superb at his job, intimidating in an iceman kind of way. He sometimes leaves the team and does private jobs for Dyle." He added grimly, "I'd bet Shaw was one of those jobs. It was Jaden who took me down in my hotel room that night. I didn't have a chance against him. It wouldn't surprise me if he was the one who planned and carried out your abduction. Dyle was very disappointed that the first attempt against you failed. He'd want a sure thing this time."

"Anything else?"

"Only that each one of those men carries an automatic rifle."

". . . which brings us back to your violent-death scenarios."

"Exactly."

Kendra glanced around. The two entrances were situated on each end of the long room. "Any idea what's on the other side of these doors?"

"They always come and go from the door on the far side. That's the central living area. I assume the other one leads to another room or perhaps another building."

Kendra turned back and looked at the door behind her. She shook her head. "There's been a tiny bit of sand tracked in from that entrance. It probably leads outside."

She squinted at the light brown walls. "What kind of building is this?"

"Prefab carbon fiber. Light, but very strong. It's easy to transport and assemble on-site, often used in military operations. An entire village can be erected in just a few hours."

She reached out toward the nearest wall and drummed her fingers against it. It felt almost like plastic. She turned back to Waldridge. "Could an acid weaken these walls?"

"Afraid not. Carbon fiber is extremely resistant to chemical attacks. It's very similar to sturdier metals in that respect."

She nodded. "Damn."

Waldridge stepped back toward the workbenches. "But I think you're on the right track. They've given me a fairly well-equipped lab that could work to our advantage. Properly combined, chemicals can be awesome weapons. The problem is, we still need a way out. Brute force isn't going to do much for us against those automatic weapons."

"I might have that part covered," she said quietly.

"What do you mean?"

She opened her hand to show him a small rubber capsule, about an inch long. "I swallowed this before I was taken."

"What is it?"

She tore open the capsule. "Have you ever heard of a bump key?"

"Can't say that I have."

"Neither had I until Jessie decided she had to pull out all the stops and get me something more than that GPS to keep us alive. She'd used it in Afghanistan. It's a specially cut key that you insert and strike as you turn it. Each strike causes the tumblers to jump for a moment, just long enough to enable the lock to be thrown."

"It actually works?"

"According to Jessie, it works on about 95 percent of the locks out there."

"And you have one?"

"I have six. All contained in this capsule. It has to be the right size as the lock you're trying, so I brought an assortment. Jessie got them for me and showed me how to do it." She glanced at the doors on each end of the lab. "There's a good chance it will work here."

Waldridge looked at the keys in her hand. "You regurgitated that capsule when you first woke up . . ."

"I really wasn't all that nauseous. I just had to get it out."

"You might have told me."

"I didn't know if the place was bugged or anything about the situation."

He smiled. "You did come prepared for a rescue mission."

"Sorry I couldn't swallow an AK-47." She walked over to the workbench. "So assuming I can get us through that door, what do you have in mind for those chemicals?"

"I'll show you later. But we'll need to be very careful with them. Volatile."

"What isn't in this situation? I'll leave it to you. If it's got to be done, we'll do it." She looked down at her side. "But everything would have been simpler if I could have managed to keep that device." Her glance lifted to him again. "You're all right? Once we get out of here, you'll be able to function? That stuff they gave you didn't cause you any internal damage? You said not to the heart or brain, but anywhere else?"

He tilted his head. "What would you do if I said it had?"

"I'd have to adjust to the situation." She moistened her lips. "But it would scare me and make me angry."

He smiled. "And make you go after the bad guys for me?"

"Not right away. I'd need to get you somewhere safe

first. But I have someone who would show me how to do it later."

"Amazing," he said gently. "You must tell me about that someone. But I'm more interested in your dedication to punishing my oppressors. I feel honored."

"Bullshit." She braced herself. "Now, is there any immediate or permanent damage?"

"No. Weakness and soreness after the convulsions caused by the shots, but no damage. I'd be able to keep up with you, Kendra."

She breathed a sigh of relief. "That's good. I don't know what we'll be facing once we get—"

Kendra was startled by the sound of the dead bolt being thrown on the large door at the far end of the lab. The door suddenly opened, and two men with automatic rifles shoved a third man into the room.

The third man wore a dark hood identical to the one that had been placed on Kendra. His hands were bound behind his back, and he fell to his knees.

The men with the rifles left the room and locked the door.

"Friend of yours?" Waldridge asked Kendra.

"No," Kendra said as she moved toward the prisoner. "But I think he may be a friend of yours."

She pulled off the hood.

It was Hayden Biers.

He was dressed just as Kendra had last seen him, but his shirt was now torn and showed several bloodstains on the chest and collar. His hair was covered in perspiration.

Waldridge turned to Kendra. "You said he was safe."

"I thought he was." She picked at the duct tape binding his hands behind him, but wasn't able to loosen it. "Dr. Biers?"

"Kendra . . . I'm sorry." He tried to stand, but fell weakly back to his knees.

Waldridge quickly stepped toward him. "Take it easy, Hayden. It may take a few minutes."

Biers looked up at Waldridge as he approached. "Charles . . . I was afraid you were dead."

Waldridge grimaced. "Not yet. But Dyle is constantly persevering toward that aim."

"What happened?" Kendra asked.

Biers shook his head. "They knew Jessie Mercado was looking for me. I suppose they were watching her home and office. They grabbed me in her apartment." His gaze shifted to Waldridge. "I'm sorry, Charles. I had one job, and it was to not let myself get caught."

Waldridge shrugged. "I obviously didn't do so well at that job either."

The dead bolt rapped, and the door was once more thrown open. This time Ted Dyle entered the room. But the two men with automatic weapons were a silent threat behind him. Her gaze flew to the guard on his right. White hair, gray eyes, fortysomething . . . It was the man she'd seen when she'd been taken. That must be John Jaden. She could see how he might be in charge. There was a quiet air of authority about his demeanor and the coldness was also evident. Iceman . . .

"Good evening, Dr. Michaels." Dyle was dressed more casually than in the photo Kendra had seen, in which he was wearing a suit. Here he wore slacks and a white pullover shirt. His sleek dark hair was as carefully barbered as she remembered from that night in Monterey. "I see you're with us again. It's delightful to meet you at last. Though I've always been a fan from the first time I heard you speak. Inspiring. Really inspiring."

"And did I say all the things you wanted me to say? I understand that you were forcing Dr. Waldridge to make me dance on your strings."

"Not true, Kendra," Charles said. "They were *my* strings, and I was careful to make sure that nothing you said would be against your principles. Dyle merely wanted Night Watch to become a household name, and I could go along with that." He met Dyle's eyes. "As long as he realized that I had full control of any project in which I was involved."

"The man who pays the bills makes the rules," Dyle said. "Stubborn. Incredibly stubborn. Eventually, you'll come to realize that." He turned back to Kendra. "Did you enjoy your time with Waldridge? I wanted to give you a little time to become reacquainted. By the way you were tearing around L.A. and San Diego trying to find him, I gather you wanted that desperately."

"You're fully aware how grateful I was to Waldridge. You were there from the beginning."

"Really before the beginning of your association. I was there with the money when he was developing that stem-cell operation. I thought it had great promise. Not wonderful monetary potential, but I could see what Waldridge was working on down the road and that you were only the beginning." He inclined his head. "Quite a splendid beginning. I was very upset when Waldridge let you run out on us."

"You mean and actually have a life?"

"Debts must be paid. I've been trying to demonstrate that to my friend, Waldridge, during our time together, but he's not being reasonable." He smiled broadly as his gaze shifted from her to Waldridge, then Biers. "The band is back together. Or at least two of the three. Regrettable that Dr. Shaw couldn't join us."

"Enjoying this, Dyle?" Waldridge took a step toward him, but one of the armed guards motioned him back with his gun. "Yes, I think you are. You want to grandstand in front of a new audience instead of our usual more intimate sessions? I'll play along. You wanted to point out that you'd killed Shaw, a brilliant man who wanted only to make his work mean something? We get it."

A flash of anger crossed Dyle's face. "Perhaps if the three of you hadn't left with my intellectual property, it wouldn't have been necessary."

"It was never supposed to be just a vehicle for your pharmaceutical-sales division."

"I have a right to earn back my investment."

"You already would have done that thousands of times over," Biers muttered.

"Thousands of times versus millions of times," Dyle said. "What sounds like a more prudent business plan to you? Especially if the second questionable option requires even more research and development."

"I told you we could do it," Waldridge said. "No side effects, no lifetime dependence on our medication."

Dial shook his head. "I made a financial decision. Sorry you didn't agree. My only regret is that I let you squirrel away our project's formulas."

"You didn't *let* me do anything. The project is virtually mine anyway. I had to protect it. I could see where this was headed."

"You're holding the process hostage. We could be helping people right now."

"And then hold *them* hostage. How many times have we

gone over this? You're not getting it until it's finished," Waldridge said. "My way."

"You son of a bitch." Kendra could see that Dyle's sleek mask had vanished, and he was practically trembling with rage as he stepped closer to Waldridge. "Always have to be the great man, don't you?" He was glaring at him. "You've always been so quick to take the credit for Dr. Michaels's miracle of sight. But too often, you've happily ignored the fact that none of it would be possible without funding." Dyle turned toward Kendra, and she took an instinctive step back as she saw the sheer malevolence in his expression. "I paid for those eyes of yours, Dr. Michaels. If your idol here doesn't see fit to give me what's mine . . ." Dyle turned back toward Waldridge, and spat out, "I must insist on taking them back."

Kendra recoiled in shock. She couldn't breathe. She could only stare at Dyle.

Nightmare. Her worst nightmare . . .

She was barely aware that Waldridge had gone still beside her. "What are you saying?"

Dyle smiled. "Do I really need to say it? I believe I've made myself clear."

"Yes," Kendra said unsteadily. "Say it."

"I'm certain you've already researched me enough to know who I am, Dr. Michaels. I'm a man who gets what he wants. And if I don't get what I want from Dr. Waldridge, I'm going to take your eyes." His voice was soft, full of venom. "First your right eye, then your left eye. Is that clear enough for you?"

"You're a monster," Biers said. "We were right about you. That's why we left."

Dyle ignored him. His gaze was fixed on Waldridge's face. "One hour," Dyle said. "Then I'll come back and take

Kendra's right eye. No anesthesia. I want both of you to feel every cut. If you want to stop me, you'd better get to work, Waldridge."

He turned and walked toward the door, his whole bearing brimming with arrogance and self-satisfaction. He thought he'd played the winning card, Kendra could see. He didn't care that card was hideous and the stuff of her worst nightmares. Perhaps he had won, she was too shaken right now to tell. But she couldn't let him leave this room with a complete victory.

"Wait." Kendra stepped toward Biers. "Take your errand boy with you, Dyle. If you intend to blind me again, I don't want one of the last things I see to be this scum. I can't stand to look at him."

Dyle turned. "Excuse me?"

"Biers has been working with you." She stared at Biers. "I don't know for how long, but I'm guessing it's been since before these three men left England. It's how you were able to find Shaw and Waldridge so easily."

Waldridge's gaze was narrowed on her face. "Kendra?"

She nodded. "I'm sorry, Charles. You trusted the wrong man. Biers is in Dyle's pocket. He's playing you."

Dyle smiled. "What makes you say that, bitch?"

"I know he's been here before," Kendra said. "He probably even set up this lab. For all your precautions with the hood over my head, I know we're about ninety miles east of San Diego, somewhere in the Anzo-Borrego Desert."

"Interesting," Dyle said. "I hadn't heard that an uncanny sense of directions was among your gifts."

"It isn't. Everyone who has walked in this room has been tracking in a coarse sand that is only found there, at least in this part of the country. The remains of thousands of years of underwater life. It's very distinctive. There are granules wedged in the ridges above your soles."

Dyle looked down. "What does that have to do with—"

"Biers had the same granules wedged in his shoes when I first met him. He'd already been out here." She turned to Biers. "You wanted us to find you at your apartment. You knew Jessie would somehow be watching your place."

"That's it?" Dyle said. "Sand?"

"That, and Biers was the only other person who knew about the tracker that Jessie put in me." She felt her hip. "It was cut out of me before I even woke up. He had to have told you. Or maybe he did it himself. Charles said someone who knew what he was doing did the stitches. Did you bring him in here to put more pressure on Waldridge? Another friend whom only he can save if he gives you what you want?"

Waldridge looked at Biers with disgust. "Get on your feet, Hayden. You can stop the act now."

Still on his knees, Biers glanced at Dyle. Dyle gave Jaden an impatient gesture, and Jaden pulled Biers to his feet and cut the duct tape binding his wrists. Biers rubbed his wrists and brushed himself off before smiling at Kendra. "I did do the removal." He reached in his pocket and pulled out the small disc. He showed her the tracker and the thin battery he'd removed from it. Then he slipped the items back in his pocket. "You're lucky that Dyle told me to do it. You might have ended up with blood poisoning. Dyle's men are good with knives, but not in that capacity. Not that it would have made much difference at this point."

"I trusted you," Waldridge said to him. "Why?"

"That was your mistake," Dyle said. "Not everyone see the world the same as you do, Waldridge."

Waldridge was still staring at Biers. "Shaw is dead be

cause of you. As surely as if you pulled the trigger your-self."

Biers shook his head. "Shaw was a foolish old man. He sealed his own fate, just as you did. We were all partners in this project. Yes, you were the guiding force and held the patents. But you had no right to hijack it."

"You never told me you felt this way."

"Would it have changed anything?" Biers didn't wait for a response. "Of course not. You would just have cut me out of your plans. I was better off with Dyle. He said that he'd make me a minor partner. Do you know how much money that will mean?"

"May I point out that your time is growing shorter with each passing word," Dyle said as he glanced at Kendra. "Come along, Biers. I believe your colleague has some soul-searching to do."

Biers avoided Waldridge's and Kendra's eyes as he fol-lowed Dyle out of the lab. One of the guards followed him, but Jaden didn't move, his gaze fixed on Kendra.

She instinctively tensed. The ordeal wasn't over. "What do you want, Jaden?"

He smiled. "I just wanted to tell you that I'm glad you're here. I was amused to see how you saw through Dyle's little trick. I always knew you'd be clever. I was looking forward to the challenge of taking you out. But then Dyle changed his mind and robbed me of the pleasure."

"Changed his mind?"

"When you were doing the publicity circuit all those years ago, Dyle was thinking that Waldridge might need a martyr scenario to drive him deeper into the Night Watch Project. The death of his pride and joy, supposedly com-mitted by a hate group like the one who was fighting to make the government shut down the research? Anyway, you seemed to be the perfect candidate. He genuinely cared about you. But then Waldridge let you go about your merry way, and Dyle decided his commitment wasn't strong enough to go through with it." He smiled, his silver gray eyes glowing with malice. "But that's all changed now, hasn't it?" He turned toward the door. "With an interesting variation. I wonder if Dyle will assign me to be the one who takes out your eyes . . ." A moment later, she heard the door lock behind him.

Shock on top of shock. "Dear God, Charles. Eight years? Even that far back?"

"I had suspicions, but no knowledge of this kind of . . . evil. I just didn't like the *feel* of it. And I wanted you to be free to enjoy your life."

"And you let me go."

"It appears we were both lucky it was a joint decision."

"Yes . . . lucky." Shock and revelations and that last confrontation with Biers and Dyle were taking their toll. She felt limp now, her knees trembling. What good had any of it done? The situation was still basically the same.

No, it wasn't the same. She didn't feel as weak and ineffectual. Dyle couldn't feel as all-powerful as he had before. Both were good results in a bad scenario. And she had now been able to gauge the depth of Jaden's ruthlessness and the fact that he would never stop. Knowledge was also power. She needed any good results that came their way right now.

If you could call it good when her stomach was twisting, and she had to fight not to fall back into that pit of sheer terror.

Waldridge stepped closer to Kendra. "You're shaking," he said gently. "Don't fall apart now. You were bloody magnificent."

"I couldn't let them have it all their own way," she said unevenly. "I hate bullies, and I wanted to smack Biers when I realized what he was doing."

"Well, you slapped him down figuratively. I would have liked to do a good deal more to him." His expression was shadowed. "I was in a world where I could trust no one, and I allowed myself the bad judgment to trust Biers. He was so brilliant and enthusiastic. I suppose money and power can change people."

"He's weaker, but just as bad as Dyle," she said, remembering Biers's expression when he was looking at Waldridge. "And he's jealous of you. I'm surprised you didn't pick up on that."

"We were colleagues. I celebrated any success he made. I thought he did the same."

"And you trusted him," she repeated. "But he belongs to Dyle now. He didn't even get up off his knees without Dyle's okay. He was the one who cut that GPS out of me. If Dyle told him to cut out my eye, he'd do it in a heartbeat." Her lips twisted. "Of course, he might have to fight Jaden for the pleasure."

He muttered a curse. "No way, Kendra."

"I hope we can keep that from happening." She had to stop this shaking. "I guess you know how I'd feel about that. Dyle managed to hit a bull's-eye. No one can really know the difference unless they've been there."

"I won't let him touch you."

"You might have to let him go ahead and do it if we have to find a way to stall."

Waldridge took her in his arms and held her. Comfort. Friendship. Togetherness. "No, then we'll find another way to stall."

"How? You can't give him what he wants. You said if

you gave in, you knew it would only be signing your death warrant. Do you think he'd let me live afterward? Not likely." She pushed him away and drew a deep breath. The shaking had almost stopped. She was getting better, that moment of realizing that she was not alone in this battle was helping. "You can't do it. We'd both end up dead."

He didn't speak for a moment. "Quite possibly." His lips twisted. "Then we'd best come up with another solution. Dyle believes he's come up with the perfect mechanism to force me to his way of thinking. He knew what seeing you tortured would do to me. He was entirely serious about taking your eyes."

She had known that, and the fear had nearly paralyzed her. Snap out of it. They could get through this. They had no choice.

"Tell me about the layout of this place." She looked at the large, reinforced door through which Dyle had just exited. "Do you know where that leads?"

"Oh, yes. That leads to an office–sitting room and a kitchen." His lips twisted. "And a small room where Dyle spent a number of hours trying to convince me of my duty to him."

Torture. Would that be where she'd be taken if Dyle decided to take her eye? Don't think about it. Concentrate. "So that's the main part of this encampment? Where do the guards sleep?"

"Not in the main facility." He nodded at the other smaller door. "You said you thought that led outside. You might be right. There might be an outbuilding out there. When they were taking me back and forth to my charming little home away from home, I saw a few tents as I passed the window in the office."

"So there will be tigers behind either door. We just have to plan a way to get past them."

"Or invite them into our parlor?" Charles asked. "I believe Dyle has already issued a command invitation himself."

"That's an hour from now." She took another step back and glanced around the lab. Concentrate. Memorize everything about it. "In an hour, we won't be here."

CHAPTER
17

KENDRA HEARD FOOTSTEPS in the hall outside the lab.

She tensed, she'd been expecting it, but it still caused her heart to speed up.

They were coming for her.

Her time was up, and Dyle's men were now unlocking the door. Her hand closed behind her around the bump key she'd identified as most likely to work on the door. Her palms were sweating, and her pulse was erratic as she stared at the door. She murmured to Waldridge standing next to her at the table. "Here we go." She moistened her lips. "Good luck."

"You, too." He picked up two corked flasks filled with water. "Even if this goes horribly wrong, it's better than the alternative."

"Gouging my eyes out, you mean?" Her gaze never left the door. "Can't argue with that."

The door swung open, and the same two gunmen as before entered. Dyle wasn't with them. Too bad, Kendra thought.

She shared a quick glance with Waldridge.

Almost time.

The two gunmen moved forward. The larger of the two men, a muscular man with a handlebar moustache, gestured toward Kendra. "Time's up, lady. Unless Waldridge has changed his mind and decided—" He broke off as his gaze went down to the floor. The two men had stopped warily as their shoes crunched on a gritty mixture of potassium permanganate and glycerin that Waldridge had carefully spread on the floor. "What's this shit?"

Waldridge walked toward them with his water-filled flasks. "Only a science experiment. After all, Dyle ordered me to get to work."

He hurled the flasks toward the floor.

The flasks shattered.

The two men were instantly engulfed in flames!

Kendra and Waldridge dodged behind the nearest table.

Screams! The man with the handlebar moustache squeezed off a barrage of shots before he dropped his gun as his arm was engulfed in flames. Within seconds, the other gunman was on his knees, yelling as he tried in vain to extinguish the chemical fire on his clothes.

Waldridge whirled around. "Now, Kendra! Those screams are going to bring them running."

She was already at the smaller door, working the bump key as she'd practiced with Jessie. She positioned the key and tapped it with the mallet she had taken from the lab equipment.

351

Strike, twist, repeat . . .

Strike, twist, repeat . . .

It wasn't working!

The men's screams had become lower-pitched wails, and she realized that the horrible scene behind her was pulling her focus.

Detach. Concentrate.

Strike, twist . . .

The lock turned! She pushed open the door, and bright sunlight flooded into the lab. Beyond the door there was sand, only sand for as far as the eye could see.

She turned back at a crash from the other side of the lab. Biers, Jaden, and the other guard had burst through the primary door with fire extinguishers. Biers pointed toward Kendra. "Stop her!"

Waldridge picked up two larger flasks he had ready, and yelled to her, "Run!"

Kendra bolted out the open door and a heartbeat later Waldridge was there. He whirled around and tossed the flasks toward the second, wider strip of potassium permanganate and glycerin he'd laid down.

Foom!

Flames roared over the entire lab.

Waldridge leaped through the open door and bolted across the rough sand after Kendra as a series of small explosions rocked the lab behind them.

"What's that?" Kendra shouted.

"Ammonium nitrate," Waldridge replied. "And perhaps a few vials of zinc powder. I used everything I could find."

Kendra glanced over her shoulder at the complex that had been their prison. It was smaller than she had imagined, with beige coloring that would make it invisible from the sky. The lab was joined by a walkway to smaller structures, which must be the quarters section Waldridge mentioned.

Another explosion shook the lab.

Kendra's gaze was flying over the trucks and vehicles parked in the area.

No time to hot-wire anything.

Kendra pointed to a three-wheel all-terrain vehicle parked several yards away. "There!"

Waldridge gave it a doubtful look. "Will your bump key work on that?"

"No." She was running toward the ATV. "But it's a sport model, so we may not need a key." She practically flew onto the seat and checked the console. Relief. "We're good to go. Hop on!"

Blue flames shot from the open door.

Waldridge jumped behind her and wrapped his arms around her waist.

Kendra had already started the ATV and was gunning the engine. She pulled back on the throttle. The back wheels kicked up sand as the ATV bounded over a small dune and headed out into the open desert.

DYLE SHIELDED HIS FACE from the white-hot chemical fire that had completely enveloped the lab. The strong desert wind had sent the flames leaping totally out of control. His hands clenched in fury as he turned back to the two badly burned men who had been dragged out just before the entire building went up in flames.

One of the men, Aaron French, was clearly dead. His crispy face was a bloody scab only barely recognizable as a human being. Incredibly, the remnants of his handlebar mustache were still visible.

The other man, Dan Brill, wasn't faring much better.

He screamed in pain as Jaden and Nathan, the other security man, tried to peel off his black fatigues. He quieted only after he was injected with a heavy sedative.

Biers grimaced at the sight of the two charred men. "That could have been us, Dyle. For God's sake, you know Waldridge is a chemical genius. Why wasn't he more closely watched?"

"Are you criticizing me?" Dyle asked coldly. "Taken alone, none of those chemicals could have caused this chaos."

Biers immediately backed down. "No, you're right, of course. I'm just concerned."

"And so you should be. We'll get them back. All of my men are damn good in the desert. Jaden ran my security detail for me in Egypt." He turned to the remaining security men, Jaden and Eric Nathan, who were approaching them. "Why aren't you on the road? What do I pay you for?"

"We have two men down," Jaden said. "French is gone, but Brill stands a chance. We need to get him to a hospital."

"Later," Dyle said. "Right now we have to catch Waldridge and the woman."

"Brill is going to die if we don't get him to a hospital *now*," Nathan said.

Dyle looked down at the burned man, who was struggling to breathe. "He's going to die anyway. You and I both know that. The nearest hospital is a hundred miles from here."

"We have to try," Nathan said. "I'm not leaving him. We've been through a lot of shit together."

"You can try when you get back if he's still alive."

"That's not the way we do things, sir."

Dyle smothered his rage. He wanted to shoot the son of a bitch. But he had to work with these idiots. He had no one else at the moment. "Honorable. But two people have escaped on your watch, and they have to be retrieved." Hell, let Jaden handle it. They were his men. He turned to Jaden. "What do you think?"

"I think Nathan is right. Nathan and Brill were buddies." He looked down at the moaning man with no expression. "And compensation should be made for violating his feelings in the matter." His gaze shifted to Dyle. "Considerable compensation."

Whatever. Anything to get them moving. "Look, then suppose I give each of you a bonus of $50,000 when you bring them back."

That got Nathan's attention, Dyle noticed. Cash always did. "That's a lot of money." Nathan paused. "But you're actually paying me to let him die."

"He'll die anyway. I'm paying you to keep the mission on track."

"Fifty thousand apiece?" Jaden repeated.

He wanted to make certain his assistance in the matter was going to show a profit. Jaden never did anything without a paycheck. "Absolutely."

Jaden turned to Nathan. "We've got to look out for ourselves. That's a lot of money."

"Time's wasting," Dyle said.

Jaden said to Nathan, "In the same situation, Brill would take the money and leave our asses. You know that."

Nathan shrugged. "Okay. Maybe you're right."

Jaden turned to Dyle. "We'll leave Brill and start tracking Waldridge, but this is a big area. We'll need help. I want your okay to call down to Mexico for reinforcements from Koppel's team to come up here to give us support."

"No, how many times do I have to tell you, this mission is confidential."

"It won't be confidential if we can't find Waldridge before they make it out of this desert."

"We'll probably find them before Koppel's team can get up here to help."

"Then you can send them back. But it will only take a few hours for Koppel to cross the border and get here. It will make the difference if we have trouble locating Waldridge and Michaels."

"Are you telling me what to do?"

"I'm telling you I'm not losing that bonus if they manage to get away. I want help." He shrugged. "Take it or leave it."

Dyle muttered a curse. "I'll take it. But if any of those men talk, I won't be shy about taking a contract out on you, Jaden."

"Expected," Jaden said. "But no one talks if I tell them not to." He reached for his phone. "Now how do you want to work this?"

"How do you think? We stop talking, get moving, and *find* them. You and I will go in my Range Rover. Nathan, you take Biers in the Jeep."

Biers looked startled. "Me? I thought I'd stay and watch over this poor fellow."

"I'm sure you did," Dyle said sarcastically. "But you're no longer on a free ride, Biers. We need all hands on deck. You'll earn that fat check I gave you. If Waldridge and Michaels get away, you have everything to lose." He turned to Nathan. "Give Dr. Biers a gun."

"*What?*" Biers said.

But Dyle was ignoring him and already running toward the Range Rover.

KENDRA PUT ON AN EXTRA BURST of speed on the ATV. There was nothing even remotely resembling a road, but the desert was reasonably flat. She dodged a line of scrub brush, noticing at the last moment that it hid large boulders that could have been fatal if struck at her present high rate of speed.

"Do you know where we're going?" Waldridge shouted over the engine.

She nodded toward the sun. "West. I can't get any more specific than that." She checked the rearview mirror. They had already put about six miles between them and the complex, with still no indication that they were being pursued. But she expected that to change at any minute.

A small dune appeared suddenly ahead of her.

"Hang on!" she yelled.

She jumped the dune, which launched them into the air. They skidded on the landing. Kendra tightened her hold on the handlebar grips, wishing that Jessie was the one driving. The wind was so strong that the ATV was being buffeted as if it were a toy, and it was nearly impossible to keep it steady.

The ATV engine sputtered.

It sputtered again.

No. No-no-no-no-no . . .

The engine sputtered out completely.

"What's happening?" Waldridge yelled.

Kendra was cursing. "I think we've run out of gas."

They rolled to a stop.

"What now?" Waldridge asked.

Kendra hopped off the ATV and squinted against the

strong sun as she gazed into the distance. Heat. Overpowering heat. The skin of her face had no protective covering, and she already felt it drying out, burning, as the hot wind blew against it. "The only thing we can do. We walk. There's a ridge up ahead, so maybe we can stop there and get out of the sun." She started toward the ridge. "We'll take shelter there and start again after dark."

"And hope they're not heading this way."

Kendra nodded. "We got one break. This wind is so strong that any tracks disappear as soon as we make them. Help me push this ATV into the scrub brush. It will be better if they don't know we're on foot. They'd limit and concentrate their search range if they did."

Delta 1904
Atlantic Ocean

It took five calls for Lynch to get through to Griffin when he was finally in the air and heading for the U.S. By that time he was halfway across the ocean, and his nerves were raw. His mood had started out that way, and the iciness of his tone reflected it. "What the hell is happening, Griffin? I don't appreciate being kept in the dark."

"Tell me about it," Griffin said sourly. "Get off my back, Lynch. I'm having enough trouble without you giving me grief. I don't have time to hand out bulletins to everyone when I'm trying to find your damn doctor."

"You'd better rethink that. Kendra is with that 'damn' doctor. I want her found."

"So do I." He paused. "Sorry. I'm worried about Kendra, too. But my director, John Howell is giving me hell about Waldridge. He's being almost as big a pain in the ass as you are about his disappearing."

"I'm only giving you hell about Kendra. Waldridge doesn't matter to me."

"Well, he matters to Howell. You could have told me about that new research Waldridge is doing. When the director read my last report, he jumped on me with both feet. There are two hot-ticket political items in Washington, defense and health care these days. He didn't like it that I'd lost a researcher who's work could sway millions of votes."

"I didn't know about it," Lynch said impatiently. "You found out about the research the same time I did. And I don't care about your damn director. I want to know what leads you've got on where they took Kendra."

Silence.

"Griffin."

"We found the truck that fits the description of the one that hit Kendra's car in Sweet Water, California. It's a tiny town due east of San Diego. That's where they must have changed vehicles." He paused. "Well, actually, it was Jessie Mercado who found it. She was scouring through all the towns along that highway asking questions and tapping her contacts. One of them paid off." He went on brusquely, "And that was where they also removed the GPS tracker. Jessie found a pad that had a little blood on it in the back of the truck. She was mad as hell. She said that someone must have known about the GPS to locate it that soon. She thinks that it might have been Biers and told us to go pick him up. We haven't found him yet. But we're checking traffic and security cams in all of the small towns around that location and seeing what kind of vehicles went through them for the entire day. I've sent out agents to interview citizens, and we're hoping for—"

Lynch was swearing. "Nothing. You know nothing. If Jessie hadn't been there, you'd know less than nothing." His hand clinched on his phone. "Don't tell me about hope. Give me results."

"We're working on it. All we need is one lead, and we'll pounce."

Lynch drew a deep breath. Now wasn't the time to go on the attack. Griffin would just get stubborn and start avoiding his calls. He was having enough frustration trying to get through this damned flight without going ballistic. "I want to know when that lead comes in. Don't make me call you."

"It's not as if you could do anything right now anyway. But I'll keep you informed." He hung up.

Griffin was right, Lynch thought in frustration. There wasn't anything he could do flying at thirty-five thousand feet above the Atlantic. He needed to be on the ground working those leads himself. Not depending on Griffin's agents or Jessie to come through for him.

And it would still be hours and hours before he would be able to take control of the hunt.

What could happen to Kendra during those hours?

Anza-Borrego Desert

As the last tinges of sunlight disappeared in the west, Kendra turned to Waldridge. "Ready?"

"Ready." His eyes were still closed as they had been for many of the hours they'd spent hiding in this crevasse nestled in a long ridge. He had made no complaints, but Kendra suspected he must still be recovering from those days of torture.

She smiled as she noticed that he'd torn off his shirttail to fashion a sweatband over his forehead. "Hey, what's this? Rambo?"

"I wouldn't presume. Though I was pretty good back at that lab, hmm?"

"You were awesome. Rambo, eat your heart out."

He opened his eyes and leaned forward. "Any idea where they are?"

"No. I haven't heard the cars in over an hour." They had barely gotten the ATV hidden and found this crevasse when she'd heard the pursuit she'd expected. Two vehicles, but they hadn't risked coming out of hiding to see who was in them. They'd just crouched here, trying to blend with the brush surrounding them. Then the vehicles had passed, and they'd heard them only in the distance for the last few hours. "They may be trying a different direction."

He nodded. "It was probably lucky that our ATV quit on us. It would have given them a dust plume to follow." He slowly, painfully, stood up and surveyed the desert around them. "I'd hoped we might see a light from a house or building somewhere around here."

"I already looked. There's nothing."

"Too bad." He moved stiffly across the uneven earth.

She frowned. "Look, if you want to stay here. I can set out on my own and—"

"Absolutely not." He smiled. "We're in this together. And don't worry about my being able to keep up. I told you I could do it, and I will. As soon as I get the kinks out, I'll leave you in my dust."

"Okay, Rambo."

True to his word, Waldridge kept a brisk pace for the

next few hours as they made their way across the rough desert terrain. The night sky, free of spill light from any large population center, shone brilliantly with the illumination of thousands of stars. After dark, the wind had died down, and the desert was still, almost silent.

Almost.

A sound, a roar in the distance!

Not good.

Kendra stopped short as she picked up on the sound. Her heart jumped into her throat. She'd hoped that they'd lost them. "Hear that?"

Waldridge listened and turned to look at her. She couldn't see his expression in the darkness, but his body language spelled out the same tension she was feeling. "Yes. Probably one of the cars that's been looking for us?"

"I'm pretty sure it is. It sounds like a Jeep. There was a Jeep back at the complex." Her gaze searched the distance. "But I don't see headlights yet."

Waldridge cocked his head. "You're far better at this than I, but do they sound as if they're getting closer?"

She took a moment to get her bearings.

She closed her eyes.

Concentrate. Locate. *See* it.

"I think . . . they're near where we ditched the ATV."

"Do you suppose they've found it?"

"They might have run across it. They're heading in our direction."

The car was getting closer.

"Because now they can also see our footprints. The minute the wind died down, we were screwed." Waldridge motioned back to the desert floor behind them, where their prints in the sand were now plainly visible. "Once they found the ATV, it was only a matter of time until they found those prints."

Right, Kendra thought, as she felt the chill go through her. It was only a matter of time, and their time might be up if she couldn't think of some way to escape the vehicle bearing down on them.

They had no weapons. There was only flat desert terrain where they were here. No real place to hide. Only cactus and sagebrush that wouldn't take long to search.

Okay, think. Look at the whole picture. Go back. Remember. Search for options. Pull a plan together.

The car was getting even closer.

Suddenly, she could see the headlights!

"Closer than I thought," Kendra said. "They'll be here in a few minutes."

"Then why the hell are we just standing watching them?" Waldridge's gaze was darting around the terrain, attempting to find an escape route. "Let's go. We can't stay here."

"No, we can't."

Because she had the plan. No weapons here, but she'd remembered another possible weapon. Flimsy, at best. She only prayed it would work.

But first she had to go after it.

She didn't look at Waldridge as she started running forward instead of away. "But we can't let them run us down either. We'd be even more vulnerable. I have an idea. Go take cover behind that brush. Okay?"

"What? Where are you going?"

She gestured toward the headlights. "There."

"That's crazy. I don't care what kind of—"

"Don't say another word." She glanced over her shoulder, and said fiercely, "Stop *arguing* with me. I don't have time. I'm going to do this. I can make it work. Now hide. I'll be right back."

"Kendra!"

She blocked him out as she sprinted toward the headlights, jumping over brush and cactus plants along the way. She needed to cover three to four hundred yards for her plan to work, but the car could be on top of her before she got there.

What then?

Don't think about that. Just keep pushing . . .

The Jeep's engine revved harder. It was closing the gap fast. Had she been seen?

No. The Jeep was slowly drifting away from her.

Can't let them get too far off track . . .

She ran even faster, ignoring her aching ankle and cactus-needle scrapes.

She cut to the right, crossing in front of the Jeep's high-beam headlights.

As if in response, the car's engine roared. She'd been spotted!

She turned and ran back in the direction whence she had just come.

No shots. She hadn't thought there would be. She still had value to Dyle alive. But there had always been the chance . . .

The Jeep revved even harder.

Damn, she'd cut it close. Maybe too close.

The vehicle bore down on her with the headlights casting her long shadow on the landscape ahead. She nimbly jumped over cactus plants and wild brush. But the car mowed over them even more easily than she had.

And was gaining on her.

Shit. Stupid idea, Kendra . . . Stupid, stupid.

She leaped over the thick clump of brush she'd seen just minutes before.

Zero in on me. I'm the target. Don't think of anything, don't look at anything, but me.

There it was right ahead of her!

She skirted the wild sagebrush with just inches to spare.

Faster.

Faster.

Faster . . .

Crash!

She whirled. Just fifteen feet behind her, the vehicle had smashed at high speed into a clump of large boulders hidden by that wild sagebrush she'd just skirted.

It had worked!

Maybe.

Kendra kept her distance while she warily tried to assess the damage to the jeep and its occupants. The entire front was pulverized. Smoke poured from the crumpled front end, and the engine noise had been reduced to a series of erratic clicks.

Only one of the headlights was now functional though it was flickering on and off. There was blood on the shattered windshield.

She moved carefully around to the driver's side. A man was slumped over the steering wheel, his head oozing blood. He was dressed in the same black fatigues as Dyle's other security men.

She circled around to the other side.

She froze. There was no one in the passenger seat, but the door was now wide open.

Shit.

She whirled around, her gaze flying in every direction. Where in the hell had—

"Hold it right there, Kendra."

She knew the voice immediately. "Biers."

"Turn around. Slowly."

She turned to face him. His lips were cut and bloody, his shirt torn.

And he was holding a handgun aimed at her chest.

"This is what it's come to?" she asked. "No more brilliant scientist and partner? Dyle's made you one of his mercenaries?"

He flushed. "For the time being."

She nodded back toward the jeep. "The job didn't work out so well for your friend there. Guess he should have worn his seat belt."

"Where's Waldridge?"

"We split up hours ago. We figured it would make it more difficult for you."

"Nice try. We saw two sets of footprints back there. Side by side."

"You must be mistaken. Want to go back and check again?"

"It doesn't matter. We'll find him. Dyle has called for reinforcements. Anytime now, there's going to be a small army out here."

"It's a big desert."

"But Dyle has you again." Biers smiled. "Waldridge won't let you be—"

A belt snapped around his neck!

Waldridge leaped from the darkness and yanked Biers's head down hard against a boulder.

And again.

And again.

And again.

The gun went flying, and Kendra ran to pick it up. She

spun around with the gun aimed at Biers, but he was unconscious, his head and face a bloody mess.

Waldridge let go of the belt, and Biers fell to the ground.

She drew a deep breath and tried to smile. "Damn. You *have* become Rambo." She frowned. "But there's blood on your cheek."

"Not mine. Biers's. He splattered." He used his sleeve to wipe Biers's blood away. "Are you okay?"

"Yes, thanks to you." She walked around the car and with the gun still in front of her, pushed the unconscious driver back in his seat. She unfastened his shoulder holster and pulled out his handgun.

"Is he alive?" Waldridge asked.

"Barely. I don't know for how long. He's not going to be giving us any trouble."

She reached for his phone on the console. The screen read NO SIGNAL.

No surprise there. Few towers in this barren area.

She grabbed the walkie-talkie resting in the cup holder and held it up. "There's this, but the range is probably only a couple miles."

"Which makes it only useful if you want to chat with Dyle."

"Not likely. Too bad we can't use it to—"

She froze.

"Turn Biers toward the car."

"What?"

"Do it."

"I will. But you really shouldn't order Rambo around like that." Waldridge turned Biers's unconscious, bleeding body toward the still-flickering headlight. Kendra knelt beside him and fished through his right pocket.

Let it still be there . . .

Then she felt it! She dove deep into the pocket and pulled it out. Small, unobtrusive, but as valuable as the Hope Diamond at this moment.

She smiled. "I've got it!"

She'd produced the quarter-sized tracking device Biers had taken from her hip. She fished around for another moment until she found the thin battery. It took a few minutes of maneuvering and adjusting, but then she connected both parts together with painstaking care.

"Cross your fingers," she said. "I think we're back on the grid."

"Hallelujah," Waldridge said softly. "Then we can expect the FBI, the CIA, Interpol, and maybe your friend, Lynch, to be mounting a splendid rescue mission and get us out of here?"

"Not exactly. We're not entirely certain the tracking message is getting through." Kendra's gaze was on the eastern sky. "And if I'm not mistaken, that helicopter on the horizon may be the reinforcements Dyle's sent for."

"Shit." His gaze lifted to follow her own toward the helicopter. "So we run and hide?"

"With all possible speed." She jumped to her feet. "We definitely run and hide."

JADEN PUT DOWN THE WALKIE-TALKIE and turned toward Dyle. "Koppel's team is ten minutes out. Eleven men. A copter and three Hummers."

Dyle stood next to his Range Rover and turned toward the helicopter's airborne light in the distance. "It's about time."

"I thought you'd be pleased once you got used to the idea. It's the way to go. They should wrap this thing up in no time. His gaze went to the horizon, where he knew the aircraft and Hummers would soon appear. "You've increased the firepower since I was last down there with Koppel. What do you have going on down there below the border that you need all that personnel and equipment?"

"The cartels have been running wild. I need to protect my executives and my interests there. I hoped it wouldn't be necessary to pull them away." He gave Jaden a sour look. "You spoiled that, didn't you?"

"Necessary. Don't worry, it will be daylight soon. After that, it won't take long to round up Waldridge and Michaels."

Ten minutes later, the helicopter touched down as three Hummers pulled up and stopped in a tight formation around it.

Koppel's security team gathered around Dyle as he brought them up to speed. When he finished, Tim Koppel glanced around. "This is all the men you have here? No wonder you gave me a shout. Where's Nathan, Jaden? I don't see him."

"Out there somewhere with Dyle's pet scientist," Jaden said. "He hasn't checked in for the last hour."

"Are they in a dark-colored Jeep?"

"Yes."

"We saw it from the copter as we came in. It appears to be disabled a couple of miles due north of here. You want us to check it out?"

"No," Dyle said quickly. "I didn't bring you here to play nursemaid to those bunglers. I'll take Jaden and go myself. I told you, Waldridge and Michaels need to be your top priority. Get moving."

"WE'VE GOT THE LOCATION," Griffin said as soon as Lynch picked up. "Jessie Mercado called me five minutes ago, and the GPS tracker just started sending out a signal.

Kendra's in the Anza-Borrego Desert. That's all I know, so don't ask questions. I'll text you the coordinate app Jessie sent me."

"*Yes!*"

"How long before you land in San Diego?"

"Another twenty minutes."

"Then I'm not going to wait for you. I'm heading out right now. Do you want me to send a car and agent to the airport to bring you to—?"

"Hell, no. I'll arrange for a helicopter to be waiting the minute this flight hits the ground. Just *get* to her."

"On my way," Griffin said tersely.

Anza-Borrego Desert

"I couldn't help it," Biers whimpered as he gazed up at Dyle, kneeling beside him. "I told you, none of it was my fault. It all happened so fast. And then I thought I had her, but then . . . my head. You shouldn't have expected me to do something like this." He reached up and touched his blood-soaked head. "I'm hurt. I need a doctor."

"You fool!" Dyle's eyes were glittering with fury. "You actually *had* them, and you let them get away?" He looked at the wreckage of the Jeep with the body of Nathan crumpled at the wheel. "Both of you were fools. I thought with Nathan along, you'd be able to function like a real man, but I was wrong."

"There are footprints leading to that north ridge," Jaden said as he strode back to the Jeep. "If Waldridge and the woman are on foot, we have a chance of tracking them down if we move fast."

"You see, nothing I did was that bad," Biers said. "You

can still catch them. But first stop this bleeding, then send me out on that helicopter and get me medical attention. I might have a concussion."

"And I might need that helicopter pilot to get Waldridge out of here. You think I'd waste time on you?"

"Yes, of course. I'm important to you. You told me so. We're going to be partners. I need help, Dyle."

"Partners? That charade is over." He turned to Jaden. "He needs a doctor just like your man did back at the lab. What's your answer to that?"

Jaden smiled. "My choice? Then it's the same answer we gave Brill. That's only fair."

"You heard him, Biers," Dyle said as he turned away. "If I get Waldridge and Michaels back, I have no need of you. And I *will* get them back." He glanced up at the helicopter that had just taken off again and was flying low, lights spearing the ground below. "Hurry up with it, Jaden. We need to deal with more important matters." He moved toward the path leading to the ridge, and called back, "Don't worry about the concussion, Biers. Jaden will take care of making it go away."

"What are you—" Biers's eyes widened in terror as Jaden leveled his gun at his head. "No, it isn't fair. I was supposed to be—"

Jaden blew his head off.

And it served the stupid fool right, Dyle thought, when he heard the shot. "Done?" he called back to Jaden.

"Maybe not entirely," Jaden said. "I think you'd better come back here. We may have a problem. Or an opportunity." He dropped to his knees beside Biers's body. "He's been searched." He was pointing to the lining of Biers's pocket, which had been half pulled out of Biers's pants. "You didn't notice it when you were questioning him?"

"All I noticed was his whining." Dyle had a sudden thought as he hurried back. "Check those pockets. Now."

"The tracking device?" Jaden quickly searched Biers's pockets. "Empty."

Dyle cursed. "Then Kendra Michaels has her tracking device. If she managed to activate it, this whole area could soon be swarming with Feds."

"Shit," Jaden said as he reached for the walkie-talkie. "I'll need to warn Koppel about it."

"Wait." Dyle snatched the walkie-talkie and spoke into it. "Koppel, do you read me?"

Koppel's voice blasted over the radio, along with the sound of the helicopter rotors. "Roger."

"I need your communications specialist up there to go to work."

"Like he hasn't been working already?"

Prick. Dyle held on to his temper. "Koppel, I need him to scan this area for a signal of some kind. It's transmitting GPS coordinates."

"Do you know the frequency?"

"No. It's coming from a tiny transmitter. Start with the types of tracking signals your people use in your applications, then have him scan other wavelengths that may seem to fit the bill. If you can lock on it, it'll make your search for Waldridge and Michaels a hell of a lot easier. Time is of the essence because we could have some company here soon."

Koppel asked warily, "What kind of company? And how soon?"

"Federal law enforcement. And I can't give you a time frame. You've just got to locate Waldridge before they get here. I've given you the tool you need, now do it."

"Damn. Okay, we'll see what we can do about homing in on that tracking signal. I think we can do it. Stand by."

CHAPTER
18

"WAIT! DON'T YOU DARE takc off without me,
Lynch!"

Lynch had just turned on the rotors of the helicopter,
but Jessie's voice was still piercing enough for him to hear
her. He glanced out of the window to see her running
across the tarmac toward him. "I'm not waiting for anything," he yelled back at her. "And I don't want passengers."

"You mean witnesses, don't you?" Jessie had reached
the helicopter, and she was glaring up at him. "That's why
you wanted Griffin to go ahead. You didn't want him to
get in your way."

"Step aside, Jessie," he said coldly. "I'm taking off."

"Not without me. I don't give a damn about what you do,
whom you kill, and whether it's by the book. Do you
think I don't know what's been building up inside you?
You're ready to explode. You did your research on me? I
didn't have to do any on you. I probably wouldn't have
found anything anyway. But I *know* you. You don't play

by any rules but your own. That's why you win. Winning is important to you."

"Go away, Jessie."

She ignored the words as she took a step closer to the window. "Maybe only one thing is more important to you, and she's in that desert. So Griffin's rules won't only be ignored, they'll be decimated. That's okay with me this time. Why do you think I'm here instead of hitching a ride with Griffin? Sure, he's going to go out there with a crack-erjack team. But sitting back in his office is his boss, Director Howell, who's putting pressure to make Waldridge top priority. If Griffin has to make a choice, who would it be?" She met his eyes. "I've already made my choice. I'll keep Waldridge alive if I can, but I let Kendra walk into this mess. I was stupid. I should have realized that Biers could be a phony. I told her I could protect anyone. But I didn't protect her the way I should. So now I have to make it right." She straightened, her shoulders braced for battle. "And I can't let Griffin or anyone else stop me. Not when I have you as an alternate. I can help you, dammit. So, if you think this helicopter is going to take off without me, you're sadly mistaken."

He was silent, staring at her without expression. Then he asked, "How can you help me?"

She released the breath she'd been holding. "The usual way. I'm smart, well trained, and considered lethal. Anything else we can work out between us." She paused. "I will *not* be a witness. I see only what you tell me to see."

"You'll obey orders without question?"

She hesitated. "Yes, until we leave the desert."

Another silence. Then he nodded curtly. "Get in the helicopter. We've got to get moving."

"Right." She didn't wait for him to change his mind. She

was around the helicopter in a heartbeat and jumping into the passenger seat. She pulled out her tablet as he took off. "I figured I'd navigate. I pulled up the app, and I can track where Kendra is going and check the terrain. I'm also going to Google and try to see what other movement is going on around her. And maybe I could—"

"So much for obeying orders," Lynch said dryly. "I don't recall discussing any of this with you, Jessie."

"But you would have," she said quietly. "I'm just anticipating the order . . ." She smiled. "Sir."

LIGHTS SPEARING THE DARKNESS.

Coming in their direction?

Kendra felt the fear gripping her when she first saw those lights in the distance.

She and Waldridge had climbed atop the small ridge overlooking the large basin, and the first thing they had seen when they reached the top were those three road vehicles separating in search patterns as they thundered across the desert. The second thing were the lights of a low-flying helicopter some distance to the east.

Waldridge gave a low whistle. "Not good. What do you think the odds are that's our rescue party?"

"Not very high," Kendra said. "Even if that tracking device worked, I don't see how they'd get here in that kind of force so soon. Three vehicles *and* a helicopter?"

Waldridge nodded. "Those must be the reinforcements Biers told us about." He grimaced. "Though it's flattering he would think he would need them, I was hoping that you'd have a more optimistic take on it than I did."

"I want to be optimistic. We just can't be certain that tracking device is even working. And even if it is, I don't know if Jessie and the FBI can get here before those guys

IRIS JOHANSEN & ROY JOHANSEN

track us down." She shivered as she watched the precision of the drivers of those vehicles as they covered miles of desert, those brilliant lights constantly searching. "They seem to know exactly what they're doing, don't they?"

Waldridge reached out and gripped her shoulder. "But so do we," he said gently. "Look how far we've come against the bastards. We're fantastic."

"Yeah." She covered his hand with her own. "We're fantastic. How could I forget?"

"I have no idea. See that it doesn't happen again." Waldridge looked to the east, where the sky was just beginning to lighten. "But it's going to be tough for us to move after it gets light. Maybe we should try to find some place to burrow down and hide."

"That might be a good plan."

But they both knew there were few places to burrow and hide in this barren desert. In these last hours, after they had left Biers, that truth had hit home to them as they had made their way over that scorched earth to this ridge.

Kendra gazed down at the tracking device in her hand then looked up toward the western horizon.

Please. We're here, but I don't know for how long, Jessie. Come and get us . . .

JESSIE HELD ON TO HER tablet computer as Lynch banked a wide turn with the helicopter.

"Did you text Kendra's current tracker coordinates to Griffin?" Lynch asked.

Jessie nodded. "Griffin and his team are on the way."

"Good."

"And Griffin requests that we hang back and coordinate our arrival at the scene with his team."

Lynch shook his head. "Griffin knows that's not goin

to happen. He's just covering his ass in case this thing goes south. Truth be told, he'd rather not be responsible for what I do out there."

She glanced at his expression, then looked away. "I can understand that."

Lynch cocked his head toward the back. "Behind our seats, there's a black canvas bag. Would you mind unzipping it and showing me what's in there?"

Jessie pulled the heavy bag into her lap, unfastened the snaps, and opened the zipper. She stared in disbelief at the bag's contents. "Holy shit."

"Everything seem okay?"

The bag contained a variety of handguns, automatic rifles, and ammunition. "It depends on how you look at it. They all appear to be in good shape and functional." Jessie pulled out a Smith & Wesson semiautomatic. "Do you always travel with an armory?"

"Not always. I had a friend meet me at the airport with some special favorites. I thought they might come in handy tonight. Would you like to borrow one?"

She patted her shoulder holster. "I brought my own, thanks."

"Suit yourself." He was gazing intently down at the stretch of desert that had just come into view, his lips tightening. "Check that tablet again. Shouldn't we be almost here?"

THEY'RE COMING THIS WAY," Kendra gasped as she climbed the ridge's rocky face. She tried to get her breath as she looked over her shoulder at Dyle's helicopter, which hovered less than half a mile from where she and Waldridge were scrambling over the rocks. Stay in the shadows. Those beams from the helicopter were lighting up everything around them. If they got much closer, they would spot them and pin them against these rocks like a collector would a butterfly.

But butterflies were helpless. They mustn't be helpless. They mustn't let Dyle gather them up. They mustn't let him win.

Waldridge swung his legs over a cluster of rocks. "I'm slowing us down," he called back to her. "It would be easier on the desert floor."

"We'd be sitting ducks down there. Keep going. You're doing fine."

Kendra gave him a gentle shove to help him over the rocks. Waldridge *was* slowing down, and she probably was, too. Moving along this high ridge was increasingly treacherous, especially as they grew more tired.

Keep moving.

Stay hidden.

But that damn helicopter was getting closer.

So close.

Too close.

She tried to move faster.

Keep moving.

Hold on until help arrives.

If help arrived, she reminded herself. She had no way of knowing if the tracking device was actually working.

Don't think about it. If they couldn't count on it, then they'd find another way.

But the helicopter drew closer. The spotlight swept over crevices and pathways they had traveled only minutes before.

Damn. She shook her head in disbelief. In this vast desert, it was as if they knew exactly where to look.

Waldridge was muttering a curse. He was obviously

thinking the same thing. "I believe it might be time to find a place to hide."

Her gaze was frantically scanning up the rock wall. "Just on the other side of this ridge is our best bet. Can you make it?"

"Do I have a choice?"

"Not unless those guys decide to pack up and call it a day."

"I don't think that will happen. Of course, I'll make it."

Dyle's helicopter moved even closer. Vegetation rustled on the hillside. The wind was suddenly filled with blowing sand.

Waldridge whirled and was scrambling over the ridge. Kendra was two seconds behind.

Light.

Her breath left her body as she cleared the rim.

She and Waldridge were suddenly bathed in white, blinding light.

Pinned.

Stabbed by light.

"Shit," Waldridge murmured.

As her eyes adjusted, she realized what she was seeing. A trap.

Dyle, Jaden, and two other of his uniformed security men stood next to a Range Rover and a Hummer. Dyle had not been in the helicopter, as she'd assumed, but one of the vehicles. Each vehicle had roof-mounted arc lights trained on the ridge, clearly waiting for Waldridge and Kendra to make their appearance.

The two security men had their automatic rifles trained on them.

Dyle smiled. "Careful. I wouldn't want you to fall."

Kendra looked up. The helicopter was now overhead

with its intense search beams trained directly on them. She
and Waldridge looked at each other.

Frustration.

Defeat.

No place to go.

They made their way down the short incline until they
found themselves face-to-face with Dyle and Jaden.

Dyle frowned and stepped toward Kendra. "First things
first. Give me the tracking device."

"Biers took it from me, remember?"

"And you took it back from him. Give it to me."

The realization hit her. "You picked up the signal. That's
how you knew where we were. Your helicopter was steering us right to you."

"Enough stalling. Give it to me."

Kendra pulled the tracker from her pocket and placed
it in Dyle's extended palm. Dyle immediately dropped it
on the ground and smashed it with his heel.

"It's over," Kendra said. "They know who you are and
what you've done. No matter what you do to us, it's over
for you."

Dyle raised his voice to be heard over the sound of the
hovering helicopter. "You don't think I've made prepara-
tions? You don't think there are scores of countries that
will deny extradition for a man of my generous nature?
Particularly if they can also reap the benefit that I'll bring
with Waldridge."

Waldridge shook his head. "You've already gone down
that path."

"I'll get there yet. I just need some more time with you."

"You've already lost," Kendra said, shielding her eyes
from the blowing sand. "Even if you won't admit it."

"Why admit what doesn't exist? I won. You lost. Now

all I have to do is rake in the pot and head for Mexico. In a few minutes, you'll both be on that helicopter, and we'll begin the new game." He smiled. "But perhaps with a few of the same inducements I used—"

A series of short pops sounded above them.

"What the hell . . ." Dyle was gazing up at the helicopter. "What's happening?"

More short pops sounded.

The helicopter whined. It sharply banked away from the ridge!

Kendra's gaze flew to the helicopter as it moved erratically off the ridge. The tall wing and rear motor were wobbling, sending the helicopter spinning on a lateral trajectory toward the desert floor.

"It's crashing," Dyle said, stunned. "What's Koppel doing? How could it be—" Dyle was quickly raising his walkie-talkie, but he froze as he saw the answer above them.

Kendra looked up and saw it, too.

Another helicopter, silhouetted by the first orange rays of dawn, rose from behind the ridge.

Pow-pow-pow-pow.

The same sharp pops they had heard earlier, blasted from the helicopter. As the aircraft swung around, she saw Lynch leaning out the open door, wielding an automatic rifle. But the target was not the crippled helicopter this time. He was aiming at something or someone on the ground.

A scream!

Kendra spun back around. Dyle's two security men were down, their heads shattered by Lynch's gunshots. Dyle and Jaden had grabbed Waldridge and were trying to take cover behind a row of boulders.

Lynch leaned back inside the helicopter as it was buffeted by the strong desert winds.

Jaden lifted his gun toward Lynch, but Waldridge leaped over and struck his arm as Lynch's helicopter turned and descended behind the rim. "Son of a bitch!" Jaden turned and struck Waldridge with the butt of his automatic rifle.

"No!" Kendra screamed, as Waldridge slid down the embankment, unconscious.

Or dead? Pray God he wasn't dead.

"Jaden, you fool," Dyle shouted. "I *need* him. Now go down and get him. We've got to get out of here. Chances are he's not alone."

She hoped Lynch wasn't alone. But she couldn't let Jaden let loose any bullets at that helicopter. She took cover behind another row of boulders, reached to her waistband and pulled out the gun she'd taken from Biers.

"You go get him," Jaden told Dyle. "I'll join you as soon as I take care of the problem here. After all, that's what you pay me for."

Dyle was swearing as he started crawling down the embankment.

"Here we are, Kendra." Jaden had ducked behind the boulder again. "What a lot of bother you've caused us. I don't relish your coming along and causing me more trouble. So I think we'll dispense with you before Dyle comes back and decides he needs you, too."

A bullet splintered rock a foot from her head.

She fired back in the direction from where she'd judged his voice had come.

Blamm!

Kendra's right arm throbbed, and her gun went flying.

Pain. Searing, horrible pain.

"Now we take care of unfinished business." She could see Jaden moving toward her. "Are you ready, Kendra? You've had a very long grace period, but all things come to an end."

A barrage of gunshots erupted from the top of the rim. Spitting sand only inches from Jaden.

"Dammit." He dove back behind the rocks. "Only a minor interruption. I'll be right with you."

He returned the fire from the rim.

"What are you doing?" Dyle was crawling toward him from the embankment. "I told you we have to get Waldridge out of here. Now do it. I wasn't able to get him up that embankment."

"And I'll take care of it," Jaden said. "Don't I always take care of everything for you?"

"Talk's cheap. Get us out of here."

"Too late," Lynch called down from the rim. "I wanted to spend a little time with you, Dyle, but Jaden shot Kendra, and I don't have that choice now."

"Kill him," Dyle shouted at Jaden. "Now."

Jaden was already firing a round at the rim.

"I've got cover and a clear view," Lynch said. "I *see* you, Dyle. Enjoy the next minute while I line up my shot."

"*Kill* him," Dyle screamed again. "You heard him." He was trying to get closer to the protection of the boulder. "Take him down!"

"Time's up," Lynch said softly.

A bullet tore through the center of Dyle's skull. His head jerked back, a thin ribbon of blood ran from his lips.

He slumped over, dead.

More bullets tore down from the rim, pinning Jaden behind the boulders.

Jaden returned the fire. "Well, Kendra, it appears the situation has changed. I may have to assess the situation and change with it. Would you like to take a little ride with me?"

"Screw you. You're beaten, Jaden."

"I'm never beaten." He crouched low, moving slowly toward the bank of rocks where Kendra lay. "Let's go."

"A hostage? Seriously?"

Jaden whirled around. Lynch was standing less than ten feet away, holding his rifle in front of him.

"You should rethink that strategy," Lynch said.

"It's worked before." Jaden spoke in a lazy drawl that belied the intensity in his eyes and movements.

"Not this time. Drop your gun."

Jaden nodded up to the ridge. "I thought you were up there."

"That's what I wanted you to think." Lynch shrugged. "I brought a friend."

Jaden nodded. "You're good." He paused. "So . . . how good are you?"

"You don't want to find out."

Jaden gripped his rifle. "The way I see it, I have a definite advantage. I'm wearing Kevlar. You're not."

"That's why I'd put a bullet in your head as I did Dyle. Drop your gun."

"Look, you just killed my employer. Somehow I don't think I'm getting paid for this job."

"I think you're right."

"So why don't we call it a day? I'll pull my men out, and we can—"

In a blur of motion, Jaden raised his gun.

Blam!

The shot was Lynch's. Jaden went down with a single bullet in his forehead.

Lynch didn't even look at him. He immediately whirled and strode toward Kendra.

The next moment he was kneeling beside her, pushing the shirt off her shoulder to reveal the wound. "Why the hell did you decide to take on Jaden? I was here, dammit. All you had to do was let me—"

"It didn't work out that way. Waldridge might have been—"

"I don't want to hear about Waldridge right now. Is this the only wound?"

"Yes."

"Is she going to be okay?" Jessie was running down from the ridge. "I'm pretty good a dressing wounds. Why don't I—"

"No." Lynch put a hand out to stop her. "She's not bad. I'll take care of her."

"Waldridge is down the embankment," Kendra said. "Jaden hurt him. He needs help, Jessie."

"Yes, by all means, go down and help Waldridge," Lynch said roughly. "Or she'll be going down herself."

"Right away." Jessie was already running down the embankment. "I'm on it."

"Satisfied?" Lynch asked curtly. "Now let me get a better look at this wound."

Satisfied? She couldn't sort out her emotions at this moment. Too much had happened in too short a time. And most of it had happened since Lynch had erupted on the scene. She couldn't get her breath as she looked down at Dyle. Dead. Brutally, horribly dead. Jaden, who had tried to kill her, with the bullet hole in his forehead . . . So many dead . . .

She looked down at the fiery wreck of the helicopter engulfed in flames on the desert floor. There were almost certainly dead down there, too.

But not Waldridge or Lynch or Jessie. Safe. All these people she cared about were safe.

She moistened her lips. "You really know how to make an entrance, Lynch. I'm impressed."

Lynch didn't answer, his hands swiftly bandaging the wound.

"You were . . ." She didn't have a word to describe that savagely efficient carnage. "Unusual."

"Not really. I was angry, and I wanted it over fast, or you would have seen unusual. I wanted to cut Dyle's heart out." He'd finished putting the temporary bandage on the wound. "I think this is just a flesh wound. The bullet seems to have gone right through it. We'll get you to a hospital to confirm it."

She looked at Waldridge, who was leaning on Jessie as they topped the embankment. "I have to go see if Charles is—"

"No. He wasn't the one who was shot. You worry about you. You can bond with him later." He helped her to her feet. "Right now, we're out of here before Griffin arrives and keeps you here answering difficult questions."

"I can answer questions." She looked at the bodies. "I think."

He shook his head. "No." He called, "Jessie!"

Jessie looked across at them. "Waldridge is okay, Lynch. Cut on his head. And just a little bruised and stiff."

"Take care of him. Griffin will be here any minute and will be whisking him away. Go with them and make certain he goes to a hospital and gets a clean bill of health."

Jessie's gaze shifted to Kendra. "You're certain she's all right?"

"Fine," Kendra said. "Dyle injected Charles with something. Make sure they didn't do any damage."

"I told you they didn't, Kendra," Waldridge said. "Believe me, dammit."

She smiled. "It doesn't hurt to check."

"They'll check," Lynch said curtly as he slid his arm around her waist and propelled her up the ridge to the helicopter. "Call me later and report, Jessie."

"I will. Last duty, Lynch." She grimaced. "Actually, a freebie since I'll be out of the desert by that time. No orders after I leave the desert, remember?"

"I remember." He glanced over his shoulder. "But while you're here, you might rush Griffin along so that he won't dwell on what happened here. I've been trying to convince him that I've mellowed since the time when I worked at the Bureau."

"Mellowed? I think you've blown that. I'll do what I can." She looked down at the desert floor. "I hear them coming. You'd better get out of here." She turned to Waldridge. "Come on. I'll give you a hand, and we'll go meet them. It will give Lynch a little extra time."

A few minutes later, Lynch was lifting Kendra into the passenger seat of the helicopter, then jumping in himself.

She leaned back in the seat and closed her eyes. The adrenaline of the past day was ebbing away, and she felt weak, shaky.

"What's wrong?" Lynch said fiercely. "*Tell* me. Was I wrong about that wound? You're *not* going to leave me now, Kendra."

"Don't be silly. I'm just having a few aftereffects from one hell of a day." She opened her eyes. "The wound isn't anything that—" She stopped as she met his eyes. She inhaled sharply. "But I'm not the only one who's having aftereffects, am I? God, I'm sorry, Lynch."

"You should be." His voice was uneven. "About a lot of

things you've done recently. We'll eventually go into all of them in detail. But right now I need a few moments to realize that you're alive and not dead. Come here." He took her in his arms and held her tight, his face buried in her hair. "Just be quiet, okay? Let me have this time."

She didn't want to speak. She felt so close to him in this moment. She'd had no time to dwell on the thought of life or death since the moment she'd been taken. It had been all action and survival. But the people who cared about her had that time. Lynch had that time. Her arms tightened around him. She wanted to give to him, take away those bitter hours of worry. She couldn't do it.

All she could do was hold him through this terribly vulnerable moment for him.

"That's all. I'm done." He cleared his throat and released her. "Now I'm back to normal." He started the helicopter. "Which might or might not be good for you. We'll have to see, won't we?" The helicopter lifted off. "But you don't close your eyes again until I get you to that hospital. I'm not having it."

CHAPTER
19

HER MOTHER AND OLIVIA WERE outside the ER with Lynch when Kendra was wheeled out into the hall by a nurse.

"Stupid," her mother said shakily as she came toward her. "Completely stupid. I don't know how I raised such a total idiot." She bent down and slid her arms around Kendra. She held her tightly for a moment. "Lynch tells me that you're not being punished for that idiocy. You're going to be okay?"

"I'm okay now. The wound isn't going to be a problem." She gave her a quick hug. "They'd let me go home now, but I got a little dehydrated in the desert, and they want to pump me full of fluids. They'll release me first thing in the morning."

"I would think they'd keep you longer. Running around that desert, then—" Dianne stopped and drew a deep breath. "Don't do this kind of thing again. It's not permitted from now on."

"Hush." Olivia pushed her aside and gave Kendra a hug. "I agree completely with the spirit of her message, but not her delivery. I'll chew you out myself, but not until you get out of the hospital, and I have you at my mercy." She turned to Dianne. "Now let her go to her room, Dianne. And we'll go to a bar and have a stiff drink and swear at her, then maybe give the tiniest prayer of thanksgiving. Sound good?"

"Excellent."

"I thought so." Olivia brushed a kiss on Kendra's forehead. "I'll see you at the condo tomorrow morning. Gird your loins, kid. You're going to hear from me."

"I'm shivering in my boots. Sorry I put you through it."

"Me, too. But I'll find a way to get back at you." She turned to Dianne. "Now give her another hug and come along. That drink is calling my name."

"Presently." Dianne thrust an overnight case at Lynch and stood frowning at Kendra. "I meant it, you know." She paused. "But perhaps I'm not entirely angry that you were such an idiot. I was proud of you, too. It was good what you did for Waldridge." She turned away. "But that's after the fact. You should have been smart enough not to have had to risk your neck for him. Next time, keep that in mind."

"I will," Kendra said gently. "I promise."

"See that you do." Dianne turned to Lynch. "Okay, get her to her room and see that they give her those fluids."

"Yes, ma'am," Lynch said. "Though I believe my job will just be to tag along with this nice nurse." He smiled, his gaze on the nurse's ID badge. "Marty? Sorry to keep you waiting, Marty. I know you have your job to do."

"No problem. Take your time." The nurse was smiling back at him with the slightly dazzled look that Lynch usually managed to elicit, Kendra noticed wearily. Sometimes it amused her, but now she was just grateful Lynch's charisma almost automatically guaranteed that things would go smoother.

Lynch turned back to her mother. "Good night, Dianne. I'll call and give you a report when I leave here."

"Tag along?" Dianne repeated dryly, her gaze on the nurse as she joined Olivia and started down the hall. "I doubt if you know the meaning of the phrase."

"Of course I do. I'm a real team player." He waved the nurse to go down the hall. "Let's go, Marty." He fell into step with Kendra's wheelchair. "Good night, ladies," he called back to Dianne and Olivia. "I'll keep you informed." He looked down at Kendra, and said in an undertone, "And you do know they'll both be on my ass if they don't receive a call that meets with their approval? So you'd better have a good night."

"You won't know if I do or not." She looked up at him as the nurse wheeled her into a room at the end of the hall. "Go home, Lynch. They cleaned me up in that ER, but you still look like you've been through a war."

"When I see you tucked in." He leaned against the wall and watched the nurse help her onto the bed. "I made a promise."

"Yes, you did." She leaned back wearily against the pillows. She was suddenly aware of the weakness she hadn't permitted herself to acknowledge before. "Thank you for bringing them, Lynch. I was going to call both of them, but I might not have gotten around to it right away."

"Imagine that." He watched the nurse move around the room. "You only had to contend with bullets and dehydration and hired killers chasing you down. Hardly worth mentioning." His gaze shifted back to her. "Anyway, they

391

knew how much you cared about them. You called your mother, and she found a letter to Olivia when she went to your studio after she flew back here. So I knew that those were two people I had to make certain to bring up to date." His lips twisted. "Of course, I might not have had the entire list. Did you send out any other touching good-bye's to anyone else?"

"No, thank heavens. Those were the only two. At the time, I felt as if it was something I should do, but I obviously made a complete mess of it."

"I wouldn't say that, but you clearly made some mistakes."

"Now that's diplomatic," she said dryly. "I can always count on you, Lynch."

"Yes, you can. Not that you've demonstrated any degree of faith that you could lately."

His voice was without expression, but she could sense the edge beneath it. He was definitely not pleased with her. How could she blame him? She had known this would be his reaction when she had deliberately not told him what she was planning to do. "You would have found a way to stop me."

"Yes, I would."

"It was the only thing I could—"

"No, it was what you chose." He inclined his head. "And I have no intention of discussing it with you when you're lying in that hospital bed. When I attack, I prefer an opponent to be on their feet."

"So you can knock them down?"

"It has a certain appeal at the moment." He turned to leave. "I'll see you tomorrow, Kendra."

"Yes." But she had to say one more thing. "You saved both me and Waldridge today. I haven't said thank you."

"No, you haven't. You're welcome." He smiled reck-lessly. "But I didn't give a damn about Waldridge at the time. I still don't. If I'd had to go in another direction, Wal-dridge would have just been collateral damage."

She felt a ripple of shock. "Charles Waldridge should never be considered collateral damage."

"Maybe not to you. I'm having a few problems with him. Good night, Kendra." He went out the door.

She lay there, only vaguely aware of the nurse dimming the lights, putting the burner phone her mother had brought on the nightstand, and leaving the room.

Lynch's words had been disturbing and so had been the leashed emotion she had sensed since she had left the ER. It had probably been present since he'd brought her from the desert, but she'd been too wired and profoundly re-lieved to notice.

And now she wasn't in any shape to probe the mental and psychological mysteries of Adam Lynch. The pain medication they'd given her was taking effect, and she was having trouble keeping her eyes open. She'd have to deal with Lynch in the morning . . .

2:35 A.M.

Her phone was ringing, she realized drowsily. The hospi-tal room was still dark, but she could see her phone screen flickering on the bedside table. Who the hell would be call-ing her at the hospital in the middle of the night?

Something must be wrong.

She reached for the phone. No ID. Maybe a wrong num-ber? But she couldn't take a chance of not answering after what she'd just gone through.

IRIS JOHANSEN & ROY JOHANSEN

"Kendra Michaels."

"You sound half-asleep," Charles Waldridge said. "And so you should be. Yes, it really is two thirty in the morning. Just another bit of blame to heap upon my head, Kendra."

She was suddenly wide-awake. "Why on Earth are you calling me at this hour, Charles? Are you all right?"

"Yes and no." He paused. "But I had Griffin call and check on you, and he said you were doing splendidly. I asked him to get your burner number so that I could check on you later myself. How is that wound?"

"Practically nothing. Why is it yes and no?"

"The physical checkup I went through showed that I was in the pink of health considering what I went through for the past week. Everyone was particularly happy that my brain functions were positively normal."

"That's wonderful." She paused. "What's the no?"

"The fact that I'm disturbing your sleep and calling you at two thirty in the morning." He added soberly, "Because I may not be able to talk to you again for a long time."

She stiffened. "What the hell are you talking about?"

"I've spent the last six hours being debriefed on Night Watch by Griffin and his boss, John Howell, the director, plus several members of congressional committees who are very interested in the progress I've made. It seems I'm an asset who can increase their political clout because I can give their voters a gift they can't get anywhere else. They've scheduled another round of talks with more committee heads this afternoon."

"And that means you may have to go to Washington or some university think tank?"

"That means I'll have to go on the run," he said quietly.

"What?"

"I know how it works, Kendra. It starts off with my being treated as if I walk on water and everyone kowtowing. Then there's a subtle change as the program is infiltrated by the money and power brokers. I watched it with Night Watch."

"It doesn't have to be like that. I know Griffin is honest and wouldn't intentionally set you up with anyone who wouldn't want the best result from Night Watch."

"Not intentionally," he repeated. "But now the word is out about what I'm doing and how successful it's proving to be. I tried to play it down, but the investigation is ongoing, and it's attracting too much attention. It's going to be a political football game, with me as the football." He paused. "And one of the senators who was sitting at that table was Robert Lockart. I'd met him before he was elected to Congress. He's an industrialist Dyle brought on board with your stem-cell procedure years ago. He was particularly interested in the commercial possibilities of it. He didn't know anything about the work I'd done lately on Night Watch, but he was exceptionally interested today. To quote Mr. Shakespeare, he has a lean and hungry look."

"But the government could protect you."

"Could it? Look at the political system. The U.S. government and economy is just as bureaucratic and self-serving as Great Britain's. Perhaps more. I can't risk letting anyone else control my work. The project is nearly finished, and I won't let it be hijacked, as Dyle was trying to do. The minute I sat down for that debriefing and watched the eagerness light up those faces, I knew what I was going to have to do."

"Run away," she whispered. "But that would have to only be the start. What else?"

"Set up a lab somewhere that's safe from interference.

Finish the final research myself. I have control of the patents, but I won't file them until I have the version I need."

"It would be very expensive."

"I have the money. When I left London, I transferred all my funds to the Caymans. Once I leave here, I start looking for a place to set up a facility and get to work."

It sounded simple. It wouldn't be simple. There would be all sorts of land mines around every corner. It would be terribly difficult. "You're positive this is necessary?"

"I'm not being paranoid. I sat there at that table, and it was déjà vu, Kendra. I could see it happening."

And so could Kendra. Waldridge's research was too tempting not to attract the supremely ugly as well as the good. "So when do you have to leave?"

"In the next few hours." His voice was rueful. "I think that Griffin was ordered to put a guard at my hotel to 'protect' me. But I can probably slip away since they think I'm flattered by all the high-powered attention. I made that very clear." He added ironically, "After all, I'm only a simple scientist. I just wanted to call and tell you what was happening. I won't phone you again once I'm in the wind. There's such a thing as plausible deniability."

"I know." She was trying to think. This was all wrong. She had thought it was over. After all he'd been through, Charles shouldn't have to run again. She could see why he felt he had to do it, but he would be vulnerable. She *hated* the thought of him alone, perhaps hunted. "That's a lawyer's term. I've always hated it. People should just do what they think is right and shout it out."

He chuckled. "Typical Kendra philosophy." He paused. "I'll miss it. If the situation weren't this potentially hazardous, I might ask you to go on the run with me. It might make life interesting."

"No, it wouldn't. As soon as you set up your lab, I'd fade into the test tubes."

"Incubators."

"See? I'm already not up to your standard."

"Wrong. You're definitely up to any standard I could devise," he said gently. "It's been a singular experience, spending this time with you. In spite of everything, it's been a grand adventure, hasn't it, Kendra?"

"A grand adventure," she repeated. "But then, that's the way it started out with us."

"True. And, when I've finished the project, I'll be in touch and we can—"

"Charles, that's not the way this is going down," she interrupted. "You're almost as clumsy at good-byes as I am. Only this isn't life or death yet. And it doesn't have to be, if it's handled right. But your disappearing into the sunset is not handling it right."

"I beg your pardon?"

"If what you say about those committee members is true, the minute you disappear, Griffin will be pressured into trying to find you. The FBI is very good at what it does. You might not even know when they've found you."

"Surveillance? I'd be careful, Kendra."

"And since you're superintelligent, it might be fine. It might not. In any case, I'd be worried, and I'd prefer not to be."

"I have to do this, Kendra."

"I'm not trying to talk you out of it. I'm just saying that if you're going to do it, it has to be done right." She tossed her blanket aside, got out of bed, and disconnected her fluid IV. "Here's what you do. Slip out of your hotel, take a taxi to the airport, and rent a car. Pick me up outside the hospital in an hour."

"What?"

"Just do it, Charles. Okay?" She hung up before he could argue with her.

A moment later, she was in the bathroom, washing her face and running a brush through her hair. Then she moved to the closet and snatched the pants and shirt her mother had sent to the hospital. She put them on, flinching as she drew the shirt over her bandaged arm. There was no way she was going to face an argument from the nurses at the front desk, so she'd have to find a way to slip out without being noticed.

She stopped and sat down before she faced putting on her shoes. She was short of breath, and her muscles were very sore.

Ignore it. She could get through this. Use this time until she met Waldridge to think and plan. She had an idea which way to go, but it had to become more clear, every detail precise.

Detach.

Concentrate.

"IS YOUR FRIEND, GIANCARLO, who owns that jet still in the country?" Kendra asked Lynch as soon as he picked up her call.

"I have no idea. What the hell are you doing calling me at this hour? You're supposed to be sleeping."

"It didn't work out that way. Would you find out if he is and will lend you his jet? I suppose it doesn't matter. You'll manage to fix it somehow. I'm heading for Montgomery Field right now. Will you meet me?"

"Are you going to tell me why you're not in the hospital?"

"I will when you get there. I'd rather you spend the time on the phone with your friend, Giancarlo. Will you meet me?"

Silence. "I'll meet you." He hung up.

Charles tilted his head as he glanced at her from the driver's seat. "You're nothing if not a whirlwind, Kendra. You're certain all this will come together?"

"No," she said bluntly. "But it has a chance. And if it does come together, it will be better than your wandering around blindly and letting Griffin find you." She glanced at him. "That's the first time you've questioned me since I got in the car. Doubts?"

"Yes, and I wouldn't be blindly wandering. I just don't have a plan in mind yet. However, I'm perfectly willing to put myself in your hands." He smiled. "Because even if it doesn't work out, I'll enjoy watching you one more time before I have to break out on my own again."

"I'm glad I have entertainment value." She picked up her phone again. "Now I have another call to make, and I only hope that I can be persuasive instead of entertaining." She was punching in the number. "Anyone will tell you that's not usually my area of expertise."

Montgomery Field

Lynch was standing in front of the hangar at the deserted airport when their car drew up before it. His hands were jammed into the pockets of his black leather jacket, and his expression was harder than Kendra had ever seen it. He gave a cool glance at Waldridge as they got out of the car. "I thought you might be mixed up in this." He turned back to Kendra. "I'm here. That's all I promised."

"Giancarlo?"

"He's ordered that his Cessna be fueled up and put at my disposal." He paused. "I told him I'd let him know later if I'd actually be using it. I don't like taking orders, Kendra."

"It wasn't an order. It was a request. I just didn't have time to make it a polite one."

"And any request should have come from me." Waldridge stepped forward. "I can understand how you wouldn't want to be involved, Lynch. You've done more than enough for me. Forget this. I'll handle it on my own."

"You will *not*," Kendra said impatiently. "It would be too easy to get screwed up. And I don't intend to let that happen. I want to get back to my kids and not have to worry about you."

"Your kids?" Lynch's expression changed the slightest bit. "What do they have to do with anything?"

"They obviously don't. Because I've had to put their therapy on hold since all this began. And now Charles is becoming all noble again, and it will probably end up having Jessie slicing me open and putting another disk in me."

"That won't happen," Lynch said grimly. "Never."

"Never," Waldridge repeated. "It's time you stepped away, Kendra."

"Not until I'm certain that this is going to work out." She was seething with frustration as she turned to him. "Listen to me. Can't you see? Lynch is *perfect*."

"At last I agree with something you're saying," Lynch said.

"Be quiet. I can only deal with one thing at a time." She locked eyes with Waldridge. "Look at him. You saw what Lynch did at that ridge. He's a damn rock star. Neither of us have probably ever seen anyone as good as Lynch at what he does."

"Are you saying I need a bodyguard?"

"Probably. But that's not what he does. I don't know exactly what he does myself. I know he fixes things. They send for him when everything goes to hell. When a government is crashing. When a cartel needs to be taken down. When someone needs to be found who people don't want to be found. I don't know what else. I don't know if I want to know. But he *fixes* things." She punched her index finger on his chest. "And you need to be fixed."

He blinked. "Indeed? Not only is that humiliating to me, but there appears to be a problem with the rock star accepting the gig."

Yes, there did, and she was probably doing this all wrong. But she was tired and worried, and her arm was beginning to throb. She whirled on Lynch. "Look, I know I'm asking a lot of you, but Charles is going to go off on his own and set up a lab to finish the Night Watch Project. He got scared off by some of the potential players whom Griffin's boss brought into the debriefing yesterday. He thinks that he could be drawn into the same nightmare he went through with Dyle. He's not going to allow it. He believes he has to go on the run."

Lynch's face was totally without expression. "Do you think he could be right?"

"Yes, Charles has been through it all before. He knows the signs."

"And what do you want me to do?"

"He needs a place that's totally safe, where he's protected, where no one will ask questions."

He smiled crookedly. "What? In this world? You're dreaming, Kendra."

"I don't think so. You have so many enemies, Lynch. You built that gorgeous house here that has every security device known to man and could repel a small army. You did that because you wanted to be able to relax within those walls." She paused. "But you're not a man who takes anything for granted. You'd prepare for the day when you might have to leave that house and go on the run yourself. You'd have a place set up for yourself that's everything I described."

"Would I?"

"Yes. And I need you to lend it to Charles for a while, then set up everyone surrounding him as if you were the one in hiding."

"If there was such a scenario, you'd be asking for a lot."

"I know." She moistened her lips. "He's worth it, Lynch."

"Is he? I really only have your opinion on that. I always like to make judgments for myself."

"But you know what he's—"

He held up his hand to stop her. "I'm thinking about it. But I have to know everything connected to the problem. Am I going to have to arrange protection for you there, too?"

She frowned. "No, of course not. Why would you have to do that?"

"It was a possibility. How long will he need to be in hiding?"

"He's not sure. Possibly a year, maybe longer."

"Is Griffin going to be involved in a search for him?"

"Charles thinks it likely that—"

"I think that I should speak for myself," Waldridge interrupted. "This is all judgment calls on my part, too, Lynch. I believe a certain amount of pressure will be applied on the pretext that I could be in danger. Griffin might feel he has to find me. I don't know about the extent of that search."

"Griffin doesn't drag his heels. Your cover would have

to be perfect." His gaze was fixed absently on the airport tech filling the Cessna. "There would be a hell of a lot of loose ends to tie up . . ."

"Will you fix it?" Kendra asked. "Is there a place?"

His gaze shifted back to her. "It's a big favor. You'd owe me."

"Of course I would." She asked slowly, spacing between each word. "Is there a place?"

He turned on his heel and started toward the Cessna. "There's a place." He was striding quickly across the tarmac. "Get on the plane, Waldridge. From now on, you do everything I tell you to do without question. Understand? You may be a god in your particular universe, but from now on your universe is limited to your lab. But if you manage to make it through this mess and win the Nobel Prize, I might even bow down and worship at the altar like the rest of your fans."

"Not bloody likely," Waldridge murmured as he fell into step with him as Kendra followed behind. "But I'm not a god, and I'm certainly not a fool. If Kendra says I need fixing, and you can do it, who am I not to cooperate?"

"Kendra needs to do some fixing herself." Lynch was looking over his shoulder at Kendra. "I take it you went AWOL from the hospital?" When she nodded, he said, "When you leave here, you go back to your condo. Leave Waldridge's rental car at a metered spot downtown. It'll be towed and the rental car company will get a call once it hits the impound lot."

Kendra nodded. "Okay . . ."

"Then you call your mother and ask her to meet you at your condo. You tell her that she's to tell anyone who questions her that she received a call from you in the middle of the night and you told her to pick you up outside the hospital. You told her you couldn't sleep, and you saw no reason why you should have to stay there." He smiled. "Considering your reputation with the FBI field office, they won't find it unusual you wanted to run your own show. But Dianne will say she didn't want to leave you alone. So like a good mother, she bunked down on the couch and was available in case you needed her."

"As an alibi?"

"Yes, you won't need one. No crime has been committed. But it might throw off anyone who thinks you have anything to do with Waldridge's disappearance. I'll lay a few more false trails for them to follow, but they'll come to you first." His lips twisted. "And Dianne will be completely convincing if it means she's doing something that will protect her hero and still keeping you safely here in San Diego."

"Yes, she will," Kendra said. "Though I don't want to involve her."

"She was mad as hell that you didn't involve her the last time. She may forgive you if you let her do this." He turned back to Waldridge. "And can you give me an idea where those incubators with the organs would be taken in London? Biers said he didn't know."

"He knew. Probably the test lab on the south side. Why?"

"Another loose end. After I leave you, I'll have to go and grab all those incubators and ship them to your new lab. You don't want anyone else to have access to them if they have a finished product."

"No, I wouldn't." He smiled. "I was worried about them. I'm glad you thought of it. That could have been a disaster."

Lynch waved his hand impatiently. "I'll need all the details about transporting. I don't know anything about keeping live organs healthy."

"My area," Waldridge said. "I'll make it easy for you to fix that problem." They'd reached the steps, and he turned to Kendra. "It seems that this may be—"

"Who's that?" Lynch stiffened, his gaze on two head-lights spearing the darkness as a car drove onto the airport grounds. "I don't like this."

"I do," Kendra said as she whirled and started hurrying toward the car that had just stopped. "I was afraid that she wouldn't make it, and I'd have to send her after you."

"Her?" Lynch called.

"Jessie," Kendra said over her shoulder. "I couldn't let Charles go without making certain he had proper security. And I couldn't expect you to stay and protect him. Jessie probably won't stay either, but she'll be able to set up a security system she can trust."

"And that *you* can trust," Lynch said dryly.

She didn't answer. She had reached the car, and Jessie was opening the driver's door and getting out.

"I HEARD HER TALKING TO Ms. Mercado in the car, and she didn't have an easy time persuading her," Waldridge said as he watched Kendra and Jessie standing there talking. "But Kendra was very determined, and Jessie finally gave in." He glanced at Lynch. "But since you've made it clear that you're going to be in charge, I'm wondering if you'll let Kendra have her way in this."

"I'm wondering, too," Lynch said. "Jessie might be useful if she agrees to the same rules I give to you. She's ex-military, and she might do it. She's smart, she's good, she doesn't make mistakes. It would free me up to go after those incubators right away while Dyle's pals are still running around in a panic after they hear he's dead. I could drop her off with you, snatch the incubators, then come back and finish the rest of the setup."

"You'd feel comfortable doing that?"

Lynch smiled as he gazed at Jessie. "Yes, I'd feel comfortable. You can, too, Waldridge."

"Then it appears your decision is made, doesn't it?" He was still looking at Kendra and Jessie as he added, "Much easier than the one you made when you told Kendra you'd take me on. That was a close call for me. It all rested on a couple of sentences, didn't it?"

Lynch's eyes narrowed on his face. "Did it? What were they?"

"The first was when Kendra was so exasperated because she'd had to ignore the therapy for the kids she teaches. The second line was when she said that of course she wasn't going with me. I believe that clinched the matter in my favor?"

Lynch didn't answer.

"But I'm curious, if she hadn't said those words, would you have just let me go out on my own, or would you have found a way to have Griffin find me in the fastest way possible?"

Lynch looked him in the eye. "What do you think?"

"You're too smart to do anything that would irreparably cause an upset in your relationship with Kendra. I'll go for the former, which, according to Kendra, might have the same result."

"Or there could have been four or five options."

"Absolutely, you're a man of limitless possibilities. But those two were the most obvious."

"And how would you have responded?"

"I would have done my best to disappear and keep Kendra from trying to rescue me again," he said quietly. "That's my real threat to you, Lynch. Our relationship is very complicated, and you don't have to worry about my ever becoming her lover. There's too much else going on that has to do with gratitude and pride and admiration. Maybe deep friendship and a hint of a father-figure image thrown into the mix? God knows what else. But the one certain thing she knows now is that we'll always be friends, and Kendra doesn't have any idea how to go halfway with anything."

"Is this going somewhere?"

"Oh, yes, most definitely. When you whisk me off to my safe little paradise, you must not ever tell Kendra where it is. Because if she ever got a hint that something was wrong with me, she'd be there in the next breath. She couldn't help herself. She has an almost maternal protective instinct about the people she cares about. That's who she is, and it will never change. I think you know that."

Lynch nodded slowly. "And I had no intention of telling Kendra where you were." He shrugged. "Though I knew I'd catch hell."

"You can tell her it was my decision." Waldridge smiled. "I always get special dispensation because of the gratitude thing."

"I've noticed."

"But think how grateful she's going to be to you for protecting me while I strive to do my all for humanity. I'm sure you'll be splendid and innovative, and we'll become fast friends while you're doing it. Isn't that better than destroying me?"

"I don't want gratitude any more than you do, Waldridge. It just confuses things and gets in the way."

"Exactly.

Lynch was silent. "And I never said I wanted to destroy you. That wasn't one of my chosen options."

"Yet."

He shook his head. "I like what you're working on. I appreciate what you gave to Kendra. I was thinking more about option four."

"And what was that?"

Lynch smiled.

"I'm not to know? A mysterious threat to hover eternally over my poor head?" Waldridge chuckled. "You're a terrible and complex man, Lynch. Maybe I should be the one to rescue Kendra."

"Really? Then perhaps option five would be better." His gaze returned to Kendra and Jessie. "Make a friend of Jessie Mercado, Waldridge. You may definitely need her if you decide to make my life difficult. But I don't think you will. You're a driven man, and you'll be too busy to worry about me."

Waldridge's smile faded. "But not too busy to worry about my friend, Kendra," he said quietly. "I've made a huge investment in her happiness. You *will* treat her well, Lynch." Then he was once more smiling. "But then we both know that Kendra will not permit anything else. However, just remember: If you don't behave satisfactorily and someday you desperately need a heart or some other vital organ, I'll see that you never receive it."

Lynch looked at him, stunned. "Damnation." And then he started to laugh. "Option six?"

Waldridge nodded serenely. "Option six."

"YOU KNOW THAT THIS isn't going to be a permanent arrangement," Jessie warned Kendra as she reached into the passenger seat to get her duffel. "I'm not going to let my business go down the tubes while I play babysitter to Waldridge at some godforsaken back-of-beyond hideout."

"I never expected that you would. I'm just grateful that you're taking the time to protect him during the initial stage and set up his security." Kendra made a face. "And I'm sorry that I can't afford to pay you the kind of money Delilah Winter would throw at you for the job. I don't even know if you'll need hazard pay or not."

"It's part of my job to make certain that I won't." Jessie smiled. "And that Waldridge won't either. I'll keep him safe, Kendra. I'll wrap him in a cocoon and won't let him out until he's finished his work. Before I leave him, he'll be surrounded by top-notch people who will answer to me." She looked at Lynch. "And to him. There's no way Lynch is going to have it any other way. By the way, where is this place we're going?"

"I don't know. Things were moving too fast. I'll ask Lynch when I take you to the plane."

"That would be helpful," Jessie said dryly. "I've moved around the world enough to have contacts almost everywhere, but I'd like to get things moving before we touch down."

Jessie was operating at her usual top speed, Kendra thought. The knowledge filled her with both confidence and relief. "One other problem: Griffin knows you had a connection with Waldridge. He might try to find and question you. I don't know if he'll cause you any—"

"I've got it covered. I left a message on my answering machine that I was visiting my dad in New Orleans. Then called Dad and told him to avoid anyone who might ask about me."

"Will he be able to do that?"

Jessie chuckled. "Yes, and enjoy every minute of it He'll leave trails and blind alleys and make certain tha Griffin's agents *just* miss me every time." She added, "Un til I get back, and they happen to stumble on my dad and me in a piano bar on Bourbon Street."

"But if Griffin suspects you're playing him, he could cause you big-time headaches. He has mega influence with law enforcement in California."

She shrugged. "I'll take the risk." She shook her head "Stop frowning. You're not responsible for me. Waldridge was my client before I even met you."

"But I managed to pull you into a hell of a lot more tha you expected to face." She grimaced. "I thought it wa over, Jessie. I didn't want you to have to go through an more because I asked you."

She smiled. "Hell, it was a grand game. Waldridge wa worth it. We both knew it. I could have said no at an time. I didn't do it. The only thing different I would hav chosen is that I'd been the one to do that last bit with you I'm alone a good deal of the time in my work." She me her eyes. "I liked having your company, Kendra Michaels."

Kendra nodded. Their experiences together had bee wild and exciting and evoked memories of her past. It ha forged bonds that she knew would last. "Another time You were always challenging me. We still have unfinishe business."

"Another time," Jessie agreed as she picked up her duff and started and started across the tarmac. "And now to fac Lynch. Did you tell him I was coming?" She held up h hand. "Never mind. I know. There wasn't time. I'll ha dle it."

A moment later, Jessie stopped in front of Waldridge an Lynch. She turned to Waldridge and smiled. "Here we a again." She shook his hand. "It's good to see you. I'm glad if there's trouble brewing, I'm going to get in on the beginning instead of the end. I'm much more effective if I can initiate preventative measures."

"Kendra says that you'll be everything I'll need." He smiled. "And that I have to put myself entirely in your hands. What a delightful idea."

Jessie shot a wary glance at Lynch. "And what do you think about it, Lynch?"

"I think that you obeyed Kendra and not me in a situation that could have gotten her killed."

"Yes."

"Will that happen on this job?"

"It might. You know how situations change, and so do solutions. But I can promise you that I won't act without immediately letting you know. Is that good enough?"

He was silent, staring at her. "You kept your word at the desert. Good enough. Get on the plane." He was glancing at the sky. "Dawn's starting to break, and the airport will be stirring. I want to be out of here in five minutes."

"Right." Jessie looked over her shoulder as she entered the plane. "Waldridge, I want to go over your complete daily routine as soon as we get in the air. I'll need it to set up a schedule . . ." She was gone.

"Trust her." Kendra took a step closer to him. "I'm not very good on trust myself, but you can trust her, Charles. She won't let you down."

"How can I not if you vouch for her? Because there's no one I trust more than you." He cradled her cheeks in his hands and kissed her forehead. "You've done everything anyone could ever hope to do, Kendra." He looked down into her eyes and said gently, "Now, let me go, my friend."

"Of course, I will. But I'll be in touch and there's email—"

"No, I won't answer. When the project's over and safe, I'll call you, and we'll meet for a drink to celebrate. Until then, I don't exist for you. Do you understand?"

She understood, but she could still feel her eyes sting with tears. "Now who is protecting whom?"

"That's what friends do. In life, it's always a trade-off." He kissed the tip of her nose. "And don't try to interrogate Jessie or Lynch." He chuckled. "Of course you will. But they'll be sworn to silence on penalty of not being invited to our party when my prison gates are thrown wide." He released her and started up the steps. He looked over his shoulder and smiled. "And you'd better have something interesting to tell me that will be worth my catching up on. It's going to be a boring couple of years for me."

He disappeared into the plane.

She drew a deep, shaky breath and stood there looking after him.

"Get going," Lynch said roughly. "Get the hell out of here, Kendra. And call your mother on the way home as I told you to do."

She turned to face him. His expression was stone hard. Angry. He looked angry. "I'll remember." She tried to pull herself together. "I know this is going to be a massive inconvenience for you, and I don't blame you for being upset."

"You're right, it's going to be a major pain in the ass, and it will last longer than I care to think about."

"If there's any way I can share the load, you only have to tell me. After all, it's my responsibility."

"Not any longer. You heard him, you're out of it." He added through set teeth, "*I* certainly heard the bastard.

How could anyone possibly follow a parting speech like that? He went straight to option ten."

She frowned. "Option ten?"

"Never mind. You would have had to be here."

"I *am* here. And I don't know what you're talking about. All I know is that I'm being closed out. The least you could do is tell me where you're taking him."

He shook his head. "No way. I'll let you know when I get those incubators to him. That's as far as I'll go." He was standing on the steps, his legs slightly parted, and his blue eyes glittering recklessly. "You want me to fix this? Consider it fixed. But it's my way, Kendra. I'm having enough interference."

"I'm not going to argue with you. I know how much I owe you for this."

"Yes, you do." He took a step closer and kissed her. Hard. Hot. Searing. He lifted his head and pushed her away. "And there's one thing I'm going to collect on right now."

She couldn't breathe. Her body felt as if it was on fire. She could feel her pulse leaping in the hollow of her throat. "What?"

"You're going to make me a promise."

She instinctively tensed. "I am?"

"You're damn right you are."

"What am I supposed to promise?"

He whirled to go up the steps. "When you start handing out all those heart-wrenching good-byes to all and sundry, I'm going to be on the list." He looked back over his shoulder, his eyes blazing, and his expression hard and stormy. "No, I'm going to be *first* on the list. Understand?"

Her mouth fell open in surprise. "I understand."

"I want to hear it."

"I promise. First on the list."

"Good. More later."

The door slammed shut behind him.

She stood there, watching dazedly as the plane began to taxi down the runway. Nothing had turned out exactly as she had intended. Somewhere along the way, she had lost control.

She shook her head as she turned away and headed for the car. By the time she had reached it, she was already recovering. It was not as if everything wasn't working out well. She would find a way to regain control of the situation. She would just have to think about it and come up with a way to do it.

Detach. Concentrate.

She looked back at the Cessna, which was now in the air. Jessie, Charles, and Lynch were on that plane. She had thought she was ready, eager, to go back to the normal tempo of her life with family, friends, and work. But she wanted suddenly to be there in that plane with them, planning, helping, on the front lines, instead of being sent home to safety.

Lynch.

She could almost see him standing there on the steps, his eyes glittering down at her. Powerful, dominant, and issuing challenges as he always did.

"More later, Lynch?" she whispered as she started the car. "You're damn right. You haven't seen anything yet."

AUTHOR'S NOTE

Since the publication of the very first Kendra Michaels novel, we've received many queries about the procedure that gave her sight. Since *Night Watch* goes into more detail than any of our previous books, this seems like a good time to pass along some of the real-life medical advances that have inspired us.

Since 1998, Professor Pete Coffey of University College London has conducted much of the pioneering work in retinal-cell regeneration and even his earliest procedures (much like the one Kendra undergoes in *Night Watch*) were successful in restoring the vision of several of his subjects. His work gave birth to The London Project to Cure Blindness, which has been pushing even more boundaries in the years since. The team is currently conducting stem-cell trials to treat Age-related Macular Degeneration, which causes blindness in over 30 million people worldwide. Other exciting cell-based blindness cures are being explored in California, spearheaded by Gabriel Travis at

UCLA and Henry Klassen at University of California, Irvine.

Spoiler alert! Don't read the following until you've finished reading *Night Watch*.

Many readers may assume the Night Watch organ reproduction project is the stuff of science fiction, but some forms of the process are actually here today. Dr. Anthony Atala is doing fascinating work with the Wake Forest Institute for Regenerative Medicine in Winston Salem, North Carolina. He and his team have taken human cells and grown replacement blood vessels, muscles, skin, and a complete urinary bladder. The ultimate goal is to re-create other vital organs that are a perfect match for patients, eliminating the need for organ donors in most cases. Atala and others have developed 3-D printers that actually *print* replacement organs using water-based solutions containing animal cells. Philadelphia tech company BioBots has actually brought such a printer to market, and although such efforts have yet to be approved for human use, serious work is under way.

Exciting times, indeed.

Read on for an excerpt from the next book
by Iris Johansen and Roy Johansen

LOOK BEHIND YOU

Available in July 2017 in hardcover from St. Martin's Press

PROLOGUE

"ANOTHER SODA AND LIME. Easy on the lime this time."

The bartender pursed her lips and gave him a pitying look. She obviously thought he was a recovering alcoholic, desperately clinging to sobriety by his fingernails.

He was nothing of the sort. He just needed to keep his wits about him.

Zachary looked up at the bar's mirrored backdrop where he could see literally hundreds of people shoehorned into this popular downtown watering hole. There was only one who interested him, though.

Pretty, strawberry-blonde Amanda Robinson sat in a corner booth. Late twenties, medium height, and a smile that lit up the room. She was surrounded by friends, three women and two men, who obviously adored her. They were finishing their third round of drinks. As always, Amanda had cosmos and gave her dark-haired friend the toothpick-impaled cherries.

Zachary checked the time. 9:45 P.M. The group, many of whom worked at the same insurance corporation as Amanda, started making noises about it being a "school night." Pretty Amanda picked up her phone and opened an app that bathed her face in a soft blue glow.

That was his cue. Zachary threw a twenty onto the bar and walked outside. The sidewalks on University Avenue were much less crowded than they'd been a couple hours before. He rounded the corner and found his car on the lonely side street. He unlocked the trunk, pulled out a large magnetic Uber sign, and slapped it onto the passenger-side door. He climbed inside, started the car, and circled around the block.

He smiled as he saw Pretty Amanda outside the bar. She and her friends were now talking on the sidewalk. He powered down the passenger-side window as he rolled up to the group.

"Amanda Robinson?" he shouted to the group.

"That's me!" she shouted.

After a few good-byes and quick hugs, Pretty Amanda hopped into the backseat. She pulled the door closed behind her.

"So . . ." he said, pretending to study his phone. "We're going to Rillington Drive?"

"Yes," she said absently. She was already engrossed in her own phone, scrolling through emails.

Perfect.

"This won't take long." Zachary power-locked the car doors as a shiver of excitement tore through him. "I promise, Amanda. This won't take long at all."

CHAPTER 1

KENDRA MICHAELS STUDIED THE NINE-YEAR-OLD boy in the wheelchair.

Just as his file had stated, Ryan Walker was unresponsive. Disengaged, borderline catatonic. He'd been that way since suffering head and spine injuries in the same boating accident which had killed his father.

It had been nine months, and although there was some hope that he might one day walk again, doctors were less sure about his cognitive abilities. He hadn't spoken since the accident and doctors were in disagreement whether the principal cause was psychological or physiological.

Kendra knew she was a port of last resort for Ryan's harried mother, Janice. The poor woman had been trying to find answers for her son at the same time she was grieving for her husband. She'd been advised to consult a music therapist after Ryan had supposedly shown a slight response to a few television commercial jingles. It was a phenomenon Kendra had so far been unable to reproduce in her studio.

Janice Walker was watching from behind a one-way glass on the studio's far side and Kendra could almost feel her despair.

Kendra studied the boy's unresponsive eyes. *Let me in, Ryan. You'll be safe here.*

She walked across the room to the keyboard. Her studio was a large carpeted room, twenty-five by fifteen feet, filled with an assortment of musical instruments, a keyboard, a drum set, and an array of woodwinds. She'd played some recordings and live guitar pieces for Ryan, but those elicited no response.

Maybe the keyboard would work better.

She sat down and turned on the console. "Okay, Ryan. Here's something I think you'll like. Your mom tells me you like Kiss. You're a Paul Stanley fan, right?"

No response.

Kendra started playing "I Love It Loud" using her keyboard to emulate the band's hard-driving sound.

Still nothing.

But then, there was . . . something.

A slight furrowing of the brow.

A pull on the right corner of his mouth.

But that was all.

Kendra finished the song without any further response from Ryan. "Did you like that one?"

No reaction.

She stood. "Well, that's enough for today. We'll listen to more music the next time you're here, okay?"

The door to the observation room opened and Janice Walker stood smiling with excitement in the doorway. "Did you see that?"

Kendra glanced down at Ryan. "Let's talk in there."

Kendra ushered Janice back into the observation room and closed the door behind them.

"That was progress, right?" Janice asked.

"Maybe. I've had clients make facial expressions like that when they pass gas. Or when they're hungry. Or for a dozen other reasons."

"I know my son. He was reacting to the music."

Kendra thought so too, but it was always better to keep parents' expectations in check. "I hope you're right."

"I am right. Where do we go from here?"

"We keep working at it. In some people, music is the crowbar that opens the outside world to them. It helps them make connections that no other kind of communication can. Those small connections can lead to bigger connections. That's the goal anyway."

"Can we come back tomorrow?"

Janice was anxious, like a starving person who had been tossed a breadcrumb. Not that Kendra could blame her. Her response would have been the same if Ryan had been her son.

"We should wait a couple days. It helps to give the brain time to process between sessions."

Janice nodded, but she couldn't hide her disappointment. "I know. It's just . . . This is the first time I've seen him respond to anything since . . ." Her voice trailed off. "I want it so *much*."

Kendra reached out and squeezed Janice's arm. "I know. If this is the crowbar that will work for Ryan, I promise I'll find the right way to use it. We just need to be patient. Okay?"

She nodded, still staring at her son on the other side of the one-way glass. "It's hard to be patient." She tried to smile. "But I believe you're doing everything you can for him. And I know you have other clients. A couple of them came in here while you were working with Ryan."

Kendra wrinkled her brow. "Really?"

"Yes. They came in through the other door, the one that leads out to the hallway."

"Ryan's my last appointment of the day. Are you sure . . . ?"

"Well, they said they were here to see you. I just assumed . . . It was a man and a woman, both well-dressed. They said they'd come back later."

Kendra wasn't sure she liked this. She had an idea who it might be, but she hoped she was wrong.

"Is everything alright?" Janice asked.

"Yes. Fine. Nothing to worry about. I'm sure they'll be back soon."

"SOON" WAS ONLY FIVE MINUTES after Ryan and Janice left, when FBI Special Agent Roland Metcalf entered her studio. He was a tall, good-looking man in his mid-twenties, and he possessed a self-effacing sense of humor that she'd always found refreshing for a man in his profession. Kendra had known him for a couple of years, and today he was with a young woman she had never met.

"Sorry to barge in on you at work, Kendra." He motioned to the woman at his side. "This is Special Agent Gina Carson. She just transferred in from the Chicago office."

Kendra adjusted the stacks of sheet music she'd picked up. "Hello."

Gina nodded her greeting with obvious uneasiness. She clearly wasn't sure why they were there.

Metcalf was strolling around the studio. "You know, I've never seen this place. I've always wanted to see what you do."

"Well, it seems you did that today. I heard you let yourself in the observation room while I was working with my last client."

Metcalf nodded. "Sorry about that. The main entrance was locked."

"I didn't want to be disturbed."

Metcalf quickly caught the nuances in her tone. "We didn't want that either. That's why we left."

"But you came back," she said without expression.

"Come on, Kendra. You *have* to know why I'm here."

"I have a pretty good idea." She continued to tidy the sheet music. "Doesn't mean that I like it."

Metcalf frowned as he waited for her to finish.

She let him wait.

After another moment he said, "Three murders, Kendra. Three murders in the last eight days, all within a couple of miles of here."

She didn't look up. "Three? I thought it was just two."

"A third popped up this morning. We're on our way to the crime scene now. San Diego PD has been handling the cases, but the FBI has just joined the investigation. My boss wants you to join us."

"Fortunately, Special Agent in Charge Griffin isn't *my* boss. So I get to politely decline."

Gina moved toward the exit. "Then thanks for your time."

Metcalf held his ground. "Hold on, Carson." He smiled at Kendra. "I need a few more minutes to appeal to Kendra's sense of civic duty."

Metcalf's partner was clearly annoyed as she stepped back toward him. "You didn't tell me she was a music therapist when you said you wanted to stop here."

"It wasn't relevant to our investigation."

"I'm thinking *she's* not relevant to our investigation."

Kendra's lips quirked. "You heard the lady, Metcalf. I'm not relevant."

"We're wasting time," Gina said. "You asked and she answered. She said she's not interested. Are we working this case or not?"

Kendra was getting more annoyed at this foul-tempered woman than she was at Metcalf. Her eyes narrowed on the agent's tight mouth and annoyed expression. She found herself suddenly feeling protective of Metcalf, not that he needed anyone's protection. She liked the guy and it irked her that this agent would speak to him with such a total lack of respect.

Metcalf, perhaps sensing Kendra's reaction, suddenly snapped at Gina. "Cool your jets, Carson. Griffin wants an extra set of eyes on that crime scene. *Her* eyes."

"I'm still missing something," Gina said sourly. "On our way here, didn't you tell me she used to be blind?"

"Yes," Kendra answered for him. "For the first twenty years of my life. An experimental surgical procedure gave me my sight."

Gina clicked her tongue. "So now you have super vision or something?"

"Not at all," Kendra said. "I'm sure my eyesight is no better than yours."

Gina turned back to Metcalf. "So why are we here groveling to a music therapist to help us on a murder investigation?"

Metcalf was obviously losing patience. "I don't grovel, Carson. I ask politely, because that's what the Bureau does when they go hat in hand to try to get help to keep a serial killer from claiming other victims. You obviously haven't spent much time reading our case files since you transferred down. If you had, you would have seen that Kendra has helped crack over a dozen cases in the past few years. Many of those would've gone unsolved if she hadn't stepped in."

Gina was slightly taken aback by the attack. "So how, exactly, has she been of—"

"I don't take anything I see for granted," Kendra interrupted. God, she got tired of going through explanations. Particularly to arrogant agents like Carson. "When I got my sight, I got into the habit of identifying and mentally cataloguing everything that passed in front of my eyes, just to make my way in a world that was totally new to me."

"I guess that makes sense," Gina said skeptically.

"That isn't the half of it," Metcalf said. "Like most blind people, Kendra had already developed her other senses to help her get by. Hearing, smell, touch, taste . . . She's held onto those skills, too."

Gina still seemed unsure. "Huh. Interesting."

Kendra shrugged. "Most investigators only go by what they see. They're missing well over half the story."

She could almost see Gina's hackles rise at her words. "Have you had any law enforcement training?"

"No. It's nothing I've ever had any interest in."

"No, you'd rather play with your instruments or try to impress agents like Metcalf here. Believe it or not, we're actually trained observers," Gina said. "It's a big part of our jobs. I appreciate that you've assisted my colleagues, Dr. Michaels, but I really don't see how you could be of any help in a case that's shaping up to be—"

"You want to show her?" Metcalf was smiling at Kendra.

"Not really."

Gina was frowning as she looked from one to the other of them. "Show me what?"

"Come on, Kendra," Metcalf murmured, his eyes twinkling. "She annoyed the hell out of you and you're no angel. You know you want to do it."

Satan get thee behind me.

"I'd rather not."

"Please. You're not the only one who took flak."

Kendra sighed. He was right, she was definitely no angel. It had been a rough day and Gina Carson had rubbed her the wrong way. "If I do this, will you leave?"

Metcalf laughed. "We'll *think* about leaving."

"Bastard." She turned toward Gina and looked her up and down.

Gina shifted uneasily. "What the hell is going on?"

"You used to smoke," Kendra said. "But then you quit for a while. Maybe a *long* while. But you recently started again."

Gina cursed. "You can smell smoke on me?"

"No." Kendra walked toward a cabinet with her sheet music. "But it's only natural for someone who's been under the kind of stress you have been under."

"What stress?"

"Moving, for one. You've lived in Chicago for most, if not all, of your life. Your parents are from there and probably their parents before them. It's also stressful getting out of a long-term relationship. You recently broke up with your boyfriend or girlfriend. Is that what prompted the move?"

Gina stared at her for a long moment. "Boyfriend. Matt. After seven years. But that wasn't the only reason."

"In any case, you're still living out of a hotel while you get your own place. You're looking to buy, not rent. For now, you're staying at the Pacific. I hear it's nice."

Gina glanced at Metcalf accusingly. "Someone told her."

"Don't look at me," he said. "And I'm sure she didn't even know you existed until five minutes ago."

"I didn't," Kendra said. "But I know you drove here from Chicago even though the FBI provides you with a company car. Maybe you did it because you wanted to bring a car of your own here, but I'm thinking it was because it was the best way to bring your pet. A parakeet?"

Gina's expression was becoming more stunned by the moment. "Cockatiel."

"A very loved and spoiled little bird," Kendra said.

"Extremely," Gina said weakly.

"You like seventies rock and Starbucks. You may cook, but you're also partial to Papa John's Pizza. And you're a tennis fan, aren't you?"

Gina appeared to be dazed. "Yes."

Kendra turned to Metcalf. "Satisfied?"

His smile was still brimming with mischief. "Come on, you're not gonna tell her who her first grade teacher was?"

"Mrs. McAlister. She had a mole on her left cheek."

His jaw dropped. "What in . . ."

"I'm joking." She turned back to Gina. "But it would've been awesome if I was right about that one, huh?"

She was silent and then said grudgingly, "It's still pretty awesome. Who the hell told you all this stuff?"

Kendra shrugged. "You did, in the first thirty seconds you were here."

"I seriously doubt that."

"Doubt all you please. It's true."

Gina was suddenly looking uncomfortable. "Okay, what about the smoking? I've been trying to hide it from my new coworkers. It shows a lack of self-discipline."

"For what it's worth, I can't smell smoke on you at all. But I can tell you've been chewing Nicorette gum. Cinnamon Surge flavor. It's on your breath."

Gina rolled her eyes. "I was trying to decide between that and Fruit Chill."

"White Ice Mint may be their least distinctive flavor."

"I'll take your word for that," Gina said grimly.

Kendra pointed to Gina's right upper arm, left bare by her sleeveless top. "There's also a slight tan line there in the exact dimensions of a nicotine patch."

Gina looked at her arm. "I quit for four years and I started up again after my boyfriend and I broke up."

". . . . which brings me to another tan line." Kendra pointed to Gina's neck. "It looks like you've been wearing a heart-shaped pendant for quite some time. Every day for years but you recently stopped wearing it. Your skin is much lighter there. With no sign of an engagement or wedding ring, that suggests a breakup. Also, your left upper arm is much more tanned than your right. That's where I got the long car trip. You drove here from Chicago."

"But you knew my parents were there. And my grandparents."

"Linguistics. You have a born-and-bred Chicago accent. Anyone who's seen *The Blues Brothers* could spot it a mile away. It's doubtful it would be quite so pronounced if your parents didn't imprint it on you. And if *their* parents didn't imprint it on *them*."

She scowled. "Right on all counts. But how the hell did you know about my bird?"

Kendra took Gina's hand and pointed to dozens of light scratches on the back of her hand and arm. "Too small and too light to be a cat or even a pet rodent. It's clearly a small bird. Those light scratches run all the way up your arm and onto your shoulder. You take him out of his cage frequently. Obviously loved and spoiled."

"But what about all those other things? Papa John's? Tennis?"

Kendra smiled. "You were holding your phone when you walked in here. You'd probably just checked messages and your main screen was still lit up. Your app icons gave you away. Papa John's Pizza, Starbucks, and the Tennis Channel. I could see that your most recent album played from your phone was The Who's *Tommy*."

Gina looked down at her phone. "Oh, man."

"You can write a biography based on a person's main smartphone screen."

"Pretty pathetic life story." Gina's lips twisted. "Pizza delivery and drive-through coffee."

It did sound pathetic, Kendra thought, and suddenly all the vulnerable details she'd pulled together about Gina Carson were scrolling through her mind. Her antagonism toward the woman was abruptly gone. She smiled. "For the record, I have the same apps on my phone. But I also saw you had the Pacific Guest Suites app which lets you use your phone to unlock your room. It's a place I recommend to my colleagues and clients when they're in town for more than a few days. And you also gave the Zillow real estate app prime placement on your screen which tells me that you're looking to buy instead of rent."

Gina nodded ruefully. "Well, I'll be more careful about who sees my phone, that's for damn sure."

Kendra turned to Metcalf. "The dog and pony show is over. Time for you to go."

"I said I'd *consider* leaving. I just did that and I've rejected the idea. At least not until you agree to come with us to the crime scene." He coaxed, "What would it hurt? Just a quick glance around."

Kendra shook her head. "I have real work to do. My work."

"Dr. Michaels." Gina Carson's voice was hesitant. "I know I probably came on too strong with you. It's a habit I have. Maybe it's a little worse right now because I'm the new kid in town. Everything's pretty strange here for me right now. I just want you to know that if you're not doing what Metcalf wants because you're pissed off at me, that I'm not going to give you any trouble."

Shit. Those words had been hard for Gina. All she had was a tough façade and that damn cockatiel in her life right now. This was becoming more and more difficult for Kendra. "I'm not pissed off at you." She made a face. "Not any longer. I just don't want to get involved in another case right now."

"I know you don't," Metcalf said. "Griffin told me I'd have trouble convincing you. I was hoping that you'd think that I was so charming and loveable I wouldn't have to pull out the wild card Griffin gave me."

"Wild card?" Kendra repeated warily.

"Griffin told me to tell you something."

"I can hardly wait to hear what it was," she said dryly.

"He said you owed him."

Kendra cursed. "He's playing *that* card?"

"He really wants your help on this."

That was clear enough. Griffin had recently been help-ful when a friend of hers was in deep trouble. He'd given her manpower and lab time when he had no official obli-gation to do so. She had known his help would not be without strings.

Now he was cashing in.

"Okay," she finally said. "I'll visit this one crime scene with you and take a look around. That's it."

Metcalf nodded. "That's all I'm asking."

But one thing could lead to another, and she would have to be the one to call the halt. Her last case had been both physically and emotionally draining, and she needed to step back and heal for a time. She didn't *need* this.

But evidently she was going to get it.

Just one quick look around. That was going to be her limit.

"Let's get this over with," Kendra said. She turned to Gina. "And when we're finished, you can use that Papa John's app to order me a medium Meat Lovers pizza. I'm starving."

METCALF OFFERED HER A LIFT to the crime scene, but Kendra turned him down flat. She preferred to follow in her own car. She didn't want to be stuck there any longer than she needed to be.

Within minutes she turned onto Holt Street and im-mediately found herself at a police roadblock. She saw Metcalf waving his badge at the officer, then pointing back to her. The cop waved them through.

It was a block taken up by Kimbrough Elementary

School on one side and a two-story apartment building on the other. In the middle of the street was a large white tent, approximately ten by ten feet. Kendra counted no fewer than a dozen uniformed police officers on the scene plus several detectives and forensics personnel.

She parked behind Metcalf and walked toward the school with him and Gina. "I'm guessing the tent isn't a PTA bake sale," she said grimly.

"San Diego PD put it up to spare the kiddies from what promises to be a horrific sight."

"Great. Thanks again for the wonderful afternoon."

"Aw, come on. What would you rather be doing today?"

"Root canal. Colonoscopy. Having my fingernails removed with a pair of pliers." She stopped outside the tent. "I smell gasoline. Something's been cooking." The realization hit her. "Something . . . or someone."

"Exactly," Gina said. She grabbed the tent's door flap. "Ready for this?"

No, Kendra wanted to tell her. She wasn't like them. She could never get used to the sad, horrible stories that greeted her at these crime scenes.

She nodded. "I'm ready."

Kendra ducked through the flap and stopped cold. There in the center of the tent was a charred woman's body bound to a desk chair.

Her breath left her.

It was the work of a monster.

A police detective had entered behind them. "It happened around eleven thirty. The principal saw her burning out here. He ran out with an extinguisher and put it out."

Kendra still hadn't adjusted to the shock. There were

wisps of strawberry-blonde hair and a face that was half gone.

Kendra looked away.

Detach.

Concentrate.

"Burned alive?" Gina asked.

Kendra shook her head. "No. She's been dead for a few days."

"How can you tell?" Metcalf asked.

"The odor. It's not just charred flesh, there's been decomposition."

The detective nodded. "The M.E. was just here. He backs that up. He says she's been dead a few days at least."

Kendra made herself turn back toward the corpse. Corpse. That's right, think of her as an object, a puzzle. Not as a woman who'd had a life, friends, lovers. "Do we have an ID?"

"Not so far," the detective replied. "We've just started running her against missing persons."

Kendra studied the corpse, trying to pull anything from it she could. "If that doesn't pan out, you might canvass some of the high-end hair salons. She used a Japanese hair conditioner that isn't common around here. Tsubaki."

Gina jotted this down into her notebook. "I'm not sure I'm spelling it right. I'm a Pantene girl myself."

"I know." Kendra knelt beside the corpse, which was still dripping with extinguisher foam. "Did anyone see her deposited here?"

"Not so far," the detective replied. "We've done a preliminary canvass, but no one reports seeing her before the fire."

"Probably a truck with a ramp. The chair could have been rolled out quickly, set on fire, and the truck took off before anyone noticed." Kendra looked up. "It's my guess her body was taped to the chair at a fairly active construction site. You should start there."

"What makes you say that?" Metcalf asked.

She pointed to the castors which were covered by a chalky powder. "That looks like silica dust which you'll find at many building sites. The body was already in this chair when it rolled across the dust and kicked some up." She gently lifted the corpse's left pant leg. "See? It's not underneath the body."

"Very good," Metcalf said.

There was nothing good about anything connected to what had happened to this woman, Kendra thought. Certainly not the fact that Kendra was able to see what had happened to her. Why hadn't someone been able to see it before it happened?

Three more investigators entered the tent as Kendra examined the corpse's high-heeled shoes. "It's obvious she's been dragged. There's more construction dust here, too, but it's different."

"Different how?" Jennings asked.

"It's darker. Looks like residue from cut granite."

One of the investigators shone his high-powered flashlight over the shoes. "Wait!" Kendra said. "Keep that light where it is."

She squinted at the pool of extinguisher fluid beneath the chair. The mirror-like surface reflected the seat's underside. There was something there . . .

"Someone give me evidence gloves."

Four pairs were suddenly thrust in her direction. She took a pair of plastic gloves from Metcalf and slid them on. She peered underneath the chair which was relatively unscathed from the fire.

Affixed to the chair's underside was a shiny silver pouch.

Kendra peeled it off and stood up.

"What is it?" Gina asked.

"Maybe nothing," Kendra said as she loosened the pouch's drawstrings. "But this seems like it might be made from a fire retardant material." She pulled two items from the pouch. "A set of keys and a pair of eyeglasses."

"Hers?" the detective asked.

"Maybe, but I doubt it." She opened the glasses. "These are men's spectacles, probably for a face larger than hers was. And the keys have a tag for a supermarket loyalty program. Meijer's."

"It's a Midwestern chain," Metcalf said. "If these things aren't hers, what are they doing here?"

"Your guess is as good as mine." Kendra put the items in Metcalf's hand. "The smell is getting to me. I have to get out of here."

Kendra lifted the tent flap and slid outside.

"Wait." Metcalf was following her. "That's it?"

"Yes. That's all I got." Her nostrils still burned from that horrible stench. She didn't break stride. "Catch the beast who did this, will you?"

"It would be easier if you helped us."

"I already have."

"You know what I mean."

"Not this time, Metcalf. Tell your boss that I consider my debt repaid."

Metcalf nodded. "I'll tell him. Between you and me, we're still in the position of owing you."

Kendra finally stopped. No use running away. She was

far enough away that she shouldn't be able to smell the terrible odor, so it must be her imagination.

"You've never owed us a thing," Metcalf continued quietly. "Thanks for coming out here today."

"Sure. I'm certain you'll get him. Whoever it is, he's very concerned with calling attention to himself."

"You've given us a good start."

She nodded toward the tent. "Your partner's very attractive. I'm pretty sure she's interested in you."

Metcalf shook his head. "Your powers of observation have seriously let you down. She barely tolerates any of us."

"It's a defense mechanism. She's probably lonely, trying to start a new life for herself in a new town."

"You're cutting her way more slack than I am." He shook his head. "Anyway, she's really not my type."

"Don't tell me you're one of those guys who's threatened by strong women."

He smiled at her. "Not at all. It's a quality I find most attractive."

Kendra turned away slightly. Metcalf was smart, good-looking, and a nice guy. She liked him, but she couldn't return that romantic vibe she occasionally got from him.

"Then maybe you should give her a chance." Kendra cocked her head toward her car. "I'm outta here. Good luck with your case."

HAD KENDRA MICHAELS MET Pretty Amanda yet?

Hard to say.

Zachary sat on the park bench and unwrapped his sandwich. As much as he wanted to be watching the activity in front of the elementary school, he knew better

Only amateurs lingered near their crime scenes. Profilers studied behavior traits in what they assumed were people like him. It was one sure way of getting caught.

He was no amateur.

And there was no one like him in all their books and charts.

Still, he would have been thrilled to see Kendra Michaels admiring his handiwork.

If, that is, she'd even been brought into the case. He had already been disappointed twice before, so there was no guarantee she was there this time either.

Patience.

It was a plan years in the making. He could wait a little while longer.

He took a bite of his tuna-and-peppers sandwich as he watched the collegiate soccer team on the practice field. The goalie, a strapping young man named Todd Wesley, was doing well today.

Zachary smiled. A good way for the young man's teammates to remember him.

Strapping Todd was a creature of habit. After practice, he'd grab a smoothie from the little shop on the corner before going to his apartment for a quick shower. He'd eat while watching television, then spend an hour on his sofa surfing the web until his girlfriend got off work at the campus library. She'd swing by and the two of them would go out to dinner.

Zachary shook his head. Did Strapping Todd know how monotonous his life had become? He certainly would've done things differently if he'd known this would be his last day on earth.

No matter. Tonight would be different.

Very different.

Because this *might* be the one that would catch Kendra Michaels's notice.

And when she finally gave him the attention he deserved, the game would be on . . .